CHILD OF
NORMAN'S END

CHILD OF
NORMAN'S END

By
ERNEST RAYMOND

CASSELL & COMPANY LIMITED
London, Toronto, Melbourne
& Sydney

First Published • 1934

Printed in Great Britain
at
The Chapel River Press, Andover, Hants
F150 234

TO

LELLA RAYMOND

PART I

CHILD OF NORMAN'S END

I

SOMEWHERE between Earl's Court and the river you will find the place. Two centuries ago it was a pleasant hamlet standing on the level fields that stretched to the river's rim ; to-day, well, there is hardly a green thing anywhere and never a water bird ; and Norman's End is but a parish cut from the crowding houses and the straight intersecting roads that lie between Earl's Court station and the southern turn of the Thames. Clearer direction I must not give you. Learned persons say that the name is a corruption of No-Man's-Land, as the river levels were called when they were fens, and the water birds flew screaming. I do not believe it, because a little way back from Norman's End Lane, which is now the roaring business highway for these parts, there is an old mansion called Great Normands. You might have a task to find it, so hidden behind shops and houses it is, but I have a fancy that once upon a time it gave its name to a hamlet over the fields.

It is not the old mansion whose derelict garden we shall visit so often in the course of our tale ; it is just one of the many gentleman's houses that were dotted among the cabbages two centuries ago. For by then, you see, the great city had crept a little closer, and men had drained the fens and turned them into market gardens. There were market gardens everywhere, as far as eye could reach; and the people called them Fulham Fields. And out on the fields you could see these country mansions hiding behind their dark cedars and tall elms. You might have seen six or eight of them in an afternoon's walk along Norman's End Lane —no roaring thoroughfare then but a winding cart road—had you thrown your glance over the fence all the time and looked across the fields to the distant river, where the tall sails went by. They were much affected by artists, these pleasant seats; and many a man famous in his day lived in one or another of them: Bartolozzi and Cipriani the painters, and Edmund Kean the player, and that most celebrated novelist of George II's time who was the friend of Johnson and Boswell but little loved of Harry Fielding, as all may divine who read " The Adventures of Joseph Andrews." His was the derelict garden that we shall have occasion to visit, you and I, on the business of our story.

Ah, Norman's End where the wild birds screamed! I could spend a page or two sorrowing over the changes that were to come upon you, fast as the dissolving views of a phantasmagoria. Not really so fast, of course, but they seem quick and continuous and diaphanous to one who sits here like a god, chewing a pen and considering the past centuries as they stream over the face of Norman's End. First the fens; then the market gardens; and after the gardens the long streets—and oh, surely it is sad to think that where once they dug lettuce and leek they were soon to dig kitchen and pantry and cellar—rows upon rows upon rows of them! Yes, I find it sad to-day, even though I was one of the

children who frisked with the maids in those underground rooms where, a hundred years before, romped
mole and rabbit and worm.

It was somewhere in the second half of Victoria's
reign that the long streets of houses began their march
over the fields. Tall houses; prosperous middle-class
houses requiring two maids apiece; and in due time
they had covered every inch of green ground, and Norman's End Lane, from being a country road, was a
street of blazing shop-fronts and rattling drays and cabs.
The new roads ran straight, but Norman's End Lane
twisted in and out, and in and out; and no one
remembered that it was the twist of an old hedge-
bordered lane. Nor do you remember to-day, as you
swing in your bus along it. Do so hereafter, if you
can find it.

The outer fringe of Queen Victoria's prosperity had
passed over Norman's End. Even so; but what then?
Athens had a golden age of a hundred years length;
Venice enjoyed her glory for a few centuries; but the
golden age of Norman's End endured but fifteen years
or so, from the second Jubilee of Victoria to the
coronation of George V. (We all had two maids then.)
But it was perishing even as it bloomed; the motor and
the electric railway were carrying prosperity farther and
farther afield; and quickly those staid houses went
down into maisonettes and flats, and a different type of
children played in the streets. The accelerator on the
motor car condemned our Norman's End; and the
conductor rail on the permanent way finished it; and I
think there was seldom a little social system which the
Everlasting Flux so quickly slew. It will be our
occupation now, and for me a rather wistful one, to

catch at something that happened in these highly respectable years of Norman's End.

I shall speak of but one part of this considerable parish : the central part ; the best part. To aid you in picturing it I shall call it the Square Quarter Mile. Imagine five residential roads running parallel, and closed in at the top by Glastonbury Road, which lies at right angles to them, very quiet and sedate, and at the bottom by the run of Norman's End Lane itself with its streaming traffic. Pause, while you master this picture ; it will heighten your enjoyment of this excellent tale . . . Now imagine these five roads crossed twice, by Wentworth Avenue and Bertrand Avenue ; name the middle road of the five Conyers Road ; realise by an effort of the imagination that it must form a T-square with Glastonbury Road ; now go over this paragraph once again to make sure that you have the picture perfect ; and you will have all that you need to know of the Square Quarter Mile, the centre and the crown of Norman's End.

It is the best part because it has the tallest houses. Streets of smaller residential houses parade all round it, and away to the left they leave gentility behind and become very poor indeed ; but we shall not visit in these parts. Enough to say that among the houses on the left of the Square Quarter Mile stands St. Alban's Church, immensely important to the tale ; and among those on the right Trinity School, where we all went as boys. If to-morrow you flew this way from the direction of Earl's Court you would see the grey spire of St. Alban's rising on one side and the twin red towers of Trinity on the other ; and (though you would not see them because they sit low among the private houses) you might know that in the neighbourhood of Trinity were the private schools " for the daughters of gentlemen," such as Lammas, to which Cynthia Coventry went, whose tale it is.

The church on the left, the schools on the right. And in my day the children, who were the big feature of the place (or so it seemed to me then) walked right to school for six days of the week, and left to Divine Service on the seventh. On weekday mornings before the sun was high, you watched them sauntering towards the schools with their satchels on their backs, and in the evening you heard them returning for tea, with their voices at echo amongst the houses ; on Sundays you saw them walking with their fathers and mothers to the church, and heard only the sound of their feet.

What more shall I tell you ? Glastonbury Road is the best of the roads, and it was here that Cynthia lived. Conyers Road is the next best ; Wentworth Avenue with its line of plane trees—ah ! Wentworth Avenue presents us with a most interesting fact. It crosses, as you remember, the five parallel sisters, but it also separates one epoch from another. If you walk across it, coming up Conyers Road towards Glastonbury, you walk right out of the stucco age into the red-brick age. All the houses so far have been tall pretentious houses of grey-brick and stucco, with balustraded porticoes and deep areas where the kitchen windows are barred against the burglars ; but now they are all of red-brick and gabled, and it is possible that their doors and windows are painted green. Their areas are wider and lighter ; their steps are less steep ; their facades have exchanged pomposity in favour of picturesqueness ; and we have entered a cosier age.

And yet both divisions are unmistakably Norman's End. What is it that keeps them one place like this? Is it that the window boxes with their geraniums and marguerites are the same in one part as in the other, and the long tresses of virginia creeper hang alike from the stucco and from the red-brick walls? Is it that the holland blinds and lace curtains are much the same in all the windows of the Square Quarter Mile, and the hearth-stoned steps are as white between the red-brick piers as under the stucco porticoes? Or is it just the quiet of the pavements that links them together?

But stay! I am speaking of it as it looked forty years ago. I know not if it has this unity now.

I am speaking of it as it looked in Jubilee Year. Probably the hearth-stoned steps are not so clean now, because thrice as many people cross them, and they are a No-Man's-Land among the tenants. Probably the windows show curtains of a distressing variety, and a box of geraniums only once in a way. Surely all is changed but the strong-built walls. The lamplighter crosses no more with his twinkling pole from gas-lamp to gas-lamp. The doctor's coachman drives him no more from house to house; nor, waiting with the empty brougham, walks the sleek horse up and down. The fly-paper man with the gummed paper tied around his top hat and all be-spattered with flies—comes he this way any more? Comes the man with the muzzled and waddling bear? Comes the old groundsel-peddler with a beard like the prophet's, who would offer his yellow blooms to our faces diving beneath our windows? And the old tinker with his decorated wheel before him, and his ragged wife at his side, and his melancholy cry behind, "Any knives to grind? Any chairs to mend ? If I'd as much money as I could spend, I shouldn't be crying, Any chairs to mend ? "

I don't know. I think not.

In Jubilee Year, 1897, though Norman's End was entering upon its golden period, and though the factors that should work its decay were already shaping in the same despotic city that had ordered its creation, none the less its building was not yet complete. So nearly merged are life and death, blossom and decay, in the everlasting flux of things. Town had not wholly conquered Country, and there were green wastegrounds here and there among the tall houses. These were unfenced hollows, dropping down from the pavements, and ablow in summer with nettles and sorrel and high grasses, among which ran the yellow of charlock and the white of ground-elder. One of these, a fine rectangular playground, was right opposite Cynthia Coventry's window, occupying, in fact, the very corner where Conyers Road met Glastonbury Road.

No. 22 Glastonbury Road is the house to which in 1894 Tom Coventry came, bringing Old Mrs. Coventry his mother, Hilda his wife, and Cynthia his child ; and its strategic position was good. As an observation post it could hardly be bettered, though this interested Old Mrs. Coventry more than Tom or Hilda (I am not so sure about Cynthia). Standing almost in the centre of Glastonbury Road, it commanded a view down the length of Conyers Road ; it commanded the pillar box beside which a lamp-post was most conveniently placed so that one could see who was posting his letters in the darkness of a winter evening ; and it commanded this wasteground where the children of one's neighbours romped and played.

Look well at Cynthia's house. It is one of a long uniform row, red-brick and four stories high; it has hearth-stoned steps and a tiled space before the hall door; on every sill the window boxes are bright with geranium, marguerite and lobelia, and down the red walls hang the long tresses of creeper. The ground-floor windows are the windows of Tom Coventry's study; those of the first floor are Cynthia's outlook on the world in which she finds herself existing; those of the story above light up Old Mrs. Coventry's bed-sitting room; and, in reference to these last, it is odds that, should a step break the quiet of the pavements, the old lady's face, with its black hair parted in the middle and its eager little eyes, will lift above the geraniums to see what's afoot and to hope that it's something exciting.

Let us call back a summer sun of forty years since, and invite it to light up an afternoon long dead, that we too may see what was afoot on the pavements commanded by Old Mrs. Coventry's window, at five of the clock.

II

THE sun slanted down upon Conyers Road; and far down among the stucco houses a door opened. From under the portico a woman stepped on to the pavement and turned sharply in the direction of Glastonbury Road; a plump little woman of forty, sailing along under a large hat whose trimming of tulle stood erect from a bed of mint and roses. Her big-topped sleeves made her shoulders seem twice as wide as they were; her bodice did all that was possible to give her the hour-glass figure of the time; and her skirt swept the dust from the ground, except where she lifted it behind and unveiled a peep of white lace petticoat. Evidently a private excitement was driving her on, for she moved rapidly; and I think she was warm beneath her veil, as she crossed Wentworth Avenue and entered the red-brick world.

Her steps rang on the pavement, and the face of Old Mrs. Coventry rose at her window, stealthily. The plump little woman crossed the road and went up the steps of No. 22, thereby forcing Old Mrs. Coventry into a somewhat cock-eyed stance, if she was to see down the wall of her own house. Why was Rose Damien calling at this hour? It was not Hilda Coventry's At Home day, and even for a woman as intimate with the Coventrys as Rose Damien, five o'clock was a strange hour. Did she bring interesting news?

Old Mrs. Coventry's ears were well-keyed instruments, and she heard the bell ring in the basement far below. She heard Ada, the parlourmaid, showing Mrs. Damien up the first flight of stairs to the drawing room, and she could detect that Mrs. Damien was breathless. Then she heard her daughter-in-law hurrying in her weak and flighty fashion to greet the visitor.

The drawing room door closed; and Old Mrs. Coventry remained standing in her room—a *petite* old lady in a boned black dress, with a sharp little face, black hair parted under a lace cap, and tiny jet eyes which now stared behind their steel spectacles, while her tiny ears listened. The door had been shut a whole minute; and Old Mrs. Coventry was not a woman to stay for two minutes outside a closed door. Before another ten seconds had passed she was lifting her skirt out of the way of her little feet and hurrying down the stairs. That exasperating Hilda should not shut her away from any interest in the drawing room.

She did not enter at once; and within the room, on the drugget laid over the carpet, Mrs. Damien and Hilda Coventry sat opposite each other. Mrs. Damien sagged heavily in an arm-chair, with her feather boa thrown back and her parasol against her knees. Her bosom heaved; and it might have occurred to a wittier woman than Hilda to think that Rose Damien's bosom would have made a good lectern for a fair-sized bible. Hilda, long and slight, leaned forward from the sofa, with her shoulders a little rounded, for she was a weak thing, Hilda: it was a common remark in our parts that "Young Mrs. Coventry" was a weak creature because her restless old mother-in-law had drained the vitality from her.

Mrs. Damien had told her news. Abbott, her husband, had come home with two splendid seats for the Jubilee. Abbott couldn't go himself, so Hilda must accompany her. Abbott, being a stockbroker in the city where they were speculating in seats, had been able to get these two at a ridiculous sum; he had these special advantages, of course.

Rose Damien, let us here point out, was proud of Abbott. She spoke often of his advantages. Not that he was a striking person, either in ability or in appearance. He was a spare little man, of small neat features; always well-dressed for his work in the city but merely competent in its discharge. He liked peace and quiet, so when Rose fussed, he did what she wanted. She had fussed about these tickets, so he had got them for her; just as, a year or two ago, she had fussed about his becoming a churchwarden, and now, twice a Sunday, he walked up and down the aisles of St. Alban's, allotting seats and lending hymn-books, in frock-coat and white waistcoat slip. In short, a trim and trite little man of no great importance in the world; but Rose Damien, who was a fat, managing, confident, positive woman, had need to be proud of him, for her own satisfaction, and accordingly was so. It was only his special advantages, she said, which had enabled him to get these two seats.

Hilda clasped her hands together and cried, " Oh, how lovely ! " but dropped immediately into sadness and defeat as she asked, " But what about Mamma ? "

" What about her ? " demanded Rose Damien vigorously.

" Well, you know what she is. She can never bear to be left out of anything. She won't like it at all."

Rose said she was very sorry for poor dear old Mrs. Coventry, but she didn't see that it could be helped. Abbott could never get another seat, and Mrs. Coventry must allow Hilda to go alone for once. Yes, there was no doubt about that. Mrs. Damien said it very easily and positively; she didn't live with Old Mrs. Coventry.

"She won't like it," sighed Hilda, shaking her head. "When I went to Lord Tennyson's funeral without her, I didn't hear the last of it for days. She cried when she read that the choir had sung his 'Crossing the Bar.' She so loves anything pathetic like that."

"Well, I'm afraid there's no help for it," said Mrs. Damien. "She'll have to put up with it, that's all. It hasn't been easy to get these two tickets; and there's an end of it. She must resign herself to staying at home for once." And she felt herself a vigorous woman indeed, compared with Hilda.

"I don't know. . . ." worried Hilda.

"You give in to her too much," declared Rose. "I always say it to Abbott: you give in to her too much."

"Oh well . . . anything's better than having a row," sighed Hilda.

"Is it? I'm not so sure. I'm not so sure. That's where you're weak, I think, Hilda. Believe me, I've nothing against old Mrs. Coventry; we all think she's a perfect dear in many ways, a perfect dear—but it isn't good for anybody to have their own way all the time. I'm sure *I* wouldn't put up with it. . . . No, no," added Mrs. Damien very emphatically, as she contemplated with satisfaction the picture of herself declining to put up with it. "You must put your foot down sometimes. Firmly."

"It doesn't do any good," Hilda explained sadly.

"I think *I* should make it do some good. You must——"

But it was at this point that Old Mrs. Coventry, standing without, suspected, very justly, a conspiracy within. And she entered the room, peering behind her steel spectacles. She justified her arrival very pleasantly, though Hilda suspected that there was discipline for her in the words. "I suppose there's no reason why I shouldn't come in. Hilda knows how I always like to come in when *you're* here, Rose. I heard from Ada that it was you. How are you, my dear?" And she kissed Mrs. Damien on both cheeks, holding both her hands. "And how's Abbott? And the boy—how's little Leo?" On hearing that Abbott and Leo were very well, she declared that Leo was getting tall for his age and Rose must see that he didn't outgrow his strength, as if Rose could in some way determine the stature of her son. Only at this point did she consent to release the hands of her visitor, and to breathe, "Yes . . ." The "Yes" was a mere meaningless sound to accompany her as she sat down.

She sat down in silence. Hilda had no courage to tell the mission of her friend, and Rose, despite her brave words, showed no sign of doing this for her. She fingered her dress, her boa, and the handle of her parasol instead. It wasn't *her* business, she told herself, to pick a quarrel with the old lady.

"Yes . . ." breathed Old Mrs. Coventry, looking from one to the other. She had remarked the silence, of course, and was more than ever certain that it veiled a conspiracy. They were concealing something from her. Few thoughts could exasperate her more. Her eyes bored into them. Her head nodded a little. Her lips

went forward and back, as she prepared to be rude.
She never had the least objection to being rude to her
friends. You had better understand at once that it was
almost incredible the way this little old lady could savage
her friends and yet retain them. They always forgave
her the next day. Perhaps it was because she forgave
them so readily ; perhaps it was because, when not
stabbing them with pointed words, she made a great
play of affection, holding their hands and patting the
gloves ; more probably it was just this, that she was the
best audience in the whole of Norman's End, ever ready
and eager to listen if they had a wrong to rehearse or a
tale to whisper of their neighbours. She listened with
gimlet eyes and a patting hand, and then poured out her
agreement and her sympathy. Avid for life, of which
too little came to this tall, narrow house, she was glad
to take it at second hand from the lips of her friends.
And they came round with it. They couldn't do without
her ; for with Old Mrs. Coventry they were sure of
steadfast listening, ardent agreement, and fluent sympathy.

This afternoon she opened with what might be called
the family gambit ; that is to say, she hit hard at Hilda,
and Rose took the bruise.

" Of course, if Hilda has something to talk to you
about that she would rather I didn't hear, I won't stay.
So often nowadays she has secrets from me. I don't
know why, I'm sure."

" Not at all," corrected Mrs. Damien hastily. " We
. . . There's nothing secret, I'm sure, is there, Hilda ? "

" No, no. Of course not. There's nothing secret,
Mamma. You imagine these things."

" Imagine ! " The old lady tossed her little head,

" I'm not quite a fool, though Hilda seems to think so, sometimes, I *must* say. I've been called many things in my life, I dare say, but I can't remember that I've ever been called a fool ; and I *do* wish she'd realise it sometimes ; I do really ! "

" Nobody thinks you're a fool, dear Mrs. Coventry," soothed Mrs. Damien.

" You don't, I know, my dear ; but Hilda does, I often fancy. She thinks I don't see when she's keeping something secret from me, whereas I see always— always ! And I so dislike all this secrecy. Why can't she be frank with me ? Everybody knows that I desire nothing but her good. I'm sure I've never given her reason to think I wish her anything but well. I'm sure I've always tried to show that I desire nothing but the happiness of her and Tom. Isn't he my only son, and haven't I tried from the very first moment to surround him and his with happiness ? I'm sure I've been a good and considerate mother if ever there's been one. And why should she——"

" Now, now," protested Mrs. Damien, perceiving that the old lady was working up for tears. " Now don't be angry with Hilda. She'll tell you everything that you ask her, I am certain. Why, we all love to tell you our little news because we know how kind and interested you are. . . . Well, Abbott is home, so I had better be going now. He never likes me to be away for long when he's at home. He likes to tell me anything of importance that's happened in the city." It was another of Rose's healing fancies that Abbott liked to do whatever she was resolved he should do, whereas, often enough, he had no strong desire that way. " Good-bye then, Hilda. Good-bye, dear Mrs. Coventry."

Old Mrs. Coventry rose too. " Oh, please don't go on *my* account. I beg you not to. I will go myself, and then Hilda can talk to you alone. I can see that that is what she wants to do, and I always know when I am in the way."

" I have no desire to talk to Rose alone, Mamma. *Won't* you believe me ? "

" Well then, what is it—*what* is it that there is between you ? "

" Nothing, nothing, Mamma."

" Don't be an idiot, Hilda. I've no patience with you—no patience at all. Anybody can see there's something. *You* tell me, Rose, if Hilda's too obstinate to do so. I quite understand that you feel it ought to come from *her*, but if she's in one of her moods and won't speak, *you'll* tell me, I'm sure. Is it something about Leo ? "

" No, no. Nothing about Leo. If there were anything the matter with Leo, I should be the first to tell you, dear Mrs. Coventry."

" Yes, you know how interested I am in all your little news. And I always stand up for poor Leo, don't I, Hilda ? Well now ; sit down and tell me what it is."

She sat down herself, leaned forward, and fixed her eyes on Rose ; who sat down too, put her boa back from her neck, and adjusted some trimming on the high slope of her bosom.

" It's nothing, dear Mrs. Coventry. Nothing at all, really. It's only that Abbott has been given two very good seats for the Jubilee, and I asked Hilda to come with me. He's really been very fortunate to get them at all, but he has influence, of course, in the city. . . ."

The old lady stared behind her spectacles ; she stared

for many seconds without being able to speak ; and it is possible that no child who had been told that her brothers were to go to the pantomime without her could have suffered a more sick disappointment. Her lips trembled ; her eyes filled. But she controlled herself and saw her course ; she must sound the pathetic note, and so hit hard all round.

"Of course Hilda must go. You and she go together, my dear. I won't say I hadn't hoped to go with her, but she'd rather go with you, I'm sure. I quite understand. The young people must stick together, and the old must stand aside."

"Oh, but you mustn't think that——" began Mrs. Damien.

"Of course I think it ! But I don't mind, my dear." And she took both of Mrs. Damien's hands in such a way as to leave Hilda most uncomfortably excluded from the connexion. "You two go and enjoy yourselves. Perhaps I can find somebody to take me, or I can go alone. Perhaps I'll find somebody who won't mind that I'm old. Or I can see the pictures of it in the illustrated papers. . . ." If Old Mrs. Coventry was the best listener to other people, she was also the best listener to herself ; she could be deeply moved by her own words. She was much moved now, and withdrew one hand to find a handkerchief.

"Perhaps Mr. Coventry will take you," encouraged Mrs. Damien.

"As if Tom would take me anywhere ! " snapped Old Mrs. Coventry, after blowing her nose till it was red. "Tom ! " And she dismissed her son with that sound. "And I sacrificed everything for him, God knows."

"Oh, *you* go, Mamma, and I'll stay," sighed Hilda.

" I shouldn't dream of going.   Rose doesn't want to
be landed with an old woman like me.   It's all right,
Rose ; don't you worry.   I want you young people to
be happy.   It's only that I'd rather Hilda told me things
to my face instead of conspiring behind my back.   After
all, I've had my time.   There were those who were glad
to take me once.   When the Princess of Wales came
to marry the Prince, Captain Abadie took my mother
and me, but I was young and attractive then, though
you mayn't believe it now.   They used to say I was like
the Empress Eugenie."

How far her likeness to the Empress Eugenie would
have shaken her lip and broken her up we shall never
know, because at this moment the door flung open, and
Cynthia burst into the room.

Cynthia was nine years old ; a slip of sexless humanity
with deep chestnut hair hanging round her face and a
fringe along her forehead.   Her shepherd's-plaid dress
was untidy from play, and one stocking hung down over
her boot.   Whether she would be beautiful hereafter
was still an open question.   In figure surely yes, but
her face was still soft and indeterminate.   Promise of
beauty peeped, maybe, in the large eyes lit with excitement, in the moving nostrils which were that rare thing,
a pair of identical twins, and in the wide full-lipped
mouth which the ardent speech broke open.

" Oh mummy, could I go out and play ? Rob Ingram
and the Ellison boys have just arrived on the wasteground.   Could I ?   *Could* I ? "

" You mustn't burst into the room like that," rebuked
her mother.   " There are visitors here."

" Oh, I'm sorry," exclaimed Cynthia, skipping with
impatience.   " Could I go ? "

"No, no," said Hilda. "The evenings turn cold. And I don't think children ought to go out and play in the cold, do you, Rose?"

"Yes, I do," answered Mrs. Damien.

When, like Rose Damien, you are very conscious that your character is of superior force to your listener's, you like to display that force, sometimes by correcting your listener's confusions, and sometimes by sharply disclosing a viewpoint completely opposed to her own.

Hilda looked up startled and annoyed; but Rose drove confidently on: "I think it is good for them to get out into the open. It isn't as if they'd meet any but children of their own class about here. I'm sure I wish Leo would go out more often and play with the others. I'm sure I have to force him out sometimes. I tell Abbott to *make* him go. But you know what Leo is. Upon my soul I wish he had more of **Cynthia's spirit**."

Hilda moved her head a little pettishly. She was angry at being always talked at by Mamma and corrected by Rose Damien. "Please don't encourage the child," she said. "It's absurd."

"Absurd?" If Dr. Johnson had been told by that poor booby of a Boswell that he was absurd he could not have expressed more surprise, more throttled indignation, than Rose Damien now. Hilda Coventry to call her absurd! *Hilda Coventry!* Unfortunately it deprived her of words. "Absurd," she repeated. "It's not absurd."

"Then can I go, mummy?" said Cynthia. "Can I go?"

"No."

"But they're playing 'French and English,'" submitted Cynthia as if that materially altered the argument.

"It's not the least absurd," said Rose Damien, to no one in particular. "I think I know what I'm talking about."

"Oh *please*, mummy."

"*No.* I don't choose that you should go, and that's enough. The evening's getting cold."

"Oh no, it isn't, mummy," assured Cynthia. "It's boiling."

And here we must emphasise that, whenever Cynthia Coventry wanted to do anything, the mood of all nature, in her view, was not only congruous but enthusiastic. If she wanted to stay indoors, she expounded volubly the patent fact that there was wind, or a dampness on the ground, or a threat of rain in the sky. If she wanted to go out, and Hilda thought it too cold or too hot, she declared, with aggrievement widening her eyes, that the weather had quite changed and was now the very opposite of all that her mother supposed. Mr. Guilder, her vicar and her great friend, used to say that, when she grew up, she must disguise herself as a man and become a barrister because, if her heart was in a cause, she could plead it as no one else. Before such pleading one felt ashamed that one had been so foolish as not to see the glaringly obvious fact or so cruel as to condemn what was manifestly free from all blame. If ever she was tried for murder, said Mr. Guilder, she must defend herself because no one would be within a hundred miles of doing it as well as she. Defending herself Cynthia was indeed at her best and most fluent. She never pleaded guilty. In all her nine years she had never once admitted to her judges that she had sinned. Always she could show most lucidly that it was a fortuitous combination of circumstances that had produced the undesired incident, and not any guilt of hers. When on one occasion she was wildly swinging a skipping rope and hit the unfortunate Leo Damien on the face, she ran home to tell her mother how terribly sorry she was, but that Leo had really put his face in the way. Mr. Guilder was present at this explanation, and at once commissioned her to defend *him*, should he ever stand charged with larceny ; and Cynthia, looking up at him, loved him the more for this raillery.

So now she reiterated, with wide, aggrieved eyes, that the weather was boiling. *Truly* it was. *Honestly* it was.

Hilda stamped her foot weakly. " That is enough. You are not to go. I have said so."

" Oh bust it ! " muttered Cynthia, beginning to sulk.

" And you're not to say ' Oh bust it.' It isn't ladylike. Don't you realise that people won't like you if you're rude and use these slang expressions."

" I don't care," said Cynthia. " I shall like myself."

Rose Damien guffawed, and Hilda turned on her. " I wish you wouldn't laugh at the child when I am rebuking her——"

" Nonsense, nonsense," smiled Rose, who had decided that one couldn't treat seriously anything so absurd as Hilda Coventry correcting *her*. " Nonsense, nonsense."

" I know my own child," rejoined Hilda, who now looked as sulky as her daughter. " I know that she gets over-excited and hot. She can never do anything quietly."

" Oh I *don't*," cried Cynthia, outraged, " and I *can* ! "

" That's enough. Run away and read some nice book."

" But I don't *want* to," expounded Cynthia, as if this were conclusive. " Honestly I don't." Something like tears stood in her eyes, for when she wanted a thing badly, nothing else in the world mattered, and she could hardly conceive that it was going to be denied her. Nice books? She hated them. The evening sunlight was on the wasteground, and Rob Ingram and the Ellison boys were running and shouting among the high grasses. "Oh please, mummy, *please* may I go? I'll keep absolutely cool. Absolutely. And it's roasting out."

"Cynthia, do what I tell you. Sit quietly in your nursery and read some nice book and enjoy yourself."

"I'll go and sit there," agreed Cynthia, "but I won't enjoy myself."

"Oh yes you will."

"No I shan't. Because I don't want to."

"Of course you'll enjoy yourself. You love reading."

"But I don't *want* to enjoy myself," explained Cynthia passionately, as if driven beyond endurance by the stupidity of people who couldn't see the obvious. And in her desperation at the unreasonableness of her mother —was it not roasting outside?—she thereupon risked all. She risked her very life.

This is a great moment in Cynthia's early years; it is heroic, because she is offering all. One utterance alone can give her the necessary relief. She has often thought of uttering it but has never before dared to, because like all the other children of her time and place, she is well versed in her Bible and knows that God may strike you dead if you lay a hand profanely on the ark or speak a sacrilegious thing. Cynthia believes this with such perfect simplicity that she has always shuddered when by accident she has laid another book on top of her Bible—which, according to Mr. Guilder, one must never do. And yet she has often been tempted to submit her bible to this profanity just to see the heavens fall. In the same way she is often tempted to a blasphemy. She is being so tempted now, and has made up her mind to yield. She is ready to break a lance with God. After all, what does life matter if one is forbidden to play with Rob Ingram and the Ellison boys, when the sun is on the wasteland? She moves away pouting; and at the door tosses her blasphemy from a rising wave of tears: "I don't *want* to enjoy myself, and not even God can make me do what I don't want to do." And she is out in the passage, waiting for death.

Nothing happens there. Nothing but the voice of her grandmother on the other side of the door, "Oh, you naughty, *naughty* little girl!" and the ticking of the clock in the hall below, and the quick thumping of her heart. Grandmamma's reproach is not interesting her; it seems a small affair compared with the question as to what God is deciding to do.

Nothing apparently. And she goes back to her window to stare at the boys playing on the wasteground, and to wonder what He is thinking, and to be a little unhappy at what she has done. For, however she may plead her innocence aloud, however she may proclaim to the world her freedom from all sin, her heart knows better. It dissents always from the best of her speeches, and remains unconvinced. In fact, during most of this her tale, whenever we shall see Cynthia running, playing, or sitting at her window—yea, right up to her twentieth year and beyond—we may assume that she is keeping company with a remembrance of guilt.

III

CYNTHIA took her eyes from the wasteground and looked down the length of Conyers Road. Coming up the road was a man. A tall man in middle life, of habit just beginning to become full. Her eyes descried the top hat, the short black coat tightly buttoned over the white waistcoat, the striped trousers and the grey spats ; and her mind immediately supplied all the rest—a moustache meeting close-cropped whiskers on full cheeks (which gave him, people said, such a likeness to Parnell) a pair of sad, absorbed but gentle eyes, a high white collar with a thin black tie, stiff white cuffs falling over the wrists, and a rolled umbrella in the big gloved hand. Her father. She raced out of the house to meet him, and her race was given a remarkable quality by the conflict between her eagerness to meet her father and the necessity of stepping on every coal-hole if bad luck were not to supervene.

Tom Coventry did not see her at first. Only his tall, full body was walking up Conyers Road. His soul was in a land of iridescent light. All things were good in this fair country where the gracious towers of one's dreams took shape in a soft, soothing air. It was a land of his own creation, and the usual hour of his translation there was when his office desk was locked for the night, and the door closed, and his body stowed in a District Railway train, and his newspaper lowered to his knees. Sometimes, however, he would pay it a quick visit between one letter and the next in the quiet of his office. Not difficult this, because, as Secretary of Deacon's Ecclesiastical Trust, he was master of his time, and had a room of his own, with a closed door, a thick red carpet, and a window overlooking Great Smith Street, Westminster. No one could say nay to him if he chose to rise from his desk and stand at the window for a little, with his hands on the base of his spine. Or to walk around the room and look up at the engravings of illustrious butcheries: Trafalgar, Balaclava, The Thin Red Line, and Waterloo, with Blücher and Wellington shaking hands over the illustrious mess. He was not seeing the pictures, of course, because his soul was in the iridescent land.

It was Hilda who had caused him to create this kindly, insubstantial place. If we are romantics it is so often our wives who quicken this creative gift in us. But Tom Coventry had warrant above most of us. He was as romantic as any other man cast in the foundry of Norman's End, and he had built up his cloud-hid country out of plentiful material indeed—to wit, the difference between what Hilda was and what he had dreamed she would be. How had he come to marry her, for whom he felt nothing but a kindly antipathy? How? Unable to see reality, Tom Coventry was unable to see the answer to this question, because it lay in the same inability to see reality. He had seen a long, languishing, corn-haired girl and invested her with a fabric of dream. He had married her, and she had turned into Hilda. Good God, into Hilda! Into Hilda, whose ceaseless inconsequent chatter drove him into his study (and into the iridescent land), whose

C

chatter was inconsequent just because it was ceaseless, and ceaseless just because she was a very silly woman.

Now he saw her distinctly, and it is probable that, out of business hours, she was the only reality he saw. He didn't exactly dislike her, because he had sense enough to see that the blame was his own, and kindness enough to pity her, but he recoiled from her. He recoiled from her colourless hair, her long thin limbs, her drooping back, and (most of all) her walk with the toes turned outward. Great Heaven, those outward-turning toes! I assure you his pain was very real when he thought of them. He had not foreseen them. He had not foreseen anything in Hilda ; and he suffered. Strictly moral in act (wherever his thoughts might stray) he had no one else but her ; and he was very hungry. This evening in his pearly dreamland he had met a different woman, an exquisite creature who had stroked his hair and laid her cheek against his. He had even—let the truth come out—run away with her, and they two together, encouraging and rejoicing in each other, had achieved famous things in the world. And Hilda and his mother, hearing of the fame, had learned what a jewel they had had in their midst and not understood.

But at Norman's End Station he had descended from the carriage not unhappily as he thought of his home and his chair and his dinner ; and he had decided, walking up the station stairway, that his high morality would not suffer him to do Hilda such a wrong. " One must live up to the highest that one sees," he thought. " I will bear my burden. I am one of those who is destined to be always alone."

No wise man was near to whisper him that he was

a contented as well as a discontented man ; that, like a cat on the cushions, he loved the comfort of his familiar home, the oiled ease of old habit, the sweet, drugging ecstasy of his dreams, and, yes, the warmth of his resentments. How he would have repudiated the idea that he found his yoke easy and his burden light !

One way of escape from Hilda was to dress exceedingly well, and so to feel that in this matter at least he was all that a man might be. But Tom Coventry's dress was not as good as he thought it. It was clean, close-fitting and well-pressed, but its total effect was old-fashioned. Walking, when business was done, in a gracious land where fashions did not change but stayed as they had been in his youth, he never perceived that in the real world men were making subtle changes in collars and ties and the position of watch-chains and the cut of the moustache. No doubt his tailor did his best for him, but it was by little things that he managed to achieve an out-of-date look. For example, no one to-day wore the collar and tie that he was bringing up Conyers Road. Or again : he had not yet observed that with full evening dress no man wore a black tie and all wore patent shoes. He would go to a party, feeling that he had attired himself very well and was a credit to the room ; but the young men were smiling.

He was feeling very well dressed this evening ; and I think I did not mention that he had a white carnation in his button hole. He also swung his rolled umbrella now and then, or smoothed its tight folds to make them even smoother. And adjusted the high collar beneath his chin.

Soon he saw his daughter running with a remarkable zig-zag action towards him. And since this looked like love and a welcome his heart leapt. Not that I may write anything so agreeable as that " Cynthia was the one perfect thing in his life." There was no perfect thing in his life—only over yonder in his dreams. She could stab him most cruelly if her hair was untidy, or her nose untended, or her eating unmaidenly. And it was often unmaidenly, for Cynthia did most things enthusiastically, and her eating was far too enthusiastic for grace—even for decency sometimes. They didn't eat like that in the country of his dreams. The only thing he would have wished her to do enthusiastically— namely, the kissing of her father—she scamped. She would give him a peck, and run to her play. And he did not tell her how she had hurt him, but took up his book again, and his burden with it.

This evening, however, as she ran towards him, she certainly looked a graceful wild animal, and loving withal. And a hope jumped in him. Between this first glimpse of the child and her arrival before him he saw her growing into a tall and beautiful woman, accompanying him in travels all over the world, caring for him in the days of his widowhood, delighting in him when he was a handsome old man, and throwing herself on to his death-bed to sob out, " My darling, darling father ! " He pushed his umbrella under his arm-pit so as to have both hands ready to welcome her.

She took the hands—but a little too casually for his content—and fell to walking at his side. He put his arm along her shoulder as they walked on, and the thought ran through him that it would be pleasant if she suddenly flung an arm around his waist and squeezed him affectionately. But she did not. Instead she poured forth her desire to play on the wasteground with Rob Ingram and the Ellison boys.

Anxious to-night to do all that would buy her love, he said yes, certainly she could go and play for a while.

" Oh may I ?   May I ?   May I go now ? "

" Yes, if you want to, my darling."

" And will you tell mummy ?   Will you tell her you said I might ? "

" I'll make it all right with your mother."

" Oh, *cheers !*   And tell her I'll keep absolutely perfectly cool."

He nodded ; and she was gone. There she was, running away from him again to the playground at the head of the road, with her legs swinging.

He sighed ; and flew away to his happier land.

IV

WHEN Rose Damien returned to her house in Conyers
Road and walked upstairs to remove her hat, she saw
Leo, her son, lolling with a book in his playroom.
This incensed her. Would nothing ever induce the
boy to go out and play like other boys? Nearly ten
years old, and for ever mooning with his toys or lolling
with a book. No wonder he was pale and weedy. Ten
years old, and still afraid of boys if they were bigger
than he. Because that was the truth of the matter: he
was afraid of them, and it sickened her to think that she
had a weakling for a son. Having a high opinion of
her own vitality, she was determined to get some
gumption into her son. Having likewise an unworried
conviction that she was right in all her views, she held
it for truth that the best way to put gumption into a
milksop was to harry him into the companionship of
" real boys " who would knock him about and so make
a man of him.

" Oh Leo ! " she protested at his door. " There you
are. Always moping indoors ! And don't shrink
whenever anyone comes near you ! Why aren't you
out playing with the others ? I saw them having a fine
time on the wasteground. Abbott ! "—she had gone
to the banister and was calling down the well of the
staircase—" Abbott, here's this boy stuffing indoors
again. Tell him to go out."

Abbott was sitting in the morning room when this voiced dropped down from on high. A well-cleaned little man, as we have heard, with groomed hair and neat features, he was still in the spruce attire that he carried to the city—except for a homely old coat that he had donned on returning, in a resolve to be cosy. Very different the loose and stained old coat from the rest of him, but I have an idea that it expressed the real Abbott Damien much better than the white waistcoat-slip and stern collar. It was the jacket, I suspect, in which he would have liked to spend his Sundays, if Rose hadn't made him a churchwarden with a frock coat, stiff cuffs, and gold watch-chain. So now: he would much rather have left the boy in his room and himself in his chair; but the path to cosiness didn't lie that way, so he took off his gold-rimmed spectacles, came to the foot of the stairs, and called, " Leo. Go out as your mother tells you; " after which he returned the gold spectacles to his nose and went back to his chair.

His voice reached the second landing where Rose Damien stood at Leo's door. " There ! " she exclaimed triumphantly, as if God had spoken from Sinai. " Get along out and try to be a man."

If Rose had sickened to see him lolling in his chair, Leo had sickened to see her standing at his door. There was nothing he hated more than playing with boys who made fun of him. And especially if Rob Ingram was among them, because Rob was three years older than he and had a habit, if one blundered in the game, of taking a kick at one's behind. It was not a hard and ill-natured kick so much as a gentle and joyous one, but it was humiliating to receive, and the other children laughed. This evening he had so hoped to escape from the real world with its kicks and its ridicule into the imaginary world of "Alfred at School" which he had been reading last night till his eyes tired. In that imaginary world Leo Damien played often a hero's part, whereas, down in this hated world of Conyers Road he could only be what a powerful mass-suggestion had made of him, and that was a furtive and shrinking waif, a target that quivered under the blows.

But his mother stood there, and one didn't argue with this fat and bustling woman any more than with Rob Ingram. He slunk from the room without a word, and no one knew, save himself and God, that he was suffering like a victim walking to his execution.

A bullied boy is never without guile, and Leo had a method of postponing as long as possible his departure into the street. He retired into the privy on the first landing, shot the bolt, and prolonged his stay there for a considerable spell. There was comfort in that bolt. But soon he heard his mother's voice calling, "Abbott, I don't believe that boy's gone yet. Tell him to go;" and his father's unenthusiastic "Leo! Go out as your mother tells you;" and he knew that his respite was at an end. With a pull on the chain he published to the house that his delay was blameless, and unloosed the protection of the bolt. Humming to show that he was not really afraid, he came down the stairs and passed out into the street.

Fifteen minutes earlier Cynthia had run from her father to the wasteground, but had not immediately joined the children in their play. Rob Ingram was there, the largest of them and their leader; and Grant Ellison and Gus Champion, his two henchmen, and Jack Trevelyan and Ernest Ellison, two younger boys who had an alliance of their own; and there was one girl, Aline Guilder, the vicar's daughter These six were playing "French and English," for the children of Norman's End, like their parents, provided house-room for many an idea that was twenty years out of date, and, in spite of 1870 and an imperial figure on the German throne, they still supposed that the French were the natural enemies of the English, and rightly abhorred.

Six children, and for "French and English" the sides should be even! Cynthia, who two minutes ago was pulsating with hope, now trembled with anxiety: perhaps they would not ask her to play. Would they? Oh would they? With her heart irregular and her knuckles at her mouth, she stared hard at the cannon-ball head of Rob Ingram, believing that this must make him look up and see her. He did so, but, unwilling to address directly a child so much younger than himself, he shouted to Grant Ellison, "I say, man, there's the Coventry kid! D'you want her?"

Hope and anxiety rent Cynthia, as her fingers stayed nervously at her lips. Truly life could be too painful at times.

"Well, man," grumbled Grant from the other end, "We shall have to have someone else if we have her."

Her heart emptied. Her eyes swung back to Rob, but without hope. Rob Ingram, however, had a mind to take her. "French and English" is a military game; and Rob did not differ from other generals in thinking that his dignity was enlarged if the cannon fodder was plentiful. "Well, look along the road, man," he ordered, "and see if there's anyone decent in sight."

Grant ran up the bank and looked down Conyers Road. "No. No one," he said.

"Oh well then. . . ." Rob accepted the disappointment with equanimity; it was not death to him, as to Cynthia.

"Wait a jiffy," cried Grant. "Here's Face Damien coming."

A contemptuous laugh from Rob: evidently Face Damien was a joke.

"Poor old Face!" he cried. And Ernest Ellison and Jack Trevelyan ran up the bank to see the approach of a fool. Jack, eager to stand well with Rob, shouted, "Lord-a-mussy, did you ever see such a drainpipe?"

"Never mind," answered Rob. "We'll make old Face play. Only I'll have the Coventry person, mind you." And, turning to Cynthia, he shouted, "You! Come along, whatever you call yourself."

Cynthia rushed down the bank to her joy.

And meanwhile Leo Damien came onward to his pain. Passing the last of the houses, he appeared in view of all the children; and here he stood above them, hesitating.

"Lummy!" cried Rob to Grant Ellison. "What an ass!"

"Hallo, Face!" cried the others. "Hallo, Stinkpot!"

Leo smiled as if he enjoyed their pleasantries.

"Look here, Face," shouted Rob. "'Joo want to play 'French and English'?"

"I don't mind if I do," answered Leo, putting a brave face on it. "Yes, thanks awfully, I should love to. . . ." and Cynthia, watching, knew dimly that he was trying to appear what they thought he ought to be ; and a spasm of pity went through her.

"Right then," shouted Rob. "Come along. You're on Ellison G's side, and for pity's sake don't let him down, because he's rather annoyed at being given you."

The game began ; eight children crossing and re-crossing one another on a square of tussocky grass, where the charlock ran and the daisies, and the nettles stood high under the bank, and the pavements and the house-backs framed the scene. Their voices pierced the evening ; and the voices of the boys were no different from those of the girls. Cynthia, playing with wet brows, dishevelled hair and storming breast, found time to wonder that anything which was such a thrilling delight to her could be such manifest unhappiness to Leo Damien. His movements fascinated her : she felt drawn to watch him. She watched him shrinking from the bull-like rushes of Rob Ingram, or making a brave effort, against all his inclination, to stop Jack Trevelyan. She saw his sickly grin when they shouted abuse at him. She noticed that he refused to run away when Rob charged up to him, bringing a merry and encouraging kick. He just stood and grinned that he might earn a record for being as other boys. Odd : his pain stirred a funny exaltation in her, as well as a sharp pity.

In her excitement and her interest she did not perceive that a figure had paused upon the pavement and was looking down with an amused and admiring gaze upon the children at play among the nettles and the flowers. But there was such a figure : a short, wide-shouldered man with a magnificent face ; wearing a clerical frock-coat and a tall hat, and holding a black bag in his hand.

This is the most remarkable figure in Norman's End. This is the explanation of much in Cynthia, and a potent force in her destiny. So, before she looks up and recognises him with a shout, I must tell you all about him.

V

THIS Norman's End was plainly a little kingdom, and over it reigned a king. They called him the Uncrowned King of Norman's End. I marvel to think of the power that was the Rev. Wilfred Guilder's. I can scarcely believe what I recall of his church whose grey spire dominated our roofs even as Mr. Guilder dominated his people. Not a resident in that Square Quarter Mile (at least none that I knew) but went along the pavements to St. Alban's on a Sunday ; not a woman but discussed parochial gossip and little else at her At Home days ; not a child, whether seven or seventeen, but believed quite simply that St. Alban's was the most important thing in his world, and Mr. Guilder the highest authority, and the many activities of the parish where children had a place—the Guilds, the Bazaar, the Pantomime—a source of the jolliest hours. Even the great tall boys of Trinity School walked unquestioningly to church ; and as for the girls of Lammas, they went joyously up the steps of St. Alban's and divided their worship between the God Whom Mr. Guilder preached and Mr. Guilder himself. The church had to be enlarged in our time to take the people who crowded there ; the Bazaar broke its own record year by year ; and the Christmas Pantomime spread its repute far beyond our borders. Of the Trinity boys it is hardly exaggeration to say that, in the end, half of them were in the church, and most of the rest on the stage. And of the girls of the Guilder period you will find many doing pious work in various parts of the world, and others starring in the provinces.

And yet St. Alban's had no gorgeous ceremonial to help it, and no fine music. Its services were the simple broad-church services of the time, and its music (so said the few who knew anything about it) was abominable. It had only Mr. Guilder.

I bow to his memory. He was a good deal less than a saint, but he must have had greatness somewhere or he could not have done so great a work. His gifts were as much those of the actor as the priest; but the priest was in him as well as the actor. He was a martinet with his four assistant curates, but they admired him, and speak well of him now. And it is always difficult to believe much ill of those whom the children loved. His appearance helped him, no doubt. Though short and broad, he had the face, as Mrs. du Pré used to say, of a senior archangel. The fair hair, beginning to grey, was parted in the middle and waved down to the ears like an ageing woman's; but there was nothing feminine about the keen eyes, the straight thin nose, the thin determined lips, and the huge wide shoulders. Some likened him to a fighting saint of the Middle Ages; others to an actor manager of the current century—and indeed his resemblance to Mr. Wilson Barrett in *The Sign of the Cross* was extraordinary —and most agreed that he could have been a Don Juan, had he cared. Enemies avouched that he did care.

But if enemies spoke ill of his character, there was no speaking ill of his work. Nowadays we are accustomed to see the church struggling against odds: at Norman's

End, in the Guilder reign, it was triumphant, jubilant, masterful. Perhaps it was the last great day of the church. Or perhaps this Norman's End, where a perfect middle class had silted up, was well made to be the church's last happy ditch. We did not know that we were a perfect middle class, but I suspect that Mr. Guilder did, who had humour and wit in his eyes and few delusions about his people. To be the perfect middle class is to stand half-way between all things ; and we stood half-way between Society which ended at Earl's Court (if it got so far) and the People who began near the river ; half-way between town and country ; half-way between religion and worldliness ; between High Churchmanship and Low Churchmanship, between Victorianism and that which was to come, between the Machine Age in its pride and the same age in its dismay, and between Security and the collapse of all our old and comfortable things.

But there is one thing difficult to understand about Mr. Guilder. Often I think and think about it. He taught us much that was good, I am sure, but how came he, an intelligent and gifted man, to teach us so much that seems ridiculous to-day : that nothing must ever be allowed to stand on the Bible, for instance, or that each of our peccadilloes crucified our Lord afresh— terrifying doctrine that haunted our childhood and is not gone from the shadows yet ! Was it that he was the product of his age and could believe it all in some way that we, turned in the sharp lathe of a subsequent age, can no longer understand ? Was it that he had gifts for oratory and organisation, but none for theology, which didn't interest him ? Or was it that he just gave his people what they expected ? But then he could hardly have taught it to Cynthia and the rest of us children. He liked us too well, I think, to treat us so cynically.

Cynthia looked up and saw him as he smiled down. Leaving all, she ran to him, crying, " Mr. Guilder! Mr. Guilder! Mr. Guilder! " because the abounding life in her compelled her to say such delightful words three times. And when she had got up to him and taken the hand that he extended, she stared into his face with nothing more to say, her breast panting.

" And how's our Cynthia? " asked Mr. Guilder. " Take your time about answering, Miss. Take your time."

" I'm all right. Where are you going? "

" I am walking back to the Vicarage."

" Oh may I come with you? *May* I? "

" But what about the combat down below? "

" Oh, I'm tired of that. It's getting mouldy. Besides, if I go off with you, they'll let Leo Damien go; and he's dying to, I can see. *Honestly* he is. They keep bumping into him."

" What? Not on purpose? "

" Yes. They think it's funny, but I don't think he really likes it."

" Poor Leo Damien: he's always in the wars, isn't he? "

" Yes; and I'm certain he'd like to go home. *Honestly* he would. So may I walk back with you? Oh, *please*."

" My dear, I shall be honoured. Come by all means."

" *Cheers!* " murmured Cynthia, under her breath.

And they walked off together through the summer light, a short broad man in black garments and a slip of a skipping girl. They were not many steps from the wasteground before Cynthia decided to ask him an important question. Uneasy about the blasphemy she had spoken that evening, she was in a mood to take expert advice upon it. That sense of sin which is the gift of Protestantism to its children had been worrying in her heart, even as she ran from base to base in Rob Ingram's game, or bumped with a scream into Aline Guilder; and now she felt that she would like to hear from Aline's father, who knew everything, that God has not cast her out utterly. Evening was in the streets; and the dusk and the darkness were near.

So, leaping a little that she might not appear too much ashamed, she told him the story. He did not laugh at her. Instead he looked sideways down at the upturned, seeking eyes, and surprised her with the words, "But Cynthia: unconsciously you spoke the absolute truth. God *can't* make you do what you don't want to do."

"Oh yes He can!" declared Cynthia, somewhat shocked.

"No."

"But *why?*"

"Because He has given you free will. He was so sure of you that He has left you free to do what you want. His confidence in you was so enormous, you see; His trust in you so huge. And He hasn't misplaced it, I know."

Cynthia was silent for a few steps. This Divine trust was touching her; and she was thinking that she would like to be worthy of it. She saw in a vision a long, holy life stretching before her. Mr. Guilder had raised this vision in her many times before, and it was never wholly to disappear; it was to fight with her, and for her, for the rest of her days.   And to-night, as an obvious first step towards it, she refused to spare herself in her confession ; with another small skip she insisted on the completeness of her crime.   " Oh, but if I spoke the truth, it was only by accident, I'm afraid ; because all I wanted to do, really, was to say something profane. Honestly I did."

" Then I'm afraid the devil was beside you, tempting you," said Mr. Guilder.   " You mustn't let him win, Cynthia—

> " There's a wicked spirit,
>   Watching round you still,
> And he tries to tempt you
>   To all harm and ill.

> " But ye must not hear him,
>   Though 'tis hard for you
> To resist the evil
>   And the good to do."

" I suppose there really *is* a devil ? " asked Cynthia, when he had finished.

" Of course there is !   Who's been telling you there isn't ?   Now look here, my child : when you grow older, people will try to make you believe that there's no such thing as a real personal devil, but don't you listen to them.   Remember it's the devil himself working through them, because one of his most subtle temptations is to make people deny that he exists.   Then he's free to tempt them with twice the chance of success."

" I see."

With all the force of his personality behind it this

doctrine went straight into her soft, receptive mind that night—to live there among the shadows for many a long year. I tell of it because it is one of those things in Mr. Guilder that bewilder me. Here was a doctrine, you perceive, that carried its own preservative within it, like canned cream ; it cut the ground from under you if you approached to the attack ; it knocked you down if you dared to question it.

But she did not remark this, nor her vicar either. They walked along together, out of Glastonbury Road into Parson's Road, quite satisfied with its fairness. Mr. Guilder was now comforting her with the assurance that, if the devil was always near her, so too was Jesus, ready and waiting to help her. And because He was always there, watching her, she mustn't wound him with these little acts of rebellion. She didn't want to hurt Him, did she ? But one thing was certain : He would forgive her at once if she was contrite and asked His forgiveness on her knees, as she would that very night, he was sure. Cynthia promised that she would—indeed she was looking forward to it keenly— and they were free to talk of other matters.

" What are you going to do now ? " she demanded.

" Have dinner."

" Lucky *thing!* And what are you going to do after dinner ? "

" Well, then I have a Class for Sunday School teachers."

" Oh, *may* I be a Sunday School teacher when I'm old enough ? I'd love to."

" I shall insist upon it."

" How soon ? "

" When you're sixteen, shall we say ? "

" Oh *joy !* And can I be a district visitor too, and have a district, like Mummy ? "

" When you're eighteen."

" Oh hurray ! But what I'd really like to do would be to be a proper clergyman."

" And why do you want to be a proper clergyman ? "

" Oh I don't know." She skipped into the gutter and back again on to the kerb, at his side. " It must be so lovely running bazaars and pantomimes, and dressing up in a surplice and preaching in a pulpit with everybody staring up and thinking there's nobody like you."

" But is that quite the motive for setting about the work ? Shouldn't you do it for Jesus' sake ? "

" Oh yes, I'd do it for that too," agreed Cynthia.

" I'm sure you would."

Thus prattling of Jesus in the evening light, they came to the vicarage, hard by the church's wall. The vicarage had a narrow garden of gravel and shrubs ; and at its low gate Mr. Guilder halted, to bid her good-night. She looked up at him as if expecting—or hoping for—something ; and he stooped and kissed her on the forehead. Instantly she threw her arms about his neck in gratitude and love. It was an embrace that would have lifted high the heart of Tom Coventry—but such offerings are not for fathers. Mr. Guilder accepted her kiss with a smile, and when it was over, put her gently away and patted her head. " There, there ! " he said. " God bless you, my dear. Run along home now."

Greatly happy at this agreeable close to the day, she ran off, turning to wave a hand when the distance justified it. And Mr. Guilder stood at his gate, watching her. He watched till she was round the corner of Parson's Road and out of sight. Then he went through his gate. She had stirred anew his affection for all the children of his parish, and he was wondering if there were more he could do for them. That his work among the children was the purest of his labours he knew very well, and, feeling of a sudden heavy and sorrowful, he hoped that it might weigh a little in the balance against pride, display, egotism, and secret, illicit hungers.

VI

In Cynthia's memory the Diamond Jubilee was associated with a high thrill. One night just before bedtime she became aware that there was alarm in the house. Downstairs her mother was moving about the passages in agitation ; and twice her father came to his door and called out that there was no need to get excited. Her father, she had noticed, was always impatient with her mother when she got fussed and flurried. He rebuked her for such panicking, and himself became a model of calmness and self-control—an offensive model, Hilda thought. " It will probably turn out all right," he called this evening ; " for God's sake don't fuss ; " and went back to his room shutting the door. But a little later her mother was ringing for the servants and consulting them in undertones. Ada, the housemaid, passed Cynthia where she stood eavesdropping on the first landing, and, being a raw girl with an appetite for alarm, drew a vivid pleasure from telling the child that her grandma was lawst and no one knew where she gawn. " Your ma thinks she may have had an accident in the streets, being that short-sighted as she is, but the master says he'll give her a little while longer before he starts arstin' the p'leace. But law ! your ma isn't half in a stew, and the dinner's doin' to rags. If I was her, I'd step round to the p'leace myself."

This was a thrill. Cynthia hoped, of course, that her

grandmother had not had an accident, but she could not deny a leaping desire that *something* should turn out to have happened. After this promising opening any other issue would be an anti-climax. The certainty that she desired this, and no less, seemed very wicked to her, till she took comfort from the knowledge that she couldn't bear the old lady to be hurt, but would be content if she had fainted somewhere, in a way quite pleasant to experience. Even this seemed rather unkind and was doubtless the work of the devil at her side ; but she couldn't pare down the hope any further, and took it with her to bed.

Old Mrs. Coventry had left the house about four o'clock. Ever since Hilda and Rose Damien had told her that they were going to the Jubilee without her she had been enduring the birth-pangs of a resolve ; for days and nights she had been enduring them ; and now, at four o'clock this afternoon, she was delivered of the resolve, a fine kicking infant. She would go off alone to see the decorated streets. It would give them a lesson. It would punish Hilda and Rose and Tom to think of an old woman sitting alone on the top of a bus and staring out from her solitariness at the gay decorations, because no one wanted her. They would be ashamed when she returned home and told them where she had been.

In cape and bonnet she slipped from the house as guiltily as Cynthia might have done. In Norman's End Lane she got into a bus that took her to Hyde Park Corner. At Hyde Park Corner she had difficulty in getting to the top of a bus that would pass through the decorated streets, for many other people were engaged on the same enterprise, and however she might hold her umbrella aloft and run for the vehicle's step, there were others more active than she. A kind young man, however, took pity on her (as her craft had foreseen) and bustled her on top of a green bus and put her in the best seat of all behind the driver, where she was soon as happy as the happiest sightseer on the highway that day. She exchanged her fervencies with the passengers behind. She shared her laughs with the woman at her side. She was even arch with the driver, who was facetious and talkative. The luxuriant decorations, the streaming people on the pavements, the lively crowds on the bus-tops or in the wagonettes, the voices and laughter on the air made up an invigorating draught for this little old lady who so loved life and could never get enough of it.

Surely no such decorations had been seen before: Venetian masts with bannerets taking the breeze and festoons of evergreen stretching from mast to mast and across the roadway, so that the bus carrying the bonnet and egret of Old Mrs. Coventry passed beneath openwork awnings of greenery; huge gas-lit stars and monograms—" V.R.I."—between the windows of high buildings; " 1837-1897 " everywhere; mighty stands blocking out whole facades and built into every corner, and all festooned with red, white and blue; favours on every man and woman in the crowd; coloured ribbons plaited in the tails and the manes of the horses, or entwined in the wheels of the bicycles; gas-jets spiralling up the columns of one building, and fairy lamps ready to illuminate the outline of the next—I tell you Old Mrs. Coventry took fire with loyalty to her Queen and with pride in her Empire! " Come the four corners of the world in arms, and we shall shock them ! " Tears were very near the surface as she peered through her spectacles at all this ebullition of a nation's love. Her lips shook and moved.

Always the tears came easily to Old Mrs. Coventry's eyes. As witty Mrs. du Pré used to say, " she could turn on the waterworks at the least provocation ; " and anyone who witnessed her wiping her eyes or blowing her nose at some tale of duty done or suffering borne would have supposed her compassionate indeed. So she was, up to a point. She did not, it is true, give money to the stricken, because she kept a very tight hold on her few possessions, but she gave largely of her sympathy which cost her nothing because it was effortless, inexhaustible, and wholly pleasant. This evening it was the sight of love that made her lift her veil and touch her eyes with her handkerchief and blow a low note on her nose—while the driver turned his head to see what ailed her. The mottoes on the triumphal arches played the devil with her lips and eyes. " God save our Queen ; " " Our Hearts thy Throne ; "—these were disturbing enough ; but when across the face of a stand she saw " In every Heart one Prayer, God save Victoria," it choked her. She bowed her head till she had recovered.

Such mounting emotion cried for relief ; and when the bus stopped at St. Paul's, she tripped quickly down and, though her buttoned kid boots were hurting her now, climbed the steps of the cathedral, passed into its echoing darkness, and knelt and prayed. She prayed for the Queen and the Empire, and rose feeling all that serenity, humility, and self-satisfaction which follow prayer. She felt right with God. Coming out through the door, she saw the poor box, and, to sustain this

feeling of goodness and to add value to her prayer, she
fetched a sixpence from her purse and dropped it in.

In St. Paul's Churchyard she saw another bus which
was going on towards the Mansion House where there
were more decorations; and, quite unable to leave
anything unseen if there was an opportunity of seeing
it, she contrived to push and hoist herself aboard.
These parts she could not bear to leave till she had seen
the first iridescent monograms and the first gas fairy
lamps spring into light—and in fine, it was after eight
o'clock before she was homeward bound in a District
Railway train.

As the train steamed towards Norman's End apprehen-
sion came. What would they say at home? She
was not afraid of Hilda whom she knew she could bully,
but she was a little afraid of Tom. Her attitude to her
son is illuminating. Never was there an old woman
more regular at church; never one who could get
hotter (and ruder) in her support of the proprieties—
the word " moral " was for ever on her lips and she
fully believed that she believed in it, but it was not
there for the reasons she supposed—and yet deep down
in her heart she despised her son for being so moral.
It was dull. Deep down in her heart she admired the
gay libertines. But though rather despising his apparent
strictness she was sometimes afraid of it; and to-night,
sitting in her corner seat, she began to compose
arguments that would show how completely the wrong-
doing was Hilda's and his. For she was like her
grand-daughter in this, that she invariably protested
that it was fate, or the other person, who had erred, and
not she. The difference between these two was that
Cynthia, however indignantly she might argue her

innocence, was often troubled by the sense of sin, whereas Old Mrs. Coventry had no such handicap.

Her return through the door of 22 Glastonbury Road was a small sensation. Hilda flurried out in the uncontrolled manner that her husband despised; Ada delayed on the basement stairs that she might hear the story; the cook leapt up them for the same purpose; and even Tom consented to come to his study door, but in good order.

" Where *have* you been ? " demanded Hilda petulantly. " What a fright you have given us ! "

Fright ? Cynthia herself could not have looked more surprised at this unexpected and unwarranted attack.

" Fright ? Why should you be frightened ? I've just been alone to see the decorations."

" It wasn't right of you to go alone like that, telling us nothing."

And here Old Mrs. Coventry drove home her stiletto. " Nobody would take me, so I went alone."

" Ridiculous ! " began Tom.   " You know that——— "

But his mother was much too good a general ever to listen when anyone opened an attack. She always knocked out such an attack by a sally-in-force of her own; and whether the sally was irrelevant or not mattered nothing, so long as the enemy lost the initiative.

" It's not ridiculous ! Not at all ! I'm nearly seventy, and there'll never be another Jubilee in my lifetime. Hilda and Rose Damien might have thought of that, I *do* consider, instead of thinking only of themselves like all young people to-day. I don't suppose I shall see a Coronation either. I'm sixty-seven, and we can't tell what'll happen : I may be bed-ridden when the Queen goes. I'm sure it's wonderful I'm as active as I am; everyone says so. Let me have what pleasure I can, while I am still able to enjoy it—that's all I ask, and I don't see that it's much. If I'm not to see the Jubilee, don't grudge me a look at the decorations. *Please* don't do that. *Please*, I beg of you. It's not my fault if I'm interested in all that concerns my country, and *you're* not. I don't ask anyone to take me, as far as I'm aware; I can go alone. Have I asked anyone to take me? Have I——"

"Don't talk such nonsense," interrupted Tom. "I would have taken you to see the decorations. I was arranging only to-day to take you all. Cynthia ought to see them, and now you've spoiled everything."

"Oh, but I'll go again," said the old lady promptly and brightly. "Yes, Cynthia must see them. It's something she'll remember till she dies, and I doubt if even she'll see another Jubilee in her lifetime, unless the Prince of Wales goes before the Queen. The triumphal arches are wonderful. Most moving. One says, 'Our Heart thy Throne' and another, 'In every Heart one Prayer. . . .'" but she couldn't continue this one for the gathering tears.

So to-morrow they took the decorated journey again, all four of the Coventrys. Cynthia sat beside her grandmother in the front seat of a bus, and she could have had no better companion: the old lady was abreast of her in interest and enthusiasm. If Cynthia observed something exciting her grandmother insisted on seeing it too. Her spectacles were directed everywhere. Soon the mottoes on the arches were playing havoc with her again. She turned to Hilda and Tom in the seat behind and explained that the Queen was beloved because she had always been moral—which statement, in its beauty, seemed to shatter her self-control, for her lips shook with unshed tears. Cynthia gazed over the side of the bus : she was always embarrassed when granny's emotions were getting the better of her.

After this trip the Jubilee was frothing in Cynthia's head quite as much as in her grandmother's. She talked of little but the Queen and the Empire. Did the Queen eat always off gold ? Did she have hundreds of maids to dress her, or did she have to pull on her own stockings ? How many dresses had she ? Was our Empire the largest the world had ever seen ? How much larger was it than anyone's else's—for a child's philosophy of life is always vulgar. It is the philosophy of the largest helping. Some of us grow out of it as we grow older ; most of us don't, and then we become millionaires, or admirers of the same. Or militarists. Cynthia was every inch a militarist. Was our navy *ever* so much bigger than anyone else's. Could England beat any three nations put together ? Four ? Five ? Would it one day conquer the whole world ? Cheers !

And by this time the loyal inhabitants of Norman's End had decorated their houses too. The stucco balconies or the red-brick walls bore shields of radiating flags, and the red, white and blue of the Union Jack on the shield picked out the colour of the scarlet geraniums, the white marguerites, and the blue lobelia in the window-boxes. Look ! the very flowers had turned patriotic. Hurray, hurray !

And then on the Sunday morning before the Jubilee a Thanksgiving Service was to be held in every church in the land. By half-past ten the bell of St. Alban's was calling all loyal subjects, and Cynthia was looking from her window to see the people coming out of their houses and walking quietly along the pavements to church. See! there were the Damiens appearing from under their portico far down Conyers Road—Abbott, as churchwarden, would have his work cut out to-day. There went the Ellison boys with their mother; here was Rob Ingram with his people—oh why couldn't they start straightaway? She was quite ready. She stood in her white muslin dress, white cotton gloves, and black stockings and shoes. On her head was a big Leghorn hat, trimmed with flowers. And her grandmother was ready. Grandmother had been ready as soon as she, and was now standing in the hall, impatiently tapping a foot on the tiles, or calling up the stairs " Come, come, we shall be late. *Hilda*, do come along! " Hilda called that oh dear, she was coming; and soon they were on the pavement walking silently to church. When they turned a corner and saw the crowds pressing up the steps of St. Alban's Old Mrs. Coventry quickened her pace, exclaiming, " Oh, do come on! We shall never get a seat." In the half-darkness of the church they were met by Abbott Damien who escorted them up the nave to a pew some dozen from the front. But Old Mrs. Coventry would have none of this. In a loudish whisper to Hilda she explained that she would never see anything so far back as this, and such a service would never be held again in any of their lifetimes. Leaving Abbott where he stood, she descried a seat two from the front and hurried towards it, Cynthia most skilfully following.

When Cynthia had knelt for a prayer, she sat back and lifted her eyes to scan the church she knew so well. The first thing that she observed was a large Union Jack hanging down from the centre of the rood-beam, immediately beneath the cross. The roof of the church was so dark that the flag seemed to emerge gradually out of the darkness like something in the process of being created, but not yet complete. No other decoration anywhere ; just a single flag at the foot of the cross, swinging like a punkah in the draught up there.

This was the Guilder touch.

Oh great, stirring day ! The people were pouring in, and every pew was packed, and the sidesmen were fetching chairs from the vestry and from St. Alban's Hall across the yard. Abbott Damien, very neat in frock coat and waistcoat-slip, was putting people into the chancel itself, in a row of chairs before the choir stalls—so great was his authority. Cynthia felt proud that he was their friend. Way back in the church-warden's pew Rose Damien watched him too, and was great by proxy. Old Mrs. Coventry had her spectacles up, and was studying it all. And when Cynthia, turning her head, saw a crowd standing many deep at the back of the church and whispered this interesting news, her grandmother exclaimed, " Where ? Where ? " and turned to see it too.

Now a noise of a congregation rising. The choir and clergy are entering. They take their places, and all eyes seek Mr. Guilder as he passes into the vicar's stall. The organ booms the familiar opening bar of a hymn ; a thousand hands pick up a thousand leaflets from the pews ; and the mighty pæan bursts forth : " Now thank we all our God, With hearts and hands and voices." The hearts of all are full, and their throats too. It is an apotheosis of Britain and her Queen.

It is also, in smaller fashion, an apotheosis of Norman's

End and its King. Cynthia stares up at Mr. Guilder
in his stall. He is so important and yet her friend.
Let the truth be stated at last : Cynthia has a happy,
guilty secret ; she loves Mr. Guilder better than
anybody—better even than her father and mother.
In fact, ever since she learned from Ada that " gurls
are like as not to fall in love with gentlemen
much older than theirselves " she has been in love
with Mr. Guilder ; and to be in love with someone
is, by definition, to love that person better than your
father and mother. Sometimes, so strange is her
leaning towards an occasional blasphemy, she has been
tempted to say, " I love him better than God." To-day,
staring up at him in all his glory, she is being strongly
tempted to say it, because she feels it would be doubly
blasphemous in church. Anything might happen.
She does not do it, but contents herself with staring at
Mr. Guilder in his stall.

Now he is in the pulpit ; and the congregation, sitting
down, is hypnotised into silence as it waits for the great
event of the morning. Cynthia turns to one side that
she may see him better, and she is not the only person to
think he looks magnificent up there, with his fair greying
hair parted in the middle and waving down to the ears,
and his keen-featured, thin-lipped face gazing over his
people. He leans on the pulpit lectern—and he has
begun. Very quietly he has begun, because he knows
the power of his voice to command and hold an interest.
" *Jubilate*," he says. " *Jubilate Deo*." Ten years before,
in an earlier jubilee, they had celebrated the queen as a
woman ; to-day they were celebrating her as Britain
itself—Britain at the highest peak of its power and its
greatness. In every sphere—in science, in literature,

in trade, in empire—God had been pleased to vouchsafe greatness to a nation which, with all its faults, had taken its stand on the Holy Scriptures and the homely virtues. And of this nation how perfect a symbol was their beloved queen, a simple, home-loving, chaste, and motherly woman. (Old Mrs. Coventry wept.) Well might they rejoice in the Lord for her, and for all of which she was the symbol. As a nation they might learn from her. She bore her greatness with simplicity, taking it from the hand of God in Whose service it must be used. Let them also have faith in their greatness, and yet bear it with humility, laying it all at the foot of the cross—and his hand pointed to the Union Jack floating slowly in the twilight under the rood.

It did not occur to Cynthia or to anyone else in that church—not even to Mr. Guilder, a man gifted but not intellectual—that an imperialist flag and the cross of Calvary were two symbols that harmonised but ill, or that this inspiring address was of a piece with all the Diamond Jubilee celebrations in being less a tribute to the Empress Queen than a glorification of Ourselves as the Boss Nation which had made good money, conquered the world, donned the millionaire's fur coat, and would now put a diamond pin in its tie. Rather did all agree with Mr. Guilder that they should kneel down and thank God for their successful blend of worldliness and other-worldliness.

Mr. Guilder certainly had a talent for effect. In every other church in the realm the people rose to sing the Jubilee Hymn; we alone in St. Alban's, at the bidding of our vicar, sang it on our knees. Good Bishop Walsham How wrote this hymn for the Jubilee; and as I remember it now, I am glad that our attitude

E

was humble because I cannot see that his words were. On our knees and softly we sang :

> " *For every heart made glad by thee*
>   *With thankful praise is swelling* ;
> *And every tongue with joy set free*
>   *Its happy theme is telling.*
> *Thou hast been mindful of Thine Own—*

none of us blushed as we sang this—

> " *And lo ! we come confessing*
> *'Tis Thou hast dowered our queenly throne*
>   *With sixty years of blessing.*
>
> *O Royal heart, with wide embrace*
>   *For all her children yearning !*
> *O happy realm, such mother grace*
>   *With loyal love returning !*
> *Where England's flag flies wide unfurled,*
>   *All tyrant wrongs repelling,*
> *God make the world a better world*
>   *For man's brief earthly dwelling.*"

But our interest is less with a Jubilee than with Cynthia who knelt there, a small expression of the nation's mood, jubilant, exulting, sanguine, questioning nothing and fearing nothing. I see her as a gift thrown up by life, as the grass is thrown up and the trees and the weeds ; or, if you like, as the flowers appeared in the still unconquered fields of Norman's End. Life rises full and strong in her, so that she is eager, generous, foolish, bursting to give herself to someone or to something ; rich, pliant, dangerous material for people and circumstance to form as they will.

VII

MEMORY foreshortens the time of childhood so that events which were really far apart seem nearer together than they were. No doubt the street salesmen, such as the fly-paper man and the old groundsel-peddler, did not come so often along the camber of Glastonbury Road as it seemed to Cynthia in after years. Nor the wandering entertainers such as the man with the bear and the highlander with his lass. But, seen in retrospect, her ninth and tenth years seemed a constant jumping up from her play on the floor and a running to the window at the sounds of minstrelsy without. Strange visitors from that outer world in which she found herself existing were coming up the road. Bagpipes, bagpipes ! It was the highlander and his lass ; and possibly if they saw her face at the window (and maybe her grandmother's face at the window above) they would throw down the swords in the form of a cross, and the kilted girl would do a leaping dance among them, while her partner played a merry accompaniment, one toe beating time. Or a barrel-organ shattered the silence without warning of any kind ; and there was the little unshaven Italian looking up at the windows and touching his black curls, while his monkey in the red jacket, the best beggar of them all, leapt and swung on its chain and touched its forelock too. Or a doleful cadenza on the wind instruments jumped her to her feet, and the German

band in its peaked caps was assembled at the corner of
Conyers and Glastonbury Roads. But best of all—
far away the best of all—was the one-man orchestra.
You recognised him in the distance by the monotonous
beat of his big drum. The drum was fixed on his back
and he beat it with a stick tied to his elbow ; bells were
hung on his pagoda-like hat, Pandean-pipes tied under
his lips, and I forget what instruments he played with
his hands and his knees and his feet. He too, if you
looked hard enough, could be induced to place his stool
at the pavement's edge, and sit down and give you a
protracted performance. I protest these things do not
happen any more. The occasional drunkard who has
lost his way in the Square Quarter Mile does not go
rolling homeward, singing his song ; for we are a soberer
nation now. Nor does the man fall down in a fit and
hit his head an alarming crack on the pavement, and the
crowd gather round him, and Ada run out with a cup
of water in Christ's name—at least, perhaps he does
this still, but it doesn't seem such vivid entertainment
now.

And one day Cynthia heard a hammering outside.
A hammering, just beneath her window and across the
road. She ran to the window and saw men building a
hoarding round her wasteground. What did it mean ?
Old Mrs. Coventry and Hilda, being equally interested
to know what it meant, ascertained the news before the
day was done. Flats. A huge block of flats was to be
built on this corner site. Cynthia inquired what flats
might be, and her grandmother said they were a new-
fangled way of living, in a tone that left Cynthia with the
idea that flats were not altogether nice ; which made the
building of such dubious homes all the more interesting

to watch. Cynthia watched often and long. The walls rose higher and higher ; the scaffolding shot above them into the sky ; daily the same cheery men, with hods on their shoulders, mounted the ladders whistling and singing ; daily the bricklayers, unafraid on their dizzy platforms, slapped bricks on to mortar, or came to the edge of death to haul up a pail with rope and pulley, winking at Cynthia when they saw her face at the window.

But the Square Quarter Mile was perturbed. All the talk at the At Home days was given to the flats. Hilda's visiting cards bore a neat imprint, " Fourth Wednesday," and every fourth Wednesday she sat in her drawing room (the drugget being up) by a three-decker stand of cakes, and a table laid with her best cups and saucers, waiting for the visitors who should remember her At Home day ; while down in the basement Ada sat looking as smart as possible in her long black dress and her white cap with streamers, waiting for the front-door bell. Very early in the afternoon Old Mrs. Coventry brought her crochet down to the drawing room, so as to be there before the first of the visitors and to miss no word of the talk. And there the two sat, in a drawing room with a golden mirror over the mantelpiece, curtains of Utrecht velvet and lace in the windows, a display of pampas grass in one corner and a spread of bullrushes in another, and a standard oil lamp extending its pink silk shade over tables and stools, like a frilly benediction. Perhaps it is fair to suggest that the incoherence and the frilliness of the room was a good expression of two unordered and pretty-pretty minds. They liked it well, though the charm of the bullrushes was somewhat spoilt by a tendency to burst at any moment over the carpet and the linoleum.

One by one, or in pairs, the ladies came. Rose Damien, the Ingrams, the Ellisons, the Trevelyans, Mrs. and Miss Hoare (neither Hilda nor her mother-in-law could bring herself to say "the Hoares"), Mrs. Guilder and others. The talk would be general at first and then split itself among pairs; and a watcher might have noticed how each lady in a pair, having a stronger desire to speak than to listen, would often address her partner at the same time as her partner was addressing her. Each lady, no doubt, would have liked to be heard by her partner (or should we say "her opponent"?) but if it might not be so, well, the talking was the thing that mattered. Then perhaps an exciting question would be thrown across the pairs, and the divided talk would suddenly coalesce and become general again.

Such a babel was in progress one At Home day when the flats were nearing completion. Old Mrs. Coventry was in the thick of it; in fact she was leaning forward in her chair that she might be in the thick of it. The subject was the flats, and she shook her head, as if far from happy about them. Unable in these quiet streets to satisfy her zest for the spicy stuff of life, she was wont to call upon her imagination to minister to her needs, and this afternoon she was disposed to believe some very pungent things about the flats.

"I don't like it, I must say," she said, shaking her head. "What sort of people we shall get living right in front of us I don't know at all."

"And I quite agree with you," said Mrs. Ingram, a tall and angular but not very effective woman. "I fear it will change the whole character of the neighbourhood."

The agreement delighted Old Mrs. Coventry. "It

will lower its whole tone," she continued emphatically. " You don't know *who* may come."

" Hardly the class we've been accustomed to," suggested Rose Damien. " Abbott says some of the rents will be fairly high but others within the means of any prosperous little shopkeeper."

" Good gracious ! " said Mrs. Ingram, as if she hadn't realised it would be as bad as that.

" Yes," Rose Damien affirmed with nods. " Yes."

But this was not what Old Mrs. Coventry had meant. She had meant something much more racy than this. So, pursing her lips in dislike of her fears, she repeated, " You don't know *who* we may get. All this building of flats savours more of Paris than of London. I don't think we are getting any better in England, I *must* say. Yes, flats are a convenient place for a certain type of people . . . Mmmm. . . ." and her lips pursed again and her head nodded knowingly.

" Quite so, quite so," said Rose Damien softly, and nodded sadly.

" And they are calling them St. Alban's Mansions, I hear."

" It oughtn't to be allowed," said Mrs. Ingram.

" I doubt very much if there'll be anything saintly about them," laughed Old Mrs. Coventry, something wickedly, for she would have been a wit of the outrageous type had she lived in the eighteenth century and been true to herself. " And there's another thing "—this time she turned to Rose Damien and lowered her voice that the talk might be theirs alone— " come a little closer, Rose. Hilda must tell you. Hilda, come and tell Rose what it is you've noticed. I don't think it's right what they're doing.

"Tell her what, Mamma?" inquired Hilda, drawing up.

"You know. About the windows. Perhaps Abbott will advise us if anything can be done."

"Well, it's obvious," said Hilda, glancing round to see that none of the others was listening, "that the front of the flats is going to face Conyers Road and the side wall is going to face us. That mightn't be so bad, but—but——"

"But what, my dear?" Rose encouraged.

"Well, the side wall rises straight from the pavement, and from the nature of the windows we can only think that they are—well—the kitchen and the bathroom and —er—so on. . . ."

Old Mrs. Coventry nodded vehemently her opinion that Hilda was speaking truth. "And it's not nice," she said.

"Fancy turning such windows on to Glastonbury Road, which was always a good road," said Hilda.

"I doubt if it's even sanitary," suggested Old Mrs. Coventry.

Rose laughed. "I'd rather they faced your road than mine. And I suppose they had to put them somewhere."

"They should have put them at the back," said Old Mrs. Coventry with conviction. "They should have put them at the back. I wonder if it's too late to do anything about it now. We must ask Mr. Guilder about it, Hilda. It's a scandal. I am only waiting to see if they put frosted glass in these windows, and then I shall speak to someone about it. And Tom ought to take steps. He certainly ought to take some steps."

Alas! the flats were finished, and the glass went in; and there could be no doubt that the lower panes in these side windows were of frosted glass patterned with fleur-de-lys.   And it is a fact that Hilda and her mother-in-law did ask Mr. Guilder if anything could be done about it.   One day when he had come to see Cynthia they took him behind a closed door and asked him this question, either because they believed in his power to alter the whole architecture of the flats, if he put his mind to it, or, as is more likely, since one of them was no fool, because they didn't mind if they talked sense, so long as they talked something.

Mr. Guilder glanced across at the offending windows. " Yes," said he, laughing. " It looks as though they are going to show you the seamy side of their life." And both ladies thought this a very daring remark of Mr. Guilder's, and evidence of what a broadminded man he was ; for whatever else happened in Norman's End, it was accepted that Mr. Guilder could do nothing wrong.   The elder lady giggled and gave him something of a roguish look.

In the safety of the streets the children discussed the flats too, between one game and the next.   Surely it was only in Norman's End that children of such gentility played in the streets.   But play there they did ; and I suspect it was the green wastegrounds that began it.   And once it had been granted that they might play in the streets, where there was no danger of their meeting any but nice children, their games were little different from those of the children in the slums.   With a piece of chalk they limned cricket stumps or goal posts against a side wall and played the seasonable game.   Or they chalked on the pavement a jumping-off line and competed in long-jumping, which could be painful indeed when one jumped far.   Or they trooped off towards a livery stables in a lowlier part to stare at the grooms washing down the wheels of broughams and dog-carts and to get a nervous delight when one of their bolder spirits, such as Rob Ingram, went forward on to the setts and took a hand with the hose.

It was Rob Ingram who, when the wasteground was boarded up, conceived the idea of playing cricket against the pillar box in Glastonbury Road. This pillar-box was well placed for a wicket, since a good forward drive would send the ball right down Conyers Road opposite, and a square cut or a leg hit would send it up or down the length of Glastonbury Road ; and the most likely stroke of all, a strong pull to the left (which is the only stroke that girls seem capable of, and most small boys too, for that matter) would lift the ball high over the hoarding, count for a six, and involve some interesting climbs over the unfriendly barricade and up the deserted scaffolding. And Rob Ingram, returning from his discovery of the ball (he generally discovered it first) would give the rest of the children his views about the flats. " They shouldn't have built them," he would say. " My father says that if he had known they were going to build them, he'd have taken steps. I must say I wish he had. After all, this has always been a neighbourhood of ladies' and gentlemen's children, and now I don't mind betting we get a lot of Sunday School kids here."

" Go on ! " said Grant Ellison incredulously. " Sunday School kids can't afford flats. They'll be pretty awful, I expect, but they won't be Sunday School kids. This isn't a District."

"I don't know," said Rob unhappily. "I don't know."

" Sunday School kids ! " pondered Grant. " My hat ! "

" If they aren't District children they'll be something almost as bad, you bet," said Rob. " Flats are like that. A rotten lot of people get into them. I tell you what, men : we shall have to band ourselves into a sort of Defensive Alliance against them."

" Oh yes ! " cried Aline Guilder, the vicar's daughter, skipping delightedly. " Let's ! "

" Yes," continued Rob, glad that they recognised his wisdom. " I mean to say : we can't have a lot of Cads trying to join us."

When completed, however, St. Alban's Mansions were seen to be handsomer places than anyone had surmised. Built of red brick and white stone, they rose four stories high. Their paint was dazzlingly white. They had wide mosaic steps that swept up to the main entrances, and a porter in uniform. And the ground sloping down to the basement flats was fenced by an ornate railing and planted with privet, box and laurel.

The Square Quarter Mile was comforted. The flats had lowered the neighbourhood a little, but not as far as it had feared. It remained only to learn who the tenants would be. Who would come ? This was the question in all the drawing-rooms. It was the question on the pavements where the children played. Who was coming, and when ? But the windows of the flats stared blank and uncurtained, declining to answer.

And then one evening after tea, just as the children, with shouts and pouts and laughter and sulks, had arranged the field for cricket, and Grant had taken " middle and leg " to play the bowling of Rob, they saw in the far distance of Conyers Road a pantechnicon. It was coming towards them. Slowly behind its two great Clydesdale horses, it lumbered nearer and nearer. So clear was the evening air that you could see the blue smoke trailing up from the pipe of the driver, where he sat aloft, with the reins lying slack on the horses' cruppers. You could see a drift of blue smoke floating sideways from the back of the van, where the men lolled in comfort on the tailboard. And you could hear the enlarging *klip-klop* of the iron hoofs on the metalled road. It came straight on. It turned neither to right nor to left at Wentworth Avenue, but ambled and bumped across it, and came straight on into the red-brick world.

The first of the tenants? Yes, the van halted near an entrance to the mansions; the men jumped off the tailboard and crossed to the pavement; the driver came down from his high place and, forcing up the horses' heads and shouting at them and cursing their tosses and rears, backed a wheel against the kerb; the horses, come to rest, pawed at the ground and jingled their harness; and, while faces appeared at windows to see what was invading the peace of Conyers Road, the men in their aprons of white calico or green baize threw open the van doors and began to toss on to the pavement sacking, ticking, shavings and straw.

Immediately the children were arrayed on the pavement to contemplate the passage of the furniture. There was a silence: Rob Ingram picked up a straw to chew, this being the best of all aids to contemplation; Cynthia, with her hands at her sides, just stood and stared; Leo Damien drifted about behind the others, glad that the game was postponed and, with it, the chance of his provoking public laughter by a failure with ball or bat; Grant Ellison patted one of the horse's on flank and quarters till told that " that there off 'orse is a bit sev'age sometimes," when he returned to the company on the pavement ; Aline Guilder, coming from the vicarage in search of a game, ran up to this higher entertainment—and, in brief, there was a representative gathering to greet the furniture of the new arrival.

The men in the aprons, jovial fellows, were quite pleased to have a public for their art this evening. One of them, a long, wiry, knuckly fellow in a white apron, called " Ed," was especially communicative, both with his tongue and his winking eye ; another in a baize apron, shorter and stouter and called " Freddy," was terse, but showed a pretty wit, all the same. Ed broke the first dramatic silence by the offer of a jest, as he and Freddy staggered to the steps with the first heavy piece. " I'd rather climb six stairs than sixty with this 'ere cathedral," said he. " And it's the top flat too. 'Eave it up, Sandow."

" Sandow yerself ! " said Freddy.

" Now he's engry with me," explained Ed, with a wink to the boys. " One, two, and up she goes ! "

The men were amused, it seemed, by the character of to-night's job, and ready to share their amusement with the standers-by. When Ed returned from upstairs, he winked again at the company and said, " This is a rum un' we're movin' this journey. Gaw-blimey ! Not arf ! "

" Why, what's he like ? " asked Rob Ingram.

" Like ? " The word demanded too much of Ed's descriptive powers. " Like ? I dunno. Like nothin' I've seen before. He's got curly 'air and a big beard. Artist, you see. Like—what's he like, Freddy ? "

"Like Gawd Awlmighty," grunted Freddy.

"No." Ed rejected this description. "No, he's not quite like that."

"Like Gawd Awlmighty when He was younger," amended Freddy. "Least, *I* thought so."

"'Ere! Mind the children!" Ed rebuked him. "Talking like that! It's Blarsphemy. Besides, he's not quite like 'Im. He's too pleasant and effable."

"Yes, he's effable all right; I'll say that."

"A jolly kind of cove, I thought. 'Ere, give us a lift, Freddy, with this Town 'All. Now, out of the way, young cockolorums."

Struggling with a cupboard they staggered up the steps and out of sight, reappearing soon at a window of the top corner flat, from which Ed lowered them another wink. Cynthia was pleased to see them up there. It meant that it was a flat directly in front of her windows that had been let to this interesting man.

"You'll see some furniture in a minute," said Ed, when down on the pavement again. "If I 'adn't seen the feller and known he was a Nartist, I'duv said he was barmy."

"Why what's the matter with it?" demanded Rob.

"'Taint the sort you'd 'ave in your 'ouse, young gent. Nah, I reckon it'd upset your ma and pa. All comic shapes it is. And coloured. Mad, I thought."

"Shall we see it in a minute?" asked Aline Guilder.

"Well now, I wonder! P'raps yes, Miss Curious, and p'raps no. 'Oo can say?"

"What's his name?" asked Rob.

"'Oo?"

"The artist chap."

" O'Kelvie.   Yuss : Mr. O'Kelvie.   Of course, that looks like he's an Irishman, which'd account for a lot too.   But I put it down to the art meself."

" Has he any kids ? " pursued Rob.

" Any what ? "

" Has he any children ? "

" Children ?   Well now !   I dunno.   Has he got any nippers, Fred ? "

" Hah should I know ? "

" Don't be so short with me !   I reckon he 'as.   I reckon there's a boy somewhere.   We've moved enough of them toy trains and guns and what-all.   Yes, there's a boy somewhere, but we ain't seen 'im."

" 'Ain't seen a missus, neither," grunted Freddy.

" Nor we 'ave, come to think of it !   'Aint struck his missus anywhere about.   Where's she, do you suppose, Freddy ? "

" I reckon he done 'er in."

Ed considered this view, came to a decision, and spat in the gutter.   " I shouldn't wonder," he agreed. " Yes, thet's about it : he done 'er in ; and I don't blame 'im.   And now he sings all day long.   He was singing and humming and sucking his pipe all the time we was movin' him.   He takes life easily, he does ; anyone can see that—come as you like and go as you like, but please shut the door—see ?   Not like me, worrying and cussing and making everyone's life a misery. Well, good-evening, young sirs ; I can't stay talkin' with you.   I 'efta earn my livin', I do.   If the foreman cops me, he won't kiss me good-bye when me day's work's done—see ? "

Freddy nodded his head at the children and explained tersely, " He reckons he's a comic.   Kiss *'im?*   Gawd ! "

" No, he won't," concluded Ed. " And then I shan't sleep to-night—see ? "

They carried more furniture through the entrance, most of which seemed commonplace enough, though there were one or two pieces of strange shapes, probably made by the artist himself. At one time Ed brought out an unframed canvas wrapped in sacking, and by the light in his eye one guessed that he thought this an even better joke than the furniture. " This is a picture and a half. One of his own, I reckon. Would you like to see it ? "

" Yes."

" Well then you shan't ! "

" Why not ? " demanded Rob.

" Because it wouldn't be good for a young shaver like you. This is a pair of what you call ' Noods.' Thet's why I wrapped 'em up in a piece of sacking—to keep 'em warm. No, it wouldn't be good for you, my lad. I'm not sure that it's very good for me, neither."

" Come along ! " persisted Rob, not without a knowing look, for he was nearly fourteen now. " Give us a look."

Ed lifted the sacking for a second that Rob might see, but lowered it before Cynthia could get near it—which needed quick work. " There you are ! " said he, justified. " Didn't I say so ? Adima Neve. Like as two pins." And he whisked them up the steps.

" There was nothing much wrong with that, as far as I could see," Rob explained to the others, authoritatively.

Ed returned and continued to be informative about the pictures. " He wouldn't let us handle his best pictures. ' Not on your life,' he says to Foreman. So he's taken some of 'em round in a keb to his new stoodier; and the others are being took round, along with the stetues, by men that's properly trained—not by common removal men like us. Oh no. He thinks they're all that good, you see; but *I* don't. Daft—some of 'em—I thought."

"Where's the studio?" asked Rob, spokesman for all.

"At the back of an old garden, about a mile from 'ere. The garden of a gloomy old house about five hundred years old, or as near as makes no difference. Gloomy? Gaw, I never saw the like of it. Looks like there'd been a murder there once, and nobody's lived in it since."

"I know!" exclaimed Rob. "He means old Ashgar House—the place with the big gates. Ripping place, *I* think. And it *was* lived in a little while ago. I remember quite well: there was an artist living in the house itself and using the studio at the bottom of the garden."

"*Was* there now? You don't say so? Well there's no accounting for tastes. I wouldn't be found dead in the place. I'd go stark, starin' mad there."

"*I* shouldn't," said Cynthia suddenly. "I should love it."

Ed, the jester, looked at her, touched his cap, and said, "Yes, miss. Thank you"; and moved off to the van; while she felt rather silly and blushed, for one or two of the boys had turned to grin at her. She was edging away a few steps when Ernest Ellison cried, "Look! Ingram, look there! You chaps, look there!" and pointed down the road. All eyes followed the direction of his finger.

"My goodness!" murmured Rob.

F

And Grant Ellison whistled.   The rest of the children stared in silence.

Coming along the pavement towards the pantechnicon was a singular and arresting figure.   He must have been six feet tall, but the largeness of his head and the breadth of his chest discounted some of the height.   He had a light brown beard of that soft curly fineness that no razor has spoiled, and brown curly hair under a wide-brimmed black hat.   His tie, more like a black sash than a cravat, took the breeze with the gaiety of a flag. He wore a black overcoat across his shoulders with the sleeves falling empty, so that it hung about him like a cloak.   One would have supposed him a giant from among the Balkan anarchists, had his beard been darker, his skin less fair, and the swing of his cane less merry. To judge from the freshness of the skin and the liveliness of the eyes, he could hardly have been more than thirty-two or three, but in view of the beard the children thought him fifty ; and the timider of them made ready to run.   Here, plainly, was Mr. O'Kelvie, master of the furniture.

" No need to 'op it," said Ed.   " 'E won't eat yer. He's a decent sort."

The children stayed.

Mr. O'Kelvie came up to the men ; and Cynthia could not take her eyes from that large round face with the fine beard and the crisp curls, under the black halo of the hat.

" All aboard ? " asked Mr. O'Kelvie of the foreman, who, maintaining the dignity of a foreman, had taken no part in the conversazione of Ed and Freddy and the children.

" Not quite, sir.   Getting on."

"You seem to have an audience. Are these the local savages?"

"Some of their nippers, I expect, sir."

"H'm. They look much the same as other children."

"Very effable they are, sir. Very nice-spoken and chatty."

"Fine kids, some of 'em. How do these blasted pavements breed 'em?"

"It's bacon and eggs every morning, I expect, sir."

Mr. O'Kelvie swept the whole neighbourhood with his eyes: tall houses, clean pavements, white hearth-stoned steps, and trim shrubs behind the railing of the flats. "I'm afraid their bodies are better than their brains," he sighed, shaking his head, and bringing his eyes back on them.

"Some of them were for doing a guy when they saw you coming," said the foreman, "but we told 'em you was quite safe."

"Ha, ha, ha!" Mr. O'Kelvie's laugh was an assault on the quiet of the street. "Safe? Well, I suppose so. Don't know that any of us are safe, if it comes to that. It depends, it depends, it de—— glory be to God, what horses! God forgive me for not noticing them before"; and he went and stroked the near horse on poll and crest, haunch and quarters. "Look at that breast and shoulder —there's power for you! Look at those fetlocks. Ah, be javers, and I suppose you work with these creatures all day, and never once thank God for the privilege you have of looking at them. Ah, what a thigh you've got, my boy! what a cannon, eh? It's meself that'd give me soul to be able to model something half as good. Well, well, God rest your soul——" and he patted the animal good-bye and returned to the foreman, leaving

apparently, the Irish brogue on the horse's back.
" Well, I'll go up and see how much you've broken."

" And shell I come up and 'elp you look, sir, in case
you get tired ? "

" Ha, ha, ha ! " Mr. O'Kelvie was delighted. " No,
you'll come up and see if we can find you a drink. And
bring your lads too, if you think they deserve it. I had
a crate of something sent up. Lemonade, I think it
was."

" Now you're being funny, sir."

" Ha, ha, ha ! Do you think so ? Well, bring 'em up
when you've done, and take it or leave it—just as you
like. Good-bye, children." And he broke into something between humming and singing—" There is one
that is pure as an angel, And fair as the flowers in May
. . ."—and carried the air—and the overcoat swinging
on his back—into the mansions and out of sight.

Ed winked at the children.

They had not spoken at all since this substantial
figure appeared. Somehow his appearance and passing
had made them all feel rather small ; and, now that he
was gone, Grant Ellison turned and grimaced at Rob,
as if he would ask what he thought of *that*.

And Rob, who didn't like feeling overawed, gave him
his answer. " I don't feel he's a gentleman," he said.

VIII

GREAT was the interest in the large fair man in the top corner flat. Exactly who he was, what he was, and how he lived were questions canvassed for many weeks after his arrival. Where was it he went to every morning? Those who cared to bring their eyes to the windows saw him departing down Conyers Road, the wide black hat on his curly hair, the overcoat slung on his shoulders like a cloak, and his cane swinging and slashing in his hand, as if the joy of life rose even from the pavements of Norman's End and in imagination he could see where once the high ragwort grew and the grass plumes bent in the breeze. And who was the boy who after a week or two had joined him in the flat? An open-faced lad of eleven or so, very like the round-faced, bearded man. A son? These two, it would seem, took their baths together of a morning, for daily the rich baritone of the man could be heard singing, " They call me the gentle maiden . . ." and the happy treble of the boy joining in the chorus, along with the splash of water. " Disgusting," said Old Mrs. Coventry with her lips ; but her heart was with them.

Father and son, no doubt ; but where was the mother? There had been no sign of a woman as yet, and it really seemed that these two were " pigging it " together up there.

Gradually the other flats filled up; but these new tenants had little interest for Old Mrs. Coventry, since, as far as she could see, their affairs were quite regular. All except one: she was not sure about the lady who had come to the best flat of all, the first-floor flat at the corner. This woman was altogether too lonely, and too well-dressed in her loneliness, and too slim and elegant and daintily powdered, to be wholly respectable. One felt also that she was "advanced": her curtains were quite different from the lace of everyone else's windows, and her maid had a French look with that absurd little apron and stiff frilled cap.

Here was matter for speculation at Hilda's At Home days; and imagine the interest when Mrs. Ingram brought a rumour about this woman—a rumour that exactly confirmed Old Mrs. Coventry's surmises. "They say," said Mrs. Ingram, "that she's quite well known in Society as 'Lord Brok's widow,' but of course they use the word 'widow' as a joke. You know how easily some people joke about serious matters. Lord Brok is still alive; and she is actually the widow of a Mr. du Pré. Or at any rate she goes by the name of Mrs. du Pré." All eyes were on Mrs. Ingram now, and Old Mrs. Coventry asked what then the word "widow" might mean. Mrs. Ingram shrugged her shoulders: it was difficult to say aloud, but they must surely guess. The connexion had never been known officially, so Mrs. du Pré had been able to move in quite good circles. But now for some reason or other Lord Brok felt obliged to bring the relationship to an end—or to pretend to do so—for he was still very fond of her, and you could be pretty sure that when she went off, dressed in her theatre cloak, she was going to meet him. And so they called her his widow. And of course there was little doubt that he paid for the flat.

"Just what I thought!" cried Old Mrs. Coventry. Pretending to be appalled, she was really pleased. Surely there was never an old lady whose words were more in conflict with her inmost thoughts (though these thoughts were seldom conscious, I think). She pretended to believe that such people as the O'Kelvies and Mrs. du Pré were letting the neighbourhood down, and she really believed that, thank God, the neighbourhood was coming alive. A few blossoms of vivid, defiant, and joyous life were appearing in front of her very windows. "That's the worst of flats," she said. "I always knew that we should get some very shady people." She called them "shady," but, unknown to herself, she believed that silly, dull people like Hilda and Mrs. Ingram stood in the shadow, while people like these enjoyed the sun.

"And that poor little boy!" she added. "Being brought up with no religion at all, I suppose! Not even baptised, if you ask me! It's wicked. Something ought to be done about it. Mr. Guilder ought to look into it."

Rumour of Lord Brok's widow had reached the children too, but they did not understand it. These children, playing on the pavements, were very innocent. Even Rob Ingram who laid down the law on so many points knew less of life than he supposed. Not being as good with his books as his authoritative utterance suggested, he had yet to leave Trinity Preparatory School for the larger corridors of Trinity itself, and so was still fairly innocent. And in a break between the games he looked up at Mrs. de Pré's curtains and deplored the arrival of such a person in their midst.

"They call her Lord Brok's widow," he explained. "A bit thick, isn't it?"

"What does that mean?" asked Grant Ellison.

"It means he pays her, you ass. They always call them widows. Pays for the flat and all that sort of thing."

"Well, I don't see why he shouldn't. Why shouldn't he give her money if he likes her and he's got plenty of chink?"

"Because it's not sporting to take a man's money like that. It's not ladylike. After all, it's taking a lot of money for nothing, isn't it?"

Rob would have been indignant if told that Cynthia Coventry had a clearer brain than he, but it was so: Cynthia, listening to his wise talk, could see that it was inadequate and ill-informed. And this persuaded her to pursue some inquiries of her own. She asked Hilda what exactly was meant by the phrase "Lord Brok's widow," and Hilda gave her a flurried and retreating answer, "Oh, that's nothing," which was the sure way to show the child that it was certainly something. She asked her grandmother and drew a much more interesting answer, for Old Mrs. Coventry got a relish from speaking on these lively matters, even when it took the form of reproof to a child. Her beady little eyes fixed on her grand-daughter and she said, "I pray it may be many years before you know what it means. And don't ask that question again!" which swelled the child's wonder to bursting point. She asked Ada, and Ada said mysteriously, "Arst a p'leaceman! I ain't going to tell you, Miss Cynthia, but I know what I think. I've got long ears and they pick up most that's floating around. You can take it from me that that lady's no better than she need be. In fact, she's a wrong 'un, with all her fine clothes, if what they say is true."

No wonder that the windows of the first floor and the top floor flats fascinated Cynthia as much as the windows behind which prisoners or lunatics are locked may fascinate you and me. She hurried to her own window to see the departure of the large jolly man who had no religion and the round-faced boy who would without doubt perish everlastingly. Also the slim and beautiful lady who was unsportsmanlike enough to take Lord Brok's money for nothing.

And then came the evening when the light danced on her wall. The sun was low and bright that evening, and she had turned from looking out at the street to resume her play with the toys on the table. And suddenly she became aware of a square of light dancing and flitting on the wall opposite her. It seemed alive; it ran up the wall-paper, it rested like a golden influence on the handle of a cupboard, it sought out corners and felt its way along the ceiling. With a pounding in her breast and her fingers at her teeth, she wondered at the miracle. Some sense that its direction came from the outside world drove her back to the window, and at once the light was resting on her eyes and playing there, so that she was dazzled and blinded. Dodging clear of it, she looked across the road and upwards. There at the window of what could only be his bathroom was the round, grinning face of the O'Kelvie boy, who was flashing the sun's reflection into her room with a shaving mirror. Horrified, she turned back into her room. That boy had never been introduced! And yet he was flashing this light into her room and grinning into her face.

It seemed so shocking that she could not tell her people, and instead she told Rob Ingram one evening when he was discussing the O'Kelvies. He was scandalised. He agreed that it was disgraceful. " I shall stop it," he said. And thereafter he and his friends, with Cynthia as a member occasionally co-opted to their councils, spent some pleasant times planning how to stop the cheek of the O'Kelvie boy. They agreed that they must lie in wait till they could see a repetition of the offence. So on an evening when the sky was unclouded and the sunlight slanted on to Glastonbury Road, they instructed Cynthia to stay in her room, and went and hid in doorways and round corners to watch. And soon the sun in the wide heaven and the O'Kelvie boy in his window met and shook hands : the O'Kelvie boy held the hand of the sun in his mirror, and lo ! a trembling light flashed up and down the red brick of her house and over the hanging creepers and in at her window. Rob and his henchmen emerged from their lairs. What confounded cheek ! By golly ! they'd put a stop to it. Rob went straight to the pavement beneath the O'Kelvies' windows, and, looking up at the round face of the boy, cried, " Here ! Stop that ! "

The boy jumped at the voice, but—you will hardly believe it—he only grinned and turned the light straight into Rob's eyes, as if he didn't give a damn for him. " My heavens ! " exclaimed Rob. But the boy had disappeared and shut his window with a bang.

This meant War. Rob assembled the others, and they agreed that only war could wipe out such an

insult. They would catch the cad one night and mob
him. They must teach him a lesson, once and for all.
And in the following evenings they might have been
seen on the prowl, like Red Indians stalking their prey.
But whether the O'Kelvie boy had realised that it was
war or had decided at the same time as they to open
hostilities I do not know, but he certainly got in the
first shot. It was an evening when a milk-white flaky
cloud lay across the arch of heaven, but the sun had
dropped below it, throwing the shadow of the Glastonbury houses right across the street and a man's height
up the wall of the flats opposite. The rest of the high
wall was washed with its light. Such an evening must
surely draw the O'Kelvie boy to his top window or
lure him into the grateful air, and the children crept to
their hiding-places, to watch and be ready. Grant
Ellison and Aline Guilder were stalking along under the
side wall of the flats were the shadow lay, when—
Ernest Ellison saw it all from the other side of the road—
the arm of the O'Kelvie boy appeared at the window
of his bathroom, and, turning down a cylindrical and
perforated tin such as often lives behind such windows,
peppered the unsuspecting Grant and Aline with a red
disinfectant powder.

" Hang it ! " said Grant in dismay.

" My goodness ! " exclaimed Rob, leaping out. " He
shall pay for that. Why, some of it went in her eye ! "

They all walked away from this exposed place for a
Council of War. The Council of War made a Plan of
Campaign. Thirty talkative minutes it gave to the
plan, during which its members were seldom more
exultantly alive. By a stratagem they would lure him
to a quiet place and there give him a lambing. It was

the only honourable thing to do, for had not some of
his stinking powder gone into a girl's eye ? Grant
Ellison, who had more brains if less authority than
Rob, suggested that they sent him a mysterious letter
inviting him to present himself at six o'clock the next
evening at the wasteground between Wilbury and
Goodwood Avenues, where he would hear something
to his advantage. When Rob doubted whether this
last clause was quite fair, Grant said that of course it
was, because it would certainly be to his advantage to
learn that he mustn't give them any of his lip. Which
satisfied Rob ; and as President of the Council he
announced dramatically, " All on the wasteground at
five-thirty to-morrow. It'll be an ambush ; " and he
and Grant went home to pen the letter.

This wasteground was the last that had not gone
down beneath the march of the long roads. It was a
little to the right of the Square Quarter Mile on the
way to Trinity School. You will not find it there now.
But on that evening of the ambushing of Michael
O'Kelvie, a rectangle of countryside peeped up defiantly
here, with pavements on three sides of it, and the
side-walls of houses on the fourth. Defiantly indeed,
for it was all ablow with high bearded grass, willow
herb, chickweed, hedge mustard, sow thistle, and
shepherd's purse ; and the white butterfly danced over
all. The children, converging upon its centre, where
Rob and the Ellisons awaited them, walked knee-deep
in grass and flowers ; but they did not heed this, nor
care, any more than they heeded the blue infinity of the
sky arching over their little world, for they were children
of the firm pavements. All were there : Cynthia was
there, because she was craving (not without guilt and

shame) to learn what devilry they would work on Michael; and Leo Damien was there, weedy and wistful and sad, because his mother had just driven him out " to go and be like other boys." Under Rob's orders, the girls and younger boys stole to hiding places behind the houses, while the more important boys took up privileged positions in a hollow behind the high screening grass. Only Rob stood or strolled in the midst of the wasteground. Cynthia, peeping from a brick pillar, looked with palpitating heart at the point where Michael, if he came, would first appear.

Long ages passed; the girls began to giggle; Grant Ellison cocked up his head above the grass and offered a humorous remark to the soft evening air; and two hidden voices started a song in muted tones:

" I'll be your sweetheart if you will be mine;
All my life I'll be your valentine . . ."

" Shut up! " commanded Rob.

Then another boy deliberately broke the silence with an artificial noise in his nose, and repeated it at regular intervals; and the girls giggled; and Ernest Ellison said loudly, " He won't come at all. Of course he won't! "

" Shut up! " said Rob to them all, with a certain monotony.

And the O'Kelvie boy did come. He came sauntering round the corner of the houses into their view. Quick whispers announced this, and a vast silence. Every eye gazed at a victim coming to slaughter. There he stood, high on the pavement and grinning down at Rob in the midst of the grass; and most of them observed for the first time what a sturdy, strong lad he was. Even within his norfolk jacket, Eton collar, and knickerbockers—knickerbockers which, made long after the fashion of those days to allow for growth, and buckled at the knee, were now crumpled into two interesting accordions—even within these trappings you could deduce a depth of chest and a strength of limb worthy of his father. And a strong sense, too, under his cap. He stayed in his place, grinning at Rob, instead of coming down the bank into a possible jeopardy.

"Hallo," called Rob.

"Hallo," called Michael O'Kelvie.

And then silence. Rob, not having foreseen that the interview would take place across half a meadow, and not possessing a brain which was at its best when taken at a disadvantage, could think of nothing to say or do. And he was not helped by the sound of a giggle rising from the grass behind him.

At last he ventured, "I say! I've got something to show you. It'll interest you."

"Well, bring it up," suggested Michael.

"No, no. You come and see it. It'll interest you. It will, really."

"I don't believe you've got anything."

"Yes, I have. Honour bright!"

"Absolutely honestly?"

Rob thought over this and decided that there could be no doubt whatever that he had something to show the cad, so he answered, "Yes, *rather!*"

Slowly, suspiciously, Michael came down the bank towards Rob and through the grass, till he was facing him. Cynthia, her lips parting, felt her heart drumming against her breast.

" Well, what is it ? " asked Michael.

" It's *this !* " said Rob.   And in a trice he had got behind the boy, put his knee into the small of his back, pulled on his shoulders, and laid him flat on the ground.

" That's for peppering——" he began.

But he had no time for more.   Michael, red as the creepers in autumn, and wild as the gales in winter, was upon his feet and charging at Rob, with his round head down and his arms swinging like hammers.   Rob fought back ferociously, but he was blinking and dazed by the suddenness of the onslaught.   The other boys rushed from their hiding places, but, forgetting that their appointed task was to lynch a cad, stood around and watched with a gaping interest this fight between their captain and his prisoner.

And Rob, who was not having by any means too successful and happy a time, saw them between his blinks and blows and called out, " Here ! do something, you fellows ! "

Thereupon some of them set on to Michael, trying to manhandle him and pull him to the ground ; but he swung about towards them, and with his head still down and his Eton collar flying, thrashed out at all comers furiously and blindly.   They dodged aside from this rain of blows, with the result that Michael fought a way through to a figure which had stood on the outside of the ring, merely pretending to take part in the fun. His blind fist found the stationary and unoffending figure of Leo Damien, and, glad to have met a substance so unresisting, pummelled it as if eager to kill.   Leo at once gave ground, ducking and dodging.   Michael, following this line of least resistance, rained his blows mercilessly on the retreating figure, while the others laughed. Leo ran. Michael ran after him. The other boys, roaring with laughter, ran too, till, making a ring round the fighters, they prevented one of them from retreating any further. Michael then went for Leo " like one o'clock " as Rob said afterwards ; but it was not so much like one o'clock as like a clock gone mad with its two hands racing round and recording sixty hours a minute. He was pounding and milling Leo, who bent and doubled beneath the punishment.

" A fight ! A fight ! " cried Rob, perhaps relieved at this change in the character of the evening. " Fight between Face and O'Kelvie ! Keep the ring, men. Two to one on old Face ! "

The boys roared and cheered ; and it was clear from the nature of the cheers that they were all on Michael's side now.

He apparently had no objection to fighting one of them singly instead of all of them together, and after drawing back, staring round at the ring, and taking a breath, he went at it again with multiplied vigour. Leo lifted up both arms to protect his face, and Michael, finding that there was only defence and no attack, looked up from his milling, saw the position, saw the unguarded spot beneath Leo's heart, and, having had many a jolly boxing lesson from his father, hit the spot with a powerful blow and stepped back to watch his opponent crumple up. All breath gone from Leo's body, he could only collapse into a sitting position on the grass, while the crowd jeered. Michael, fully understanding his blow and its result, stood above him victorious and panting, while the crowd, quite unaware of Leo's helpless condition, shouted to him to get up and go on. He only stared at them like a hunted and helpless animal. And when he could breathe again, he rose and, turning from the scene, moved as if to slink away.

Jeers and groans greeted this move. But after one look back at the outburst, he moved away through the grass, never looking round any more, but sometimes lifting up his head and looking at the sky as if he neither heard nor minded the chorus of ridicule that followed him.

" Cowardy, cowardy custard ! " they cried.

And Cynthia, who had been compelled to watch the fight because she was fascinated by their cruelty to Leo, now took an almost intolerable thrust of pity, as she saw him slinking away like that and pretending not to mind the jeers. Who would have thought that pity could pierce so deep and sit there aching so ? She could almost have cried, " Oh, oh, *oh !* " in her hurt. This sight of Leo Damien slinking from the wasteground, defeated and despised, was one of the sharpest memories of her earlier years.

Meanwhile Michael, flushed and panting with victory, announced, " Now I'll fight any other of you. *I* don't care."

" No," said Rob rather quickly. " You won that. Didn't he, men ? Yes, I reckon you won that fair and square. So now we'll make a Treaty of Peace."

" What did you want me for ? " panted Michael.

" Well, we couldn't have you peppering Aline Guilder, see ? " answered Rob almost anxiously. " Some of it went into her eye, you see."

" I'm glad," said Michael.

Oh, why was he intransigeant like this ?

G

"Well," explained Rob, "we thought you were scarcely a gentleman if you'd do a thing like that."

Michael's answer was amazing. "Nor I am," he panted. "And it's the last thing I want to be."

"*What?*" cried Rob.

"No," affirmed Michael. "My father says it's the last thing he wants to be. He says gentlemen are slaves tied hand and foot. And that they think they're mighty fine but they're mostly afraid to do what the other fellows aren't doing."

"But that's nonsense," said Rob, though in his heart he wondered for the first time if it was. Luckily the wonder didn't last.

"All the same," explained Michael, who might love to echo his father but was child enough to have all a child's snobbery, "my father's descended from the Irish kings."

"*Is* he?" said Rob, much impressed. "Then you *must* be a gentleman, whatever you do."

"Yes," agreed Michael. "I suppose so." He was quite happy to have the best of both worlds. "And my father's famous," he added. "Somebody's written a book about his work."

"H'm," said Rob doubtfully, and got back to something he could understand. "I'm glad about that because I think we should like you to join us. But we thought you ought to know that our people don't altogether approve of all that your father does, and I agree with them, I *must* say."

"My father says he doesn't give a hoot what the old witches think," said Michael.

At least, Cynthia supposed that the word shot forth on his panting breath was "witches." It sounded more like " pitches," but that didn't make sense.   But she wasn't sure at all, and the way the boys giggled and turned to look at the girls threw such a doubt over the word that she decided not to speak of it to her people.

Soon they were playing " French and English " in the long grass, with Michael one of them ; while Leo Damien wandered alone in the quiet streets, knowing that it would be unwise to return into his mother's view before twilight sank upon Norman's End, and happy children came home from play.

IX

THE problem that had occupied the At Home days for some time was whether or not the ladies should call on Mrs. du Pré. Old Mrs. Coventry thought they ought to do so, because by now she was most anxious to do so. After all, said she, whatever the rumours might be, they *knew* nothing definite ; and in common Christian charity they ought to call on her until she was officially condemned.

" Besides," she continued, " it'd be extraordinarily difficult, living right opposite the woman and not knowing her. I'm sure I'm always passing her in the road and I don't know which way to turn. And in church too. She's most regular at church, and I see she's contributed to the Assistant Clergy Fund. I must say I think we ought to call. What a pity Mr. Guilder isn't here. We could act on his advice."

Mr. Guilder after a sudden and alarming illness had gone away for a three months' rest. That he had left behind him four large and muscular curates did not help the ladies in their difficulty. They thought of curates, not as priests charged with the cure of their souls, but as fresh and agreeable young men to whom it would be quite impossible to talk about Mrs. du Pré and Lord Brok. With Mr. Guilder, on the other hand, all things were possible.

Suddenly a second question joined the problem of Mrs. du Pré. That had happened which made it possible for them to call on the O'Kelvies. A woman who was plainly the mother of Michael had arrived at the top flat; and from the laughter and merry voices that you could hear across the road you adjudged these people the happiest family. The woman called herself Mrs. O'Kelvie, and there could be no doubt she was O'Kelvie's wife—or you could suppose so if you were anxious to call. And Old Mrs. Coventry was now most anxious to call. She was longing to see the inside of that remarkable top flat. Her impatience fermented and swelled till it could brook no more delay, and she commanded Hilda to get her hat and come along. On Hilda's consenting, the enthusiastic old lady declared, " Yes, come along. It's right, I'm sure. We can't treat people rudely if we live just opposite them ": and, lifting the front of her skirt, hurried up the stairs to dress.

She was in her room on the second floor before Hilda had left the dining room. Here, after changing her dress, she sat on a chair and buttoned up her kid boots with a hook, tossed it aside, and rose to seek in the wardrobe for her best bonnet with the bird's wing, and for her cape that was so handsomely beaded for smart wear. By now Hilda had arrived in her room across the landing, changed her dress, and was pinning on a large hat with feathers. This fixed, she drew open a drawer and unrolled a spotted veil from the section of broom-handle on which it slept. She tied the veil behind the brim at the back, threw her fur boa across her shoulders, buttoned on her gloves, and picked up her muff.

But all this took time, and she could hear her mother-in-law beating her foot impatiently on the landing without. "I'm coming," she called; and the two ladies were ready. They set off across the road, and their silk petticoats *frou-frou'd* as they walked. But they were dressed in more than tangible clothes. Each, unknown to the other, wore a consciousness of security in virtue and a resolve to be a little gracious and condescending to these dubious people, Mrs. O'Kelvie and Mrs. du Pré.

Soon they stood on the landing outside the O'Kelvies' front door. Through the door came the rich baritone of O'Kelvie singing as he worked, " Little Dolly Daydream, Pride of Idaho . . ." but as they touched the bell, his voice stopped abruptly. A silence, as of death, took possession of the flat. Then they heard the song gently resumed and brought along the passage as if Mr. O'Kelvie himself were coming to the door. They braced themselves for the meeting, and Hilda hastily adjusted her veil. The door flung open, and Mr. O'Kelvie and the ladies faced each other.

It would be difficult to say which side of the doorway held the greater surprise. Mr. O'Kelvie saw an old lady and a young one dressed up in their best and obviously contemplating a call. The ladies saw a huge bearded man clad in nothing but a pair of oriental slippers and a gay dressing gown that left unveiled the fair hair on his breast. The curls on his head were tousled and his beard seemed almost as rough.

Hilda could speak only with her eyes; and her eyes spoke only her discomfort. It was her mother-in-law who recovered first and hastened to save the faces of them all.

" Oh . . ." she began. " It's . . . Is Mrs. O'Kelvie at home ? We just came to call. We live just over the road. Yes, we came to call on your wife."

" Christ ! " exclaimed Mr. O'Kelvie.

The word slipped out before his guard was awake. Angry at his carelessness, lest it had offended them or made them seem unwelcome, he addressed himself at once to be courteous and kind.

" Oh, I'm sorry, but my wife has gone away again. She only came for a week or two. But do come in for a little. It is most kind of you to call."

" Oh, I don't think . . ." demurred Hilda, hesitating.

But her mother-in-law, having got so far, had little mind for turning back.

" It's very unconventional, I'm afraid," she twittered, " but . . ."

" Oh, everything's unconventional here," answered Mr. O'Kelvie. "Come in. Come in, do. At any rate I can show you some pictures that'll interest you. Yes, my wife went away last week."

" And will she be back soon ? " asked Hilda in her best calling manner, as they walked along the passage.

" No, she's not coming back," said Mr. O'Kelvie.

" Oh. . . ."

Neither lady knew what to reply, and both were wondering into what strange world they had penetrated, as he led them into the dining room. Presumably it was the dining room. There was a table pushed against the wall with the remains of a meal on its bare top, and an odd assortment of chairs about the floor, some high-backed, some long and soft for a lazy man. On the dove-grey walls hung extraordinary pictures. Nothing delicate or pretty about these pictures. Pattern stared boldly from them and colour shone violently. Surely such unashamed colour was hardly nice. And the subjects of one or two of them were not the kind that one liked to be seen looking at, with a man in the room. Hilda looked at them once and then kept her eyes away from them, but Old Mrs. Coventry, having once put her spectacles up, kept them up and allowed her eyes to stray back to the pictures again and again.

"Do sit down," begged Mr. O'Kelvie; "and, by the way, you must forgive my clothes. I was working when you came in, and in warm weather I like to feel absolutely free. Do you know, I sometimes think one could argue that an artist has to be anti-social, up to a point—else how can he be completely himself and really say something individual and new?—and one way to get into the mood for good individual work is to get out of your clothes, ha, ha, ha! One can get into a real rebellious mood then. Don't you think there's something in it?"

"I really don't know," stuttered Hilda, who hadn't the foggiest idea what he was talking about.

"Yes, one's quit of all concessions to the world then, and can see it as it really is. 'Off with these lendings!' ha, ha, ha! Though I don't know, by the way, why I should suppose that you knew I was an artist."

"We had heard that you painted," said Old Mrs. Coventry.

Perhaps O'Kelvie thought that this was a little like saying to Charles Dickens, "We had heard that you wrote," but he only smiled and said, "Yes, I paint and sculpt too."

"And I think my little girl knows your little boy," said Hilda, trying to take her share in the talk.

"Oh, is that your little girl over the road? God, she's a flame, isn't she?"

"A what?" inquired Hilda.

"She's a radiant and leaping bit of life. I've noticed her."

"I'm afraid we don't think her very beautiful as yet. She may become so."

"Beautiful!" cried O'Kelvie. "Of course she's beautiful! Every child is."

"Oh, I don't know. . . ." demurred Hilda.

"Oh yes. What else can they be, unless they're sick or deformed? They're alive, aren't they? My God, the children knock me silly sometimes! I stand at that window and stare at them. What movements! I feel I must get their movements on canvas or burst! What energy! Beautiful? You'll be telling me that a driven wave isn't beautiful next. Must be. Can't help it."

But this was not what Old Mrs. Coventry had come to learn. She did not like talk that she did not understand, so she turned the conversation into a channel that interested her and was empty at present. "And did you say," she asked, "that your wife was away for a long time?"

"She's away for good," said O'Kelvie.

"Oh. . . ."

"Of course she'll come back and see us sometimes. She always does. She's a very good sort, Maggie."

"I see . . ." said Old Mrs. Coventry, in that tone which implies that one sees a little but not much.

"Perhaps I had better explain that my wife and I divorced each other about two years ago, but we are still the best of friends, and she came the other day to see that we were happy and cosy in the flat—just to give us a friendly look-up and a sweep round, ha, ha, ha!"

" I see."

"It's all very simple," said O'Kelvie, smiling upon them for fear they should be shocked and offended. " It may seem strange to you, but it's really astonishingly simple and sensible, when one comes to do it.   One can't understand then what people have been making the fuss about."

" But what about the little boy ? " asked Old Mrs. Coventry.

" I'm keeping him, and she's got the younger one. Of course Mike often goes and sees his mother, and we're all very happy and contented.   That's why I came to this comic—to this part.   Maggie found the flat for us. The pup's got to be educated somewhere, I suppose, and Trinity's no more idiotic than any other school, so I thought he might as well go there, while I worked in my studio in Ashgar Terrace.   Did you know there was a studio there ?   It's in the garden of old Ashgar House, where old What's-his-name entertained Johnson and Boswell, and wrote his rather stupid novels.   You must come and see the garden one day, if you like ghosts."

" Ghosts !   Oh, how exciting ! " cried Hilda.   " Is it haunted then ? "

" One can imagine so if one likes. . . ." said O'Kelvie, hiding his despair.   " Yes, I think it must be.   Old ghosts with powdered wigs.   It's derelict now, but there's an ancient mulberry tree that's seen a great deal."

" And did you paint those pictures there ? " asked Old Mrs. Coventry, whose eyes had strayed to the wall.

" No, not I ! "

She therefore felt free to say what she really thought of them.   " They're rather strange, aren't they ? "

"Oh no," he laughed. "I don't think so. That's a Manet."

"A what?"

"A Manet. He gave it to me just before he died. Come; you must look at them better. This is a Camille Pisarro, and that's a Lucien. They both gave them to me when I was in Paris."

"I see . . ." said Old Mrs. Coventry, peering close at them through her spectacles.

"And this is a Degas, though I don't think it's one of his best." And he began to discuss rhythms, planes, and masses with them who had never heard of such things before. "See what I mean here. This one's a Renoir."

"They are famous artists, I suppose?" inquired Hilda; and her mother-in-law, who had kept quiet rather than reveal her ignorance, thought what a fool Hilda was, thus to give herself away.

"Well, yes, I suppose so . . ." sighed O'Kelvie. "And now, if you like, I'll show you a little of *my* work. I've improvised a studio here at the back."

"I'm sure we should love to see it," said Hilda.

"Perhaps your pictures will be famous too, one day," chirped Old Mrs. Coventry.

"What? . . . Oh yes . . ." O'Kelvie called up all his humour to annoint this wound, and led them into a room where an easel turned towards the north light, a table stood behind it, littered with tubes, brushes, mahl-sticks, palette knives and cans of turpentine, and against every wall lolled canvases and folios and frames. Here he showed them one canvas after another, and fortunately his spate of exposition, criticism and dislike saved them from the necessity of offering an opinion.

They could not have done so, for the pictures had stunned their thoughts to a stand-still. " Yes, very nice, I'm sure," was all that the elder lady offered ; and Hilda said, " I always think it's so nice to see where anyone works." And they went back to the dining room.

" And now if you'll just wait here," said O'Kelvie, " I'll make you some tea."

" Oh no. No," they hurriedly protested. " No, please not ; it is much too early."

" Oh yes ! Yes, you must ! My tea is excellent."

" No, we really must be going. We have other visits to pay. Come, Hilda." And they rose. " It has been most interesting, I'm sure, hasn't it, Hilda ? "

" Well, of course if you can't, you can't," laughed O'Kelvie, " but I'm sorry, because I believe you'd have liked my tea better than my pictures. Some other time, perhaps."

They were now walking along the passage to the door.

" Well, good-bye," he said at the door.

" Good-bye, Mr. O'Kelvie. It was most kind of you to show us your pictures. Especially those that you've painted yourself. Some of them were very pretty, I'm sure."

" Yes," said he ; not that this had any meaning, but because he was anxious to be pleasant. " Yes, certainly " ; and his zeal for their happiness even brought him out on to the public landing in his dressing gown and bare legs. " Good-bye," he repeated, as they went down the stairs. " God be with you." And his door closed.

They went down the stairs rather quietly. The condescension with which they had been prepared to treat the O'Kelvies had been defeated and driven back

on itself; and perhaps for that reason it was all the
more ready now to deal with Mrs. du Pré. She at
any rate would not be so different from their expectations
and so destructive of their superiority—no, not when
you recalled Lord Brok. Both ladies, of course, when
they heard O'Kelvie's door close, expressed their shock
at his life; but in Old Mrs. Coventry the shock was
official rather than real. In reality she was feeling
enlarged by this contact with life. Hilda, for her part,
muttered that either Right was Right and Wrong Wrong
or they weren't, and imagined that she had disposed of
the offender upstairs; not perceiving that he would
have been delighted with such a statement as a basis
for a jolly discussion, answering, " Yes, that is the
question ! And supposing they aren't ? " Hilda, in
fact, was a little peevish and very ready to encounter
Mrs. du Pré as they stood outside her door.

The maid opened to them; and neither would have
admitted that her smartness and her obvious superiority
to Ada at home had hit their condescension an initial
blow. Nor when they were in the drawing room did
they allow its " chic-ness," and its difference from any
other room of their acquaintance, to deal them the
second blow. And when the door opened, and Mrs.
du Pré swam graciously towards them, a tall, slender
woman as perfectly appointed as the room, they warded
off the third blow with exemplary courage—the courage
of despair.

Now Mrs. du Pré, though she came smiling and
with outstretched hand, had come to slay. She was
by no means a bad woman, for no woman can be this
who has humour and sense, and who has been loved;
but the ladies of Norman's End had been slow to call

upon her, and that rankles with the best. She took the hands of her visitors in the friendliest way, said how sweet of them it was to come, and sat down before them, smiling.

They explained that they were near neighbours of hers, and she raised her eyebrows in surprise. They lived quite near? Did they really? What, opposite? Now which house was that?

Inwardly Old Mrs. Coventry bridled. One likes it to be known that one lives opposite. One deems oneself sufficiently remarkable to have been noticed, going out and coming in. And Old Mrs. Coventry, who knew the homes of everyone within eyeshot of her window, simply did not believe that this woman was speaking the truth. She pursed her lips forward and back, but said nothing.

And Mrs. du Pré continued happily on her way. Exactly opposite? Why, she was as delighted as she was surprised. Then did they know that tall, rather sad-faced, and *most* attractive man—a little like Parnell, with his cropped side-whiskers and moustache—who went to the station every morning. He was rather a pet, she thought, walking along all silent and thoughtful as if probing deep into the problems of life. It was Mrs. Coventry's husband? Not really? Oh dear, oh dear, oh dear! Then she had said the right thing, hadn't she? Because truly she had always admired him. Oh! why then of course the little girl that sometimes ran to meet him was Mrs. Coventry's daughter? How delightful!

Hilda, somewhat appeased by this (unlike her mother-in-law who wasn't deceived in the least), expressed the hope that Mrs. du Pré was liking the neighbourhood.

" My dear," exclaimed that lady, " I think it's the dearest place. It's so *amusing* ! I've never known any place like it, have *you* ? I'm enjoying it immensely. It's so—so *funny*."

Not understanding, and somewhat taken aback, Hilda inquired what she meant.

" Oh, you must feel how funny it is," protested Mrs. du Pré. " It tries to be such a lot of things that it just isn't, does it not ? I mean, it tries to be Society, and it just isn't ; it tries to be saintly, and it just isn't ; it tries to be the last word in modish behaviour, and it's all just behindhand ; and—oh, I don't know what I mean, but it's the sweetest place. You must feel it yourself, I'm sure." And Mrs. du Pré lifted her eyebrows as much as to say, " Two women of the world like you and me must agree on this, mustn't we ? "

Hilda by now was not too pleased. She felt the rapier pricking her, but was not sure where and how. " I must say," she answered, " I have never thought of it like that."

" Oh, but you must have done," protested Mrs. du Pré brightly.

Hilda crumpled her brow, trying to understand, but Old Mrs. Coventry snatched the sword from her nerveless fingers.

" We have some very well-known people here," she declared. " Perhaps you haven't met them yet."

" No ? Is that so ? " queried Mrs. du Pré, quite unoffended and much interested.

" Yes. There's Stephen Easter Crane, for instance, the novelist. She lives in this very road."

" What, the woman who wrote ' Barry's Daughter ' and ' The Man I Chose ' ? Does she really live in this road ? Oh yes, I should like to meet her. I always want to know whether people like that really believe in what they write, or whether they do it with their tongue in their cheek. I think they must have their tongue in their cheek, don't you ? "

" Why ? " snapped Old Mrs. Coventry.

" Well . . . " Mrs. du Pré smiled and her head went to one side as she sought for an answer. " It's so—so *naïve*, isn't it. I mean, between ourselves, it's rather nursemaid's fare, don't you think ? It's not taken seriously anywhere, is it ? "

" There are people here who take it quite seriously, I'm sure," said Hilda, who had enjoyed " The Man I Chose " very well.

" *Do* they ? " Mrs. du Pré was most interested at this revelation. " Well, isn't that an illustration of what I mean ? People here are really quite unsophisticated, are they not ? And so—so out of touch. And they are quite impressed, are they, with such a very tenth-rate artist as the Easter Crane woman ? Well now ! But ' artist ' is hardly the word—and that reminds me, have you seen our Assyrian Lion upstairs ? He's a bit out of place here, isn't he, because I believe his work is very fine. Or should it be Assyrian Bull ? I never know. How on earth did *he* get here ? I have a great friend who is really *au fait* with the latest movements in art—er—Lord Brok—and he thinks highly of the Assyrian's work. He was much amused to learn that the creature lived two ceilings above me."

Her easy mention of Lord Brok left her visitors without a word. Hilda sat in her chair with confused eyes, staring. But Old Mrs. Coventry's eyes moved sharply to a silver-framed photograph of a handsome man in uniform, and the movement did not escape Mrs. du Pré.

"Yes, that's Lord Brok," she informed them most naturally. "I have known him ever since I was about twelve years old. He used to come to my mother's place in Derbyshire when I was a child. It's been a life-long friendship. And he's been very kind to me since my husband died. He's most amused at my coming here, but I tell him that it's the most restful little backwater—so quiet and still and untouched by Time. I call it a little pocket of Yesterday. It *is* all that, you'll agree?"

A backwater—Out of touch—Unsophisticated! And yet all so charmingly said that they didn't seem to be included in the description, though feeling in the deep of their hearts that they ought to be there! This was defeat.

"We like it well enough," said Hilda, empty and drifting.

Mrs. du Pré perceived that the time had come for mercy. "So do I," she affirmed enthusiastically. "I love it! And I tell you one thing that's quite perfect about it. Your Mr. Guilder. What a face! And what a voice! No wonder they all worship him. I declare I do myself. A little more height and he'd be too good to be true. 'Ambrose' I call him—don't you think it suits him? 'St. Ambrose'—though he's no saint, I'm certain! He ought to be a Lord Chancellor, or a Mayor of the Palace in some old dynasty. Yes, he's a very bright spot in Norman's End. . . . Oh, *must* you go? Not so soon? . . . "

Our two Coventrys returned home stripped of all that fine confidence in which they set out. They walked

H

very quietly, and it was not till they were on their front door steps that the older lady said, " A most dangerous woman ! " But she didn't really believe this. In her heart she was resolving to enjoy the society of Mrs. du Pré, and to hear more of Lord Brok, and to discuss with her the shortcomings of Hilda and Rose Damien and her son, Tom.

X

THE Square Quarter Mile accepted Mrs. du Pré but not Mr. O'Kelvie. Mr. O'Kelvie had admitted his wrong-doing and so was beyond forgiveness; but his laughter still rang across the road, irritating as a fly at a horse's ears. Mrs. du Pré returned the calls diligently, went to church regularly (if a shade too radiantly) and even did her portion of church work in a " district." She came rustling in her silks to the At Homes, and, though all agreed that her talk was too *risqué* by far, they enjoyed it and felt oddly braced up by it. It is always a tonic when first you hear someone who dares to be witty and to say aloud in the drawing room what you have only thought in the passage. Her wit was ruthless but not unkind : you felt that it was flushed through with an affection for her victims. At Hilda Coventry's she would make fun of that plump Mrs. Damien " with her neat little dog, Abbott, so like a whippet in his winter jacket; and her weedy son, Leo, who was less like a lion than any boy she'd ever seen "; and at Rose Damien's she would be daring indeed about that poor darling, Tom Coventry. " My dear, he may be over forty and threatened with fat, but no one's awakened him yet. I've no doubt he's a very fine Secretary of Queen Anne's Bounty, or whatever it is, but that doesn't alter the fact that he hasn't moved an inch from the schoolboy who's afraid to do what the other boys aren't doing. He's never got free. A pinch of freedom would do him all the good in the world—he's so potentially attractive with his big frame and his great sad eyes! Someone ought to take him in hand. He wants a woman to laugh at him when he's pompous and silly, and to tell him that we like them better when they're not quite so correct—someone who'll point out that men's fashions have changed the weeniest bit in the last twenty years—instead of that fluttering nonentity he's tied to. What he wants "—and her eyes danced with mischief—" is to be cited as a co-respondent in a divorce case. It'd be the making of him. And with a mamma like his he ought to be capable of anything." In short, Mrs. du Pré's opinions, unless you discounted them as merry talk, matched poorly with her regularity in church and her evangelistic work in her district.

At this time the Boer War spread its fever of patriotism over England, and Cynthia entered her thirteenth year.

Cynthia at twelve years old had still the wild grace of childhood. Her womanhood was peeping at breast and hip, but she herself did not seem to have noticed it, and it had endowed her as yet with neither awkwardness nor constraint. She went quite simply and childishly to her school with a satchel on her back and a packet of biscuits and a thousand crumbs mixed up with her textbooks. She was in love, of course : we know that she was in love with Mr. Guilder, but this was a love so whole-hearted and thorough and uncomplicated, so simple, so much like any other permanent part of her life—say her return home from school in the evening or her falling asleep at night—that it made for serenity and not for conflict and dismay.

And it was associated just now with a very lovely

experience. Cynthia, deciding that she must practice all that Mr. Guilder preached, else were her love worthless, was trying to be good. Not so as the others should notice it, which would be beastly, but in the inmost chamber of her thoughts, and as between herself and God. She was mortifying the flesh by secret asceticisms and finding them a source of satisfaction and joy : she would give away her toys or her share of sweets just in proportion as she wanted them ; she would make her kindness to her grandmother match any temporary hate ; she would say long prayers and read long psalms behind her bedroom door—and the whole experience was filling her (when she remembered it) with a luminous ecstacy.

She had not yet arrived at her destination, which was to love God at least as well as she loved Mr. Guilder, but she was struggling on to that goal, and she drew great comfort from the man who said, " Lord, I believe ; help Thou mine unbelief." When after a self-examination prolonged and severe she was obliged to admit that the goal was far distant, she would say, " Lord, I love Thee ; help Thou mine unlove," and thereafter be at rest.

Much of this sanctity was due to her confirmation. She had lately been confirmed. Mr. Guilder said he believed in confirming them young, and while she was still only eleven she went under the bishop's hands, with no ungenerous vow of self-consecration ; and now she went every Sunday morning to her communion, when the early sunlight was on the pavements, and the blinds were still down in the windows, and the birds were twittering in an unawakened world. Or if it was mid-winter and the sun unrisen, she went through the darkness past the lighted kitchen windows to meet her God. The church she so much loved would be still and quiet with the sparse congregation, and its stillness and quiet were only emphasised by the few gas-jets burning. And there on her knees before going up to partake of the mystery, she offered up all her ambition as a sacrifice to God, in union with the sacrifice on Calvary.

Ambition ? What ambition ? Yes, Cynthia was sorely tempted by ambition nowadays. She would have liked, if God stood not across the path, to go forward to an enormous fame, which would put her photograph in all the stationers' windows like the picture post-cards of Marie Studholme and Mabel Love. But Mr. Guilder had told the children what the cross meant—it was a symbol of " crossing out the I "—so Cynthia abandoned the hope of fame. Or rather she abandoned the deliberate pursuit of it. There remained yet the hope that the tale of Cynthia Coventry who had abandoned glory for goodness would echo down the ages. And when she heard the ladies talking about the genius and the popularity of Marie Studholme and Mabel Love, she knew what she had given up, and sat alone and quiet with the knowledge.

Very happy, these days of self-oblation. Perhaps her only unhappy hours were between tea-time and supper when she sat alone in the playroom at her home lessons. These were two dark hours and always dreaded. At school she was happy in her work because there was no chance of freedom and therefore no division in her mind, and since her abilities were at least as good as the next girl's, she quite enjoyed exercising them and showing them off. But at home when there was every

chance of pushing the books aside and running out to
play, when her window called her and the voices of
children could be heard in the streets, when there was
a saffron light in the sky over the brilliance of Earl's
Court Exhibition and her season ticket for that
illuminated paradise burned in her pocket, then the
strain of holding herself to Henri Bué's French Course
or the Second Latin Reader was a sick distress.   Nearly
all the force of her nature was directed to other activities,
and this split in her brain quickly became a headache.
And because the effort she gave to the books was fettered
and strained back by a hundred other desires she simply
couldn't understand the words.   She couldn't make
sense of the Latin pieces which at school, in competition
with other girls, she could have construed triumphantly.
Her natural force, spreading wide over happier hunting
grounds, wouldn't run in the single channel and overthrow the resistance.

One evening she sat at her table with her task before
her.   She had wrestled with the Latin sentence a score
of times without knowing anything more about it.
" Oh, *I* don't know what it means, *I* don't know, *I*
don't know," she bore witness to the empty room, and
by this reiteration disabled herself further.   And it had
been no help to hear the voices in the road, to jump up
and see Rob Ingram and his friends going down Conyers
Road towards the " Ex." Her eyes saw the Latin
words no more, because her mind was seeing a wide
space with gas-lit fairy lamps surrounding a bandstand
and outlining the facades of sixpenny side-shows and
festooned along a green enclosure. It was seeing a
three-arched stucco entrance in Norman's End Lane,
and the clinking turn-stiles behind it, and then the

covered way along which one ran to the jewelled grounds.
It saw the red season ticket and felt its texture.
Banishing the visions, she drove her eyes to the book
again, but it was no good ; they filled with tears ; and
after one brief effort at control, she dropped her head
upon her arm and sobbed.   It was absurd, but the
tearing up of a battlefield depends, not upon the dignity
of the cause, upon the violence of the battle.   She let
the impulse to cry have its way ; and it tore through her,
while her head lay on her arm.

But then the door handle turned.   Somebody was
coming in.   Immediately she lifted her head and turned
her face to the window, that no one might see her shame.
But her refusal to turn round betrayed her as surely as
if she had shown her tear-stained face.   She heard the
intruder's abrupt halt, and then his familiar voice.

" Cynthia ? How's Cynthia ? Hard at work ? "

Mr. Guilder.   He must have called on her mother and
looked in to see her before he went.   She could not turn
and look at the same time.   Oh, this was awful !   What
was she to do ? The seconds passed, and she was doing
nothing.   It was like a horrid, unnatural pause in the
motion of the world.

" Cynthia, Cynthia ! "   His finger under her chin
had turned up her face.   " What's this ? Why, my
darling ! . . ."

In a moment of acute pity he had undoubtedly called
her " my darling."   Her eyes shone up at him like wet
pebbles.

" I can't do this," she explained and pressed her lips
together to control a sob.   " And I hate it."

He looked whimsically at the book.   " Latin," said
he.   " Filthy stuff, isn't it ? I've forgotten all I ever

knew. Come, we'll do it together. You shall teach me." And, drawing up a chair, he sat at her side, actually putting his arm around her shoulder. And she, in her gratitude for this and her affection, leaned against him. I doubt if she had ever been happier. Nay, certainly she had not : a child's love may differ in degree from yours and mine, but hardly in essence ; and were we ever happier than when within the arm of the one we loved ? And the astonishing result was that, all desire having been drained home from Earl's Court Exhibition and concentrated on her present delightful occupation, she just translated the Latin (with a few aids from Mr. Guilder) as if she were bilingual and this her second tongue.

"Why, good heavens ! " exclaimed Mr. Guilder. " You can make hay of it ! What were you crying about ? "

" It didn't seem easy till you came in," she said, looking up.

And it seemed to her that he smiled down affection-ately and drew her against him tightly. Had she known more of the world, she would have known that he had drawn her almost hungrily.

She was very happy now ; and when he went she didn't want to go to the Exhibition any more. She wanted to walk about with exultant thought. " I have given myself to you," she said to his absent figure, " and I'm so frightfully happy about it. I shall never want anything more if I may just love you." It was all so simple. There was never anything more simple.

XI

CYNTHIA was not the only person in the house who felt drawn by the colour, the music, and the lights of the Exhibition. Her father liked very much to wander there, cigar in mouth, after dinner. But he liked to go alone. He would not have enjoyed it in Hilda's company, whose voice with its silly talk went on for ever, and who chafed him so with her hundred differences from the woman he imagined at his side. In the warm evenings of summer he liked to treat himself to one luxury; he who did not usually dress for dinner or smoke cigars, liked to put on a stiff shirt and dinner jacket, hang his heavy gold watch-chain across the waistcoat, set a cigar between his lips, and, having arranged his opera hat two quiet degrees from the straight and picked up his rolled umbrella, fare forth to the Exhibition grounds, where he sat in the exclusive garden of the Welcome Club and felt superior to the unprivileged crowds on the gravelled space outside.

Do you remember the garden of the old Welcome Club, marked off from the gravel of the common people by a rustic railing, a line of plane trees, and an arcade of fairy lamps ? Do you remember its chain of sheltered alcoves where you could dine *à deux* behind the trellised vines ; and its lawn with the tables and wicker chairs dotted about where you took your apéritif or your coffee and watched over the railing a multitude strolling round

and round the bandstand ? To your left the common-
coated people sat outside the cafés, sipping their lemon
squash ; over the way the lamplighters with their long
poles lit up the white lamps that outlined the paste-board
palaces ; and in the bandstand, now a dazzling crown of
lights, the scarlet-coated grenadiers (Lieutenant Williams
conducting) played the music of *The Geisha* or the songs
of the Boer War. The twilight faded from the sky, the
fairy lamps brightened, putting out the stars, and the
sky became a velvet blackness over the jewelled scene.

Well, one warm and gracious evening Tom Coventry
entered the Club garden and, passing the tables with his
cigar in his mouth and a cornflower in his button-hole,
sought a chair where he could see the crowds, think his
long thoughts, and perhaps be near a pretty face. He
found a long wicker chair and dropped into it, well
content. He liked drawing at his cigar and dusting the
ash from his fine evening dress ; he liked the blend of
melancholy and romance that the music stirred in him ;
he enjoyed looking at the beautiful faces that passed
him by ; and I would not say that he disliked the stab
of disappointment and hunger that was his whenever
he saw a young " masher " with his arm around his girl,
or (if it comes to that) an old masher on the Welcome
Club lawn with an enchanting young goddess at his side.
He so wanted a goddess too.

He sat alone, of course. In his heart he knew that he
did not belong to these macaronies of the Welcome
Club ; that he lacked their confidence with the waiters
and their ease with the women ; that he would be
clumsy and timid if he sat with one of their sparkling
queens ; and he sought consolation in thinking that he
had chosen a better path than they, preferring honourable

work at a modest salary to leading the idle life or grinding big money out of the labours of the poor. No, his goddess would have to be one with whom he could be at ease and even smilingly superior ; her divinity would have to reside in her goodness and simple beauty, not in her high manner and wealth—but what was this nonsense ?—he was married and over forty and getting fat, and he would never walk with a goddess in the garden of the Welcome Club. Only the second-best hope was left to him : one day, if Cynthia became beautiful, he might walk in romantic parts with her, rejoicing in her feminine charm, and feeling a proud father.

With a sigh he got up and strolled towards a chair, nearer a group of lively young people. And as he walked, a voice called to him, " Mr. Coventry ! Don't pass me."

He stopped and looked down at Mrs. du Pré who sat there alone, in evening gown and opera cloak. In pink velvet and silk she lay spread along a wicker chair, her head lying back to look up at him and her feet crossed before her.

He stared down smiling, not knowing at all what to do. What was the proper thing to do when a solitary woman, who was a friend of your wife, accosted you in a public place ? Could you sit with her or must you wait for a chaperon ? Pretending the ease of a man-of-the-world, he just smiled down ; and she saw right through the smile to the awkwardness behind.

And being a frank woman, she tried to see her own thoughts. What was her game now ? She knew that the pity, blent with exasperation, for the shy, taboo-ridden male which lies deep in most women was stirring within her. She knew that in some mischievous chamber of her being the sleeping temptress had risen on her arm. This instinctive temptress wasn't seeking him for herself—the idea of an intrigue with Tom Coventry was ridiculous to her who had known a lordlier lover—but she was restless to toss into such fallow ground the seeds that would quicken him to liberation and to life. In a word, she looked up at Tom Coventry, and he down at her, and the everlasting mischief was at work in the garden.

"Why not sit down for a little ? " she invited with laughing eyes. "You are alone, aren't you ? "

"Yes . . . Yes, I'm alone."

"Then come and sit by a lonely woman. I'm never at all sure that I ought to come here alone, but what am I to do ? I *won't* stay in my silent flat, and I *won't* be denied all enjoyment by a lot of silly rules. And anyway, I don't suppose it matters for an antique widow like myself. Sit down."

"Certainly, certainly," said he, somewhat facetiously. And he sat down beside her, and tried with hearty talk to conceal his awkwardness. The evening was very warm ; not a breath of air disturbed the leaves of the plane trees or the flames of the coloured lamps hung among their branches. Over the rustic railing came the *suff-suff* of ten thousand feet treading round the bandstand, and the murmur of voices ; and over this barrier of sound the music of the band. Far behind it all were the shrieks of the passengers on a switchback railway. The band was playing an air *pianissimo*, and he exclaimed for the sake of something to say, " Oh, I love this tune ! " and gently beat time with his hand.

" ' I hear the soft note of an echoing voice,' " supplied

Mrs. du Pré, adding, " and on a night of deep blue velvet too !—oh ! forgive me for such an idiotic remark, but I'm feeling so sentimental to-night. I'm in a very bad way, Mr. Coventry. I've let myself go, and I'm sinking deeper and deeper into the morass. I shall be maudlin soon."

" Really ? "

" Yes. I'm feeling just as I felt the first time I went in a gondola at night along the canals of Venice."

" And how did you feel then ? "

" Oh, I don't know. I thought of all the people I had loved and who had gone from me as all do. Dear me, dear me ! . . . What is the meaning of it all, Mr. Coventry ? "

He shook his head, and gazed down at the light of his cigar.

" I suppose you've loved lots of people in your life ? " she asked.

" No," he promptly answered, really imagining that this asceticism would impress her.

" Oh, but you must have done. You're the sort."

" What ? " He turned towards her, interested. " What do you mean ? " he asked. Few sentences had ever given him more pleasure.

" You're the sort that women like. You must know that."

" Oh, but I don't think so." He said this as a concession to modesty, not because he wanted her to believe it.

" Yes you are. You are, believe me."

" Why do you say that ? "

" I don't know. Any woman knows the sort. Yes, I'm sure many women have loved you."

" Before I was married, you mean ? " he asked, for he had now suddenly changed the character in which he would like to appear, and was ready to hint that he had been much admired before his marriage.

" Why yes, of course, of course ! We can't have anyone falling in love with you now. That would never do ! "

" No, I suppose not," said he in the same vein ; but the picture she had drawn of someone falling in love with him was a sweet ache at his heart.

" Oh, but I feel pagan to-night ! " she exclaimed abruptly, beating her hands impatiently on the wicker arms of her chair. " Do you know, Mr. Coventry, I sometimes wonder why, at this stage of history, we are still content to be tyrannised over by an old Hebrew martinet who had to keep his riff-raff in order in the desert. Because that's what it comes to. We're all content to hand over our liberty to that shocking old Moses. We're content to walk about, bereft of all beauty and happiness and seeking solace in an apéritif or in a cigar because that silly old man said we must. *He !* Confound his impertinence ! Tell me, Mr. Coventry, why should I, Gladys du Pré, sitting in the Welcome Club of the Earl's Court Exhibition, in about the hundredth year of Victoria's reign, obey that nasty old man ? We daren't stir hand or foot because of him. He's knocked the richness and loveliness out of life for how many hundred generations ? And just because his rabble of slaves needed a tight hand ! Why do we put up with it ? Why do we knuckle under in the way we do, and think we're being mighty noble and good, when in our heart of hearts we know that we're just being timid and afraid ? We're spineless."

It is an experience with us all that certain sentences in books or in talk have been as a blinding light to us, opening up a new country and determining the direction of our lives.   It was so with these words of Mrs. du Pré. For the first time in his life Tom Coventry, who had supposed that he could present no more admirable character to the world than that of a highly moral man, saw that in the eyes of free people he might seem much more praiseworthy as a rebel.   For the first time he saw that what had appeared very fine to the unsophisticated people who had been his friends might, to more critical minds, appear slavish and cowardly.   And as, like most of us, he was more occupied with the opinion of men than with the truth of God—or rather, would have delighted to find a new truth which accorded better with his desires—he began to feel that he was seeing a new light and would follow the road it showed him. He would be a rebel and free.   The band at the moment was playing a *pot-pourri* of popular airs, among which he recognised the *Barcarolle* of Offenbach ; and, proud to have distinguished it unaided and to have acquaintance with such a high-sounding name, he exclaimed, " Oh, I love this tune !   The *Barcarolle*.   Offenbach's," and hoped she thought him musical.   Fortunately he did not know that she was taking compassion on him for the simplicity of his taste.   Then to justify his past life in her eyes, he asked, while the band played on : " But what if you happen to believe in that old morality ? You can put yourself under the yoke willingly not timidly."

" Oh well . . . of course . . . if you *really* do that," assented Mrs. du Pré, " if you really believe that God appeared in person to an old bedouin in the desert and laid down the rules for ever, why then there's nothing more to be said. But often I wonder if they're anything more than the lynch law of an old wandering tribe."

Tom Coventry nodded his head over his cigar, meditating; and Mrs. du Pré, working herself up to fervour, proceeded with delicate waves of her hand. Weren't we old enough now to do what we liked so long as we didn't hurt other people? Love, for example —what they called an " affaire " could give unsurpassable bliss for a little while to two people, in a world that was not too full of happiness, and it needn't hurt anyone else. It was a matter for themselves and no business of Society's at all. " I quite agree that one mustn't hurt others; in fact, I sometimes believe that that's the only creed I've got; and now I suppose you're thinking me an abandoned woman."

" Not at all," assured Tom Coventry; " Not at all."

" No, don't, because I'm not, really, but——" and she suggested that it was at least possible, was it not? that we were still savages fearfully accepting the taboos of the tribe, or schoolboys still afraid to do what the other chaps would revile us for doing, or dull-witted dogmatists without the critical faculty to rise and judge our chains.

" It may be so," Tom Coventry nodded.

" Yes, it may be," she concluded. " And to-night I think it is. But there! We middle classes are all like that."

Middle class! Every word increased the revelation to Tom Coventry. He was ashamed of himself. Humiliated. Ashamed to think that he had arrived at forty-five and never had the critical faculty to see this truth, or the strength of character to say, " I will stand alone. I care naught for the hisses of the timid herd.

I

I will do what I want to do so long as I hurt no other."
To think that he had always been a slave, a disciplined
savage, and middle class ! To none but himself would
he ever admit that he had been all this ; to Mrs. du Pré
he would pretend that he had long ago considered all
her arguments and decided against them ; but he knew
well that he had been heavy dough into which the leaven
had only now been tossed. It was working in him, and
he felt enlarged. He felt emancipated. In one moment
he had stepped out of childhood into the adult's freedom.

But that she might think him no simpleton he defended
his past austerity ; he said that Society must fall if no
one obeyed the rules ; and she said she quite agreed—
she would have rules for the mob who must be kept in
order and fortunately were docile enough, but the top
men, the aristocrats, had always taken advantage of their
docility to lead their own lives. "There they are, the
mob !" said she, pointing to the dense throng moving
in slow rhythm round the bandstand. "Dear, good,
amenable souls ! What should we do without them ? "

And again the heady yeast dropped into his mind.
He was not content to imagine himself less than a top
man and an aristocrat. God, how had he been such a
dullard as to stay among the docile mob so long ? His
chin sank to his collar as he gave himself to thought.
Mrs. du Pré smoothed an empty glove between two
fingers of one hand. . . .

The bandsmen were packing up their instruments ;
Lieutenant Williams, his baton under his arm, was
coming down the steps of the bandstand ; and some
of the crowd was wandering off to other parts of the
Exhibition grounds. So interesting had the talk been
that they had not noticed when the music played and

ceased. It must be half-past ten already. Tom Coventry, still in the power of his past, whatever his resolutions for to-morrow might be, rose to go home. It did not occur to him to do anything else, for he always went to bed at eleven.

Perceiving this simplicity, she smiled up at him enigmatically ; and he wondered what the smile meant. He did not altogether like it. He felt uncomfortably that she thought him a simpleton. But that didn't matter. He *had* been a simpleton, and he must forget it, along with all uncomfortable memories of her and her opinion. The past was past. Life began to-morrow, and no one should think him a simpleton again.

" Good-bye, Mrs. du Pré."

" Good-bye, Mr. Coventry."

" Oh but wait. May I see you home ? " He strongly hoped she would say no. It would be awkward taking her up Conyers Road in full view of his own windows.

" No. Please not. I am going to enjoy the warm air and the people a little longer. I hate being escorted, because I cherish my independence—I really do ! Good-bye."

In the same opera hat, white shirt, and dinner jacket Tom Coventry went out between the turnstiles into the night traffic of Norman's End Lane, but he was a different man within the clothes. As he walked up Conyers Road, he saw, not the long pavements between the tall houses, nor the halo'd gas-lamps retreating to the vista's end, but the free life that stretched before him, in the pride of full day. He saw himself finding what he wanted and taking it easily. And as he looked at the radiant pictures his heart was almost sick with hope. Perhaps a prisoner, released and walking in the free streets, feels little more. A policeman was standing in the yellow-light of a lamp post with his oil lantern in his belt. " Good-night, constable," said Tom Coventry. He said it graciously, for he walked in the royalty of freedom.

XII

THE figure of Mr. O'Kelvie, a man condemned by all
her people, still exercised its fascination over Cynthia.
Why, the man was even a pro-Boer, so Rob had said,
and the only one she had seen! Everything was wrong
about him; and if she saw him coming gaily down the
steps of the flats, she stared after him till he was out of
sight. If she went down her own steps, she always
looked up at the windows of his high flat, wondering
what went on behind their curtains. And more than
once she had made a secret and guilty journey to Ashgar
Terrace that she might stare at the grey wall of his studio.

About this studio there was everything to stimulate
the imagination of a child. Ashgar Terrace was in the
cheaper, but still cosy parts of Norman's End. At
the corner of Ashgar Terrace you might see in winter the
Italian chestnut man, and, as you passed him, you went
through the hot air from his stove and the smell of his
sizzling chestnuts. Sometimes his station was occupied
by the hot potato man who had a taller stove with an
iron sun at its top, and on each of the sun's iron rails a
baked potato was impaled. Such kerbstone vendors
never profaned the Square Quarter Mile. Down one
side of Ashgar Terrace went little grey-brick houses
with areas, porticoes and balconies, and down the other
side the long garden wall of the old novelist's mansion.
The houses were of the nineteenth century, the garden

wall, with the fruit trees peeping over it, had a stone in
it which said:

THIS WALL IS

THE PROPERTY OF

MR. J$_n^o$. J$_s^a$. SALTOUNE

1795

About midway in the wall, flush with it, indeed a part
of it and, as it were, a continuation upwards of it, rose
the grey, blank wall of the studio.   No window was in
it anywhere ; the top light was in the roof.   Only a
long, narrow, perpendicular, and rather terrifying slit,
through which the larger canvases were drawn out to
the vans, broke the blankness of the wall, and this was
now shuttered by a panel of greening wood.   There
was an old blistered door with a rusty ring-handle over
the lock and pictures chalked on it by the ruder boys.
It was a door that looked as if it had never been opened,
and in fact it seldom was : O'Kelvie approached the
studio through the garden of the untenanted house.

You could not see the house from Ashgar Terrace
because the garden was long.   If you wanted to go
and gape at it, you had to go all the way round to
Norman's End Lane on which it fronted ; but Cynthia
often did this, because if ever a house looked haunted,
it was old Ashgar House.   Its shallow forecourt was
guarded by a dwarf wall surmounted by an iron
pallisade fence ; the gates were flanked by tall brick
piers with stone balls or urns on top ; within the
forecourt, among dusty shrubs, an ash tree rose and
drooped ; and between its leaves you could see the
ivy-hung walls and the dead windows of the old house.
At the side, behind gates of exquisite wrought iron,

was a courtyard of sunken cobbles—cobbles from which in the old novelist's day the horses of Dr. Johnson's coach, pawing, kicked the sparks. At the back of this courtyard was a coach-house with a low passage-way through which you could see the sunlight on the unkempt garden.

After the old novelist's time I imagine Mr. Saltoune had the house ; and much later an artist of the pre-Raphaelite brotherhood. It was he who made the studio at the bottom of the garden with the terrifying slit through which came his larger panels very well known by you. He died ; and Patrick O'Kelvie came, but only to the studio. Ashgar House stayed untenanted and decayed.

Cynthia, after staring at such a place of gloom and mystery, walked round again to Ashgar Terrace to have a look at the back wall of the garden and the studio. She was too young to think that here came a metalled roadway and the pavements of the nineteenth century beating up against the dark old wall ; too young to think that, where once upon a time the market gardeners had worked, the nursemaids now pushed their perambulators, and tinkers cried their trade, and, on the balconies opposite, ladies sat and sewed beneath their striped sun-blinds. She stared up at the studio wall. Had you not been told that Mr. O'Kelvie, who was not a good man, worked behind that wall, you would have found it difficult to associate wrong with so quiet a road. But work there he did, singing perchance, " They call me the gentle maiden . . ." or other variations of his favourite airs. And left and right ran the garden wall.

Now a garden wall behind which there is reputed

wrong is an invitation to a boy to get over it, and to a girl to get through it. Cynthia and her great friend of this period, Aline Guilder, were soon resolved by hook or by crook to get over this wall and to see the south side, and possibly the inside, of the studio. Splendid curiosity of vital youth, the beginning of all knowledge ! And yet they supposed it very sinful—but this didn't lessen the attractiveness of their project : it added its own spice. Cynthia at this time must have effected a compromise with her desire for sanctity, or else, as is more probable, come down from the heights into a temporary trough : one cannot stay on the heights for ever.

You will have guessed why Aline Guilder was her greatest friend at this time. Cynthia liked to be with her and to talk of her father. She would tell Aline that it must be marvellous to be his daughter, and would be surprised sometimes that a daughter's view of a man could be so different from his lover's. " Oh, Daddy was quite all right," said Aline, and no more. And now these two children had a new link in their great resolve to adventure into the shadowed O'Kelvie world.

Both shrank back from approaching the studio by crossing the cobbled yard before the dead windows of the house and doing a nightmare run through the garden. But the only other way was through the blistered door of the studio itself where it fronted the pavement in Ashgar Terrace. And looking down upon this spot were the windows and the balconies of the respectable houses opposite. How appear innocent to those watchful windows ? It was Cynthia who found a plan. They would play with a ball on the pavement and accidentally send it over the wall, and then ask at the studio door for permission to pass through and retrieve it.

So one golden evening, when they knew by his song that O'Kelvie was within, a red ball sailed over the wall, and they stood staring at each other.   They had done it ! Could they go on ? Aline apparently could not : she could only giggle and retreat ten yards away.   So Cynthia, though her heart had gone mad and her face turned crimson, went to the door and timidly knocked. Too late to retreat now ! Or was it not ? Aline, little coward, thought not ; and immediately ran another twenty yards towards safety.   For a second Cynthia decided to play the bell-ringing urchin and run too ; but she hesitated and didn't ; and that hesitation determined her life story.   The cheerful humming came to the door ; it opened ; and O'Kelvie stood before her, in a dusty butcher-blue blouse thrown open at the chest, his fair curly hair disarrayed.

He stared.   He saw before him a twelve-year-old girl, in skirt and blouse with a big sailor hat on her chestnut hair, her eyes dilated and frightened, her cheeks guiltily flushed, and her full lips quivering as if troubled by a nervous giggle.   Round the crown of the hat was a ribbon with " H.M.S. Perseverance " on it—a long word so that he had to glance all round her, to learn the name of her ship.

" Please," she said.   " We've sent our ball into your garden.   Would you mind if we got it ? "

O'Kelvie stared at her long enough to make her feel uncomfortable.   And yet there was a dawning grin at his lips.

" Did you send it on purpose ? " he demanded.

" *No !* " Cynthia denied—deep in her trough.   And

then, observing that he was still examining her with a doubting grin, she guessed that the other answer would impress him more. So she admitted, " Well . . . yes . . . we did."

" Glory be to God, and did you then ? "

" Yes. . . ."

" You deliberately threw it over ? "

" Yes."

" Against the peace of Our Sovereign Lady the Queen ? "

" I—I'm afraid so."

He nodded significantly. " Magnificent ! And why, madam, why ? "

" Well . . . I'm awfully sorry . . . but we wanted to see your studio."

" A blessing on your darling hearts, and so you shall ! Come in ! Why knock ? Come straight in, Miss Perseverance. Hi, you ! " This was to Aline, drifting out of range. " Come along. You're in this, I'm sure. Come along, you two slabs of curiosity."

" Oh, we're not really," Cynthia apologised.

" Yes you are, and don't be ashamed of it. Curiosity's a fine thing, and don't you let 'em tell you it isn't. Now what do you want to see ? "

" Is this your studio ? " asked Cynthia stupidly enough ; for the barn-like room in which they stood was filled with studio easels of varying shapes ; canvases of all sizes hung from or leaned against the stone-coloured walls ; a trestle table, long as a shop's counter, was littered with palettes, brushes, oil colours, crayons, cleaning rags, chisels, callipers, plumb-lines, ash-trays, and a hair brush and comb ; on other parts of the floor stood a clay bin, a pedestal, and a model's stand ;

casts and busts and tin cans stood arrayed on the shelves ; and over all was a pleasant smell of turpentine and paint. In addition to the tools of his craft, three comfortable arm-chairs and a long couch grouped themselves round a gas fire.

Very readily he led them round, explaining all things : how a painter mixed his paints and a sculptor used his chisel ; why this picture of his was beautiful and that one foul ; how he turned the revolving stands and worked the easels up and down ; why this figure was over-modelled and yonder statue lifeless ; and how the callipers measured a model from cheek to nose. He seemed delighted with their interest and hardly stopped talking at all. " Anything else ? " he inquired when they had tried half the tools and worked every handle in the place. " Anything else, Perseverance ? Command me."

" Oh please," said Cynthia, " might we look through that funny slit ? "

" Why, certainly." And, undoing two wooden bolts, he pulled away the long narrow panels ; and all three looked out, one head above another, into the daylight of Ashgar Terrace.

" What a place to pot at people from ? " was Cynthia's comment.

" I must try," said O'Kelvie. " Should we do it now ? "

" No. . . . Oh no," said Cynthia. " No, we'd better not."

" All right then," agreed O'Kelvie, replacing the panel. " That's settled. We'll do it some other day. And now what else can I show you ? "

" Could we—could we see the garden ? "

"And why not, why not? Though it's gone back to the jungle, mostly. But perhaps you'll see the ghosts."

"*Ghosts?*"

"Yes, a little fat man in a white wig; and perhaps another with a paunch and a rolling gait and a beaver hat, God rest his soul. The Doctor!"

"Oh, you're stuffing us!" protested Cynthia.

"It might be so; and then again, I might be speaking the truth of God. But come and see for yourselves. Can't say I've seen 'em myself, but I'm always hoping to. This way, my pretty ones." And he led them into the long garden.

They were surprised to see that a wall ran down its centre, dividing it into two parts, and that the studio was at the foot of the western part. For fifty yards from the studio all was orchard trees in a sea of tall or tumbled grass. They walked through the trees and the scents of the summer evening till they came to the dividing wall. In this wall there was a door through which they passed on to a moss-green path between wall and lawn in the eastern half of the garden—if that could still be called a lawn which was more like a hayfield, rank and thrown. O'Kelvie, walking along the path under the lee of the wall, pointed to an old mulberry tree which grew against the bricks and overhung their coping.

"That old tree has seen things," he said. "A century and a half ago it saw the old novelist walking up and down and thinking out his silly novels, and now it sees me walking up and down and tearing my hair as I think out a great statue; because, believe me, it's a very much greater man I am than he."

"Are you?" laughed Cynthia, as if he were joking.

"Don't laugh, don't laugh, madam. With all my

heart I believe it, and it's not myself that'll be telling you a lie. Listen : your people teach you to be truthful, I'm sure ; but what do they do when someone asks them if they think they're rather fine chaps ? Lie. Lie like the devil on Sunday. Well, now you're looking at the only person you'll ever meet who thinks he's a genius and heartily says so if anyone asks him. Mark me well, it's a fine example I am for you. What will we do now ? "

They had left the lawn, passed through the arch under the coach-house, and were standing in the cobbled courtyard, with the dead windows of the mansion gazing down upon them. The beautiful wrought-iron gates, opening on to the traffic of Norman's End Lane were before their eyes. Half open, for no one troubled to close them now. These gates, and the fact that Mr. O'Kelvie was standing unashamed in his butcher-blue blouse, with naked throat and ruffled hair, for all the hurrying world to see, hinted to Cynthia at a quick farewell and a departure by the way of Norman's End Lane.

" I think we ought to be going," she said.

" Not a bit. You can't be going yet. What about the ball ? "

" Oh bust it ! Yes. Yes, there *is* that."

" Ha, ha, ha ! " roared O'Kelvie. " It's not in Heaven I'll be meeting you, the thumping lies you've told this day ! Come back and get the ball and have some tea."

" But I say ! aren't we being an awful nuisance ? "

" Nuisance, is it ? Devil a bit. You're being an inspiration, my children. I'm loving you—loving you for being interested in my studio, and having the spunk to throw your ball over the garden wall. I call that terrific. And I know all about you too. You live opposite me with the bright-eyed old lady."

" Yes ! Oh, I'm *so* glad you know that ! "

" But I forget your name, God forgive me."

" Cynthia Coventry."

" No doubt. And your little friend is——? "

" Aline Guilder."

" Guilder ? Ah, Guilder's your father, is he ? A very fine head. And a clever man too, so I suppose you've no brains worth speaking of, Aline. Children of clever men never have. Michael hasn't—at least I can't say that I've noticed them as yet."

" I know *your* name," said Cynthia.

" Do you now ? "

" Yes."

" And what is it then ? "

" O'Kelvie."

" It is. Patrick O'Kelvie it is, the Lord be praised."

They found the ball and returned into the studio where O'Kelvie insisted on making tea. In vain they protested that they had had their tea long ago ; O'Kelvie declared that he hadn't had his, and no one went from his studio without refreshment and the blessing of God. He took a very black kettle off the floor and put it on a gas trivet. Then, drawing up a small table, he spread a newspaper on it, and on the newspaper a loaf of bread, a paper of butter, a pot of jam, and a cake and three cups. Turning from this work, he saw Aline staring at the model's stand, and suggested, " Jump on to it, child. Jump up and pose."

But Aline held back, shaking her head.

" Oh may *I* ? " asked Cynthia.

He nodded ; and she leapt up and stood there, while Aline giggled.

"Now pose," commanded O'Kelvie, laying his head to one side and considering her. "Let's see. Let's see. Fling your arms wide as if welcoming someone eagerly."

Cynthia tried to do this.

"There you are ! " cried he. "Good ! 'Youth Welcoming Life.' Beautiful ! Rather pathetic. Keep it up, child ! Hold it ! Think of all the wonderful things that are coming to you ! Splendid ! O my dear . . . that's very beautiful. . . Hold it ! . . ." And he walked a few paces backward to study the pose. "Now think that some of them will probably hurt a little. You realise that, don't you ? It's sad, but it's so. How would you stand if something that you loved more than anything else—some toy or other—broke in your hands ? See, it's broken ! Nothing'll ever put it together again. Never, never, never ! "

Pleased with his praise, Cynthia tried to express what he wanted, and instinctively shot her two closed fists, with thumbs upright, to her teeth, bending her head to meet them, while her elbows pressed into her sides as if to control herself from a complete breakdown.

With deep appreciation O'Kelvie shook his head gently. "Disillusioned ! My poor child ! Oh, jump off. It's too sad—too disturbing." And putting his hand under her armpit, he jumped her off. "Sit down on the couch till I make you the tea. I wish I had better to offer you, but it's summer, and the hot potato man isn't at the corner. Whisht, whisht, the kettle boils ! "

He made the tea in the pot, cut three thick slices off the loaf, spread them generously with butter and jam, bade them fall to, and himself ate his meal precisely as they did, with very large mouthfuls, long swills of tea, and rapid eager talk.

After this exciting close to their adventure they affirmed that they really must go.

O'Kelvie dropped again into broad Irish, as he liked to do when his spirits were high. " Well, and it's been rale dacent of you to come. Let you be coming again one of these fine days." And he opened the door for them into Ashgar Terrace.

" Good-bye, and thanks most frightfully," said Cynthia. " It's been too gorgeous for words."

" Not at all, not at all," said he cheerfully. " Good-bye, and the blessing of God go with you. It's myself that'll be praying for you." And he stood on his step in his blue blouse and ruffled hair, watching them along the pavement and waving a huge arm when they turned round.

They waved back and disappeared.

Instantly he turned back into the studio, thrust his hands into his trouser pockets, thought profoundly for twenty seconds, and then went out into the garden. Head down, he walked among the orchard trees. He wandered from the trees and, passing through the door in the wall, paced the path between the lawn and the mulberry tree. The visitation was upon him. An idea ! A creative idea ! For an hour he would be unapproachable, possessed, misanthropic, wild-eyed, waving away those who came near him. His fingers would scratch his head, run through his curls, and play in his beard. If brother artists approached and saw him thus, they would whisper to one another, " Keep away, keep away ! The mood is upon him ! The curse is upon our Pat!" and slip away, his wild, unseeing eye looking after them.

"Grief?" No, that was trite. "The Price?" The price of consciousness? Perhaps; for the price of consciousness was pain. The body taut and straining upwards, the elbows pressed to its sides, the fists shot to the mouth, and the head lowered over them. In stone. The whole figure tapering to the shoulders like a Hermes, and still: the visual expression of the price to be paid for blood and breath.

PART II

I

THAT stretch of time which carried Cynthia into her
fifteenth year seemed always in retrospect to have topped
a peak and turned downward. One morning the
paper-sellers ran along Glastonbury Road, crying,
" Death of the Queen ! " and at once, in their staring
silence, the people felt that a peak had been reached and
henceforward their English story must dip down to a
lower level. Why they felt this I do not pretend to
know. They spent a few last days on their peak
burying their Queen, and then settled down to the
slightly diminished grandeur under the king. " The
King "—strange word ! There was now a king in
England.

Old Mrs. Coventry, gossiping with her friends, shook
her head over the new king and pursed her lips rather
doubtfully. She said that he had never been as moral
as his mother ; and in her heart she admired him the
more for this. This it is safe to say : no one in
England enjoyed the funeral of the queen, and the
mourning services that followed it, more than this
loyal old lady. When she heard that they were going
to fire eighty-one guns in honour of the queen's age,
she nagged and harassed Hilda for not wanting to come,
and hurried off to a point in London where she could
hear them properly : and she heard them and wept.
When she heard that they would proclaim the King

at Temple Bar, she hurried and doubled there; but alas! though she ran along the pavements, bumping into some people and sliding past others not too carefully—strain on her face and sometimes a despairing tear in her eye—she arrived too late. She had missed the rich costumes and the loud trumpets and the Garter King of Arms. All she saw was the red cord across the street, but she stared at this and was moved thereby. She was glad to have seen it.

She forced Cynthia and Hilda to come and see the Funeral Procession (not that Cynthia wanted much dragging, who was six paces ahead of them most of the way). Hilda feared that the crowds would be too great; but her mother-in-law said, " I never heard such nonsense! We can get there early and stand near a policeman. We'll take some sandwiches and get there before the crowds arrive. It would be ridiculous not to go. Such a thing may never happen again in any of our lifetimes. I can't understand you. I can't really."

So very early in the grey winter morning these three walked past the high mansions draped in purple and white, and along by the ropes of laurel festooned from mast to mast, till they came to the wide space in front of the Achilles Statue in Hyde Park; where they tried to keep near a policeman, but found it difficult because he would keep moving up and down. As far as possible Old Mrs. Coventry dodged after him, back and forth; and where she went Hilda and Cynthia went too. Then the crowd began to thicken, and suddenly a swelling movement pushed a great section in front of them, and three weak women, of whom two were very small, were surrounded; so that all the old lady's exercise

was wasted, and a passionate tear spurted in her eye.
It wasn't fair; it wasn't fair, she complained. It was
a disgrace; it was so un-English, and the people ought
to be ashamed of themselves. She talked loudly at
those in front, in a way that made Cynthia wish herself
invisible, or dead; but the people, well placed now,
affected not to hear. Soldiers in their spiked helmets
took the places of the policemen, to keep back the
crowd; and this was too much—Old Mrs. Coventry
could see the helmets and no more—so by a wholly
unscrupulous and wholly successful ruse she pushed
Cynthia in front of her, saying, " I'm sure these gentlemen will let a little child see. They can see so easily over
your head. I'm sure this lady won't mind your going
through. She has probably a little girl of her own; "
and, pushing Cynthia, nothing loath, like a wheel-
barrow, she came like a good gardener behind. One
couldn't leave a child alone in that great crowd.
Splendid! Nothing in front of them now except the
line of soldiers; and Old Mrs. Coventry had her plan
for seeing over their shoulder-straps : Cynthia carried
a folding wooden stool, and after they had taken turns
to sit upon it while waiting for the Procession, or while
eating their sandwiches and chocolate, they held it in
readiness to be dropped to the ground and stood upon,
when the great queen went by.

And so they waited long hours. The huge crowd,
it seemed to Cynthia, were finding it difficult not to
enjoy a smothered jest now and then, but were trying
well and courageously. Silence for two hours is a strain
on the best, particularly if the best be London's best,
and one or two of them broke down under it, indulging
themselves in a joke and a snigger furtive and low.

But when the word went, " It's coming ! " the men all removed their hats, and the women wiped their eyes ; and Cynthia admired them very much for being so polite and loyal. Inflated almost off the ground, she was straining on her toes to see, till she heard her granny whispering, " Stand on the stool ! Stand on the stool ! Quick ! Quick ! " and saw her turning and explaining vaguely to some thousand people behind that the child might never see such a thing again in her lifetime.

Cynthia saw the gun carriage go by, with the King sitting rather dumpily on his horse behind, and just behind him an erect and martial figure with a peaked cap and moustaches upturned. This horseman caught the eyes of the people, and of Cynthia as well, more than the King. They said afterwards that he was the most striking figure in the procession. Where got he this odd, arresting quality ? He was not a tall man, and one of his arms, for those who could see, looked shorter than the other and rested suspiciously on his thigh. Time is a mystery, and if the past can invest a man, can the future too ? It was the Emperor of Germany.

" It's the Emperor of Germany, the Emperor of Germany ! " cried Cynthia, forgetting to be silent.

" *Where ? Where ?* " exclaimed Granny excitedly. " Oh, I didn't see him ! " And she sounded so disappointed, and strained so to see, that Cynthia hopped off the stool and told her to stand on it instead. And Granny, determining to present the crowd with a *fait accompli*, jumped on to it, and, with her steel spectacles up, stared over the shoulders in front of her. Poor King ! He looked rather heavy and old. Magnificent Kaiser, to have come to the Funeral like this ! Her tears dimmed her glasses ; and after a while she stepped off the stool, giving a quick guilty look at the people behind. And now neither she nor Cynthia saw much more, but heard the bands go by and the clip-clop of the horses on the road.

The last of the lances had sailed by, the last of the music had died away, and the crowd was moving and breaking up. Recovering Hilda who was not far off, they copied other people in picking each a laurel leaf from the Venetian masts as a souvenir of the day, and walked quietly homeward through the park.

" I'm glad I saw that," said Old Mrs. Coventry.

Then on the following Sunday there was the service in St. Alban's Church. Breakfast seemed hardly done before they saw the people on the pavements going silently towards St. Alban's. The children went by with their parents. There went Rob Ingram in his black coat and top hat, very silent and solemn. There went the Ellisons. And look : down the steps of the mansions came Mrs. du Pré, very smart indeed in her black silks and short sealskin jacket. Very soon all the Coventrys were on the pavement too, as silent and ceremonial as the rest. They followed the slow stream of people into the church and saw that it was nearly full.

In ten more minutes it was packed by an even larger crowd than it had held on the Jubilee Sunday.

They had come to pray, to mourn, and to be thrilled. And thrilled they were. Again and again the shiver of appreciation passed through them, and their throats swelled. Mr. Guilder is at the lectern : he pauses, closes the book, and looks at the people as he finishes the lesson on the words, " Man goeth to his long home, and the mourners go about the streets." Mr. Guilder is in the pulpit, and a great silence awaits his text. As always, he allows it to wait, and then, leaning on the pulpit, gives out the text. " And I saw a great, white throne." Very quietly he speaks of the throne from which a very tired but very dutiful old lady has just stepped down. He tells them first of its greatness. He paints for them a picture of two lines of grey warships, stretching from the Isle of Wight to the mainland. Coming very slowly between them, escorted by destroyers which seem scarcely to move on the still water, is the lonely little *Alberta* bearing on its deck a coffin with a white pall. The huge grey hulls boom forth their greeting and their grief as it passes, and the echo of the minute guns rolls down the straits. Behind, and very sadly, steams a larger yacht, the *Victoria and Albert*, bearing the King ; and behind that a larger one still—a white ship among the grey—the *Hohenzollern*, bringing an Emperor from the Continent, for that coffin ahead holds the Mother of Kings. It is the Queen coming home to take her last farewell of her people. Seemly picture this, of an island throne, simple and domestic in its heart, but guarded by the leviathans of the sea ! But greater than its greatness is its whiteness. Sixty-three years before, when they told Victoria that she was Queen, she bent her young head and murmured, " I will be good," and now, after sixty years of service to her people, all the world proclaimed her Victoria the Good. Mr. Guilder pauses, and leans on his pulpit again. Then he reminds them of him who has stepped up to that great, white throne. He bids them pray for him. Never a man called to so high a responsibility and so great a task. God save the King. They are to remain on their knees, he says, while the Dead March is played, employing the time in thanking

God for his mercies to England (Mr. Guilder is no musician). And then they are to rise and sing the national hymn with hope and trust in their hearts. God save the King.

And all the time they kneel and pray, and all the time they stand and sing, a high wind roars and buffets round the church, shaking, it seems, the rafters up there in the darkness of the roof ; and when they pass out again into the sunlight and the driven dust, they are nearly blown round the corner home.

II

I ALSO was of Norman's End, and I think often now of our eager interest in the Royal Family and the Navy and the Empire. Was it that, doomed in our lives to a quiet mediocrity, we had need to be great by proxy in the persons of our kings and our Empire builders? Rose Damien was great by proxy when she drove her Abbott up and down the aisles of St. Alban's as its churchwarden; did we, partly for the same reason, drive our great warships out to sea? Was it that, circumscribed from adventure and enterprise, and disciplined by the social system to office desks and domestic chains, we united ourselves with the Empire and roamed abroad with that? Roamed with the Flag to dominion and to danger? Were Throne and Empire and Royal Navy, in part, an escape from Norman's End? And if so, did we seize our chance and escape from it all, when the guns opened and the ships put out to war?

Consider the literature of Old Mrs. Coventry, in her sitting-room on the second floor. She read Ouida and Marie Corelli and Hall Caine, who were vicariously Christian in her behalf; but she gave an even vivider interest to the journal, *M.A.P.* or "Mainly About People," by the agency of whose pages she left that room and lived in very high society. She lapped

greedily at the more imperial newspapers—the *Express*
and the *Mail* appeared about this time—and fought the
South African war more loyally and viciously than any
" gentleman in khaki " on the veld. She knew the
easier poems of Kipling and blew her nose over *The
Absent-Minded Beggar*, though disapproving of the line,
" It's rather more than likely there's a kid " : she thought
that rather vulgar, she said, and a reflection on our
Tommies, who were moral, surely. But she turned
against him when he produced *Recessional*, and reminded
an At Home day that he was only a War Correspondent
after all, and her husband, the Judge, had always said
that regular officers looked down upon War Correspon-
dents as—you know—not quite out of the top drawer.
She read her Omar Khayyám when everyone else was
doing so, and declared that it was lovely ; but when Mr.
Guilder suggested, laughing, that Omar was a tippling
old reprobate and his song a glorification of paganism,
hedonism, and free thought, she said, " Oh, is it ? I
didn't realise it meant *that*." But most of all she read
in newspapers and books about the Royal Family. She
talked a deal about John Brown, Mrs. Langtry, the
Baccarat Scandal, and a lady morganatically married at
Malta. To be sure, in all their mighty dominions, the
monarchs of Britain had no more loyal and dangerous
old lover.

Almost on the heels of the Funeral—so it looks in
memory—came the Coronation. We brought down
the shields and the flags from the box-rooms, and
decorated our red-brick houses just as the merchants of
London decorated their stores and their streets. We
prepared for celebration ; and suddenly the king fell
sick, and the decorations hung limp on the houses, and

the festoons of flowers swung sorrowfully over the streets. Old Mrs. Coventry was immensely impressed by the dramatic illness of the king. She hinted that it was a warning from God that, before he was crowned King of England, he must consider well his past life and vow to be as serious as his mother. It was a lesson to the world, she affirmed, and how, after this, anyone could deny the existence of God passed her comprehension.

However, when His Majesty was pronounced out of danger, London determined that she wouldn't be deprived of her fun and set off to see the decorations before they were taken down. We children, being older now than in Jubilee year, chartered our own private bus ; and we climbed aboard it, and drove off.

It was a superannuated green bus " to seat twenty-six persons, twelve inside and fourteen outside " ; but we were all outside. All of us were there : Rob Ingram, the Ellisons, Mike O'Kelvie, Leo Damien, Gus Champion, Jack Trevelyan, the Guilders, and Cynthia Coventry ; and we took it in turns to be the conductor on the step, informing would-be passengers that it was private, and to sit next the driver, either holding the reins in a quiet road or hearing his political views. The driver had a hat like Mr. Pickwick's and was, said Cynthia Coventry, rather a lamb.

The streets were hardly less crowded than in Jubilee days. A black river of pedestrians flowed along the pavements, tossing on its surface coloured-paper torches, comic paper hats, coloured balloons, and long peacock feathers called " tittlers." It went with a rumour of many voices, an occasional *toot-toot* from a cardboard trumpet, a tune from a mouth-organ or an accordion, or a full-throated chorus of the song :

> " *On Coronation Day,*
> *On Coronation Day . . .*
>   *We'll all be merry*
>   *Drinking whiskey, wine, or sherry,*
> *On Coronation Day . . .*"

" To seat fourteen outside "—but the children on the top deck of that bus didn't sit much. They ran from side to side to see a fine decoration or a particularly jocund section of the crowd. Only Leo Damien sat alone, looking down upon the people. Leo, being thirteen now, was less the shrinking target than he used to be, but he was still by nature the " odd man out " ; and Cynthia felt the old quick pity for him when now and again he made an effort to lark with the others. Boisterousness hung so ill on his thin, spare, diffident body. At one time her pity was so strong that, using his seat and the one in front of him as parallel bars, she swung to and fro and tried to talk to him ; but, making little headway against that diffidence, she soon dawdled off. He was happier, she supposed, when he sat alone and looked over the side of the bus, thinking his own thoughts.

But Chance had it that he provided one of the greatest entertainments of the evening. The bus turned out of the main road into quiet squares and fetched up at a thrilling spectacle—a hansom and its horse lying on their sides in the roadway. Empty for a moment of driver and fare, the cab had moved off, fouled the kerb, and crashed on to its side.

" Stop the bus ! " cried Rob Ingram.   " Here, stop the old bus ! We must see this. The horse may be dead."

The driver obeyed ; and since Rob, sixteen now, immediately descended the steps of the bus to have a nearer look at the horse, most of the others followed him. Leo followed too, so as to be like them. Rob, being of the metal that didn't hesitate to discourse with bystanders, soon obtained all information and gave it to his friends.

" Its leg's broken."

" What ? "

" What did you say, Ingram ? "

" Its leg's bust, and they've sent for the horse-slaughterers."

" What for ? "

" To eat it, of course—what do you think ? To shoot it, ass. Its leg's broken, and it's suffering hell."

Instantly Leo, by a kind of reflex action, drew up his own leg and clasped its knee, while his mouth drew in a long *siff* through his teeth as if he were in pain. Grant Ellison, having observed this, roared with laughter and pointed it out to the others.

" Look at old Face ! I say, you chaps ! Look at old Face Damien. He's holding his own leg. At least he did, but he's dropped it now."

From standing round the horse they turned to stand round Leo, who went as red as the flags on the houses.

" The horse has broken his leg, Face," said Grant Ellison, acting as showman to a performing animal. " The bone snapped with a ghastly crack."

Despite an effort at control, Leo slightly bent his leg and drew a sharp breath between his teeth.

"Ha, ha, ha!" laughed the boys. "Make him do it again, Ellison."

"Smack went the bone!" said Rob Ingram, determined to do the trick himself. "And oh *goroo!* the jagged bone——"

Again Leo's knee moved slightly in sympathy.

"My Godfathers and Godmothers!" mused Rob, lost in contemplation of this strange new fact in natural history.

"Here, Face——" began another—but the driver called out, "Look 'ere, young gents, I want my supper if you don't. You can play that game on top here, if you want to"; so shouting, "Hold tight, all!" they ran to clamber aboard again; while Leo, quite unconscious of what he was doing, *limped* there.

"He's limping, he's limping!" shouted Grant Ellison, delighted with his find. "Did you ever in all your life——"

They looked back and roared with laughter. Leo blushed, but laughed too, and mended the limp.

The bus moved off towards other decorated streets, but now the boys had a new game. They stood about Face Damien where he sat, and tried to induce more of these remarkable phenomena.

Rob Ingram, standing taller than the others, took the lead. He would say abruptly, "I say, Face: did you know that Coldchurch Major had accidentally gouged out an eye with his knife?" and lo! before he could stop it, Leo's hand had shot to his own eye and pressed hard on it. It was extraordinarily funny, and they crowded round to watch. As an entertainment it bettered the decorations, which were now getting stale.

K

Once before Cynthia had been moved by pity to walk up to Leo and try to be kind. It was after a service at St. Alban's Hall. Mr. Guilder, unable to house his congregation, even after the enlargement of the church, had conceived the idea of organising a separate service for the children in St. Alban's Hall. St. Alban's Hall was nothing but a large parish building with a large assembly hall upstairs and smaller rooms down below. Its brick walls were colour-washed a cold green ; its stone stairs were uncarpeted ; its furniture was a score of trestle tables and a thousand or so of parish-room chairs, some of which were broken ; and its few pictures were no more than stained and spotted engravings of Doré or photographs of the Men's Club Cricket XI, with Mr. Guilder in the middle of them, wearing his silk hat. Round its walls went a varnished dado with gas brackets above it, whose shades of white opal glass were rather like our house-maids' cuffs. If you were to visit St. Alban's Hall to-day, you would think it a bare, depressing place ; and yet to us children of thirty years ago it was as nearly a paradise as we could find. What it is to be uncriticising, zestful children who can turn a barn into a paradise ! As it was in actual fact it offered no subject for a lyric ; as it was in our thoughts it was as well worth a book of lyrics as any daisied meadow lively with butterflies and the games of children. We didn't trouble about the stone stairs (we went up them too fast) or the stained pictures or the broken backs of the chairs (indeed we broke a few of them ourselves) ; we only knew that here took place the Bazaar, the amateur plays we wrote and acted for the common kids of the Band of Hope, the Children's Dances, and above all, the Pantomime.   To see those gaslights dim before the curtain went up on the Pantomime !

And now there was this Children's Service, which was as nearly jolly as any divine service could be ; and anyhow was a welcome relief from Morning Prayer with our people at the church.   Mr. Guilder sent all his Sunday School children and instructed the " ladies' children " that they must go too and set an example. We went ; and though you may not believe it, a thousand children or more crowded into the large hall upstairs, where a tawdry little altar was erected in front of the stage ; and to hear them singing—nay, roaring, " Once in Royal David's city," or " Around the throne of God a band " was enough to wet the eyes of angels—though we did not suppose this as we sang ; we supposed that we were just singing rather shamelessly, or, as we phrase it nowadays, " making whoopee." Among other ideas for this service Mr. Guilder conceived that of inviting those of the gentlemen's sons who were over sixteen to act as sidesmen ; and they were much pleased to accept, and to feel like Mr. Damien as they walked up and down the gangways, escorting late comers into seats, presenting hymn books, collecting money, and whispering to nasty little street arabs that they were to behave properly or there'd be the devil to pay.   Rob Ingram was very good at this sort of thing and made a fine sidesman.

All of us younger " ladies' children " were very regular in our attendance, as Mr. Guilder desired ; but whether we set a good example is not so sure.   We sat in a block in front, away from the contamination of the sticky little district children—who smelt, so our boys said, and were not wholly prejudiced.   And here, under orders from his mother, Leo would join us. But that confident, positive, and therefore stupid woman always insisted that he should come to the service in his top hat. Now Leo's head was rather long than round (as if the occiput, where they say the affections lie, were well developed) and thus his top hat, if it was to fit him lengthways, had to be rather too wide at the sides. And with such a hat Mrs. Damien would send him among a thousand children of the cockney streets ! Good God, woman ! could you not see that, if his walk up the gangway with this hat in his hand before a mass of tittering children was a *via dolorosa* enough, it was not to be compared with his departure from the building with the hat on his head, when the children were pouring into the sunlight.

One morning he came to where we sat in a block, and found a seat among us. And it happened that to-day the service was to be conducted by Mr. Booth, a newly arrived and very gentle curate to whom we felt in much the same relation as we did in a class-room at Trinity with a master whose discipline was weak. We prepared for a practical joke or two beneath the level of the chair tops. One joke to-day was not very good—except in so far as any joke in church seems excessively funny : it consisted in passing our hassocks one after another, with our compliments, to Jack Trevelyan at the end of the row, who was to pass them back to us, one after another, with his compliments, during the sermon. We giggled over this festivity quite a lot, and Leo Damien, trying hard to be like us, rather overdid his mirth, so that Rob Ingram, hearing him and walking up the gangway to quell any disorder, gave him a peculiarly dirty look that hinted at retribution after the blessing.

And, sure enough, at the service's close, when we were all flocking out, we saw Rob and Grant Ellison, another sidesman, waiting by the door to arrest Face Damien. Rob stopped him on the landing at the top of the stairs, told him that they weren't standing any monkey-nonsense from *him*, and gave him, like a good church-warden, a kick on the behind—not a severe one, but one that encouraged a shamefaced walk down the cold, stone stairs.

Cynthia saw it all ; and Rob's dullness and injustice astonished her. Hadn't he the brains to see that Leo was the least of the offenders ? Why, she herself had been much worse than he. It was idiotic ; it was a shame. Rob was a filthy pig—and when she was out on the pavement and saw Leo in the distance walking home alone under his wide top hat, the acute pity stabbed her, so that she ran after him and, breathless and flushed, spurted out, " I think Rob's a cad. Did he hurt you ? "

" No, not much," said Leo.

" Oh, I'm glad," she panted.

" Yes," said Leo.

" Because I mean, I was much worse than you were."

" Oh, I don't know," demurred Leo.

" Oh yes I was ; and he never kicked me."

" I don't mind," said Leo.

And then, since he didn't seem able to pursue the conversation, she was forced to do it herself. This pause was awkward as they walked along.

" He's a sidey beast," she offered.

" Yes," agreed Leo.

" He *shouldn't* have kicked you like that. And before all the district children ! "

" *I* don't mind," repeated Leo ; and this time there was an accent of defiance in his words. It was an accent she had never heard before. It was a note quite strange.

He spoke no further. She began to feel uncomfortable ; and the more she dug in her mind for friendly phrases, the less she could force them up, and the " soppier " they seemed if by chance she got them into sight, so after a dozen more paces at Leo's side, she said, " Well, so long, Leo ! " and turned back to her friends.

The story that Rob Ingram had kicked Leo down the stairs after divine service reached Mrs. Damien in her morning room in Conyers Road ; and she was very indignant, not so much with Rob for having done his duty, as with Leo for having submitted to the indignity. " If I had been you, I'd have hit him back. Wouldn't *you*, Abbott ? Did *you*, when you were a boy, put up with treatment like that ? I can't understand why he hasn't more spirit in him. I'm sure if I had been a boy I'd have fought anybody who tried to kick *me*. Why, when he kicked you, didn't you strike him back ? It's so unmanly."

Leo stared at her in bewilderment. Surely this was a very foolish woman. What was she talking about ? How could he set upon a giant like Rob ?

And Cynthia, when she heard Mrs. Damien's suggestion, was equally amazed at it. Leo hit Rob ? What was she thinking of ?

Neither child saw the answer : to wit, that Rose Damien, being a fool as all self-opinionated people are, did not perceive that while boys of thirteen and sixteen look very much the same generation to adults, a tall broad lad of sixteen may sometimes seem grown-up and a giant to children three years younger.

III

St. Alban's Hall ! To talk of it is to remember the Pantomime, to which (between you and me) I have been aching to come since I started this tale. Am I right in believing that the Annual Pantomime at St. Alban's was no ordinary production, or am I magnifying the things I knew as a child ? People who were grown up then, and are old now, assure me that I am right, so I will tell of it as I see it still. Also something happened when we played Cinderella that bore heavily on the developing future.

Think not then that this pantomime was the least like any other parish theatricals you have seen ; for they are usually very small ale indeed, if not matter that bows our heads in embarrassment and shame. To begin with, whatever the furniture of the auditorium was like, we had a fine stage, with trapdoors, lights, and scenery ; and we had a young genius for our director. The Pantomime was an event looked forward to all the year— the rehearsals, the dressmaking, and then, oh, the smell of grease paint, the glare of the naked gas footlights, the matinee day when Mr. Guilder stood us a feast between the two performances, and lastly, lastly, lastly, the Last Performance, the Last Night, when there were speeches and cheers and chocolates and the last sad-happy walk home with the grease paint still on our faces, to be rubbed off with cocoa-butter nor applied again till twelve slow months had gone! We performed the show before the Sunday Schools, the Band of Hope, the Mothers' Meeting (jolliest audience of all! How they shook their fat sides when the Baroness came on with his—her, I mean—" Hello, girls ! ") before we threw it on the public. By then it was perfect ; and the public paid at the doors for six performances ; and Old Mrs. Coventry was at them all, I think, with her spectacles up. Bless you for that, little grandam ! I'd as soon play before your two shining lenses as before any two delighted windows in the world. It is dead now, our pantomime ; dead this twenty years and more, but I should like to make it live again in a book. Go up again, old lights ! Jangle again, old curtain bell ! " All ready ? Then Right ! " says Lance Guilder.

Lance Guilder was our director and genius. We have not met him before, because he was too old—though he was on the Coronation bus. He was seventeen or eighteen when we were thirteen or fourteen. Quite unlike his father, he was a short, slim, wiry youth, with a small snub nose—but enough ! I must say no more ; Lance is out in the world now, producing great plays, for which, by the way, he still builds the scenery as he built ours, thirty years since, and I must not speak of his nose. Let me say only that, if he had not his father's body and face, he had his theatrical genius. The Pantomime was his inception and creation. Into it he impressed all the children of the parish—all the ladies' children, that is. From mid-November he was rehearsing us on the large stage in the echoing, empty hall. Quiet and unperturbed, like a great captain, he played the martinet, and we suffered him to do so. We all obeyed him ; even such as Rob obeyed him. I see him now, rehearsing us again and again in tireless pursuit of the best, making the scenery with laths and canvas and hammer, trying out the coloured lights, practising the sheet-iron thunder, the magnesium lightning, the roar of the rain, and generally wielding the storm.

If Cynthia had a word of praise from him, she ran all the way home to tell her people. Conceive then the day when he told her that she was to play the chief part, Cinderella. This was history. This was great history, I suggest, if history is to be measured by the depth of the emotion suffered. " Sorry," said he ; " but I've no one quite so suitable." Play the chief part of all ! It was unbelievable. She raced home to tell the family and Ada and Cook. But she told none of them that her heart was going madly and her stomach had turned sick. The doctor always insisted that she over-excited herself, and if she told them this, they might stop her. But terror took her now lest an illness came and forced her to abandon the part ; and that night she lay very quiet in bed, saying over and over again, " I will *not* think about it, I will *not* think about it." And in the next weeks she never saw a piebald pony, or glimpsed the new moon, but she said to herself, " I wish I may keep quite all right, and do it better than anyone else has ever done it."

The day of the first rehearsal drew close, and now a second terror seized her, lest, in her nervousness, she did it badly, and Lance, who spared no one, so that the Cause were served, should supersede her by another. She prayed for ability at her bedside. The first rehearsal came, and the second, and she learned for the first time that joy and suffering can sit very near together.

Our pantomime was built on the best models of the

day.   Lance Guilder wrote it, and it was whispered that he went to all the pantomimes the previous year with his note-book in his hand and his scruples left at home. So before the drop-scene went up and discovered Cinderella at her hearth, there was a dark and alarming prologue in front of it : the Demon King and the Fairy Queen declared war, while the lightning flashed and the thunder rolled.   What an agony Cynthia endured as this scene played itself along towards the moment when she must be unveiled and speak.   She caught her turbulent breath, she yawned, she prayed that no one would come speaking to her, she wiped a moist brow and tossed her warm hair backwards.   She almost decided that the joy wasn't worth the suffering, as she heard the closing lines :

> *Demon King (to all his little demons)* : To your
>   mischief hasten ! Get you gawn !
>   *But enter Fairy Queen (Aline Guilder) in a flash
>   of lightning.*
> *Fairy Queen :* Not so, foul prince, and all your
>   loathsome spawn !
>   This evil that you fashion shall not be !
>   Who threatens Cinderella fights with me !
> *Demon King :* Ah curse you ! Ever must you cross
>   my path ! You shall not touch this girl beside
>   her hearth !

(The libretto, I have said, was Lance Guilder's, but his genius lay in production.)

> *Fairy Queen (breaking into a silvery laugh)* : Ha, ha, ha,
>   *ha !* Ha, ha, ha, *ha !* Why, prince, you make me
>   laugh !
>   Just hearken ! I beside her christening stood,

And vowed that I would bring her naught but
   good.
So do your worst ! The stage is set !
I scorn you all, and I'll defeat you yet !

Yes, my God, the stage was set, with Cynthia at her
fender, and her heart beating the band ! Supposing her
voice didn't come ! Supposing she fainted as the drop
went up, and fell flat on her face before all the people !
Supposing—but the drop had gone up, and her voice
did come—no terror seemed able to stop it—and blessed
confidence came with it—not much, but some. She
got through her lines and her business, and Lance said,
" That's all right. That'll do."
Phew, what a relief !
As the rehearsals went on, the torment stilled, and they
turned to pure joy again, though the terror of the First
Night loomed ahead, making a nightmare in her dreams.
So happy and hot did she look, tossing back her hair
at the rehearsals, that you would have had difficulty in
believing there was a settled sadness in her heart ; and
it may be that she often forgot it. Or else that this
settled sadness was one of her great happinesses.
Certainly she liked to sit alone with it for hours. And
to be ordered about by Lance Guilder, who was his son,
brought a sweetness too. She was nearly fifteen, and
conceived that she could now examine love intelligently.
As a matter of fact she was as ignorant of its implications
as a child of six ; she believed it to be a spiritual emotion
only ; and the kiss, the only outward expression she
could imagine, she saw always as a sacramental giving,
never as a carnal taking. But she could realise that this
sacramental thing must ever be denied to her and

Mr. Guilder. What then? Love, even when hungry and unsatisfied, could be a very ennobling experience (she had heard him say so); and in her, as in other great women, it must bear fruit in great works. What these works were to be she had not finally decided, because they changed with every book she read; but they would bring her fame in the end. And in her biography it would be written: " The secret of Cynthia Coventry's greatness—that which made her one of the best-loved women of her generation—has never yet been given to the world. It can hurt no one now. It was simply this: that she was loyal all her life to a childish love." She might even as she died (rather young) tell the secret to Mr. Guilder himself, saying, " I never loved anyone but you. There is no harm in telling you now. Think kindly of me, won't you? "

These, being pleasant rather than painful dreams, left her free to be quite happy at the rehearsals—even ecstatically happy. But let it not be supposed that her performance, in its early stages, was remarkable. She had no great talent as an actress; and her nervousness prevented her releasing what little she had. One does not do one's best when one is repeating one's lines parrot-fashion, and Panic is playing the drums on one's heart. It is a fact that Lance Guilder, who was encouraging her to her face, was shaking his head despairingly behind her back.

But whether or not Cinderella's godmother was watching over her child and determining that she should not be misrepresented on any stage, or whatever the cause may have been, there came a force from without— it came like wind and thunder—and transformed a commonplace actress into—well, into Cinderella. I assert that the actual tale of what happened to the actress playing Cinderella is as good a story—aye, and the same story—as the lovely fable of Cinderella itself.   There came a fairy (if a rather heavy and thunderous one), a transfiguration, and the people's applause.

Thus.   In the Palace scene Cynthia had an entry such as leading ladies dream of.   The whole company stood ringed on the stage in ball dresses of silk and satin (one only imagined these during the rehearsals, but they would be shining there on the night) ; the Prince strutted to and fro, bewailing the absence of Cinderella ; the music reached a climax ; the trumpets sounded a fanfare (two Trinity boys, off, with their cadet corps bugles) the crowd parted ; and at the vista's end stood Cinderella, in a glory of white satin and diamonds.   She tripped towards the Prince, and he in full song cried, " Her beauty blinds me so, I cannot see " ;—and this was our Cynthia !—" Tell me, tell me, gentles, is it she ? " And the chorus, instead of answering this perfectly simple question, kept well within the convention and sang, " Tell him, tell him, gentles, is it she ? " which left him no better off than he was before ; except that he was able to proceed :

> *Prince :* Nay, keep your answer, for my heart replies.
> My heart proclaims her, not my eyes !
> It is, if I mistake not, Cinderella !
> *Omnes (in chorus) :* It is, if he mistake not, Cinderella !
> *Prince :* Again, ye trumpets ! Sound your loudest blast ! (what was the good of having two buglers if you didn't use them ?)
> For Cinderella has arrived at last !

You will agree that this was a great entry, and one to make Lance, the producer, cry to the chorus, " Louder ! Louder ! " They were most willing to sing it louder and louder ; and it chanced that their young voices reached Mr. Patrick O'Kelvie, passing in the street below. Now, that man is worthless who is not moved by the voices of children roaring in riotous song ; and Patrick O'Kelvie was a good pound less than worthless. He halted ; he yielded to more than a little emotion ; and, being an impulsive and fearless person, he promptly pushed open the doors and doubled up the stone stairs two at a time, to learn what might be the cause of this inspiring noise. Seen by only a few, he stood at the foot of the hall, in a big hat, and cape of winter serge, watching Lance as he drilled his ensemble. And when at length the movement on the stage was brisk, the tableau pleasing, and the top note a triumph, he startled them all by clapping loudly and booming, " Bravo ! Bravo ! " And straightway he sat down on the nearest chair to enjoy some more of this excellent entertainment.

Lance turned his head once, but showed neither pleasure nor resentment.

He quietly continued his task.

" All again ! " he ordered.

And once more, with cries of " Louder, *Louder !* " " Hammer on the piano, Miss Wright ! Smash the keys ! " he drove the whole episode through to the entrance and recognition of Cinderella.

I suppose it really was rather moving. Anyhow, it moved Patrick O'Kelvie—so much so that he felt the visitation upon him. He felt the surge of creation. Not Cynthia had stirred it this time, whom he had not recognised, but the whole picture, with its colour, movement, and ordered ecstacy. It raised the unrest that could know no peace till it had found an outlet. He shifted restlessly on his chair, he half rose to his feet. he emitted soft exclamations, and at last, remarking a flaw in the tableau, he jumped up and came towards the stage, his cape flying and his rich voice calling, "No, no!—excuse me—forgive me, won't you?—but that won't quite do. It's so nearly beautiful that it's worth making perfect. May I suggest something? Do you mind, Mr. Producer? I—I rather deal in this sort of thing. It's plastic, you see, plastic."

There was vision in Lance Guilder. For one second a shade of irritation passed over his face, and then he saw that the suggestions of a well-known sculptor and painter like this O'Kelvie man would be of great value to the work he was creating. He even saw on the programmes, "Tableaux by Patrick O'Kelvie." And, preferring, like a good artist, the glory of the work to his own credit—or may be expecting additional credit—he stepped aside.

"Please," he invited. "Please tell us anything you think."

And O'Kelvie thereupon began to re-dispose the tableaux, with great enthusiasm and volubility. As prolific as a force of nature, he scattered among the children his ideas about sculptural masses and pyramidal compositions, expounding his meaning with horizontal or perpendicular extensions of his arms; till Lance knew for sure that he was watching the work of a better man, and nodded and said, "I see . . . Yes . . . Absolutely . . . Oh, absolutely! . . ."

Then O'Kelvie, laying hold of Cinderella's shoulder,

said, " And this child—she must move differently, I
feel—if you'll forgive me.   Come, my dear, you're doing
it so beautifully, but just a point or two ! Nothing much.
I'll show you what I think, and Mr. Producer needn't
accept it if he doesn't care to.   I don't know the least
thing about stage production, but I have an eye.   By
the mercy of God I have an eye much better than most.
I see instantaneously what ought to be done, and no
doubt I should have been one of the world's greatest
producers, if I had chosen that art, ha, ha, ha.   Ha, ha,
ha, ha !   Now this is what you must do."   And he
instructed her in every movement and pose, and, turning
to Lance, inquired, " How's that, sir ? "

" Absolutely," agreed Lance.   " Quite . . . Oh,
absolutely."

" Say if I'm wrong.   I beg you to say if I'm wrong.
I know nothing about it really."

" No, no.   It's better.   Much better."

" Ah ! " sighed O'Kelvie with much satisfaction, as
if he were wiping his mouth after a good meal.   " And
now should we run through it all again, Mr. Producer,
but just as you like, please."

" All again ! " ordered Lance.

So they rehearsed it all again, with O'Kelvie standing
at Lance's side.   At the finish he boiled over with
praises, suggesting no more than one alteration in
Cynthia's attitude.   Leaping on to the stage, he took
her hand and showed her what to do ; and when she
had done it, patted her shoulder and said, " That's right,
my dear.   Now you're perfect."   And Cynthia, being
nearly fifteen, was quite pleased at being patted by him
and called " my dear."

Meanwhile Lance had been meditating, with a pencil

knocking against his teeth. And he said, " I say, Mr.
O'Kelvie : would you . . . would it be too much to
ask you to come one day and look through the other
scenes ? "

" Why, delighted, sir ! " exclaimed O'Kelvie. " Delighted ! I haven't enjoyed anything so much for years.
You bet your boots I'll come."

And all the children clapped.

" What ! Eh, what are you doing ? " he cried, looking
up at them sharply. " No, don't do that. I beg of
you not to do that, or I shall weep."

At which they roared with laughter, none being old
enough to see that this was the simple truth.

After this he came many times to the hall ; and his
loud laughter, his bubbling excitement, his mild oaths,
and his quick sideway apologies for the same enchanted
the children. " Isn't he divine ? " said the girls. " Isn't
he a knock-out ? " said the boys. " I don't feel he's a
gentleman," said Rob Ingram, " but he seems to know
what he is talking about, I *will* say." In his moments
of tumultous imagination, which sent him charging like
a bull into the midst of the ensemble, he lost all tact,
and all sense of the weight of his body and the strength
of his grip ; but he never lost kindness ; and the
children loved him, even when their shoulders ached
from his fingers. And it is certain that he loved them
too.

And if Cynthia began to act her part better, she owed
it to this strong imagination that was playing on her.
One day he took her aside, out of Lance's hearing, and
whispered with engaging mystery, " Sh ! I must show
you one or two things alone. May I ? You're so nearly
perfect that we must get you quite right. I'm full of

L

ideas about you, but I don't like to keep charging in over Mr. Producer's head. They're sensitive, these theatrical gents. May I suggest to you one or two things on the Q.T. ? Nothing much, really."

Cynthia skipped with pleasure. " Oh please do ! "

" You're not too conceited to be told ? "

" Oh no. I'm not conceited at all."

" How can you say that, when vanity rides you like the devil ? It does surely ? "

" It doesn't. *Honestly* it doesn't ! I know I'm doing this frightfully."

" And isn't that a lie ? You know you're getting quite pleased with your performance. You know you haven't an ounce of humility in your system."

" Yes, I have. Oceans of it. *Really* I have ! "

" Wait. Where have I seen you before ? Who are you, miss ? I've thought all along I knew you well. Kindly tell me at once who you are. I know your voice as well as your face . . . don't I ? "

" Well, you ought to ! And I think you might have done sooner."

Cynthia had long been disappointed that he had not recognised her. A living conflict of impetuosity and self-distrust, she had never dared visit his studio again, nor accost him in the street, for fear of " being a nuisance " ; but she had hoped that he had thought much about her and sometimes been impressed by her from his window. Apparently he had done nothing of the kind, and the thought was sad. She reminded him of a walk in his garden, looking for a red ball, and of her home across the road ; and he stared, and recognised her. " Why, of course, it's *you*, isn't it ? Glory be to God, it's you. But that must have been three years ago.

You were much smaller then. And you were dressed differently."

"Naturally," smiled Cynthia.

"And I never look out of my window now. Can't stand the same row of houses, day after day. Can't stand the same virginia creepers. And I'm afraid I walk along in rather a dream, seeing nothing but my own pictures—or I should have studied you more earnestly. But this is splendid! This settles everything! You'll come along to the studio again, and we'll run through your part. When shall it be? To-morrow morning, eh?"

"Oh *yes!*" agreed Cynthia. "Oh *cheers!*"

So next day she went along to the studio with her part in her hand. And they had hardly begun the lesson before the urge was on the master, so that he paced up and down and prophesied (I had almost said "raged up and down"). The ideas spouted up, and he poured them into poses and gestures that she must imitate. To see this huge bearded man in his smocked grey overall playing the girl Cinderella with all the sadness of the world in his eyes, and his hands clasped between his knees, as he sat on a tiny stool, made Cynthia sometimes shriek with laughter, and sometimes giggle silently. He looked so like a huge farm hand who had lost the cow he was milking. But it taught her much. Her imagination, if not original, was brilliantly responsive; and it was now alight.

"Don't laugh!" he would flash at her, when, lifting his Cinderella face, he caught the movements of her mouth, "God in His heaven, don't stand there grinning at me! Confound your impudence!"

"I'm sorry," she would stutter, "only——"

" You were laughing at me. Here am I pouring out a vast creative stream for your advantage, and you stand there——"

" I'm so sorry——" and she tried to control her mouth—" but the stool's so small."

He got up from it quickly.

" Cynthia Coventry. Are you all that in my idiocy I have imagined, or are you no more than a giggling schoolgirl? Are you the greatest disappointment of my life? If so, say so. But of course you are. You are like all the others and have a brain of wool. Clearly."

" Oh, no," she protested.

" You say no ? "

" Yes."

" Have you, then, vision above your years ? "

" Yes, *rather !* "

" I doubt it."

" Yes, I have. Lots of it."

" You have ' oceans ' of it, in fact ? "

" Absolutely. Tons of it."

" Tons. Then you can see *something*—just a little *something* of what I've been labouring to show you ? "

" Yes, all of it. Please go on."

" I question if I will."

" Oh bust it ! *Yes. Please. Please* go on."

" I will then. But I have no doubt it is an expense of spirit in a waste of shame. Now then, my child, where were we ? " The pretence of anger was gone, and all was sunlight. He enjoyed these abrupt transitions. " Yes, we'll break their stupid hearts. We'll have them snivelling at the beauty of it, all over the hall. Why, Cinderella is easily the loveliest part in all the fairy tales. She's life itself. She's everyone's frustrations, and everyone's imprisonment, and everyone's dreams. She's me—yes, half my dreams are in ruins, and I await my godmother still. She's you—or you will be her, one day. She's the little bright-eyed old lady who lives with you, and who has such longings as you'd never guess. She's Guilder—Guilder in the privacy of his study. And we'll make 'em see all this, and weep. Have no fear. And not a word to Mr. Producer; this is our secret. Come, my blessing, sit down. Sit. There's your fire——" he put a turpentine can at her feet—" and let's see you sit here sadly, while your swines of sisters have gone to the ball, bad cess to them! . . . No, don't shake your head—don't move, don't move! It's reticence that'll break their hearts; never exaggeration. Just stare into the flame and see all your wishes fulfilled there, and yet without any hope. *That's it!* Don't move, don't move! . . . Hold that! Hold! Now listen—but don't move— your mamma is in the audience; she has had her dreams long ago, and maybe she keeps some of them still. It's sad, isn't it? Your papa is there, watching you; he has dreamed—oh, how he has dreamed! and the fairy godmother never comes, and he remains imprisoned and frustrated still. Break his heart, my dear. Be you his symbol, and he'll weep, he'll weep into his opera glasses. Yes, that's it—hold! hold! Every man and woman in your audience is tied to the pots and pans of life, and the cloud-cap't towers, the gorgeous palaces, rise only in the flames of their hearth-fires. Show them all that! Show it once and for all in your attitude and your eyes. Have you got it? That's it! . . . Now the faintest shiver and sigh. That's IT! Oh my God, I'm weeping already."

"But Lance Guilder says——" began Cynthia, turning her head.

"He'll see! He'll see!" cried O'Kelvie. "Directly you've done it, he'll see that it's right. He has imagination, and he needs must love the highest when he sees it. Or if he doesn't——" and here he whispered—"do it on the night, my child. He won't see you, but the audience will, and believe me, he's a great man, but I am a very much greater."

They passed to the scene after the godmother had appeared and vanished.

"Stand now," he commanded. "Face the audience. Quite still and straight, feet and legs together, hands clasping at the breast. Listen—don't move—your dreams, and all their dreams are coming true. Is it possible? Who can believe it? No, no, it's too good to be true. But godmamma has promised it. Love is coming to those that want it, and world-wide fame to the fools like me who've dreamed of it so long, and a prince for every one of the housemaids, and yes, a bishopric for Guilder. See? You are them all; and all, all are going to the ball! After years and years of disappointment the incredible joy has come. Keep still—lest you die of it. Oh, it hurts almost, doesn't it? Hold! That's it! Now light up your eyes, light 'em up! Smile *so* happily, and yet a little sadly. Now slowly spread your arms wide apart in a welcome and gratitude that still can't believe—and if Mr. Producer doesn't drop the curtain at that point, he's a fool. Phew! It's exhausting; but what a genius I am!"

"You are," said Cynthia. "Now *I'd* never have thought of all that."

"But you're young, little one," encouraged O'Kelvie, much pleased. "Phew! I'm tired."

So it was that Cynthia triumphed in her part of Cinderella. Everyone agreed that, pantomime though it was, and merrily though she played her livelier scenes, she had contrived to get into the rôle something that was beautiful—something of the wistfulness of life. And she had done it with such taste and reticence, the wiser ones declared, not without amazement. This praise lit up a joy in her eyes, and, since O'Kelvie had made her vow to tell no one of his " little efforts," she was able, without cheating at all, to take the credit.

The last night! What a champagne cup is a last night, sparkling with exultation, and yet flushed with sorrow! Everyone came a second time to the last performance, to hear the speeches and to see the flowers and the chocolates. Everyone mentioned in this tale was there, and five hundred more—the Ingrams, the Damiens, the Ellisons, Mrs. du Pré—you could see them sprinkled about the black mass of the audience. And Cynthia, as all the others, played above herself on this last night. One always does. Exultation and sorrow are meeting and fermenting ; and of emotions such as these is the power of the artist born. Cynthia, sad that the Pantomime was nearing its end, caught a glimpse of that saddest of all sad truths, the transience of every gay and lovely thing ; and, unconsciously perhaps, she put the vision into her part, and the people felt it there. The applause for Cinderella, at the end, surpassed that given for any other ; and in all her life she hardly knew a greater hour.

As for O'Kelvie, he was—well, I can only say that, very early in the performance, the urge came upon him, and he was straitened till he could do something with it. These fifty children, so vivid, so happy, so vital—this was the unconquerable energy, rushing up from the earth and rioting before his eyes. As soon as the speeches were over, and Auld Lang Syne was sung, and the people were leaving the hall, he came buffeting through them towards the stage, passed through the side door, leapt the stairs on to the stage, and, crying " Marvellous ! Marvellous ! ", allowed the pent-up creativeness to express itself in the only possible art-form, which was a hug and a kiss to each of the lady principals. And having a fine sense of form, he brought this offering last of all to Cinderella herself. And it happened that Cynthia, seeing what was approaching, turned up her face quite innocently for the kiss, so that it fell upon her mouth. He was hardly aware of this, but Cynthia was ; and it thrilled her more, she thought, than anything that had ever happened to her. Her cheeks were hot, but her heart happy, as he lifted his head and patted her shoulder. " Bless you," he said. " You were better than wonderful."

" Oh, but *you* did it all," she murmured, with grateful eyes.

" Not a bit. Don't believe it. I could have done nothing without the material. Do you think I'd have troubled with you, if I hadn't thought you'd got it all there ? When I'm going to make a statue, I choose my stone. And listen, Cinderella beloved, I sobbed at one time—not loudly, not so as the multitude could hear me, but a good, honest gulp, so beautiful you were ! "

And again he patted her shoulder, and passed on to shake hands with the boys.

And Cynthia told her mother, who was waiting for her outside, "If I live to be a hundred, I shall never have another night like to-night. It was absolutely too wonderful for words."

IV

O'KELVIE spoke nearer the truth than he knew when he said that to Cynthia's father the fairy godmother was yet to appear. Nearly three years had passed since Mrs. du Pré dropped into Tom Coventry's thoughts her sweet but dangerous seed. All those years he had been dreaming of what he would do, now that he was free; but he had done nothing. What has happened for the last twenty years is likely to go on happening for the next three, unless some drastic new factor is introduced into the old sum of things; and Tom Coventry had introduced as yet no more than a resolve to act when the opportunity came. It did not come. Ever since that night at Earl's Court Exhibition he had been looking round for the one who would be to him all that he needed, but she did not come into view. Certainly it could not be Mrs. du Pré herself. He was afraid of her knowingness. He did not want someone who looked pityingly down on him, but someone who looked adoringly up. Someone young. Someone who thought him brilliant. Someone who thought him a top-man, proudly free; who walked her streets exalted with the joy of his love and mazed at the wonder of it. And between two letters at his office desk, or in a stroll round the carpet, his heart trembled with anticipation, and his throat dried with thirst, as he thought of that young new lover. He wandered down the next three years looking for her, happy in his hope. Then in his glass one morning he saw grey in his moustache and his cropped side-whiskers (though his eyes and skin still looked clean and fresh and young, he thought). Fifty was near. Fifty! And undoubtedly there was a tightening about his smarter coats and fancy waistcoats. He pulled them straight as he thought this. Fifty! His forty-eighth birthday went by and goaded him most vigorously.

It caused him, among other things, to cock an anxious eye at his health. Hitherto, with his lordly superiority to panic, he had always scoffed at those gentlemen who never knew a day of sickness, nor yet a day of happiness for fear of it. And now he became a secret member of their gang. He enjoyed the strength and health of an ox, and yet—if his breath gave out after violent exercise (which he took now for fear of the fat) he wondered about heart-failure; if he made a mistake in his accounting, he experienced a sharp alarm lest his brain were weakening; if spots floated over the letter before him, he immediately tested his sight by holding the letter far from his eyes and near to them, or by propping up an open book on the chimney-piece and walking backward till he could read it no more; and, if, as sometimes happened with Tom Coventry, he felt an onset of good cheer, he stopped in the midst of the exhilaration to wonder if it were really *spes phthisica*. This, the sharpest fear of all, since his cheeks were ruddy, caused him to get a volume of the Encyclopedia from the office cupboard and read the article on Phthisis.

It was all related to his great hope. He must not decay before she came. "No," he would say aloud to the picture of Waterloo, "I must act. I must do something while I have time."

But what ? What opportunities offered in his daily
journey from breakfast table to brown mahogany office,
from office to dinner table, and from dinner table to
study ? Moreover, with those who knew him already,
he was handicapped from a forward step by his religious
professions. For though as an honourable man he had
resigned from prayer when he resolved to sin, he had
not ceased altogether from attendance at church. That
would create too much talk, he had thought ; and from
talk his shyness recoiled. He went along sometimes to
Morning Service with his women. Partly for their
sakes, thought he ; partly for their sakes. For the
child's sake.

But this meant that he would have to find his happiness
far away. Where ? The question was nearly always
with him, in his train, in his office, in his study
at home. It was a mixture now of hunger, desperation
and determination ; and though he did not know it,
the swelling and the bottling-up of this compound
meant that it was ready to break forth and pour over the
first soft face that looked kindly on him. One day he
jumped up from the office desk and went to the window
and looked out at Great Smith Street, Westminster.
" It is no good just dreaming," he thought. " One
must rise and create one's dreams. And I shall do it !
I shall do it ! If one's whole heart is set on something,
one creates it. Now then, how ? " And with his
hands on the base of his spine he watched the traffic of
Great Smith Street but saw none of it. " How ? "

What did other men do ? They met loveable and
gracious women in their social round, but he—whom
could he hope to meet among these timid, slavish,
taboo-ridden people of Norman's End ? Docile,

uncritical, herd-minded—that was what they were.
Middle class.   What did the free men do ?   Sometimes
if they were business men they loved their secretaries—
hallo ! was he on the track now ?   He stood still and
taut.   He did not know that he resembled a portly stag
which has sighted something and stands motionless,
alert, and gazing.   Many men were employing lady
clerks in their offices to-day ; the halfpenny newspapers
were giving whole columns to " the invasion of the city
offices by the modern young woman " ; and it would
cause not the least remark if he introduced a lady typist.
He was master here, and his committee had complete
trust in him. Trust. Trust. The word did not add
to his happiness, but he pushed it aside . . . And, to
do him justice, he was wanting some pretty thing to
love much more than he was wanting a mistress, in the
fullness of the term.

In these offices he controlled one old clerk who had
served Deacon's Ecclesiastical Trust for thirty-five years,
and two young ones.   Could he sack one of the young
ones ?   Young Michaels was not too satisfactory—
but no !   " No, I don't like it," muttered Tom Coventry,
setting his teeth.   " I can't sack him just because he
stands in the way of my schemes. Savours too much
of Uriah the Hittite . . . I can't ! "   He sighed, to see
a pretty fancy fade and pass ; and a voice within him
taunted, " There you are !   You haven't the courage to
be ruthless.   You'll be the prisoner of your own poor
middle-class conscience for ever.   A bigger man would
cut fearlessly through to his desires."   This taunt never
failed to rouse him ; and he brought his fist slap on to
his palm.   " I'll do it then !—but no, I can't, I can't. . . .
If to refuse to offer up a young man for my own

ends is to be middle-class, then I must remain middle-class for ever."

No, the more he examined it, the more certain he was that he couldn't sacrifice young Michaels, pup though he was. And, after all—oh, comfortable memory !—not even Mrs. du Pré had recommended that. She had said that one mustn't injure other people. Yes, thank heaven she had said that ! No, he would have to wait till old Ellsworthy retired in two years' time. Really fifty then. Was one too old at fifty ? Not if he kept himself trim with exercise and diet.

However it happened that, shortly after this, young Michaels, who had long been discontented, resigned of his own will. And Tom Coventry felt that God—stay though ! it could hardly be God—that Destiny was rewarding him for his restraint. Now !

Some three weeks later he might have been seen sitting at his desk in the brown mahogany office with his head bent towards a list of names on his blotting pad and his hand poised over the table-bell. But one would not have seen the irregular action of his heart, the undefeatable shame in his mind, and the sweet expectation in his throat. The list was a list of applicants for the vacant post, who were now waiting on chairs in the Trustees' Committee Room. His palm fell on the bell-press ; it screamed its message to the clerks outside ; and Tom Coventry felt as if he had sounded an irrevocable decision.

" The slave market," whispered an inward voice, in the ten seconds pause that followed ; and his heart jumped in dislike of the word. But he put it away, and smoothed his moustache.

Young Tristram appeared at the door.

" Show the young ladies in, one by one," said Tom Coventry, affecting a business-like indifference.

" Yes, sir."   And young Tristram went.

" The slave market," repeated the voice.

" Bah ! " retorted Tom Coventry, but without conviction or happiness.

One by one they came.   He rose with a kindly smile to meet each as she entered that she might not feel that, even though she was poor and had to earn her living, he respected her less than the greatest woman in the land.   At one after another he gave a single glance and decided that she was not for him ; but, unable to disappoint her at once, he asked all the expected questions and promised to write to her in a few days.   And as each left, he rose to hold open the door for her ; and then hurried back to his chair that he might give the next one the pleasure of seeing him rise to greet her.

Odd, uneasy interviews, to him who knew that he was considering each and rejecting her, not as a typist but as someone he could love.

" The slave market," said the voice.

" No, no," he protested.

But his conscience, which had lived and toughened too long for Mrs. du Pré to slay it at a word, prodded and stabbed him.   At one time it whipped him so severely that he said to young Tristram, " Wait a minute before you send the next," and returned into his room and shut the door.   He walked the thick carpet for a while and looked up at the picture of *The Thin Red Line*. What was it that Mrs. du Pré had said ?   Again he saw the Exhibition lights, and the crowds moving round the jewelled bandstand, under a sapphire sky.   She had said, first, that a free man would be a fearless creator of his own life, not a timid, taboo-ridden schoolboy; and secondly, that a secret love might give happiness to two people while hurting nobody. Good. " Show in the next, Tristram."

" The slave market," said the voice.

" Nonsense."

But as it happened, none of these applicants answered to his need at all, so at the afternoon's close he had offended the restive conscience in thought only, not in act. But the conscience did not spare him because of this. I say it sat on his empty lap, prodding him, all the way home in the train. Tom Coventry, like his daughter, had been too often to Mr. Guilder's church and was martyred by a sense of sin.

The next day at three o'clock more applicants were due to arrive. His luncheon would hardly pass his throat because he had fed on excitement and rashers of wind. All the luncheon hour he was glancing at his watch, longing for the interviews, lest *she* were there. None the less, on returning to his office, he hung his coat on the hat-stand as negligently as if he had forgotten all about the candidates; and when young Tristram reminded him, he said, " Oh yes, of course . . . It's to-day, isn't it? Show them in."

And he sat at his desk and laid the conscience low by repeating, " A free man creates his own life," and " If love is welcome to both, whom does it hurt. I only want to get a little happiness before I'm too old, and to give her all the happiness I can."

The first applicant entered. Though at once rejected, she was given the same gentle courtesy, and the same unwarrantable hopes, and escorted like a countess to the door. And then the second entered. Miss Evelyn Penry, 15 Cooper Street, Stoke Newington.

Where is it that beauty lies? Is it in the object beheld or in the gaze of the beholder? And poetry, where is that? Is it within the essence of reality, or does the vision of the poet create it there? Does he put it where, without him, it would not be? Or, lest we become too metaphysical, we'll put the question thus : how much of a woman's beauty is really there, and how much is drawn up from the hungry heart of a man and given to her gratis and for his own joy? To Caliban, lonely, resentful, but with a poet deep in his wicked heart, a woman less lovely than Miranda, I fancy, would have been fair in his eyes. To Miranda, who had encountered no man on the island save her father and Caliban, all men when they first appeared were beautiful. To Miranda even I would have been a poem. And, as for Ferdinand, who was a well enough youth but no great song, I am sure, she thought him an Apollo and put her hand in his straightaway. It is when we are young men, says Kingsley, that every goose is a swan and every lass a queen. I wonder. How about when we are fifty? How about when we are middle-aged and no one has loved us for a long day? Evelyn Penry's features were quite undistinguished, but they were soft ; her eyes were not brilliant with intelligence, but they were bright with youth ; her mouth was no rich flower, but it smiled pleasantly as you chaffed her ; a glance might have told you that she was unsophisticated, affectionate, kind, good to date but probably quite ready to abandon goodness in the disconcerting way of many girls with naïve faces who are won so much more easily than their anxious wooers imagine (or wholly approve)

M

—in brief, Evelyn Penry was an ordinary girl of ordinary prettiness, and rather more than ordinary affectionateness ; and Tom Coventry saw her as beauty, romance and life.

Moreover, attraction breeds attraction ; she saw that he liked her and instantly liked him. And he perceived this ; and since a man is always at his best with those he feels are fond of him, he was merry with her and witty and gallant ; and often she laughed back at him, and her eyes were bright. You would never have supposed that it was the same man who sat so little at ease and doing such poor justice to himself, in the company of Mrs. du Pré.

" But you are young ? " he asked.

" I am twenty-six."

Twenty-six from forty-eight left twenty-two. Oh why had he not met Mrs. du Pré ten years sooner ? Old enough to be her father. No, hardly, hardly.

" You don't look it. You are sure you are not adding a year or two for a change ? "

" Oh no."

" I see." His eye caught sight of a ring on her little finger ; and an unreasoning jealousy and disappointment pierced him. " You are not engaged ? "

" Oh no."

" Nor likely to be ? "

" Oh no."

" I am glad of that. Because we don't want you to go getting married all at once and leaving us just when you've learned the ropes."

" Oh, I don't think I shall get married for a long time, if ever at all."

" Do you think you would like the work ? "

"Oh, I'm sure I should love it."

"Very good, Miss Penry, I will write to you in the course of a few days."

"Thank you so much." And as she walked before him to the door, she added artlessly, "Oh, have I any chance?"

He smiled indulgently, and touched her on the shoulder: O'Kelvie could not have done it better. "I must not say. But I will write in a day or so."

"Thank you so much, Mr. Coventry."

Then she was gone; and very empty the office seemed without her. He began his letter at once, intending to post it in three days time.

V

IT will be plain by now that where there was a dweller in Norman's End, there was a conscience pricking and rebuking him. All our friends had it somewhere; and it was an honour to their hearts if not always to their heads. The steeple of St. Alban's Church watched over it. Rob Ingram may have been an exception, but I should not like to swear to this, tall and thick and dictatorial though he was now become. Old Mrs. Coventry was not really an exception: she had as pretty and sentimental a conscience as any, but she had also a neat little reflex mechanism by which its murmurings were immediately satisfied and silenced. Mr. Guilder carried on his wide shoulders the best head in the place, but when he walked the well-known pavements in his silk hat and clerical frock coat, a conscience walked with him. He knew well—no enemy better—that there was much in his thoughts that matched ill with his sermons and his counsel; and he knew that where the priest is less than a saint, the people lose, though they perceive no fault in him; and his conscience drove him to work harder and harder for their good. At least the organisation of the parish should be as perfect as hard work could make it; and perhaps in the last day God would take this into account, and allow it to stand against the things that worried him; and mercy would fill up the rest.

So he started his " Service for Boys and Young Men who have Thoughts of Taking Holy Orders." It was held twice a year, in Lent and Advent, at eight o'clock of a spring or winter night. Only the gas lights of the chancel were lit, and not many of them, and the boys sat in the choir stalls, and Mr. Guilder, in black cassock and cincture, stood at the sanctuary steps, or walked up and down between the rows of lamp-lit faces, telling them of the joy that a priest's work might give them if only their consecration were sure.

Most of the boys were Trinity boys, but some came from the districts, which the Trinity boys thought strange. Rob Ingram went along to the service, and, when asked by the others if he wasn't in the Army Class at Trinity, and whether he was thinking of the Church instead, he replied carelessly that " he had thought of it sometimes." He attended the service before he sat for his first Army exam., and again after it, perhaps because the examiners, to his distress, had shown no such confidence in his fitness for the Army as he enjoyed himself. Grant Ellison attended because Rob Ingram was there ; and Leo Damien came along, not because he had thought himself of taking Orders, but because his mother had thought of it for him. She had set her heart on it and induced Abbott to set his heart on it too ; and she cast Leo forth into the night ; and he came to the choir stalls, bringing his own thoughts. He wouldn't have minded attending the service, which was a quiet hour in the half-lit church, if his mother, conceiving it a very solemn occasion, had not insisted on his getting into his Eton suit and wearing the overarching top hat, so that, when he emerged out of the darkness of the nave and mounted the chancel steps, holding the hat at his breast, the Trinity boys grimaced and the slum boys tittered. It was a convention in this small congregation that the Trinity boys, being Gentlemen, occupied each of the front rows, and the slum boys, being Cads, the back rows. Leo, then, found a place in a front row, put the massive hat under the seat, and, kneeling down, pretended to say a prayer. And if a slum boy behind him muttered, " Say it into the 'at, sir," he pretended not to hear. In good time he left his knees and sat back, opening a hymn book and pretending to be quite unconscious of his black embarrassment under the seat.

Mr. Guilder's steps echoed in the empty nave ; he appeared in the chancel ; and all the boys dropped to their knees, while he knelt with his face to the altar and prayed for these younger servants of God. Then for half an hour he talked to them quietly, sensibly, and not unamusingly ; and they listened with staring eyes, for they were children still, let Rob and Grant be nearly eighteen, and Leo but three years younger.

The address at an end, they sang " The Church's One Foundation " and went out into the starred or rainy night.

Leo's walk home was seldom a happy one. For, though Rob and Grant and their friends were too big now to rough-handle him, or even to hold direct converse with him, they were quietly amused by his thin figure under the wide top hat as it went along the dark and empty pavement ; and, ready to take the night air together, they would walk twenty paces behind him, all the way to his door in Conyers Road, that they might miss no moment of a delicate diversion. And Leo Damien walked ahead of them, pretending an unawareness of their footsteps on the flags, their murmuring voices, and their low-pitched laughs. He turned beneath the portico of his house, and heard them go swinging by, towards the lights and the traffic of Norman's End Lane.

Leo pushed the bell, broke a blister on the dark green paint of the door, and thought his own thoughts.

VI

AND meantime the rehearsals in the studio had started the happy friendship between O'Kelvie and Cynthia. She would go sometimes to the studio and sit curled up in a chair to watch him painting or modelling; and he, once a thought-paroxysm was over and quiet work occupied him, liked to see her there. He liked her as one likes a pet animal who admires one, and whom one can admire. For Cynthia was now fifteen, with her hair tied at the neck in a bow and two small maturing breasts behind which there was palpably a kind feeling for him. Women debated whether she was really pretty, but no man would have worried about it. If a girl has deep chestnut hair, a clear skin, a really perfect nose, and two bright, impudent eyes, he will ask no more. O'Kelvie found her a pleasant furnishing for his room, as she sat with feet tucked beneath her, on couch or chair. And she did not worry him by arriving too often. Always afraid of " being a bore," she allowed weeks to elapse between one visit and the next; and O'Kelvie, when at length she reappeared, would pause at his easel, stare at her as if she were his greatest sorrow, and say, " Cinderella."

" Yes, god-mamma."

" Why have you left me so long without a visitation ? "

" Oh, I don't know. I don't want to be a bore."

" Say that again."

"I was afraid of being a nuisance."

He continued to stare, his palette fallen to his side; while she grinned and awaited a further remark. It came.

"Unhappy girl! I gave you an invitation, and God in His mercy gave you a good pair of legs; and still you did not come. It is not to be forgiven. Sit down. I have nothing to say to you."

"Well, that'll be a change," said Cynthia, moving to a chair.

"*What do you mean?* The Lord forgive you for that word! 'That'll be a change'—there's no meaning in it. Would you suggest that I——"

"Oh, I don't know. They say that women talk, but——"

"Sit down before you say something you'll regret." She sat down.

"Come whenever you like," continued O'Kelvie in one of his abrupt transitions. "Walk in, walk in. You can be sure that if the moment's unpropitious, I shall hurl you out."

"Well, if you'll promise always to hurl me out by the scruff of the neck——"

"I swear it."

"And if you're sure your manners won't prevent you."

At this he laughed with his broad-chested gusto, and swore she was the first person who had accused him of manners.

"But I think you've got lovely manners," objected Cynthia.

He dropped his palette to his side again, to consider this most interesting view. "*Do* you now?"

"Yes. A little boisterous, perhaps, but——"

"Boisterous?"

"Yes. And rather rude sometimes, but anyone can see that you're frightfully kind underneath it all, and wouldn't really hurt a fly."

"That'll do, child. Kind? Nonsense. Hurt a fly? Poof! You've been reading some housemaid's stuff. Hurt a fly?—whoever listened to such a little fool? Stay there, and keep quiet, the clack you're making."

"All right. *I* don't want to talk."

Nor was his welcome of her wholly selfish. He chose to think that she was a bundle of fine possibilities which were in danger of being cramped and blunted by her environment, and that he was the man to save her. It was a pleasing idea, in the service of which, when an hour's work was done, he talked, and talked, and talked, either standing near the easel or raging up and down.

She came one day to the blistered door in Ashgar Terrace and timidly knocked, nervous that he might not want her. However a lively note in his "*COME in!*" quite reassured her, and she entered and saw him at his easel in an old dressing gown and carpet slippers. His throat and ankles were bare, but he did not seem to mind this, even if he was conscious of it.

"Ah, it's Cynthia. Well now, it's pleased I am to see you. Come in. My house and all that's in it is thine. Kick all that muck off the couch, pull it up, and make yourself at home."

"Are you sure you don't mind?"

"Not a bit, not a bit, not a bit." Like all cheerful souls, O'Kelvie had a habit of sounding his good cheer thrice. "I love little children. One day I'm going to start an orphan asylum. Kick it all off."

She did not kick it off, but made a corner for herself and curled up on it. And soon he began to talk. Except for a few pauses when he was lost in his work, he talked for two hours. That it was brilliant talk she was old enough to see. She felt ideas rushing in upon her and enlarging her. No one, she was thinking, had ever taught her so much with such careless ease. When an exciting idea effervesced too far, he dropped palette and brush to his sides and stood facing her to pour the good stuff over her, his eyes alight with interest in what he was saying and with admiration for its profundity. She prayed that he would go on and on. But suddenly he stopped. He clapped his hands to the sides of his head and stood there staring before him. He lowered the hands to his hips, while the eyes still stared. He muttered an expletive, but it was addressed, not to Cynthia whom he was no longer seeing, but in greeting to something he saw within his head. A creative idea had been born of the talk. He began to pace up and down, and to pause and bite his thumb-nail. He stopped and looked at her, but without recognition, because he was looking right through all concrete things at the idea projected from his mind. For a moment he recognised her and, waving a dismissing hand, said, " Run away, child. I mustn't talk. If I talk to you, it'll take the cream off my creative ability. And I've only a small trickle at the best. Run away, as you love me." She rose and went towards the door, but something pathetic in the movement made him cry out, " No, no ! Wait. Promise me you'll come again. I love having you, except when I've got to worry out an idea alone. I love seeing you there. Promise me you'll come again."

"Oh but——"

"Promise !" cried he, stamping impatiently.

"Yes, I'll come."

"But do you mean it ? Say after me : ' Pat O'Kelvie loves working with an audience.' "

She said it, laughing.

"And now say : ' Especially if it's Cynthia Codrington.' "

She said it, only substituting " Coventry " for " Codrington."

"Eh, what ? " inquired he, at this name.

"Coventry," she repeated.

"No, Codrington," he objected.

"Coventry," said Cynthia, adamant.

"Well, have it your own way," he allowed. And on that compromise she went.

After a while she took to going more frequently ; but she told no one, neither her people at home, nor the children at school. She so loved it—and perhaps this was one reason why she told no one. She was satisfied now that their friendship was strong enough for him to turn her from the door with a " Go ! Go ! My batteries are beautifully charged, and you'll empty them, you'll empty them ! You make me talk, sitting there and looking as though what I said was worth hearing— bless you—but it'll drain off all the best of my force if I start gassing to you ; and my voltage is high to-day— devilish high. Go, my blessing, and God go with you." If on the other hand he greeted her in broad Irish she knew that all was well. " Faith, and it's myself that's glad to see you," he would say. " And

it's a great swell you are this day.   Sit down ; " and
she would leap happily on to the couch, either curling
her legs under her or lying back with her hands behind
her head. " Please talk," she would then beseech him.
(No wonder he welcomed her.)

At first his talk galloped about in safe fields and
visited no ground that threatened her complacency.
It was mostly his theories about art, which quickly
became, as with all strongly egotistic natures, an
enthusiastic exposition of himself.

" I am myself alone, Cynthia. Listen. I admire
Bouguereau. Would you believe it ? Yes, I admire
him in parts. When I was in Paris, it was the fashion
to laugh at him and his kind, and to see no good in
anyone except Manet and Degas and that crowd. I
alone kept my head. I knew that there was more in
Bouguereau to admire than there was to make you
vomit. There always is in anyone who has been
famous in his day. Bound to be. Little people see
only the nasty and are sick. In fact, I alone in the world,
I sometimes think, have perfect balance and proportion.
I can see good in Leighton and Landseer. Think of that :
even in Leighton and Landseer. And therefore I
belong to no school. School ! I should think not !
To belong to a school is to admit yourself derivative,
isn't it ? I know I have this perfect balance and
proportion because, whenever an artist fellow takes up
one argument, I immediately see the opposite and am
compelled to give it to him. Compelled to do it in
common justice, Cynthia. If he's pro-Ruskin, I'm pro-
Whistler ; if he's pro-Whistler, I'm pro-Ruskin. They
say it's because I'm Irish, and therefore contumacious,
but don't you believe it, Cynthia : it's because I have

wisdom. All wisdom is a successful balancing of opposites. They tell me that's Hegel. It may be, but I found it out for myself, so it's O'Kelvie too."

But after she had passed her sixteenth birthday he didn't seem to mind galloping his talk nearer home. One winter day she came, and he helped her take the coat from her shoulders, and stood looking at her.

"Cynthia, how old are you?"

"Sixteen."

"You look more."

"Oh *cheers!*"

"'Cheers!'—what do you mean? Why 'Cheers!' because you're no longer a charming child? Sit down, Prestissimo."

"Prestissimo" was the name he had given her because, as he said, she could do nothing slowly, but must always dash at it at once, and at top speed. And to-day he asked what might be her name for him.

"Mr. O'Kelvie, of course."

He fixed her with the sorrowful forgiveness in his eyes.

"Cynthia, do I look a fool?"

"No. Not altogether."

"Well, do you suppose that I imagine you call me Mr. O'Kelvie in your thoughts?"

"Perhaps I don't think about you."

"Let us talk sense. Do you suppose I don't know that you've got some peculiarly stupid name for me— say 'Poll' or 'Charlie' or 'Gas-bag'? Is it 'Gas-bag,' Cynthia?"

"No, it certainly isn't."

"Well, I'm glad of that, on the whole. I like you

to like my talk. What is it, Prestissimo? Out with it. I can stand up under it."

"Oh, I *can't*."

"Yes, you can."

"Well, if you want to know, it's Rugg. R-U-Double G."

"Rugg? Why Rugg?"

"I don't know. It just fits."

"Fits?"

"Yes. Your hair's a little like a rug—and you yourself are rather rugged, aren't you—like a bear?"

"·Ha, ha, ha!" laughed O'Kelvie, delighted. "Rugg —God spare us all! Like a bear—damn her eyes! It's not so absurd as I thought. Bravo, Prestissimo!"

He was in the best of spirits, and when she was seated, opened an attack on herself, her parents, her town and her church. His ammunition was much the same as Mrs. du Pré's, but the angle from which he fired was different. "Bourgeois," said he; but his was the artist's indictment of the bourgeoisie, hers was the would-be aristocrat's. The atmosphere of Norman's End solidified, he declared, into moral stone walls. Norman's End was a spiritual prison which timid people had built for their safety. They were cowards and felt safer in their own prison. And Cynthia listened, appalled.

"But *I'm* not bourgeois," she protested.

"Bourgeois!" he exclaimed. "You're the most perfectly bourgeois little creature I've ever seen."

"*No!*" she screamed.

"You are! It comes out in your talk. You've every snobbery and every prudery that's typical of a peculiarly unhappy class. How should it be otherwise? Tell me, Cynthia Coventry how should it be otherwise? You would have to be a genius to transcend your upbringing."

"Well, I'll be a genius," said Cynthia.

"You may be," agreed O'Kelvie, quite unsurprised. "Under my tuition that miracle may come about. You have high vitality, and I doubt if genius is ever much more. It depends in what channel the super-abundant vitality runs. In Shakespeare it ran to poetry; in St. Francis of Assisi to sanctity; in Drake to piracy; and in Patrick O'Kelvie it runs to painting. In most people in Norman's End it either isn't there, or, if it is, it has run to money-making or something, certainly not to brains or self-criticism. There's your father, for instance. Do you mind if I talk about him?"

"No, because I shan't believe half of it."

"Well, I can't understand your father. He's a bit of a buck in an old-fashioned way; and in build he's every inch a man. He looks as if he ought to have kicked over the traces long ago. Everyone should kick over a few of the traces; but I'm sure he's never done anything that's not strictly *comme il faut*. And then there's Guilder. Guilder really does beat me. He has power and brains, and he's fundamentally an artist. He ought to be leading all his people to freedom. Instead he's content to be the very cupola on their beastly prison. Rather than let his vitality run into self-criticism and originality, he lets it run away into organising his parish like a successful business, which is what any draper might do. It would be different if he were a saint, but he's missed being that. No, don't tell me. I respect the saints. General Booth, for instance, is a man after my own heart; and there's a

high church fellow at Holborn, Father Stanton. He
and the General will be in Heaven when you and I
are frying in hell. But Guilder—I mean to say, his
broad churchmanship is nothing at all. It's mere
hog-wash. Either give up everything and be the
thorough-going saint, or give up nothing. All he does
is to—toss me that mallet. Thanks—all he does is to
make sinners, not saints."

" Oh, Rugg darling ! " protested Cynthia.

" Oh yes, my Prestissimo. I'll show you what I
mean. All he does is to take perfectly natural emotions
and hang labels on them which turn 'em into sin. You
like to look nice. Perfectly right and natural, and a
kindness to us all. But Guilder must go and hang a
label on it marked ' vanity ' and tell you to pray and
examine your conscience about it, and behold, you
find you're a sinner, and, as you can't possibly give it
up, you go on sinning and feel morally bankrupt.
You and I have an impulse now and then to take the
name of the Lord in vain. Excellent. A perfectly
healthy piece of creative impudence. Creativeness is
always impudence and rebellion. When Mike's being
impudent to me, I suspect he's got some originality
dawning. And anyhow, a mild profanity probably
releases a lot of rebelliousness in us, so that we're very
much nicer afterwards. But no. Guilder's label is
on it. ' Blasphemy.' Must be confessed in sackcloth
and ashes. Bah ! It makes me want to go out and
spit. And sometimes he and his tribe do the opposite.
They take a very doubtful quality and hang a good
label on it. ' Thrift,' for instance."

" But thrift's a good thing, isn't it ? "

" Is it ? I'm not so sure. I'm not sure that, as often as

N

not, the pleasant-sounding label doesn't cover a nasty parsimony or, at the best, a very feeble sort of timidity. If it's a virtue, it's never a loveable one. The loveable people in history have always been the generous, extravagant folk, never the careful, thrifty ones. No, there's something timid and unadventurous about it. But I bet Guilder preaches it to all his children, thereby destroying their lovely zest for danger. And now I'll tell you something else—confound you, what are you laughing at?"

His eye had caught the trembling insubordination at her lip.

"You, Rugg dear."

"Why?"

"You look so funny when you get worked up. Rather sweet."

"I don't believe you've been listening to anything that I've been saying."

"Oh I have! Honestly I have!"

"No, you haven't. You retired from listening long ago, and I'll tell you why—because you haven't the brains to understand any of it. You're nothing—nothing at all; and I might have known it. I was right when I told you that you'd a brain of wool, and I'm not sure that the wool is white, either."

"Please go on, Rugg dear."

"No, I shan't! Sitting there sniggering! Death of my soul, I'll not cast my pearls before *you*."

"Please!"

"No. You may be sixteen, but you've the intelligence of a child of twelve. Michael has twice your wits, and *he's* nothing, God knows. It is finished. I speak no more."

"Please ! If I say I'm sorry I smiled ? "

"I might then."

"Well, I am ; and I'll never smile again."

"Good. Where were we ? Where were we, soul's delight ? I was going to tell you something very subtle about Norman's End. Look here." He abandoned all his tools, pulled up a dilapidated chair, and sat on it opposite her. "Listen. A merciless economic system has shut them up in their little red-brick houses, away from all hope of adventure and excitement ; and what happens ? I shall tell you. They have to compensate themselves for all that they secretly crave, so they set up their respectability as something very fine indeed—which is to say, they elect to see their coward's prison as a nobleman's palace. They soak themselves in the doings of Society, on the assumption that Society is where they really belong, and it's only their ' moderate means ' which keeps them out—have you noticed that *you* never talk about your comparative poverty but only about your ' moderate means ' and never call your purchases cheap but always ' inexpensive ' ? That's your way of avoiding identification with the poor and of hanging on to the expensive classes. *You* ought to be above it, Cynthia, even if they're not. Again : they condemn with a bitter hate a person like me, because they know that I dare to enjoy much that they're starving for, and, deep in their souls, they suspect their own intelligence and fear mine——"

"Do you think you're the only person in Norman's End with intelligence ? " interrupted Cynthia.

"Aha ! " laughed he, lifting a finger in the air, like an orator about to score a point. "Aha ! You expect me to say No, don't you ? You expect me to turn all

modest and protesting, and to say, ' No, not at all ;
certainly not.'   But the answer is not No.   The answer
is Yes.   There now ! Immodest, you say ? But supposing
' modesty ' is only another of Guilder's labels to hang
round the neck of hypocrisy and lies ?   Supposing I
like the clean, white air of Truth ?   The answer is Yes,
my pretty Cynthia.   There may be another really
intelligent man in this swinish herd, but I haven't met
him yet."

" Good heavens ! you *are* vain."

O'Kelvie jumped from his seat and raised his two
fists above his head, as it might be Prometheus in
despair and raging against the sky.   " She is dull—dull
—dull, and all my hopes are shattered.   My view of
her was a bubble built of opalescence and wind.   Vain !
Vain !   She can do nothing but walk about, hanging
up the labels of her tribe.   Haven't I said that I care
nothing about being called vain ?   Haven't I said that
I prefer the man with a good conceit of himself, and
the honesty to admit it, to the craven who says, ' I've
no great opinion of myself,' and is thereby shown to
be a liar ?   Go, Cynthia, I give you up.   I make no
impression on you, and I must seek a grander material.
Go."

" No, thank you.   I've no great desire to go."

" Go.   I'm sick of the sight of you.   Are you
going ? "

" I dare say I won't."

He hunched his shoulders as if to ask, " What then ? "
And she lifted her eyebrows and inquired, " Well ? "
He gazed at her sternly.   " Are you calm now ? "
" *Me ?* "
" Yes.   Have you recovered your temper ? "

" *My* temper ? "

" Yes.   Because if so, I might go on."

" I'm in the sweetest of tempers, and have been so all along."

" Good.   Then I'll continue.   Where were we ?   Ah yes, this is the subtlest point of all."   He remained standing, but thrust his hands into his pockets.   " They enthrone religion so as to achieve greatness that way, and now they've enthroned the Empire too.   Don't you see what the Empire means to them ?   It's their way of sailing to the Spice Islands in the persons of the great pioneers.   And the Big Battleships, Cynthia ! That's where they begin to be dangerous.   I'll tell you why.   Listen.   *You're* in this.   Shut off from all adventure and power, they become Imperialists and Navalists to a man, and when one day some other country thinks that two can play at Imperialism and Navalism—as Germany seems to be thinking, with her strutting little fighting-cock of a Kaiser—and a war comes, they'll see it as excitement and romance, one and all, and offer you and the other children to be slain. See ?   The trumpets'll sound, and then there'll be no more hope for you or any of your little friends.   And now let's have tea.   Go and get some hot chestnuts from the man at the corner."

They spread a picnic on the end of the trestle table. And over the chunks of cake and the mugs of tea, Cynthia had her turn, pouring out, with a child's seriousness, her thoughts and her hopes.   And he listened as seriously.   Ceasing from folly and banter, he answered her gently always, and sometimes wisely.

VII

WHILE Cynthia reached and passed her sixteenth birthday, so did Leo Damien. And it was now that the tales about him began. Hitherto he had run true to his public past : that is to say, he had remained long and weedy and diffident, while other boys were broadening in body and strengthening in assertiveness, and his voice had not broken, nor virile hair appeared on face or arm. He still looked the " odd man out " in his high collar and ready-made Nelson knot—which were just the sort of clothes that Rose Damien would make him wear. But now something was happening beneath his untidy hair. " Noiselessly at the springtime Her crown of verdure weaves, And all the trees on all the hills, Open their thousand leaves " the strange thing was coming to birth in him—but I can only tell you what Mrs. Damien said at the At Home days. It was the sensation of the drawing-rooms.

She didn't know what had come to the boy, she said. His father had told him to do this and that, and Leo— a boy who six months ago seemed afraid to say bo ! to a goose—had flatly refused to do it. She herself had ordered him to his room after he had been rude, and he had laughed in her face. She had called Abbott to discipline him, and when Abbott came, Leo had looked his father up and down, laughed one scoffing laugh, and walked out into the night. And—would you believe it ?—he had not returned till after ten o'clock, when he went straight upstairs to his bedroom and locked the door. It had made her quite frightened. And two days ago, when his father came at her request and tried to push him out of his stuffy room, Leo had promptly hit him. He had hit his own father quite savagely. Abbott had thereupon threatened to take a stick to him, at which Leo had sat down and thrown back his head in laughter, as if such a picture could be enjoyed only in a seated position. It was so rude to Abbott. At her suggestion Abbott had gone to interview Leo's master at Trinity ; and Mr. Rustington had reported an undoubted change for the worse in the boy. From being quiet and amenable, and not without ability in the subjects that interested him, he had turned idle and impudent. Almost cynical, in fact, since he did just enough work to escape punishment, but no more. And up to this term he had tried to take his part in the communal games, but now he made no effort at all. He just languished about the field, and kicked the ball if it came his way. To laughter or ridicule he offered a kind of hardened unconcern, not empty of insolence. A very perverse boy. And whenever possible he betook himself to solitary sports, such as swimming or gymnastics. At these he was quite good, but when, seeing this, they " tried him out " for his Club Swimming Four, he took no trouble to succeed. He was a boy who refused to enter into the life of the school, and what would happen to him in the larger world, Mr. Rustington couldn't imagine.

All this Mrs. Damien told to Hilda and Old Mrs. Coventry one afternoon in the drawing room, while Cynthia sat listening. There was no doubt that Leo's

behaviour had shaken her.   She lacked the self-assurance
and aggressive conviction of former years.   It seemed to
have relaxed her figure too, so that she was now fat
and dumpy where before she had been plump and brisk.

"I simply don't know what's happened to him,"
she concluded.   "Sometimes he gives his father and
me a look that I can only call one of Absolute Hate."

Old Mrs. Coventry, who in her deep interest had
been leaning forward, touched Rose Damien on the
knee and muttered mysteriously something about "boys
of that age . . . fast becoming a man . . . a difficult
period. . . . Perhaps he needed a Strengthening Hand."

"How am I to know what he needs?" interrupted
Rose pettishly.   "He takes no one into his confidence."

"I think someone ought to talk to him very gently
and kindly," said Old Mrs. Coventry, who was having
a delightful afternoon.   She always got a second-hand
pleasure from the thought of somebody talking to somebody else about the Facts of Life.   "Some wise and
understanding man.   He might even say a prayer with
him.   A boy of that age needs all the strength that
prayer can give him.   Perhaps Mr. Guilder would take
him in hand."

"But he only laughs at religion.   That's what's so
dreadful.   He says he's an Agnostic."

The old lady stared.   "He must be going mad," she
said.

"And not only an Agnostic but a Socialist too!"

Old Mrs. Coventry touched her on the knee again.
"He should see a doctor.   I am clear about that, Rose.
You shouldn't delay before having him looked at."

"And he takes a delight," continued Rose Damien,
giving no heed in the fashion of the At Homes to her

listener's talk, " in airing before us the atheistical and socialistic views he gets from his books. I tell Abbott he should take the books from him."

" What sort of books ? " asked Old Mrs. Coventry at once, interest kindling her eyes.

" Let's see. He's always talking about Ruskin, and Morris, and Huxley. . . ."

" Oh, but *they're* all right," demurred Old Mrs. Coventry, who had no idea that they had attacked most things she believed in. " Still, it's unhealthy for a boy of sixteen to read books like that. I quite agree with you. A healthy boy should be reading Henty and Marryatt and Dean Farrar, not stuffing his head with ideas."

" And time and again," continued Rose Damien, following her own line, " I've found him reading a man called Hardy."

" That man ! " Old Mrs. Coventry, who had read his works with avidity, was shocked at last. " Oh, he's most immoral, and blasphemous too. He wrote that awful book, " Judas Iscariot," didn't he ?—no, " Judas Maccabeus "—no, what was it, Hilda ? " Jude the Obscure." Indecent from beginning to end ! Yes."

" And now he's got hold of a man called Ellis. Havelock Ellis. I was absolutely horrified when I peeped in and saw what it was about."

" What was it about ? " asked Old Mrs. Coventry. " Run away, Cynthia."

" I'd rather not say. I didn't know such stuff was allowed to be printed. I showed it to Abbott, and he was quite upset. He took the book away, and burnt it. Shaw. That's another man's name. He's reading a lot of a man called Shaw."

" Who's he ? "

" I don't know, but his ideas are perfectly appalling. Really I don't know what the world's coming to, these days."

" But can't you stop it ? Can't you put your foot down and forbid him to read these books ? "

" We do. But he only laughs and gets hold of a new book from somewhere."

" You must be firm, my dear. He's your only child, and you must save him from himself—don't you agree, Hilda ? What should we think if our little Cynthia was getting ideas into her head ? Abbott must take a strong line with him, once and for all."

" Yes, I tell Abbott that. I tell him that either he must be the master or the boy." Rose Damien shook her head in foreboding. " I feel there's a great tussle of wills coming."

In this she was right ; except that " tussle of wills " was a modest phrase for what was coming. It came next Sunday evening. The tall stucco house, No. 35 Conyers Road, looked out upon the pavement and the camber ; and its face, exactly as usual, told nothing to the passers-by of the battle raging indoors, and up and down its four flights of stairs. Leo had refused to go to church in the morning, and Mrs. Damien had said to Abbott, " You must insist upon his going to-night. We must put a stop to this sort of thing for good and all." And Abbott, not at all liking the task, said, Yes, that was what they must do. Evensong was at seven o'clock, and at a quarter past six Abbott left the breakfast room, came to the bottom of the stairs in the hall, and called up to Leo, who was in his bedroom on the second floor ; while Mrs. Damien stood just inside the door of the breakfast room, to be a strength to her husband and a witness of the scene.

" Leo," called Mr. Damien.

" Hi ! " answered a voice far up above.

" I wish he wouldn't say Hi ! " muttered Rose Damien. " It's so disrespectful."

" Get ready for church," called Abbott. " You are to come to church with your mother and me to-night."

Leo came from his room and, leaning over the banisters, called, " What's that ? "

" You are coming to church with us this evening, I say."

" Quaint optimist," said Leo.

" Dear, dear ! " stammered Mrs. Damien. " Speak severely to him, Abbott."

Abbott tried to be fierce. " Now I won't have any of that ! Are you going to get ready for church, or are you not ? "

" The answer is in the negative," said Leo.

" *What ?* " cried the angry Abbott.

" Tch, tch ! " sighed Mrs. Damien, distressed.

" Is that all ? " asked Leo, as if, in the event of his father answering in the affirmative, he would consider the debate closed and return to his room.

" It is certainly not all," stuttered Abbott. " Certainly not ! "

" I see. Well, would you mind being quick about the rest, because I'm really rather busy."

" Now please don't give me any of your insolence. You know that I don't put up with it."

" Don't you ? I hadn't noticed that you didn't. But what are you going to do about it then ? "

"Great God!" muttered Abbott forgetting he was a churchwarden.

Rose Damien sighed. "Oh, what are we to do with the boy?" she asked of the air, almost wailing. "Abbott, bring him to his senses."

"Leo!" shouted Abbott. "Do you wish me to come up and *make* you get ready?"

"Well . . ." Leo appeared to ruminate on this. "Yes, if you like. It might be amusing."

"Go up to him. Go up," encouraged Mrs. Damien. "We can't have this."

"No, we can't," said Abbott, hesitating at the foot of the stairs.

"Go up," repeated his wife.

Leo continued to look over the stairs, grinning. "Sounds like the children mocking Elisha," he suggested.

"Good heavens!" muttered Rose, as this morsel of humour fell from above. "Go up to him."

No doubt Mr. Damien felt like saying, "Go up yourself!" but he kept the words back. Instead he called threateningly, "Well, there's nothing for it," and began to mount the stairs. But there was little enthusiasm in his step, and little confidence. In truth, he felt much as Leo used to feel when Mrs. Damien drove him out to play with Rob Ingram or instructed him to fight that powerful boy. He was thinking that it was all right for her to say, "Go and fight": she was safe under cover. He reached the first landing, paused there, and looked up at his son, who, leaning carelessly over the banisters, looked down upon him.

"Now then, Leo," he appealed, persuasion being

preferable to force. "Be sensible. Don't oblige me to come up and *make* you obey."

"I have not the least intention of going to church," affirmed Leo.

"And I say you *are* going."

"All right," conceded Leo. "There's no harm in saying it."

"Go up to him," came Mrs. Damien's voice from below. "Go up to him."

"Don't worry him, mother, if he doesn't want to," called Leo.

"Go on, Abbott," repeated Mrs. Damien's voice.

"It's intolerable!" murmured Abbott. "Insolence!" And he began his ascent of the second flight.

"Excelsior," said his son, watching him.

Abbott looked up reproachfully as he climbed. "You force me to extreme measures," he said.

"Not at all," replied Leo, airily.

But he stood back from the banisters as his father came nearer ; and one knee trembled ; for the shrinking child in Leo, though going fast into memory's jail, was not yet fully overpowered, nor the key locked on him. Father and son stood face to face on the second landing. And Mrs. Damien, picking up her skirts, hurried up to the floor below, that she might see what developed.

"Now, Leo," said his father, "go and get yourself brushed and come downstairs.

"You're wasting your breath, father," said Leo. But he stared at him as an animal stares at danger. "I'm not going to do so. Why should I go to church when I fully believe that the religion they teach there does more harm than good——"

"For shame, Leo !" came his mother's voice. "What terrible things to say ! "

Leo did not listen to her. He kept his eyes on his father, and his voice turned sullen. "Why if I disapprove of it all, should I support it with my presence ? I've told you I'm an Agnostic and a Socialist."

"You a Socialist ! " Abbott laughed at him. "At sixteen. Pah ! When you're forty I may listen to such talk. But now, have done with all this idiotic posing. Are you going to do what I say ? "

"No."

Abbott put a hand on the boy's arm and tried to push him. "Come now," he began.

But Leo snatched his arm away. "Let me alone ! " he snapped.

Mrs. Damien encouraged her husband. "Make him go, Abbott. Don't stand any nonsense. He must learn to obey."

So Abbott tried to push him with both hands ; and in a second, before either quite knew how it had come about, the two were wrestling. The tempers of both blazed. Abbott was resolved to force the boy into the room, though to what end he could not now have said ; and Leo fought his father, not sure whether he was tearing himself away or throwing his father off. His high collar had flown from its stud, his ready-made tie shot all askew, his hair tossed on his head, and his eyes went brilliant with anger—though some of their brilliance may have been due to tears as well. Mrs. Damien, hurrying up the stairs and seeing them thus, was frightened. She was in time to see Leo get free one arm and, ducking his head down, crash a fist on to his father's chin. Enraged, his father closed with him

again; and Rose Damien rushed in to part them.
"Leo, Leo!" she cried.   "Oh you'll repent of this all
your life."

"Not I!" shouted Leo, but sobs racked him.
"You're bullies and cads, as brainless fools always
are!"

"Oh you wicked, wicked boy!" said his mother,
pulling at him.   "To say such things!   Leave him,
Abbott.   He's a wicked, wicked boy.   I'm ashamed of
you, Leo.   Striking your father like that!"

"Well, why does he strike me?" panted Leo.

"He's your parent.   He does it for your good."

"And I do it for his.   He's got to learn that he can't
force me to do anything I don't want to do.   And as
sure as he touches me, I shall touch him—from now,
onward and for ever."

"Don't talk so wildly, Leo.   You owe everything
to your father.   You owe your very food to him."

"Well, let him stop my food.   Let him starve me to
death.   I shouldn't mind dying.   I couldn't be more
unhappy than I am."

"Oh Leo!"   She wrung her hands.   "Oh, it's so
awful.   And on a Sunday too!   You can't mean
what you're saying.   You can't *know* what you're
saying."

"I know very well.   Let him come on again.   He can
have another like the last."

"No, no.   Leave him, Abbott.   He's out of his
senses."

"Am I?   We'll see!"   Leo tore himself from
both of them and rushed into the bedroom.   "I
shall kill myself," he cried.   "I have often thought
of doing so.   I hate everyone, and I hate life."   They

hurried after him, and saw him taking from the wash-stand a small blue chemist's bottle, labelled " Salts of Lemon. Poison," which had been used to remove ink stains from linen. Mrs. Damien screamed, and, rushing up, snatched it from him. With it safely in her hand, she sat on a chair and swayed to and fro, moaning, " Oh, what are we to do ? What are we to do ? Wicked, wicked boy."

" Well, leave me alone," said Leo sullenly.

His father stood there, shaken and bewildered.

" Promise that you'll never do such a terrible thing again," said his mother.

" I am not going to church," said Leo, as if this were his ultimatum. And he turned towards the window, where a still and rosy light was flooding on to floor and walls.

" Promise that you'll never do such a thing again," said his mother.

" If you'll leave me alone," he answered, without bringing his eyes back into the room.

" Come, Abbott," said Mrs. Damien. " I can't go to church myself now. I'm too upset. Oh dear, oh dear, how can children be so ungrateful and so wicked ? Come with me, please. I feel ill."

" You ought to be ashamed of yourself, Leo," said Abbott, to show that he was not really beaten.

" Well, leave me alone," repeated Leo sourly.

Father and mother left the room ; and Leo stayed looking out of the window ; and the sobs shivered through him. The sky was such a glamour as follows, wide-spreading, in the wake of an October sun. Very still and translucent, it seemed to reach far greater distances than the blue sky of noon. Overspanning the tall stucco houses, and sharply defining their shadows, but stretching far beyond them into infinity, it made them seem very solid and four-square, but very local and small. Local and small. Far away, beneath that spread of light, one could imagine the large, free places of the world.

VIII

CYNTHIA was feeling much older and wiser now. And one fruit of this wisdom that pleased her well was the new, protective affection she was prepared to give to her father. She was beginning to see him as a creature of the opposite sex, quaint but rather loveable; and this sight added something new to the old childish acceptance. Nowadays it seemed a pleasant thing to call him " dearest," and to lay a hand on his shoulder or to fiddle with the lapel of his coat.

And if this was pleasure to her, what was it to Tom Coventry? I have drawn him but poorly if you do not see that it was the most acceptable thing that had visited him in a disappointing world. He too was realising the sex of his daughter and observing with some tenderness the rounding and ripening of the young figure. Like all sentimental and unsatisfied men he liked to dwell often on the mysteriousness of women, and here was his daughter gathering the sweet mystery around her. He liked her soft, feminine voice. And she was showing love to him. It was wonderful. He took to bringing her little presents from town that he might strengthen that love and root it deeper and deeper; and when in gratitude she flung an arm around his waist and murmured, " Oh you're such a darling ! " he drew her against him, patted her jocularly, but said nothing because he was fighting a big battle with his tears. A sense as of something very gratifying which had just happened would remain with him long after she had run away. "Perhaps she is going to be the one perfect thing in my life" he would think, as he sank happily into his chair.

Life was improving for Tom Coventry. He liked the thought of Evelyn Penry in the office next to his. So far nothing had passed between them but his chaff and kindly solicitude and her grateful smiles. Tom Coventry was at his best with Evelyn Penry, gay, confident, witty and compassionate. That she liked him, and was even attracted to him, he could see; and that she knew he was attracted by her. It is an agreeable game when two people know that their mutual attraction is mutually recognised, but hide the knowledge behind a veil of laughter. Evelyn, sitting in his room and writing letters at his dictation was perturbed by his nearness—a flattering sight. And he, if she came close to him with papers, was shaken a little—and enjoyed the discomfort. She came with a fragrance of violets and roses, as from a woman's dressing table; and he, in a quick sideways glance, observed that her unremarkable but pretty features were dusted with powder, which gave them a rose-petal texture. Often afraid to look up at her, he saw only her hand; and its smallness, and blue-veined marble back, touched him. The nails were polished and shone like stones, and he knew that within the round wall of her shyness there was a little prisoner full of hopes and schemes. Sometimes her hand met his by accident and set his starved emotions tingling. Once when she had made a mistake in her book-keeping he put his hand over the back of hers and pressed it in laughing rebuke; and she shot a pleased look at him. By that look he believed that if one day he asked a kiss

of her—and asked it tenderly—she would not discourage him. The belief was as wine warming his
blood, and as dry air inflating his throat. Gratitude
that she should care for him, and tenderness, filled his
thoughts quite as much as desire. She so young and
pretty, and he almost old now and with no youthful
charm ; and yet she could shyly approach towards him !
It was better than he had dared to hope ; at times it was
almost incredible. Beauty was near him at last.

But how was he to advance the dalliance out of this
delectable pasture into the richer field ? The question
filled long evenings with thought. He saw himself
telling her of his great affection, and her welcoming his
words with brightened eyes ; and then the kiss. A long
kiss.

But this telling of one's love is a fence much easier
leaped in day-dreams than in the real world. Supposing
she rebuffed him ? Supposing she were wounded and
shocked ? The picture made him shiver. The
humiliation, and the toppling overthrow of his hopes,
would be more than he could bear. But she wouldn't
—something in him knew that she wouldn't. Come
then : he must take the leap, and quickly. Other men
would have dared the final bound long before this. He
must conquer this timidity. But how ? He invoked
the shade of Mrs. du Pré to come and help him.

Little did Cynthia, if she heard him pacing his study,
or Hilda, if she sat opposite him in a chair, know that
he was planning how to see Evelyn alone, and rehearsing
his speeches to her. At last he saw a plan clearly. He
would accumulate a pile of letters and detain her in the
office to help with them, and then speak when they were
alone.

"Faust and Marguerite," suggested the inner voice, inopportunely.

"No, no. A little happiness for two people; that is all."

"What would Cynthia say if she knew?"

"Nonsense. That is the old slavery of the docile herd. Cynthia is still a child and would not understand."

"Would you like her to take this little happiness one day?"

"Damn! I *won't* give in. I can't . . . now."

To-morrow then.

And to-morrow evening, when the other clerks had gone, he was there at his desk, dictating the letters to Evelyn. One by one they went aside; the pile declined; the moment for speech drew nearer; and his heart hammered. Now he was dictating the last letter, and the moisture stood on his forehead and on the palms of his hands. It was finished; it was laid aside. Could he speak? . . . Ten seconds—thirty seconds—a minute had passed. . . . No, he could not. He pushed back his chair and stood up.

"Well, that's all, Miss Penry."

"Thank you," said she, and picked up the letters to carry them to the next room and type envelopes for them.

Another voice within him cried, "Coward! Coward! Risk all. Leap." He would not be a coward. But now that he had missed the prearranged moment he would have to gain a little time. He would have to build up a new atmosphere for the avowal. As his hand took down coat and hat, he turned and said laughingly, "Half-past six. I have kept you an hour. It is a shame."

"Oh no," she lightly demurred. "That's quite all right."

"But you'll be late for your supper—of course you will!" said he facetiously. "And you're tired. Look here. I'll drive you home. Is it far?"

"Oh yes, yes . . . Oh, you mustn't do that . . . It's quite a long way."

"What does that matter? I shall enjoy it."

"Oh . . ." she said in bewilderment, but could say no more. The offer had defeated her.

"Yes, that's settled!" Tom Coventry felt a hearty man and strong. "Come along. Do your envelopes and come."

"Oh, I don't think you ought to," she persisted. "I mean, to put yourself out like that."

"Hurry," said he, pleased to be masterful. "We're late enough already."

It was winter, and already night. Together they walked down Great Smith Street into Parliament Square, where on a cab rank stood a chain of four-wheelers, their candle-lamps winking and the light of the street lamps falling on the flanks of their horses. He helped her into the first of them, observing as he did so, a smell of torn leather, old cigar smoke, and railway dust. Life could be unsympathetic enough. It should have provided a prettier setting and a sweeter fragrance for that which he purposed to do. He slammed the door to, but it flung open again; and he cursed and shut it sharply.

They were sitting side by side in the darkness.

"It's awfully kind of you . . ." she began.

"Astonishingly so, isn't it?" he smiled.

"But won't it be terribly expensive?"

"My dear, it'll break me; and I shall have to save for weeks after this," laughed he, and patted her hand. One would have supposed him perfectly at ease; but in reality his thoughts were racing round a single point. "Come. Be brave. Speak. Speak."

The cab rumbled on behind the lifting rump of its horse. Both were silent now. Tom Coventry knew that he couldn't speak with any fluency save on that of which he was nerving himself to speak. Come. Risk all. Cast the die. . . . But he could not. Lights of street lamps and of naphtha flares flashed past, throwing moving rays on the furnishings of the cab; noises of steel-bound wheels and the hooves of horses and the voices of men streamed by the window, with one sound constant in the midst of change—the clip-clopping on the camber of their own horse in front; one smell followed another—apples from a coster's barrow, bread from a baker's cart, warm dung from the roadway, and beer from a brewer's dray. But in the tiny room of the cab all was silent and unmoving, as if Time were flowing round its windows but failing to enter. Why had Evelyn ceased to speak? Did she know that something was about to happen? Did she sit there, frightened but waiting? "Come . . . Risk all. . . ." But not a word came. The frail fragrance of parma violet and rose-tinted powder blent with the dusty smell of the cab; and this again was like life—dust and decay, but flushed through with beauty. Plunge in. . . .

A slight gulp, and he had plunged. "May I tell you something?"

She did not answer; and quickly he picked up her hand. It trembled, but it stayed there.

"You know what I want to say, don't you? I have

grown so fond of you." Her hand pressed his in gratitude ; and then, stutteringly, clumsily, he told her that he was lonely and longed for some happiness.

She did not answer, but she left her hand where it rested, and gazed up at him. In the darkness he could see the brightness of her eyes, as the street lamps went by.

" Well ? " he inquired at length.

" You are not happy, are you ? " asked she. It was as if she wanted an excuse for yielding to him.

He shook his head.   " No."

" Oh my dear. . . ." And she leaned her shoulder against him and brought a hand over to find his other hand.

Tom Coventry may have been very wrong in all this, or, in other eyes, he may seem a very great fool not to have done something of the kind before ; all that I am concerned to say is that, just as the only man who can ever know what a drink of water can be is the man who has thirsted many days, so he who had not kissed beauty in love for twenty years tastes a joy the philanderer can never know.   Gratitude and tenderness have been felt in the world before, but rarely such gratitude and such tenderness as rushed up in Tom Coventry when Evelyn gave him a long kiss.   The philanderer takes his sensual pleasure only ; Tom Coventry took this, and more of it than any philanderer can find ; but he mingled with it some sweeter things.

LEO DAMIEN was gone. He had run away. That was the news that raced along the streets of the Square Quarter Mile. He had left his home in the morning as if to go to school, but had not returned in the evening. The school had reported that he had not been there all day. A whole night had passed, and he had not returned ; and Mrs. Damien was distracted. The Coventrys at their luncheon table had little knowledge of what they were eating, so busied were their minds and tongues on the Damiens' story.

After lunch Cynthia felt the Damiens' house in Conyers Road pulling—pulling. She wanted to go and stare at it. As one is drawn to stare at a house where murder was done last night, so Cynthia was drawn to gaze up at the outside of the stricken home. Pretending that she was off to buy some sweets, she set out down Conyers Road and threw guilty eyes at No. 35, as she drew towards it and passed it. It looked much as usual. Difficult to believe that there was such distress within. Its holland blinds were up, its lace curtains hung undisturbed, the stucco pillars of the portico were as yesterday, just as if no guilty boy had passed them, the hall door through which he had come was bright with new paint and polished brass, and the hearth-stoned steps were white and innocent—and yet Leo had escaped down them. Such a violent episode seemed out of place in this quiet, orderly street.

Without halting she went on to the confectioner's. She looked at its window, shook her head to convey to anyone who might be watching her that she had changed her mind about the sweets, and swung round to return to Conyers Road. Now she was able once more to throw up her eyes at the house and to get whatever of interest it gave her. As she brought her eyes down from its face, she saw Rob Ingram coming towards the house in a lazy, casual fashion. Rob was now a gigantic young man of nineteen, and she knew that he was feeling as awkward as she, to be caught like this, sloping up to gaze at the scene of a crime. They grinned at each other uncomfortably as they passed.

Old Mrs. Coventry, since hearing the news at lunch, had been athirst for more details ; and on her return Cynthia found her in the passage strongly asserting to Hilda and Tom that they should go at once to Rose with their sympathy. Tom was disputing this. Feminine panic, as we know, always drove him to an excess of calmness. " No, keep away from them," he was saying. " They are worried and don't want people fussing around. And, in any case, there's no cause for all this bother. The police will find him in two hoots. Hilda can go this evening and inquire the latest news of the maid. Hilda, you're not to go worrying them." And he passed into the study, leaving them in the hall.

" *Most* unsympathetic ! " said Old Mrs. Coventry, after she had seen his door close. " The boy may have been run over. He may be lying dead somewhere, for all we know."

" Oh no, granny," objected Cynthia. " It's not as as bad as that."

" I'm not at all sure," declared the old lady, nodding vigorously. " He's a very strange boy. He may even have made away with himself, for all we know. He's been particularly strange of late, and I don't like the look of things at all. Not at all. We ought certainly to go and see Rose—her oldest friends! I have no patience with Tom."

In the morning they heard that he was found. Ada brought the news with the hot water to Cynthia's bedroom. His pa had found him and come back with him last evening, said she; but as to where he been or what he done, she knew no more than the bed-post. She only knew what the milkman had told her. It had been a p'leace matter, she knew that. They'd had to get the p'leace on to him, which wasn't very nice for poor Mrs. Damiens, she *would* say. The young varmint, running awf and putting them all about like that! She hoped this'd learn him never to go and do such a thing again. And no doubt Mr. Damiens give him a hiding when he got him back.

Father, Mother, and Granny knew no more than this at breakfast, where the talk never left the fruitful topic. Granny even turned and asked Ada some questions when she came up with more coffee. But Ada said, No, mum, she knew no more than she told them already.

When breakfast was over, Cynthia noticed that Granny was mounting the stairs to her room with determination and rapidity. And when she herself was in her own room, to which she was obliged to go to make some amendment in her dressing which she had scamped before breakfast, she heard much activity in Granny's room above. The floor creaked with the old lady's steps as she went from wardrobe to dressing table ; drawers grated out and in ; a cupboard door shut to ; a chair was dragged along the carpet ; and no doubt Granny sat on it to pull on her boots. Cynthia guessed what was happening : without a word to anyone, without asking permission of Tom who exhausted her patience, the old lady was dressing to go out, that she mighty carry her congratulations to Rose Damien and learn the whole story. She was going to slip out quietly, quickly, and unseen.

Now this was a Saturday when none of the children had to go to school, so when Granny came creaking down the stairs—which was about thirty safe seconds after Tom quitted the house—Cynthia ran out of her door, looked up at her in her bonnet and mantle, and asked, " Oh, are you going to the Damiens', Granny ? "

Old Mrs. Coventry, three steps from the first landing, was taken by surprise. Exposure threatened her.

" What ? " she snapped. " What ? I'm going out for a few minutes."

" Yes, but is it to the Damiens' ? " demanded Cynthia, who, perceiving the old lady's guiltiness, jumped at the opportunity of employing blackmail and forcing her to accept a companion.

" The Damiens ? " repeated Granny.

" Yes. Are you going to see them ? "

Granny beat her little boot on the stair-carpet. " Yes," she admitted. " Yes. I feel I ought to go. I feel your father's wrong. . . . Our oldest friends, almost——"

" Oh, wait a minute ; I'm coming too. I must come too. Half a jiffy." And Cynthia rushed in for her hat, pulled it on, and was out again before Old Mrs. Coventry had decided how to handle this sudden threat.

Seeing Cynthia, and not wanting to wait too long on the stairs, or to have a noisy argument there, lest Hilda, who had gone down to the kitchen, came up and caught them both, she decided to accept the blackmailer. " Yes . . . well . . ." she muttered ; and led the way downstairs.

Unfortunately, in her excitement, Cynthia jumped the last two stairs and, missing her footing, slid on the polished tiles of the hall floor and banged into the hat-stand.

Old Mrs. Coventry's head swung angrily round. " Tch, tch ! Don't make so much noise," she whispered, before she realised what she was saying. And she turned an anxious little ear towards the basement.

" Sorry," whispered Cynthia ; and, having sense enough to hide a perception that the old lady had betrayed herself with these words, she followed behind, making as little noise as her partner in guilt was making —which was none at all. They got out of the house very quietly.

Under the portico of the Damiens', waiting to be admitted, Cynthia began to feel afraid of the rooms inside ; and her heart nearly jumped out of her body as the maid opened the door.

" Yes, come in," said the maid ; and showed them upstairs to the drawing-room, which was the long oblong room behind the balcony windows. Here they sat themselves down and said nothing till Rose Damien should come.

Rose came in, looking very fat and worried, and Old Mrs. Coventry at once went up to her, took both her hands, and said in a voice of deepest sympathy, " My *dear* . . ."

Rose gulped back a sob. "Well, he's back," she said. "He's upstairs. How are you, Cynthia? . . ."

"Is he?" breathed Old Mrs. Coventry soothingly. "I'm *so* glad."

"Yes. He's in his room."

It is strange how, when one of our family is in disgrace, we are apt to avoid his name and say only "He" or "Him."

"His father brought him back last night."

"I'm *so* glad. And now sit down, dear. You must be so tired."

Rose sat down; and as Old Mrs. Coventry had foreseen, there was no need to question her. With such a listener seated in front of her—one who leaned forward, her eyes behind their spectacles soaking in every word, her head nodding sympathetically, and her little gloved hand coming forward at times to touch the speaker's knee in great compassion—Rose was ready to pour out everything.

"I don't know . . ." she sighed despairingly. "I can't understand what's come over the boy. I'm sure we've tried to be good parents to him. No one could have laboured more to make a man of him——"

"No one," agreed Old Mrs. Coventry. "You have nothing to reproach yourself with. Let your mind be at peace on that score."

"Yes. But he seems incapable of gratitude or affection. Two nights ago there was a terrible quarrel between him and his father. I almost forget how it began. Something about his future. I think Abbott suggested that, if he wouldn't go into the church, he should come into his office, where there was an opening for him. And the boy said he'd much rather sweep chimneys than be a stockbroker like his father——"

" Dear, dear ! " sighed Old Mrs. Coventry.

" Said he hoped to do something productive with his life. So rude. As if his father hadn't produced enough all these years to keep him at school ! He called his father's occupation that of a parasite on Society. Such nonsense ! He gets these ideas out of the dangerous books he reads. His father asked him then what he proposed to do, as he couldn't afford to put him into the Services or the law, and he declared that he wouldn't touch either profession with a barge-pole. And when Abbott asked him what he had in mind, he said he'd like to be a market gardener. Did you ever hear such nonsense ? Said he'd like to *grow* something. Abbott mentioned the church again, and he roared with laughter and asked if we thought he'd been play-acting when he said he didn't believe anything. Abbott said he'd grow out of all that nonsense ; and from this point, somehow, the argument worked itself up and got hotter and hotter, even Abbott losing his temper and shouting and calling him a waster ; and suddenly the child laughed wildly and shouted, ' How can I live when there's nobody who understands ? ' and rushed out of the room. I was rather frightened, because once before he threatened to commit suicide, and I saw that he'd flung himself down, half-way up the stairs, in a paroxysm of tears. . . ."

Old Mrs. Coventry was staring at the narrator. So was Cynthia ; and at this last picture she took again that pang of pity. A child herself, she dimly understood what lay behind that awful cry. For a sharp second she suffered all Leo's despair, as he flung himself on the stairs.

Rose seemed inclined to cry too, so Old Mrs. Coventry

put out the hand and touched her. "Never mind, my dear. *You've* done your best. Children are sometimes like that."

Rose applied a handkerchief to each nostril and continued her tale.

"I said to him, 'For shame, Leo! Supposing the servants should see you! Get up at once.' And I called Abbott to come. But when Abbott touched the boy's elbow and told him not to make a fool of himself, Leo leapt up, as if he couldn't bear his own father's touch, and rushed up the stairs to his room. His own father who's been so good to him! In the morning he came down and ate his breakfast in silence, and we thought it wiser not to speak of the night before. He got his books as usual and went off to school—or so we imagined. But, instead, it seems he took the District train to Victoria and there got into a train for Ashford in Kent. I don't know why Ashford, unless that we were once held up there, going to Ramsgate for our holidays, and went out and had a look at the market. I suppose he hoped he'd get some agricultural employment there. He went, as calm as you like, to a commercial hotel and booked a room. In the meantime Abbott had gone to the police; and the first thing they asked was, where did he go for his holidays; because it seems that runaway children nearly always go towards places they have known. Funny, isn't it? Well, that's really all. They traced him; and Abbott went down and got him; and, would you believe it? when he saw his father, all he did was to say most flippantly, 'Well, I'll manage better next time. Who's for home?' He's not the least afraid of his father. That's the strange thing."

The tale was ended.

"And what are you going to do with him now?" asked Old Mrs. Coventry.

"He'll go back to his school on Monday," said Rose Damien emphatically. "I'm quite clear about that."

An involuntary protest burst from Cynthia. "Oh *no*, Mrs. Damien!" And her heart within her cried again, No, *no!* A child herself, she knew what would happen: the Trinity boys, all of whom knew of his disgrace, would stand around him and gape or jeer. No, no! they mustn't do that with him! They *couldn't*. They must keep him till it blew over. . . . Poor, poor Leo!

"Oh *yes*!" corrected Mrs. Damien. "We must be firm. We can't go on like this. Abbott agrees with me. He says the boy must go back to school on Monday and take his medicine. If we give in now, we're done for. Let him realise what it costs him, and he won't do it again."

Cynthia said nothing; but her heart continued to cry, "Oh, how can they be so cruel? How can they be so unimaginative and dull?"

Mrs. Damien had done her part; and it was Old Mrs. Coventry's turn. She got up, and, taking Rose's hand, who had got up too, sympathetically stroked it. "Now you're not to worry any more. You've got him back; that's the great thing. And he may turn out a fine man yet. All this violence is just a temporary thing. There, there!"— patting the hand—" don't be upset. We'll pray for him. I'll think of him at church next Sunday, and for many Sundays to come. I shall love to. And then God'll touch his heart, and

P

you'll all be very happy together. Now come along, Cynthia, we mustn't be a nuisance any more."

" I'm sure it's been most kind of you," stammered Rose.

They moved from the room, still talking ; and, as they passed on to the landing, Cynthia heard a door open on the landing above. Someone had come quietly out to listen. Leo ? The grown-ups went on talking about him loudly, with that dullness to circumstance which children find so surprising. In alarm Cynthia touched her grandmother's sleeve, and advised, " Sh ! . . . Sh ! . . ."

" What ? " exclaimed the old lady—and gave everything away to the listener.

" Oh, nothing," said Cynthia quickly.

And, still talking, the two ladies went down the stairs, followed by Cynthia, who was aware all the time of a watcher above.

Now she and her grandmother found themselves on the pavement, with a closed door between them and the Damiens.

They walked homeward, Old Mrs. Coventry talking incessantly about all that they had heard ; but Cynthia —in one of those presentiments whose source eludes our sight—suddenly turned her head, feeling certain that she would see Leo following them. And there he was, fifty paces behind. She said nothing ; and Old Mrs. Coventry saw nothing ; but when they were at their door, Cynthia turned her head again, and saw that he was still following behind, though feigning indifference. Certain that he wanted to speak to her, she abruptly left her grandmother, explaining, " I'm going to walk farther. It's so ripping out ; " and went along Glastonbury Road, and turned out of sight into the first turning, which was Macartney Road. Now, if he was really following her, she would know. She slowed her pace, and soon heard Leo's steps quickening behind. He came abreast of her.

"Hallo," said he.

"Hallo, Leo."

"I caught up with you on purpose."

"Yes. I rather thought so."

"They were talking about me, weren't they?"

"Who?"

"Mother and your grandmother."

"Yes; I suppose so."

"I heard them. And all of a sudden I thought there was no reason why I shouldn't stand up for myself a bit. I say, where are you walking now."

"Oh, anywhere."

"Why did you suddenly leave your grandmother?"

"I don't know."

"Did you do it on purpose so that I could catch you up?"

"Yes, I think so."

"Why?"

"I don't know . . ." And then, abruptly, she dropped into the language of their childish games. "Oh, it's because I'm siding with you, Leo."

To her dismay, he bit his lip at this kind word, and turned his face away.

"May I tell you all about it?"

"Please do, if you'd like to, Leo. I'm so awfully sorry about it all."

And he poured out a staccato tale, as they walked round and round the streets of the Square Quarter Mile.

He told her how he had long been saving up his weekly pocket money to run away with, and what a fool he had been not to see that it couldn't be done at his age, with so little money and with police kicking about everywhere and with parents like his. A dull couple, his parents. " I suppose I've some natural affection somewhere for Rose and the man Abbott, but I can't seem to trace it just now.   I had to surrender to the little man ; but when I saw them talking to you about it, I had an impulse to run after you and tell you that I'm not really giving in. I know what I'm going to do . . . You'll hear something in good time.   I've all sorts of plans that I've never told anyone, and I shall beat 'em in the end.   I'm bound to, because I've got all the brains.   Rose is barely intelligent, you'll agree ; and Abbott's an inoffensive little ass and mortally afraid of me.   I can't help winning in the end. . . .   Oh damn ! . . ."

This was because, in his overwrought state, and after her sympathy, the sobs would come.

She touched his fingers with hers.   " Please, please," she begged, hardly knowing what she meant.   " I think I'm so terribly on your side, Leo."

X

WE have seen that opposite Patrick O'Kelvie's studio
in Ashgar Terrace there was a row of neat little portico'd
houses with balconies before their first-floor windows.
On these balconies, when the summer evenings were
fine, the ladies of the houses would sit in wicker chairs
beneath their striped awnings and behind their iron
balustrades. Miss Hackett sat often on the balcony of
No. 17, which was almost directly opposite the blistered
door of the studio. She sat there with her companion,
Miss Bruton ; and the two did crochet or needlework
together. It made a pleasant arbour in the warm air
and under a turquoise sky : they were screened from the
gaze of the pavement by the scarlet geraniums and
marguerites and by the hanging wire baskets of pink
geraniums and creeping jenny ; while between them
and the balconies of their neighbours stood fences of
green trellis work, over which the virginia creeper hung
down like tresses of hair. Opposite them were no
windows to pry upon their quiet : nothing but the high
blank wall of the studio and the long low wall of
the old novelist's garden, with the fruit trees peeping
above it.

From her chair Miss Hackett could see much and
hardly be seen at all. You had to peer through her
balustrade if you wanted to catch a glimpse of her, as
she sat at a little table and turned the wheel of her sewing

machine. And, did you do this, she would almost certainly lift her eyes from her material without ceasing to turn and glance down at you, as you passed. She was a round little woman of fifty-five; and her paid companion, Miss Bruton, was a tall, thin, sad-faced creature, a few years younger, who used to stir a slight pity in Cynthia as she grew older, by the flowers or the grapes she put in her large hat. It seemed sad, because so futile, that this withered woman should still be attempting charm by a few grapes in her hat.

They were good summer days when Cynthia was sixteen and ran to O'Kelvie's studio; and summer faded into warm autumn; and Miss Hackett on her balcony would frequently lift her head to see the child pass indoors. Once her eyes, glancing over her spectacles, observed that the child looked up and down the road before knocking at the door. Strange! She would watch till the door closed, and then mutter to herself, or, if Miss Bruton were sitting beside her, discuss what the child might want with, going in there. And her eyes would stray to the tall blank wall, as if they would be glad to see through it. Miss Hackett loved a good talk over her sewing, and unravelled this problem at length. Shaking her head, she would say that she didn't like it at all—she didn't like it one little bit. A child like that, barely sixteen and obviously a lady, shouldn't take up with artists. She was sure her parents knew nothing about it; and really they ought to be warned. That was the second time this week that she had been there. And when about a couple of hours later, while the evening was still bright in the sky, Cynthia came laughing to the door with the great, bearded artist behind her—and he laughing loud enough

to attract the whole street—little Miss Hackett muttered
" Tut, tut ! " and " What are her father and mother
about ? "

This excellent and vital little woman was in good
shape for becoming a second Old Mrs. Coventry. Let
fifteen years pass, and she would be the same eager,
peering, active, prurient, talkative old lady. Heavier
than Mrs. Coventry, not so small and so trim, less
lovable (for we all loved Old Mrs. Coventry), but otherwise much the same. As she walked about her rooms or
up and down her stairs, she often thought of the girl
who went to the studio opposite, and she drew a satisfaction from the thought of warning her parents. It
was her duty, and it was pleasant to do one's duty.
They might be very grateful, and gratitude was always
agreeable. It could be done without difficulty, for she
had seen the father and mother with the girl at St. Alban's
Church ; and one morning she would get them alone
and gently tell her tale.

It was not an awareness of Miss Hackett's spectacles
which, after a while, sent Cynthia by the other route to
the studio of her great friend. It was simply that, being
older, she was no longer afraid of a derelict garden, and
this was the shorter way. And, having dared the adventure once, she now went always through the
wrought-iron gateway of Ashgar House, and over the
cobbled courtyard on which the dead windows looked
down, and along the path between lawn and dividing
wall, and through the door in the wall to the orchard
trees and the garden door of the studio. But O'Kelvie,
either in his absent-mindedness or because he was
talking too much to give the matter thought, would
often show her out by the blistered door into Ashgar

Terrace—and Miss Hackett was more mystified than ever. Here was that girl coming out and she had never seen her go in! One must watch more steadfastly.

A Saturday afternoon in autumn, and Cynthia rattled on the garden door, and O'Kelvie came with a song to open it. On her last visit he had raged at her and torn his hair over what he called " her snobbery and grocer's values " ; so now he flung wide the door and said, " Ah ! And it's myself that's hoping you're in a better temper than last time. If that is so, let you be coming in."

" It was you that lost your temper so stupidly," said she, coming in. " I was sweet and smiling all the time."

O'Kelvie gave no heed to this, though it was the truth. " You are calm and collected now ? " he asked.

" I am always calm and collected."

" You are really contrite ? "

" I have forgiven you, if that's what you mean."

" You mustn't heat up so easily, my dear Cynthia. You were in a poisonous mood last time, you will allow. Always keep cool."

" Shall I sit here ? "

" You must watch well that little devil of a temper, my dear Cynthia, or you will say things that in your cooler moments you will regret. I speak to you for your good. Strive after a quiet self-control, Cynthia. It is undignified for a graceful and charming young woman to rage and rampage like that. However, I accept your apology. Yes, sit there."

" Thanks. Don't stop your work because of me."

O'Kelvie was now at his modelling stand. " Have I ever done that, my gentle child ? " he asked, passing the clay from one hand to another.

"No. Only when you get worked up and start gassing."

" Start what, Prestissimo ? "

" Start gassing, Rugg dear."

" Not gassing, Prestissimo ; teaching. Teaching you to measure things by quality and not by bulk. You will remember that last time you resisted my contention that Ireland was a greater country than England by the vulgar remark that Ireland had never conquered a great empire. It is like saying that William Blake who died poor was a lesser man than John D. Rockefeller who has accumulated millions through oil. It makes me feel that you love me because I am big in bulk and not because I have an imagination like a sword."

" Please talk sensibly to-day, Rugg dear. I've come all primed up with something to ask you. Something rather serious."

" Ask away."

" No, you go on working quietly, while I get it all in order again. You've disorganised it ; and I awfully badly want your advice about it."

" My dear," said O'Kelvie, touched, " You shall have all that I can give you, but it's poor, wild, dangerous stuff."

" It isn't. It's always wonderful."

Half consciously Cynthia knew that he never liked her better than when she was serious and seeking his advice ; and half consciously she played this wide-eyed questioning as a good card ; because she longed for him to like her better and better. Last night, curled up in her bed, she had resolved to put before him what she now conceived to be the central problem of her life ; though mentioning no names and making identification impossible. Was he not himself a major figure in the problem? So, while O'Kelvie worked on, she sat searching for phrases.

He flung his tools away, wiped his hands, and said, "Now for tea!" but Cynthia was still shaping her phrases behind a silence. He cleared an end of the trestle table, spread a newspaper over it, and brought the tea-pot and the loaf; but she was still silent. He cut the bread, made the tea, and bade her fall to, and not talk so much. And she ate her bread and jam, and drank from her cup; but the phrases would not leave her lips. O'Kelvie caught her eyes, and she smiled back sadly.

"Prestissimo," said he.

"Yes, Rugg dear."

"Out with it."

She fiddled with a bread crumb; then looking up quickly, feigned a smiling ease, and said, "You see: I've long been rather terribly in love."

"I see. I thought so." He was not laughing as he answered thus; he had too much imagination and kindness for that. He said it gently.

"Or I *was*—up to about a year ago. But now— Do you think that one can love like that twice?"

"It depends on what ' like that ' means."

"It's gone on a long time now," explained Cynthia, feeling a duty to make the most of " like that. "

"I see," said O'Kelvie without a smile. "And does he love you?"

"Oh no. He's—he's very much older. He's married, in fact. Is it very wrong of me?"

"My dear, you can't talk about love being ' wrong.' It just *is*."

"Yes, that's what *I* feel," said Cynthia solemnly. "But now it seems to be fading, and I think I may be

going to love someone else. I think I began to see
how hopeless it all was ; and, as I got older, I learned
that someone else of whom I thought rather highly
didn't think him as perfect as I did, and gradually I
began to see what this person meant—and oh, it's all
rather caddish of me, isn't it ? "

" No, it's not."

" But what I want to know is—— "

" Wait a minute. Is the new person any more
available ? "

Cynthia's eyebrows and lips made a grimace of self-
ridicule and despair. " Well no, he isn't. To tell the
truth, he isn't. I'm such an awful fool, you see. I'm
so terribly ready to love."

" Does he love you at all ? "

" Oh a bit, I think. But not in my way. Not at
all like that." She looked down, and fiddled again with
the crumb on the table. " At least, not as I believe I
could love him if I let myself go. But don't talk about
him. What I really want to know is, if a love like that
can go, how can one ever believe in love again ? "

" But can't you believe in degrees of love, my dear ?
You have loved this chap and will always feel an affection
for him because of that ; but now perhaps you're going
to love someone better. And if you don't reach the
greatest heights with this new lad—well, I suppose,
you'll go on till at last you find someone whom you will
love in a way that you can never approach again. Isn't
that what happens ? "

" Yes ; that's what I try to think. But—but, oh, I
don't want to be disloyal. . . ."

" But you can't dictate to love, my dear. It dictates
to you."

"I know, I know! That's it! But . . . I don't feel at all too terribly happy about it, really."

"There's nothing to be unhappy or conscience-stricken about."

"Oh *do* you think so?" cried she, delighted at this verdict. Of a sudden, however, a new doubt dropped upon her. "But how does one know that one has reached the highest point? One always thinks one is there. I thought so with *him*."

O'Kelvie sighed. "I suppose one has to put it to the test, my dear. And perhaps to sterner tests than any you can imagine. But I really don't know." And he smiled apologetically into her face. "I've never done it myself, you see. I am a selfish brute, and no love has ever stood the test."

"Oh, I can't believe that."

"But it's so; and I could wish it were not. I think that the trouble has been that I have always given the best of my love to my art. You have a gift for loving; that's clear. I've only a gift for cutting stone."

"But perhaps you've yet to find the one you'll love properly?"

"I doubt it. Doubt it most abominably. I'm not you. Let's talk only about you. This first love of yours doesn't seem to have quite stood its testing, does it?"

"No," sighed Cynthia; and with that word she put her love for Mr. Guilder on one side, among a store of happy memories, and let the new joy have its way.

Now she talked fluently and gaily of other subjects. Her gaiety was even extravagant, as if something in her had been set free. And when O'Kelvie saw her off at the door in Ashgar Terrace and patted her shoulder,

saying, " Good luck to your new love, little Cynthia,"
she smiled up, delighted, and almost danced along the
pavement.   She gave him a last wave of her hand, and
turned homeward, filled with that warm glow which
always comes when one's strongest desires are running
free.   " Oh, there's no one like him," she kept repeating.
" He's so perfect to talk to."

Over her spectacles, needlework, and balcony rail
Miss Hackett watched all.

Two Sundays later, as the congregation streamed
down the aisles of St. Alban's to the north door, a plump
little woman, not without some pushing, followed by
whispered apologies, and some skilful navigation of her
curves round slower vessels, managed to come close to
the back of Hilda Coventry.   No opportunity could
have been more favourable, for neither the father nor
the girl had been in church ; only the mother and the
little old lady in black who always accompanied her.
So Miss Hackett had bumped into several people and
sidled between others and the pews, and now was
behind her quarry, just as they passed into the daylight
and went down the steps.   She said, " Excuse me . . ."
to Hilda, but, not being heard, felt rather foolish and
changed the remark into a cough which she hid behind
her black-gloved hand and her Bible and prayer book.
Then she gently touched Hilda with the point of the
prayer book and said, " Excuse me.   Might I speak to
you for a moment ? "

Hilda stared at her in surprise.   " Yes, yes," she
stuttered.

" It's about your daughter."

" Oh yes, yes.   She's away for the week-end,"
said Hilda, somewhat irrelevantly.

Old Mrs. Coventry, who was walking three paces ahead with Rose Damien, turned to see who had spoken to Hilda. A strange lady! What was this? The two had stopped and were talking on the pavement. Pretending to listen to Rose who was in voluble plaint about Leo, and who had been most interesting until this more interesting event had happened in the rear, she strained her ears in the direction of Hilda and her companion. She could hear nothing and was vexed. So abruptly she left Rose, in the very middle of a sentence—only she could treat her friends like this—and hastened back to the two earnest talkers, training her eyes first on one and then on the other, as they spoke.

"I was sure you wouldn't mind," the strange lady gushed to Hilda, but turned a welcoming smile on Old Mrs. Coventry as she came up. "I felt I had to speak in case—well, in case you might want to do something about it. Yes. Such a charming and attractive child as she is!"

"I am sure it was most kind of you," said Hilda, confused.

"What is it?" demanded Old Mrs. Coventry. "What is it, Hilda?"

"Yes, I felt you couldn't know anything about it," continued Miss Hackett, who, not having been introduced to the old lady, didn't answer her query. "Believe me, it was a long time before I could make up my mind, but something seemed to tell me I ought to speak. The child—— "

"What is it, what is it?" Old Mrs. Coventry beat her umbrella on the pavement, her patience no longer in control.

Hilda explained to Miss Hackett that this was the

child's grandmother, and, turning to the old lady, tried to explain Miss Hackett's story. But very soon Miss Hackett took it from her stuttering lips and explained it diffusively herself—people were apt to be thus impatient with Hilda Coventry. Old Mrs. Coventry fixed her eyes on the narrator and shot her compressed lips forwards and back. " I hope you think I acted for the best," concluded Miss Hackett. " I knew that studio hadn't at all a good name, and it was unthinkable to me that you should willingly have allowed your little girl to go there. I felt I had to speak. Yes. But, believe me, I don't want to get the dear child into trouble. That's the last thing I desire. I hate tale-bearing at all times."

" She is a very naughty girl," said Hilda. " Exceedingly naughty."

" We shall certainly look into the matter," declared Old Mrs. Coventry ; and you could see by her eyes and her lips that she would. " What can she have been up to, going there secretly like that ? "

" Yes, but don't punish her, I beg," gushed Miss Hackett. " I'm sure she doesn't realise she's doing anything wrong—— "

" If she didn't she wouldn't have kept it secret," interrupted Old Mrs. Coventry, who didn't want the story spoiled.

" Well, not *very* wrong," conceded Miss Hackett. " But I felt I had to say something. You see that studio hasn't at all a good name. He has models there, and all that. Yes, I knew you wouldn't want your little girl mixed up with that kind of thing."

" You were perfectly right. Perfectly right ! " declared Old Mrs. Coventry enthusiastically. She had recognised a bird of her own feather and, as she put it afterwards, she "quite took to her. A most tactful and sensible person." "I am sure we ought to be very grateful to you, oughtn't we, Hilda? Tell us some more about that studio. We must certainly keep our little Cynthia from such surroundings. I've never liked that man, nor trusted him. No, I wouldn't trust him an inch farther than I could see him. Most irregular he is, in his life; *most* irregular." Glancing along the pavement, she saw that Rose Damien had gone, and turned again to Miss Hackett. "Are you walking our way?"

"Yes, I can go that way," agreed Miss Hackett.

So all three walked slowly along Parson's Road and into Glastonbury Road, Miss Hackett telling all that she knew and much that she suspected, and one at least of her companions listening greedily. Old Mrs. Coventry was very happy on this slow walk. Life had become vivid and interesting; and she active and alive in response to it. And when you are happy, you feel great goodwill to whoever is with you, and Old Mrs. Coventry, talking in her turn, constantly expressed this goodwill by touching Miss Hackett's arm with her prayer book. "It was very naughty of Cynthia to go at all," she said, "knowing that we have no dealings with that man, but I am sure she went in perfect innocence." She liked the word "innocent" as she liked the word "moral": they fed her thought with the same sweet, forbidden fruit. "There is not a more innocent child anywhere, is there, Hilda? She has been brought up in complete innocence of everything. But the cynicism of that man in encouraging her when he must have known that her father wouldn't approve! I hope Tom speaks to him, and very straightly too. Goodness knows what a man like that wouldn't talk about to a child! They have no restraint and no decency—ever! I know for a fact that he told that boy of his everything that there is to be told, before the child was fourteen. Perfectly disgraceful! We can't have our Cynthia's beautiful simplicity destroyed in that way. I always say that, once you've shattered a beautiful vase, you can never put it together again."

This metaphor of the shattered vase sounded very well to her sentimental mind, and she didn't pause to wonder if it really had any meaning. Like many another sentimental and talkative lady of Norman's End she much preferred good words to good meanings.

By now they were on the steps of their house, and after prolonging the talk there, Miss Hackett left them and went homeward down Conyers Road, carrying her prayer book rather mincingly. She felt that she had done her duty. The quiet and orderliness of Sunday lay down the long pavements; and the heart of Miss Hackett felt very like Conyers Road on Sunday—clean and well-swept and quietly alight.

Meanwhile Hilda and her mother-in-law went firmly into the house. Or rather, one of them did.

"Perhaps I'll talk to the child myself," said the indecisive Hilda. "Perhaps I won't worry her father with it."

"Nonsense, nonsense!" snapped the old lady vigorously, determined not to be cheated of a scene. "I never heard such nonsense! Of course her father must be told. It's a father's business. He must go to that man and talk to him, and I hope he won't mince matters. A man like that would never listen to two poor women, and he must be stopped, once and for all. Outrageous, it is! . . . Hilda, you don't mean that you're not going to tell her father?"

Q

A child could not have looked more suddenly afraid, if told that it might be deprived of a treat.

" Oh well . . ." agreed Hilda. " If you think he ought to know."

" Certainly he ought to know ! That nice, well-meaning creature told us, and we have a moral obligation to tell *him*, I consider. He is the child's lawful guardian."

So Hilda walked towards the study door, and Old Mrs. Coventry came quickly behind, determined not to miss anything. They knew that he was in the study, because he had explained that overtime work would keep him from attending church. As a matter of fact, he had finished the overtime work as soon as the bell for Mattins ceased to ring, and was now reading " Robert Ellsmere " with no little interest in the hero's spiritual conflict.

He swung round in his chair when they announced that they had something important to tell him ; and they stood side by side and gave him the story—that is to say, his mother quickly took it from the inadequate hands of his wife and did it full justice. He must speak to Cynthia and go and see that man. He must to to-morrow. Goodness knew what ideas Cynthia might be picking up there ; she might have been meeting the most dangerous people—their Cynthia whom they had guarded so preciously ! She wouldn't trust that man to temper his talk before the most delicately reared child, and she'd little doubt that he'd talk to Cynthia as coarsely as he talked to his models, and damage her lovely simplicity ; and, as she had said before and would *always* say, once you'd damaged a beautiful vase, you could never put it together again.

LET us try to disentangle Tom Coventry's emotions when his ladies left him. He boiled with indignation against this cool fish of an O'Kelvie, and strode up and down, resolved to justify it. Damn the man for his impudence! Encouraging his, Tom Coventry's, daughter to come to his studio where, as all the world suspected, there were " goings on " of which her father wouldn't approve! But wait. Why, if he, Tom Coventry, accepted Mrs. du Pré's view of freedom, should he mind these goings on; and why should he object to Cynthia learning the way of the free men ?

" Oh *no !* "

Let him face up to it : didn't he then believe in the same freedom for Cynthia as he had won to, at some cost, for himself ?

" No, no, *no !* Never, never ! "

Very good then : how escape the dilemma : if Evelyn for himself, why not other Evelyns for O'Kelvie, and why not Cynthia, in her time, an Evelyn to some other man ?

" My God, no ! "

Oh *no !* Not Cynthia. All the training of forty years, so far from having been annihilated by Mrs. du Pré, was rising to mastery this Sunday morning. Then must he allow that he had done wrong in taking Evelyn ? Yes, if he must tell the truth, he must say Yes. That little flat on the Bayswater side of the Park which he had given to Evelyn was a place of solace and gladness but never of ease. When he shut its door on himself, he shut sweetness within, but he did not shut guilt outside. And he had to confess, since he was dealing only with truth this morning, that, fond as he was of Evelyn, and grateful as he was to her, he had tasted a tiny flavour of recoil when she had accepted his gift so easily.

No, one thing he saw quite clearly: he believed in morality for women. "Thank God I believe in morality for women," said Tom Coventry, who always thanked God when he could get back to a corner of the old safe country.

And his own actions: would he condemn them? He strode up and down with this question, till at last he admitted, "Yes, in theory I think them wrong, but I consider my own case was exceptional."

Here is the simple truth: Tom Coventry threw up self-justification in order that he might have ground from which to attack O'Kelvie. The need of justifying his wrath was greater than his need of justifying himself; because in the wrath his self-love was deeply engaged. O'Kelvie had despised him, as though he had not been there! And in such men as Tom Coventry—which is to say, in such men as you and me—*amour propre* is the factor that sweeps the board. Confound the cool villain! He knew perfectly well that Cynthia's father was a churchgoer with at any rate a declared policy of goodness, and, cynically snapping his fingers at all that, he had encouraged the girl to come secretly to his studio. "My heaven, I'll tell him what I think!" People would hear that O'Kelvie had treated him as of no account—his mother would talk of it to everybody

—very good! he'd give them something more to talk about. They should say that Mr. Coventry went straight to Mr. O'Kelvie and told him a thing or two.

For his *amour propre* had a powerful ally in his romantic heart. He saw himself as the father of the stories, hurrying to horsewhip any man who dared trifle with his daughter; and he longed to fill this rôle. And another ally, too, though working far, far below his sight : O'Kelvie was a big, handsome man who had succeeded in freeing himself from the tyranny of conscience and thereby enjoyed many things of which Tom Coventry's life was empty, and jealousy drove Tom Coventry to go to the man and justify this emptiness by a torrent of abusive words.

His thoughts were now in order ; his forces arrayed. " You leave this business to me," he said majestically to the women, when he met them again at dinner.

To-morrow evening was the time. He would return from the office and call upon O'Kelvie soon after four, which was the time that Cynthia went on her visits. A nice little shock for the man to see, not Cynthia at his studio door, but her father and judgment ! And all the next day in his office Tom Coventry was restless. Eager for the battle, since in some mysterious way it would ease deep-seated pains, he was also nervous of it. A kindly man, he much preferred amiability to raised voices and rudeness ; and he was determined to be rude —as rude as he could be. The eagerness was stronger than the nervousness, however, and he was glad when it was three o'clock and he could take the first steps. Telling old Ellsworthy that he wouldn't return that day because " he had important business somewhere," he put his silk hat on his head, pulled his black coat straight, bunched up his black tie and felt the pearl pin (he had taken pains with his dressing that morning, to impress the slovenly artist) and went out from the office. Twenty minutes later he was walking along the pavement of Ashgar Terrace towards the door of the studio, and feeling vexed with his heart that it should be up and rebellious after he had told it to be still. With the handle of his rolled umbrella he knocked on the dark old door. Now then. . . . A few seconds, and he would have opened fire. Be still, my soul; be still; we have no fear of this man . . . we are looking forward to castigating him.

Heavy footsteps were approaching on uncarpeted boards; and he braced his shoulders, felt the tie pin, and smoothed down the neatly rolled umbrella. The door swung open; and there stood O'Kelvie, in the blue blouse, his hair ruffled up, a palette in one hand, and a brush between his teeth.

"Ah," mumbled he over the brush, lifting his eyebrows at the well-dressed figure, "who-der-debble? . . . Yes, sir, wah' is it?"

"May I come in a minute?" asked Tom Coventry. "I am Cynthia Coventry's father."

"Oh yes." O'Kelvie, removing the brush, accepted the news most cheerfully. "Good. Come in, by all means. A dear child."

Tom Coventry followed him into the studio, conscious that the man had discomfited him by this breezy reception. It takes two to make a fight; or should we say, it takes two to make a castigation, for one must bend over and submit? But then he felt angry with O'Kelvie for having turned his whip aside like this, and power rose in him again.

" Mr. O'Kelvie," he began.

Unfortunately, however, the first thing that met his eye in the studio was a large canvas of two beautiful women—" Two Sisters " by Lucien Devaux ; they were nudes, and they introduced some wholly irrelevant thoughts by stirring ancient hungers and pressing on ancient wounds. O'Kelvie saw his glance at the canvas and decided that here was an opening for friendly and interesting talk.

" Indecent picture, isn't it ? " said he quite seriously.

" It is not yours then ? " inquired Tom, since one must answer.

" Lord, no. It's the work of a Frenchman who's fast becoming the rage. But I don't like it. It's rather obscene, I think."

" It's certainly rather bold," agreed Tom.

O'Kelvie turned sharply, as if this hadn't been quite what he meant. " What ? "

Tom repeated the observation.

" Oh, I didn't mean that," explained O'Kelvie. " No, I didn't mean that. The picture lacks honesty, that's what I meant. The man sets out to be perfectly frank and free, but he funks it at the last. He ends by being neither t'other nor which. That's why I call it indecent. I mean, either we're ashamed of the pubic hair or we're not."

Tom started at the phrase, as well he might, having never heard it spoken aloud before ; but the odd and unfortunate thing was that, though this was the first time that such a view-point had been put before him, he saw a gleam of sense in it at once. Much as he had seen gleams of light when Mrs. du Pré talked to him. And it wouldn't do at all if O'Kelvie started converting him to his views.   He had come to fight with the man, and he couldn't fight unless his feet were on his own ground. Best get away from this talk with its glimmering lights.

"Mr. O'Kelvie," he began.   "It's about my daughter that I want to speak to you."

"Ah yes. A dear child. Well, do sit down." O'Kelvie pushed a lot of rags and boxes off the couch; and Cynthia's father, after looking down upon the upholstery, sat where she was wont to sit. O'Kelvie stood before him, his hands in his trouser pockets, and his legs apart.

"I am given to understand that she has taken to visiting you," began Tom, rather pompously.

"Bless her, yes."

"Well, Mr. O'Kelvie . . . it is difficult to say, but . . . I have come to tell you that I cannot sanction this. In fact, I am at a loss to understand how you could suppose I should sanction it. I must say, I find your encouragement of her"—he was warming up, thank heaven!—"very difficult to explain. Very."

"What the hell——" began O'Kelvie. Because he too could warm up.

Tom raised his hand for silence, as he might to old Ellsworthy or young Tristram.   "I should have thought you would have known that I shouldn't tolerate such visits for a moment.   It cannot be unknown to you who I am, and for what sort of thing I stand. You must know that my ways are not your ways, nor my ideas your ideas.   And to encourage my daughter to——"

"God in His Heaven, man! Will you tell me what the hell you really mean?"

The tone fired Tom—much to his satisfaction. He felt his temper flame. Now he could say anything—

it didn't much matter what, so long as the words leapt
and scorched. He stood up and fixed his eyes on
O'Kelvie's.

"I mean simply this, sir. Her mother and I believe
in the ordinary decencies of life, and you, we have
every reason to believe, do not."

Something happened to O'Kelvie's mouth : it looked
square and ugly. His eyes blazed into his visitor's.
"I believe most of your so-called decencies to be
indecencies, if that's what you mean."

"Quite so. And I will not have my daughter learn
such doctrines here. She is an innocent girl, I am glad
to say, and she shall remain so."

"Innocent ? What are you getting at, man ? Do
you mean that I would seduce or harm a sixteen-year-old
girl ? "

"If you please ! " Tom's protesting hand had come
up again. "I must beg you not to use such language
in connexion with my daughter."

"Well, what the devil are we talking about then ? "

"We're talking about—" Tom Coventry hesitated,
as everyone does, who is not certain what he is talking
about—"we're talking about her getting knowledge.
And ideas."

"Knowledge and ideas ? Knowledge and ideas ? So
she does, bless her heart. And it is probably the first
time in her life that she's struck any." For O'Kelvie
was in the mood to hit now. "I gather they're not
plentiful in her home."

To a vain man few insults can sting like this. All
style went from Tom's fighting. "What do you
mean ? " he demanded, with a schoolboy's note. "My
education was as good as yours anyday, I'm pretty sure."

" Better, I'm certain. Nothing could have been worse than mine. Or more idiotic."

" Well, then . . ." said Tom, rather helpless, now that his point had been conceded.

" Well, what ? " asked O'Kelvie.

Both felt that an irrelevant issue had been introduced, and they would like to remember where the main argument had got to, so that they could get on with the fighting.

" You must have known that she came here without my knowledge."

" God save my soul, I never gave it ten seconds' thought."

" Then you ought to have done."

" Why ? Why, pray ? I happen to be a vain man, and to think myself good luck in her path, rather than danger. Why should I send round and warn you ? Dammit, man, I'd sooner have sent you a letter of congratulations that your child was being educated and enlarged at last ! And by the way, how *did* you get to know ? "

" A woman who lives opposite this place came and told us. Very rightly, I think. Very rightly indeed. A Miss Hackett."

" She came and told you ? " Now, whatever Tom Coventry may have thought of him, O'Kelvie had always shown respect for Cynthia's youth and refrained from the Elizabethan bluntness he enjoyed with his pals. But he saw no reason for this delicacy with a full-grown man like Tom. " She came and told you ? Licentious old bitch ! Sniffing around for pestilence, and determined to find it somewhere. Can't you see that it's her miserable——" but no ! I am not of O'Kelvie's metal, and cannot write it.

Inwardly Tom cowered beneath the words, but outwardly showed nothing. He did not want this man to suppose him strait-laced and a greenhorn. " I think she was perfectly right in informing us," he said with dignity. " She knew I should not choose for Cynthia to be given your ideas."

" Ideas. Ah yes." O'Kelvie said it as if he was glad to recover the main quarrel and to get his fists up again. " You mean that they will contaminate her somehow. If that's what you mean, for God's sake speak out."

" I always speak out," protested Tom.

" Right ! And you're suggesting that I am likely to ruin her mind. Is that it ? "

" Not quite, but——"

" Come, man," interrupted O'Kelvie, who was fast capturing the ascendancy. " What's the row, if I'm not ? Speak up, do."

" I have no doubt that you believe in your own ideas, but I most emphatically do not ; and I don't choose that they should be conveyed to my daughter. It seems perfectly simple to me."

" Perfectly. You mean that, though she's nearly seventeen now and nubile, you don't want her to hear all the ideas in the world, and choose among them for herself. You mean that you want to hold up her development and keep her half an idiot. You mean——"

" Not at all," demurred Tom, who felt, quite rightly, that he was being trapped.

" But, great Moses, man, it must be one or other of these things ! Either you think that I am wilfully contaminating her or you don't choose that she should meet with all ideas that are sincerely held and learn to choose among them. You want her to be ignorant rather than educated."

Tom's eyes stared bewildered. "I want her kept innocent," he repeated, helplessly.

"Innocent! Innocent!" scoffed O'Kelvie, raising his two great arms above his head in despair. "By which you can only mean 'ignorant.' And how in God's name ignorance can be a good thing for a fine young opening mind like hers beats me. My God, sir, I'll give *you* a few ideas." He was now raging up and down as he spoke, and looking very much like a caged lion when it has the red meat in its teeth. And in truth his visitor had tossed to him a topic that he loved to tear in pieces. Words and phrases leapt to his lips that he had often used in joyous talks with his friends —violent words and stinging phrases such as his soul loved. "You think that my talk will encompass her ruin. I say that's what *you'll* do. Here is a young, vital creature, all fresh and eager and pliable from the earth, and she's at your mercy. You want to shut up her young soul in darkness. You want to bind and constrict it till she's turned into one of your frightened, curious, prurient, merciless dames—Hell! I wish I could get out what I mean! God, it's awful! It's a crime, and you dare to come to me as if I were the criminal—I who have tried to let a little light into her darkness. 'Your ways are not our ways'! Damn your smug complacency! You coolly assume——"

"I assume nothing. I——"

But O'Kelvie raised his voice that he might keep all speech to himself.

"You coolly assume that you alone have any morality. Do you think that I haven't got my codes too?—though they are very different from yours, I thank my stars. They've got some red blood in them. The difference between you and me is this, that you believe that morality is to be found in a dark room, all closed up, and I believe that it's to be found somewhere in the light. You want to call every natural and healthy instinct wrong, and I say that that's a crime against life—which amounts to saying in your language that it's an insult to God. Therefore it's you that's indecent and blasphemous ; and I don't know whether you make me want to weep or to spit——"

" Will you allow me to speak ? " tried Tom again.

" No." O'Kelvie, enjoying his rage, waved him out of consideration with a sweep of his arm. " No. You've told me what you think of me, and now, by the mother of God, I'll tell you all about yourself. Listen : you're afraid to do this and afraid to do that, and because you don't like to admit that it's fear——" O'Kelvie, leaning his body forward, sent these words through his teeth at Tom Coventry, who stood upright to receive them, resting on his rolled umbrella— " because you're really ashamed of your fear, you put it on a throne and call it God. That's it ! That's what you do ! You save your self-respect by sanctifying your timidities. Pooh, it's pitiable ; and look, sir : I don't blame *you*. Your parents took you and ruined the natural vigour of your mind, when you were a little child, just as you want to ruin Cynthia now. And you hadn't the original force to break free from their fetters, so you wear 'em still and shout dirty names at those who have cast them off——"

" If we can't conduct this quarrel with dignity——" began Tom, lifting his face to the rafters.

" Dignity. I've no desire to conduct it with dignity. What's dignity got to do with a fight? All I desire, in a fight, is to knock my man out. All I desire is to say things that'll hurt. If a man comes here with an obvious intent to hurt me, I see that he goes out of that door with bigger blows to think about than any he's delivered. If he wants a fight, I see that he gets it, my boy. Fighting's fighting; and dignity's dignity; and they don't run together. You raise your voice, and I warrant I'll shout louder. I intend my blows to get home, see? "

" In that case——"

" In that case, listen : there was no reason why you should have had strength to break free from your fetters. It's only a few who do; and they're the geniuses, and you're just a very ordinary man. Cynthia may break free. She's fine rich soil, and I pray God I've dropped a few seeds into her that'll prove her salvation. That's my answer to you for smugly coming here to tell me I'd hurt her. Take it home and bite on it."

Tom, waiting on his umbrella, had for some minutes past determined to go, as soon as he could get in one last word. Deep down in his mind he knew that he was not this man's equal, but he dared not lift this knowledge into view. Instead, he tried to believe that he was acting with great dignity when he said, " This tirade only confirms me in all I thought. I have no desire to speak to you any more."

" What do I care what you think? " cried O'Kelvie, following him to the door. " What do I care whether you want to speak or not? I'll take care that you hear what *I* have to say. And one thing is this : don't imagine I shall do anything to stop your daughter

coming here.   You do your own damned dirty work!
She's your slave for another year or so, but I wouldn't
answer for her much longer than that."

The door slammed between them.

And now, upon my soul, I know not which of these
two pugilists to cheer.   I have enjoyed the bonny
fighting of Pat O'Kelvie, but my soul is moved with
pity for Tom Coventry.   I can see that this was by no
means a battle in which one man was wholly right and
the other wholly wrong.   I can see a much better show
that Tom might have put up for himself.   But what
would you?   If two Rights get going at each other,
and one of them has all the skill, the issue is inevitable.
Get the water ready, and the towel and the sponge, for
Tom Coventry, after being knocked all over the place
by a better man, has lost on points and his limbs are
shaking.   His head is bruised, and his heart, which we
cannot see, is a little disappointed.

XII

Tom Coventry had some pleasure out of it. He was always pleased with the way he spoke to Cynthia in the quiet of his study. He had spoken so gently and so sensibly, and the words had come well.

And indeed he had been fluent. One is always fluent when justifying oneself. And one always plays one's best when, after being pitted against an opponent who was unexpectedly strong, one is set to play a mere novice. It is with talk as with tennis. I who have been whipped off the court by good men have been later astonished at the brilliance, variety, and generosity of my strokes when playing against a man even worse than myself.

"Believe me, my dear," said Tom Coventry, "I have given great thought to this. . . a young girl going alone to a studio. . . you must see that it is impossible. . . I don't think anyone could call me illiberal or unsympathetic to modern trends of thought; I don't think anyone could say I am one of those who call every natural instinct wrong; who—er—put their fears on a throne, so to speak, and call them God; who, if I may so put it, save their self-respect by sanctifying their timidities. Believe me, I am not one of those who have accepted without question all the fetters that their parents hung upon them. It is simply that I have examined them, and decided that their restraints were good"—

oh, that little flat on the Bayswater side! Put it out of mind.   Why should the picture of its front door jump into view just here?—" and you can be sure that, had I not considered them good, I should have broken free from them long ago.   As it is, I feel I have no course but to forbid you to go to that studio any more."

Cynthia, who had sat herself on a footstool with her legs under her, did not interrupt this flow, but kept her eyes fixed on him for a while and then let them stray upward to the light of the window.   Reflecting this light, they looked wistful and sad.   What was she thinking?   When he had finished, she did not answer, but twisted the tassel of the footstool.

" Well ? " he queried.

She tossed back her hair.   " All right, dearest. . . But may I see him once to tell him that I'm coming no more ? "

Tom thought over this.   Yes, it would be good for O'Kelvie to see how completely he had triumphed, and to hear his decision from his daughter's own lips.   But —but supposing O'Kelvie ridiculed him to Cynthia, and Cynthia believed it!   Hateful thought.   But she wouldn't.   After his splendid words just spoken, she wouldn't.

" Yes," said he at last, " but don't believe everything he says against me."   And he smiled rather sweetly at her.

She kissed him for assurance, and ran out.

She ran to her room.   Her first emotions, as her father spoke, had been anger and rebellion, but later on—luckily her father had been fluent and continuous and long—as she saw that defiance was impossible and she must lose her happy hours with Rugg, a sadness had succeeded ;   and then, suddenly, in the midst of this

R

sadness, she had glimpsed the beauty of renunciation for her father's sake, and straightway fallen in love with it.

In her room she was thinking about it now. She did not see the real motives that drove her. She did not see that Mr. Guilder and St. Alban's Church were deep in her blood, and that she loved renunciation almost as much as she loved love. She did not see that romance and sentimentalism had seeped from the rooms of Norman's End into her being, and that she rather loved the idea of loving sadly and was almost happy in the knowledge that now her true love wasn't going to run smooth. So, shaking her head in the solitude of her room, she thought, " One thing is clear : I must do nothing that'll hurt Daddy."

And it would be difficult to say which was uppermost, the lover's pain or the ascetic's happiness, as she walked on the pavement for the last time to the studio door.

Standing in the studio with the wistfulness in her eyes, she explained it all to Rugg. " I knew all along that he'd have a thousand fits if he heard that I'd been here so often. He doesn't understand that one can be just friends. And I suppose it wasn't strictly right, anyhow —not telling them, I mean. You see, he's never been tempted himself to do anything that wasn't strictly right, so he's easily shocked."

" I say ! " O'Kelvie interrupted. " I do hope I wasn't rude to him. The more I think about it, the more I feel I was rather rude."

" Oh, I dare say he was a bit exasperating, poor darling. I nearly lost my wool with him myself last night. I think he's all wrong in his decision, but of this I'm quite sure : I mustn't do anything to hurt him. He doesn't belong to our generation, you see."

O'Kelvie smiled. "Thank you, Contemporary," said he.

"Oh, you know what I mean : in thought, anyway. He doesn't think as we do."

O'Kelvie could continue smiling down upon her, for her eyes were staring away from him at a canvas, of which she saw nothing. And, being a somewhat softer man than Tom Coventry supposed, he added no word against her father.

"All right," he agreed. "We must do as Father says."

"And I can still be most frightfully fond of you, can't I," said Cynthia, now looking up into his face, "even if I don't see you ? "

Touched, he answered. "Please be that, little Cynthia."

"And I've thought of one thing : I've learned more from you than from anyone who's ever lived, and will you send me some books sometimes—those you think will help to educate me ? Will you ? Give them to Mike to give to me."

"Of course I will, Prestissimo. And Cynthia. . ."

"Yes."

"Come again when you feel you may. I have loved having you."

"Oh, but that won't be for years and years, I'm afraid."

So the guillotine fell on those happy times in the studio.

And in the following days Cynthia was silent and sad —but happy all the same to think that she was suffering so much for her father's sake. And once you have started sacrificing yourself for a person you are likely to go on to larger efforts in the same good cause. She now persuaded herself that she must go regularly to church with her father and mother, though O'Kelvie's talk had sadly shaken her childish faith. Again she did not perceive the hidden motives: she did not know that the church would always call her. And as the weeks went by, and Sunday after Sunday she heard Mr. Guilder in the pulpit, she felt stirring anew her old love of "the beauty of holiness." Even Rugg, she remembered, had praised the "whole-hogging saints" like General Booth and Father Stanton. She would sit in the church suddenly darkened for the sermon, with her face turned upwards to Mr. Guilder where he stood under the glory of his private electric light (the church had just got rid of its spurting gas-brackets to the great advantage of the atmosphere) and she would think with all the solemnity of youth, "My life is at a critical point. Which way will it swing? Towards Liberty or towards Sanctity. I believe I could be happy with either." In this last belief she was probably wrong, for though she might hurl herself into either, the other would be calling still. She stared up at the preacher, wondering. She was only one pair of eyes in a thousand seen by Mr. Guilder—a thousand lamp-lit eyes, all half revealing that they were lost and lonely in a dark universe, and longing for guidance. Which way? O'Kelvie or Guilder?

Had she known herself better, she would have known that her will would have little say in the matter, because she would go where her love lay. She would be loyal to O'Kelvie and rejoice in her loyalty. And one Sunday evening, sitting under the pulpit, she thought she saw an idea that would bring O'Kelvie into marriage with

Guilder. Rugg believed in beauty and strove to create it in stone; she couldn't do this, but she could at least try to create it in character. What a wonderful idea! Her own character must be her marble like Rugg's, and it was quite as tough a material too! She would chisel herself into something exquisite indeed—and everybody would love and admire her. Yes, this was the saving idea; and far down in her mind it was immensely reinforced by a dictum that Mr. Guilder had once let fall. Long ago he had said it, and it had haunted her ever since. "Beauty of action alone can produce beauty of facial expression." She longed to possess beauty of facial expression, and now it might come to her as a result of her utterly selfless life. Oh, good!

And in this apprenticeship to holiness and self-mortification we will leave her for a while, quite happy. Mike O'Kelvie brought her books from his father, which she promptly devoured. If these books some-times questioned the rules of the churches, that didn't seem to matter any longer, because, whether you accepted or rejected the rules, you could always decide, unless you were a congenital idiot, which of two actions was the beautiful one, and choose it rather than the other. Unseen of the world, Cynthia tried to choose it day by day, and was happy in her struggle. Mike was now a huge young man of eighteen, and she became very friendly with him, because it was music to hear him talk of his father.

PART III

I

So now for a while there was peace in these two homes, the Coventrys' and the Damiens'. But it was a peace like the customary peace of Europe, with movements underground that might at any moment meet and detonate and crack the crust.

In their gossiping together Hilda and her mother-in-law remarked an absorption in Tom; but if they asked him what it was that knit his brows, he silenced them with a brusque, "Business. You wouldn't understand;" which, if we give a large meaning to Tom Coventry's "business" was precisely true. They noticed that his business often detained him till late in the evenings, and sometimes took him away for a whole night, which had never happened before. What did it all mean? Things couldn't be going well: more than once of late he had suggested that Hilda should try to manage with less money, and had even threatened that, if bills were not smaller, they might have to move into one of those new maisonettes in Macartney Road, and make do with one maid. "But why? Why all this sudden worry about money?" his mother demanded of him. "Has your salary been reduced?" To which he answered "No!" rather loudly and angrily, for the question had hurt his pride. His business expenses had increased, he said vaguely.

But he underestimated the acuteness of his mother.

She was not so easily deceived. In long discussions with Hilda over their sewing, she complained, " He never tells us anything ; but it's my opinion he's been gambling ; or that his salary *has* been reduced, and he doesn't like to admit it." And she nodded knowingly ; but the point of interest here is that Old Mrs. Coventry, who was quite ready to believe the most interesting things about all the men around, and secretly wondered which of them, including the sidesmen, were keeping two homes, never for a moment suspected this of Tom.

And yet it was that little flat on the Bayswater side that was costing the money, the worry, and the long forensic arguments in the train. For, sitting in his homebound train, under a top hat and within a tight black coat, Tom Coventry looked to be a single man but was really three : he was counsel for the prosecution of Tom Coventry ; he was Tom Coventry sadly in the dock ; and he was counsel earnestly defending Tom Coventry. This defending counsel was the fluent one. He was a much stronger force than his learned friend : more eloquent, more passionate, better skilled in his brief, and quite ready to shout the other fellow down and defy the judge. He could almost, with his eloquence, bring tears to the prisoner's eyes. " I must protest," said counsel, " that it is the inalienable kindness of the accused, and not his selfishness, which has landed him in this parlous mess. He cannot bear to give Evelyn less than he has given her in the past or to disappoint her of her few little treats ; he cannot bear to lessen the allowance to his old mother, which he has always paid very delicately into her small account, because it is all she has for the few bits of finery and the few hours of gaiety that are dear to her heart. She is old, he says, and may not have long to live. And he will not, gentlemen, I say he will *not* purchase his own peace of mind by cutting off his daughter's education. His love for his daughter, he has told me, is about the only perfect thing in his life ; and he refuses to sacrifice her. He even finds it difficult, when in her rapid chatter she shows her naïve hopes of the future, and her trust in him, he finds it difficult, I say—and which of us will blame him ?—to consider lowering at once their style of living—which is not high, gentlemen, not high.

" What then can he do ? My learned friend suggests that he should never have taken Evelyn into his life. We are prepared to accept that as true, though another argument might be submitted to you. But I am instructed by the accused to say that he realises well that sooner or later he will have to break with Evelyn. Evelyn herself has admitted that the end will have to come one day. But not yet. Not yet, gentlemen. You will not ask him to turn back to the old emptiness yet. He has not had much sweetness in his life ; and this is indeed sweet. The very fact that he can only see her once or twice a week, and then sometimes only for an hour or two, has kept it fresh and sweet. No, gentlemen, be merciful ; not yet.

" Besides, Evelyn is really fond of him, and he cannot bear to hurt her. He has wronged her—yes, gentlemen, the accused is prepared to admit this, though I, were I so instructed, could plead for him very differently ; but he will have none of it ; he declares that, though he has gone over and over the arguments of a certain Mrs. du Pré, he cannot get it out of his head that he has done a wrong to this girl. And for that reason, says he, he must stand by her and provide for her. Surely this does honour to his heart, gentlemen of the jury, who are men of the world!

"And yet he doesn't believe that he is a thoroughly bad man. Don't think that he believes himself a thoroughly bad man. He has wondered sometimes if he is this, but he just cannot feel it. Appearances are against him, no doubt: going to church and at the same time keeping a mistress. But the going to church has been for others' sake more than for his own. Had he been alone, he would have held back from going. But he is a family man and had to give the gossipers no chance. He had to set a good example. Laugh as you may, it *was* partly to set a good example to his child and to keep her in better ways than his that he went with some regularity to Morning Prayer.

"And the taking of a mistress—for that is—yes, I admit it—that is what it amounts to. I *will* plead a case for him. I say his step was inevitable. How could he have gone on in the old empty path with Hilda—with never any 'arms to welcome him in,' never a caress that meant anything—he whose heart was aching for someone pretty to love and someone kind who would love him? Argument is mere wind and words when something is bound to happen. Men of the world, I say he *had* to stay the gnawing hunger; it was that or madness."

So argued counsel for the defence, between St. James's Park on the Underground and Norman's End. He won his case (though prosecuting counsel was still shaking his head) and the scene changed: there was no longer a court of law in that top-hatted head bumped along in a screaming train, but a counting house.

What to do, what to do, what to do? If all
retrenchment was impossible, he must find new money
somewhere. How did men do this? They took
risks. They made money on the Stock Exchange.
How was it he had never the gambler's spirit? Perhaps
Mrs. du Pré had been right, and he was no Lord of Life,
boldly risking all, rather than sit long with those
ancient dullards, Old Custom and Old Security; nay,
he was one who sat, stupidly and prosaically content,
while the fine, bold, dashing, lordly men were taking
the high fences on the hunt for poetry and life. But
he would *not* have this said of him, nor believe it of
himself. He would risk something to win all. There
was poetry in him and courage in him, and he would
give them their run.

And he dropped into dreams of what he would do
with gambling in stocks and shares. These dreams
were so engrossing that they carried him past Norman's
End Station. He woke from them two stations further
on, and was obliged to tear and bundle from his carriage,
and wait on the platform with the shreds of his dreams.

There was peace also in the Damiens' home; and
only Leo knew that it was an armed peace.

Rose Damien, in Hilda's drawing room, reported that
the boy had quite come to his senses and was giving no
trouble. He had returned without a word to school,
and his master assured them that he was much more
amenable now, working adequately if not remarkably.
They would never make a genius of him, Mr. Rustington
said; he had neither the ability nor the force of character,
but there was no reason why he shouldn't do as well as
ordinary boys. At home he was always quiet, generally

spending his time in his room reading or making things with his tools. And really he had an astonishing gift with his hands : she would say that for him.

"Good ! Splendid ! " exclaimed Old Mrs. Coventry. "Well, I *am* glad, Rose dear."

"Yes, but I wish he were more like other boys," bewailed Rose. "I don't think it's healthy, an English boy reading all that philosophy and stuff. Why isn't he out like Rob Ingram, shooting and fishing and playing cricket. He'll have to go among men sometime. What we are to do with him in the end, I am sure I don't know. We hoped he might be a clergyman, since he doesn't like cricket and is fond of reading, but he still persists in that nonsense about 'not believing.' "

"What does he want to be ? " asked Old Mrs. Coventry, best listener in the world.

"A gardener. That's what he says. Did you ever hear anything so silly ? "

"Oh, he can't be *that*," said Old Mrs. Coventry, gazing bewildered.

"Of course not," sniffed Rose. "But that's how he talks."

"Never mind, my dear," soothed the comforter, touching her hand. "All boys talk nonsense sometimes. And I've no doubt he'll grow out of this reading phase. It can't last for ever."

The subject of Leo's future profession came up one evening when he and his father and mother were seated at dinner.

"You are nearly seventeen now," his father said, carving the leg of lamb. "Have you any clearer idea what you want to be ? "

"No," said Leo. "No clearer than before." And he took his plate of meat.

"Well, it's time you had."

"I can't have."

"How?"

"For the simple and sufficient reason that my idea was perfectly clear before. Pass the mint sauce, please, mum."

Leo, in the fashion of other sixteen-year-olds, had assumed the grand manner in his speech with his parents. Also a note of sorrowful pity for them, which was peculiarly infuriating.

"What do you mean?" asked Abbott.

"I think I've said all along that I should like to grow something. I have a fancy that I should be a poor sort of farmer, for reasons connected with the slaughter of animals which would doubtless appear weak and foolish to you (and I must say this lamb is excellent) so I can only conclude that I had best be a market gardener."

"Don't be so absurd!" persisted his mother, stamping a toe under the table.

"And why absurd, pray?"

"How can you be a market gardener?"

"With a few seeds and some soil," explained Leo.

"Don't be rude. You know what your father means. Of course you must enter a profession of some sort."

"Now let us examine this with coolness and acumen," invited Leo, helping himself to potatoes. "How can I with any happiness enter one of the professions when, as I have told you a thousand times, I hate the present order of civilisation, and perceive very clearly that all the professions are engaged in bolstering it up. You

see : strange—nay, incredible—as it may seem, I have
been speaking simple truth when I have said that I
want to spend my life breaking it down, not shoring
it up."

" *You* break it down ! " scoffed his mother.

" Yea, even I," said Leo, unabashed. " So much is
granted, is it ? Good. Then consider. The Army
and the Navy both fight for the present system ; the
Law punishes for it ; and the stockbrokers, if present
company will pardon the expression, batten on it.
Like carrion flies on a rotten carcase—but let us not be
rude. Have some gravy, mum ? The Church might
have been possible, because it ought to be in conflict
with such an enormity, even if it isn't, but, most
unfortunately, I can't believe—— "

" When you can pass your exams," said his father,
" it will be time to say whether you believe or not."

" Really ? " inquired Leo, as if interested in this new
point of view. " But what has passing exams got to
do with believing ? "

" Better men than you have believed," said his mother.

" And cleverer women than you have disbelieved,"
retorted her son.

" Pshaw ! " puffed Rose.

" Don't talk to your mother like that," said Abbott.

" But why ? "

" Because it's rude."

" But I suppose there *have* been clever women ? "
asked Leo, innocently.

" That's not the point."

" Pardon me, but it's exactly the point. I am very
willing to admit that there have been better men than I
and you, and she—— "

" Your mother's grown up, and you are still a boy."

Leo picked up this point with a genuine enthusiasm. " Now that's a most interesting point. Wait. Let's argue this. This interests me frightfully. Because is it true, in any real sense ? What I mean is : it seems to me that you supporters of the present system aren't in sight of growing up. Your whole philosophy is a child's philosophy. It's a philosophy of grab for the largest helping—which is childish, surely ? An adult gives ; he doesn't snatch. He—er—helps others on ; he doesn't shoulder and shove. Far be it from me to suggest that the most successful business man is always the biggest rogue, but I do suggest that he is often the biggest kid. He hasn't grown out of the philosophy of the largest helping. I haven't myself yet, but I'm going to try to. And, honestly, I can't see that Mum has ever grown up enough to wish to. She's hardly adolescent."

This to a woman who had been among the most arrogant and positive of her kind !

" The way you air your views ! " she sneered—helpless.

" But what else is the precise object of talk ? " asked Leo ingenuously, as one who seeks information. " Really, mum, I'm not clear. Would you have me air some one else's ? "

" I would have you realise that you're too young to talk about not believing."

" As a matter of fact, it is a great sorrow to me that I can't believe. I shouldn't at all mind being a parson and trying to convince people of the unchristian character of our present civilisation, but as I can't, and as I see that the poor victims must at least be fed— " Leo was back in the grand manner—" I feel that I shall do least violence to my conscience if I produced vegetables for them to eat, and perhaps flowers to bring a little beauty into their sordid and dishonoured lives—all of which seems to point to the occupation of a market gardener; or, at least of a florist's assistant."

" What is your quarrel with our present civilisation ? " asked Abbott.

" I have submitted one point. I have suggested that it tends to put a premium on every mean and grasping motive in human nature, and to discourage all the decent ones. It's a tribute to human nature, and to the church too, for that matter, that the decent ones survive in spite of it. Now take another point. Look at the very spot where we are now. Once it grew potatoes; now it grows a house like this."

" What's wrong with this house ? "

" Nearly everything that it stands for : you and me and mum——"

" Oh," laughed Abbott, as if about to score a good point. " And are we then worse than potatoes ? "

The point did not perturb Leo.

" Less natural," said he, cheerfully. " Less healthy; less *real*, I should say. Yes, certainly less healthy. And, mark you, I am including myself in this indictment. I'll trouble you for the salt."

Such conversations as these were duly rehearsed to the Coventrys; and Old Mrs. Coventry, when told this last remark about the potatoes, did stare in some alarm at Rose and wonder if, after all, the boy wasn't really sane. A few months later, when he had passed his seventeenth birthday, Rose came with the news that he was leaving school and going into his father's office.

" Well now ! Isn't that good news ? " said Old Mrs.

Coventry. " But I wonder, after all that talk, that he consented to work with his father."

" So do I sometimes," agreed Rose.

And Cynthia, hearing, wondered too. She did not see much of him now. He never came to parish parties or to church services ; but on one or two mornings she saw him on the platform of Norman's End, a long, lanky youth, in a silk hat and short black coat, carrying a black bag to his father's office in the city. If he noticed her, he grinned significantly, but said nothing.

II

Tom Coventry, we have observed, was not a man to give much heed to a change of fashion. Whether this fashion was the habit of his brothers or the habit of the streets he passed it by. Only the greater changes impinged upon his mind. He knew, of course, that, whereas last year he travelled home beneath the floor of London in a steam train, sitting in a small, smoky compartment with eight or ten other men, he now travelled in an electric train, sitting with his back to the windows and the tunnels, in a long corridor of a coach filled with men and girls—or, as was far more likely, strap-hanging from its roof, for no man was quicker to offer his seat to a lady, or to taste a sweeter relish in that chivalry. He knew that the Twopenny Tube was now running from the Bank to Shepherd's Bush, because its long, cylindrical tunnel had so often been his happy road to Evelyn. He had noticed that the new horseless carriages had changed their pattern and become motor-cars, and that they were now so frequent on the roads as to lift his head no more. He had read a good deal in his paper about M. Santos Dumont and his flying machines, and was ready to argue with those who doubted whether these contraptions would ever be much more than death-traps. He had a great faith in the future of flying.

But he had not related these big, central changes with

such small things as the conversion of houses in Macartney Road into maisonettes, or the building on the last of the wastegrounds of houses much smaller than any the neighbourhood had yet seen. On the whole Norman's End appeared to him much as it had always appeared. Glastonbury Road looked quite as prosperous and respectable as yesterday, and so did Conyers Road down which he walked to the station each day. And, had he gone down Macartney Road, I doubt if he would have noticed much, since he always devoted these walks to thought. His eyes would not have taken in that there were now two bells, or even three, at the sides of the front doors; that the curtains in the first-floor windows had no family connexion with those in the second floor; or that maids very seldom appeared on the step to shake a mat and glance after him as he passed. And as he had never in all the past years noticed how white were the hearthstoned steps, so now he would not have noticed that they were dimmed with many feet. Not for him to look down into the areas and see that it was seldom a plump cook who came to the kitchen door, but usually a young housewife with her head tied up in a handkerchief. This indeed would have shaken him, that the mistresses of the houses should greet the tradesmen at their own area doors. While dimly conscious of boys setting off with their books to Trinity, he would not have perceived that they were rougher lads than the Ingrams and the Ellisons of eight or nine years before. One other thing might have caught his glance and shocked it: a couple of Bluecoat boys in their yellow stockings playing with the Trinitarians, because, excellent though the Bluecoat school was, it was none the less a charity foundation. He had heard his mother and his wife bewail that there were now no old generals and admirals to be sidesmen at St. Alban's, but, as he gave only half a ear to anything they said, or, if by chance he gave two ears, was predisposed to think it silly, their little alarms didn't weigh on him heavily. He walked to his station through a Norman's End that was dead.

Not so the ladies. They had the opportunity to see much more than he, and the ability, and the desire. They *did* notice curtains and clothes and children and cooks, and they were of one voice at the At Homes, that the neighbourhood was changing for the worse. Right about the change, it is doubtful whether an Olympian observer, valuing differently from them, would have judged them right about the " worse." The neighbourhood was passing into the possession of a salaried class with incomes nearer three hundred than seven hundred —that was all. The Olympian would probably have found these people no worse than their predecessors— indeed, a few points better, since they were a few points nearer the realities of life. But the Norman's End of the Coventrys' day measured its health only by the standard social thermometer, and it felt sadly that it was getting worse. And one of the Cynthias—the Cynthia who, when O'Kelvie fulminated against snobbery, used to listen with wide, doubting eyes and answer, " Yes, my *brain* agrees with all you say, but I don't really *feel* like that ; I feel a born snob at the bottom. I know I should be ghastly upset if I woke up and found I was a baker's daughter " ;—this Cynthia, I say, was quite sure that it was getting worse.

Change. These ladies at 22 Glastonbury Road had another change to notice and discuss. A change in their man, Tom. In the last few months he had become very gentle : all had noticed it. He was, if anything, more inattentive at meals, sitting for long periods with far-away eyes and a falling jaw, as if anxiety sat heavy in his head ; but, when their questions disturbed him from such a reverie, he gave them eyes what were obviously trying to be kind, and words that were gentle. He hardly ever lost his temper with them now, nor spoke harshly. And sometimes he seemed to be going out of his way to do them little kindnesses. He kissed Cynthia very affectionately, and sometimes released his hold of her slowly, as if he would fain have held her longer.

Aye, but Tom Coventry was more worried than he had ever been. He was beaten down by worry. And in some natures, especially those that have been given a strong moral bias in youth, pain is a great creator of goodness—or of the desire for goodness. Follow Tom Coventry to-night, as he leaves the most of his dinner uneaten and walks on tired feet to his room. It is the very eve of disaster. He shuts his door, and there is little difference between your dog slinking to a corner of the garden to hide his wounds, and remember happier days, and Tom Coventry shutting his door on himself and staring out of the window at an unseen road.

Why, *why*, did he do it, he asks. He did it that he might prove himself courageous, adventurous, and free. He did it because he wanted to give Cynthia all, and Evelyn all, and his mother all. And it had failed. Failed with a roar and a crash, like the crash of a falling home. Perhaps he had never been the man to make a success of this sort of thing. Good at routine business, he had no cunning for quick, subtle gambling like this.

An old story: an initial success in which he had cleared three hundred pounds; great encouragement and excitement, and a risking of all this for larger gains; the loss of it all and more, and then desperate plunging to retrieve the position; further desperation and a vow that, if only he could just get back to the point from which he started he would leave such practices alone for ever; a borrowing from money-lenders on promissory notes alone at twenty per cent. interest—though the good routine business man in him shouted that this was the beginning of disaster—a passionate plunging with this new money—a risking of all on one last bid—and losing. What was his position now? He owed nearly fifteen hundred pounds; and he had nothing in the world but his salary of seven hundred pounds and his furniture, and there was even a bill of sale on his furniture. And there was no hope of raising more. He was done with plunging.

What then? Through silent days and tossing nights he had asked this question; and to-night he was determined to come to a final decision. If nothing went wrong he had ten more years at full salary and a pension after that. There was nothing for it but to resign himself to pay off capital and back-breaking interest during that period. He calculated that it would involve him in annual payments of something like three hundred and eighty pounds. Out of an income of seven hundred. It was staggering—but what else? Go bankrupt?

"No, I will not do that," he said, and found in these words his only happiness to-night. "I will shoulder my burden." He thought vaguely of

Sir Walter Scott. " Yes, I pay my twenty shillings in the pound, even to the Shylocks. My word is my bond ; and no man living shall call me bankrupt."

Let us not be too cynical and remark that this most honourable decision was reinforced by the knowledge that bankruptcy must jeopardise his present employment and his pension too. He truly wanted to be good ; so let us rather be glad that circumstance strengthened his arm.

He must resign himself to living on some three hundred a year. And perhaps Cynthia, now nearly eighteen, would earn a little. It was deep humiliation, but it was not starvation. And Evelyn ? Ah, Evelyn. Mrs. du Pré is routed at last : all his old nature is rising to government, and the fine old superstitions are re-conquering the land that is Tom Coventry's mind. He can only believe that God has punished him for his sin. " Because thou hast done evil in the sight of the Lord "—he feels rather like King David, and is sorrow-fully happy in feeling so, as he bows his head for the whipping.

He must give Evelyn up. The best part of him has known all along that he was sinning, and now he wants to be good again, and at peace. To rest ! To rest ! Perhaps he could see her sometimes. . . . No, the expense would be too great, and in his humility he cannot believe that Evelyn will take him without gifts. And to spend any more on Evelyn would not be fair to Cynthia, whom he has wronged enough. He will do the Big Thing. He will give Evelyn up altogether, and get his emotional happiness from Cynthia's love, and find other interests in his chair and his room and his books. He wants with all his heart to-night to do something really good, and he will do it. Tom thinks that he is making a noble resolve: we may see that the battle is only in part a battle between good and evil; for the rest it is a battle between his desire for Life and Romance and his desire for Comfort and Security; and, since Tom is over fifty and badly knocked about, Comfort and Security are winning. But, on the whole, I am glad there is no one in this room to point this out to him and deprive him of his few bleak satisfactions to-night. " No, I have done with Life," says he. He is very sad about it, and does not know that he is also relieved.

Oh Evelyn, Evelyn. To-morrow he will see her and tell her all. And now he throws himself into his chair, bringing his fingers together and preparing the words in which he will tell her. He gets some solace from the beauty of his words. " You have been the sweetest thing in my life. Always remember that. . . . But it wouldn't be fair to go on with it any longer. We have expected this, haven't we ? You are young, and must get free of me. It is best in every way, Evelyn."

And he will find her some good employment with glorious recommendations, and give her fifty pounds for herself—yes, fifty: one may as well be sold for a sheep as a lamb. The thought of putting fifty pounds in her hand to-morrow is so agreeable that he has soon increased it to a hundred. Oh, yes, yes ! What is a hundred when he already owes so much ? " And she was good to me. . . ." In the thought of putting a hundred pounds in Evelyn's hand, he is almost happy again.

Twenty hours pass. It is now six o'clock of the next evening, and Tom Coventry is coming along Conyers

Road, home.   But in that lapse of time he has crossed a bridge from one life to another.   He has said his good-bye to Evelyn, and watched her figure for the last time, as it went up a street and turned a corner. And when there was no more of her to see, he turned the opposite way, and, a little dazed, walked, as a mechanical doll might walk, to his station.   In the train he sat humpily, neither reading his journal nor looking through the window, his top hat pushed back an inch, his rolled umbrella between his knees, and his gloved hands on its knob.   If the straphangers walked over his toes and turned to apologise, he forgave them with a kind smile, as if, really, he had hardly noticed their transit.   His thoughts so drugged him that he only woke with a start to find himself at Norman's End ; and he had to tumble very quickly from the train.   His feet found their usual tracks ; and here he is coming along Conyers Road, home.

We have seen him coming home at eventide before, when his head was full of dramas known only to himself and to God—a God vaguely thought of as somewhere above the pale sky that arched over Norman's End. We see him again to-night ; he is sad—genuinely sad— but perhaps not as heartbroken as he thinks ; he is humbled, but not without pride that he is a man who has shouldered his burden.

This is an adventurer that we are seeing—an adventurer returning from his enterprise.   His enterprise was not unsuccessful at the first ; but, as he sees, he is not the sort to sustain a success, and it has ended in defeat.   He accepts the fact that he is not by nature an adventurer, and resolves that he will adventure no more.   Farewell, Mrs. du Pré.

Sad and wounded, he has but one thought now, to rest in a chair that he knows and among people who are knit into the texture of his life.   Yesterday my dog ran out of my house to enjoy life, but a passing boot crushed his foot; and he limped home, holding the injured member from the ground, and scratched on the familiar front door, behind which, as nowhere else, there were comfort, warmth, and the solicitude of friends.   Tom Coventry, with a hand that shakes, takes a latch-key from a trouser pocket and scratches it into the lock of his home.

III

" WHAT can it be ? " asked Old Mrs. Coventry, looking
up from her sewing and throwing a glance over her
spectacles at Cynthia. " Has something happened, do
you suppose ? "

" Looks like it," murmured Cynthia into her book.

And Old Mrs. Coventry lifted her ear towards the
first landing and the drawing-room. Her eyes went
with the ear, and she listened intently.

They were sitting in the dining-room, the old lady
upright in a hard chair, and Cynthia lolling sideways
in a soft chair, with a book in one hand and an ankle
in the other. Fifteen minutes earlier Hilda had been
with them, sitting at the table and turning the wheel
of her sewing machine, but Tom Coventry, immediately
on his arrival from town, had opened the room door
and said, " Hilda, I want to speak to you," and without
another word trod slowly up the stairs to a drawing-
room cold and empty. Hilda, somewhat fluttered, had
begun, " What ? . . . Yes ? . . . What ? . . ." but he
was already gone, so she was obliged to adjust her
machine for a halt, and follow up the stairs after him,
The drawing-room door had then closed sharply.

And that was more than a quarter of an hour ago.
Old Mrs. Coventry by now was restless on her chair,
and at every sound upstairs lifted her ear. Sometimes
it would seem as if Tom's voice were raised, and then

she lowered her work to listen.   Sometimes it was clear that he was tramping about the room, and she did not allow her sewing to interfere with her attention to this fact.   Once a door opened and shut, and straightway she laid her work in her lap and fixed her glance on their own door.   But no one opened it, and she, in the emptiness of time, picked up her sewing again. Cynthia, as the minutes passed, became quite as excited as her grandmother, but, having something of her father's pride in being free from such weakness, she hid the lively action of her heart behind a pretence of reading her book or fiddling with the heel of her shoe.

"I'm afraid something's happened," said Old Mrs. Coventry.

"I haven't a doubt of it," agreed Cynthia, with an unconcern worthy of her father.

"Well, well! Don't take it like that! It may be something serious. Tut, tut! you grow more like your father every day. I'm *sure* something's happened."

"So'm I."

And for a minute they remained in the same positions.

"Should I go and see?" inquired Old Mrs. Coventry, and this time she dropped the work with some finality. A word of encouragement, and she would have gone.

"Oh, give 'em a little longer."

"Well . . ." Unencouraged, Old Mrs. Coventry picked up her work again.

Presently a door upstairs opened, and both Tom and Hilda's voices could be heard. Old Mrs. Coventry, the work of her fingers suspended, remained still as marble. Cynthia looked up. The voices stopped, and they heard the steps of Hilda coming down the stairs —slow, broken steps. In the dining-room it was not alone the old pairs of eyes that stared at the door, but the young pair too.

Hilda entered, sobbing; and at once her mother-in-law rose and went to her.

"What is it, my dear? Don't cry. What has happened?" And she took her hand to pat it. "Tell us what has happened. No, don't cry."

But the more she was told not to cry, the more Hilda, who had dropped her body on to her chair and her head on to the table, cried and cried.

"What is it?" asked her mother-in-law; and then, her patience giving out, "Dear, dear! What *is* it, what *is* it? How can we help if you don't tell us what it is?"

"Yes, what is it, mummy?" asked Cynthia, more tenderly.

"He's ruined," said Hilda.

"*What?*" cried Old Mrs. Coventry; and her eyes glared at Hilda's dropped head.

"*Ruined?*" whispered Cynthia, who had risen; for there was a dignity in the word, to be greeted standing.

"Oh, speak, can't you?" commanded the impatient old lady.

"He's ruined us all," explained Hilda, blowing her nose in preparation for speech.

"Ruined us?" echoed the old lady; and Cynthia, watching, observed a change in her expression. That facile sympathy which she had always on tap for distress that she was not asked to bear had given place to alarm and indignation, now that the distress was likely to be her own. "How do you mean?"

"He's lost nearly everything, and we're going to be very poor."

"Lost *what*? Do speak up! He hasn't lost his employment, has he?"

"No, but . . ." and Hilda tried to explain. Out of her volubility these words stood high and clear enough: "Gambling. . . . Stock Exchange. . . . Overwhelming debts. . . ."

"Gambling!" At the word the old lady's beady eyes, which had been bright with curiosity, lit up with a moment's triumph. "I knew it! I knew it! I told you so! and he's lost everything! Oh, he ought to be ashamed."

"It's not as bad as that," bewailed Hilda.

"How bad is it?" demanded the inquisitor, standing at her elbow like a little black figure of doom. "For pity's sake, let us know."

"He says we shall have only about three hundred a year to live on, and that we shall have to go right away from here."

As she said this, Cynthia swung her eyes on her mother. Go away from here? Go far away, and never have a chance of seeing *him* sometimes. Oh no . . . no. . . .

"Go away? Why go away?" inquired the old lady. "I never heard such nonsense. We could move into a small flat. We can't go away. All my friends are here, and yours too. He can't uproot us like this."

"He says that it may be stupid, but he doesn't want to be seen here after he has failed."

These simple words went like an arrow to Cynthia's heart. Her lips said nothing, but her pity gasped "Oh!" Through these words, as through a door, she ran straight into the fullness of her father's humiliation; and from that moment she was on his side. Where there is pain, let sympathy rush in, and criticism wait in an anteroom.   Now she was ready to go with him anywhere.

The words didn't seem to affect her grandmother at all in this way.   " Nonsense ! He can't uproot us all," she repeated, as if pleased with the phrase.   " Just for the sake of his pride ! I'm sure *I* can't go making new friends."

" Nor I," wept Hilda.

" No, of course not ! Of course not ! I'm too old to make new friends."

As if she couldn't make new friends (or new gossips) everywhere ! thought Cynthia.   Watching the withered lips as they went forward and back, she muttered to herself, " Old Beast ! " for, if she had a capacity for quick loves, she had also a capacity for sudden and satisfying hates.   She was hating her grandmother now. She hated her ever-moving lips, her hard little eyes, her sharp chin, and the straight parting in her black hair. She hated her horny little hands in their mittens, and her marching glacé frock.   Indignation was the beginning of the fire, but when one is young, indignation flames quickly into hate.   With the indignation went also that sense of superiority to the offender which makes indignation such an exhilarating experience.

" He says we must go," repeated the helpless Hilda. " He says that if we consider him, we shall be willing to go."

" And why are we to consider only him ? " demanded Old Mrs. Coventry.   " Men are the most selfish creatures in the world.   I've not patience with him.   All my friends and interests are here.   And so are yours.   And Cynthia's too—" for the politic old lady always tried to flatter every one of her listeners on to her side—" Cynthia

T

has her little friends here. Has he no thought for anyone but himself? He's the most selfish man alive."

" *He isn't !* " cried Cynthia.

" What ! " Her grandmother swung round to her sharply, and was obviously driven off her stride by this unexpected and ungrateful desertion to the enemy.

" He isn't selfish like that," protested Cynthia lamely, and cursing the luck which had endowed her with the power to hate but not with a gift of speech that would do justice to it. " He isn't selfish like that."

" He's being very selfish indeed," declared her grandmother, on the principle that, with a child, if one has no clear argument in one's head, one can always fall back on the dignity of plain affirmation. " And why should he mind living in a small way any more than we should ? We shall have to suffer the humiliation as well as he. In what way is it worse for him than for us ? "

Cynthia sighed " Oh dear ! " and turned away in despair. Why couldn't they *see ?* Why couldn't they see that, if all must bear the poverty, her father alone must bear the shame. Oh, why couldn't anybody ever see anything ?

Old Mrs. Coventry turned to continue the argument with Hilda where the path was easier and without thorns. " But why this complete change because of a few debts ? Can't he go bankrupt or something ? "

" He says he won't do that."

" Well, he should do. He's such a quixotic fool in these matters. Everyone else goes bankrupt, I've always understood ; and then they start again, all square."

" He says he'll never do that."

" Well, then, why can't someone lend him the money ?

And he could pay back fifty of it now and then." Old
Mrs. Coventry's ideas of finance were hazy indeed.
Roughly we may say that they consisted in getting
something for nothing, which is astonishing finance.
" He lent some money to that odious friend of his—
that Johnson man. Two hundred, wasn't it ? "

" He says he has nothing to borrow on."

" Then let him get back that two hundred pounds.
That'll be something, at any rate."

" He says it's useless to try. The man can never pay,
and he won't worry him."

" Idiocy ! I never heard of such idiocy ! " She began
to storm up and down. " The man must be made to
pay. Tom has a duty to us as well as to a mere friend.
I'm sure I sacrificed enough for him."

" The man can't pay if he can't," suggested Cynthia.

" Then let Tom set to and make some. Other men
do ? "

" But how is he to make it, granny ? "

" I don't know. How do other men do it ? They
buy shares and sell them at a profit. Major Lempriére
made several hundreds like that. It only wants a little
brains."

" But isn't that the very gambling of which you said
he ought to be ashamed ? "

" What ? " demanded Old Mrs. Coventry, to gain
time. She felt that her attack was being disorganised,
as if her own battalions were shooting at her rear.

Cynthia, with eyebrows raised innocently, repeated her
simple question.

" I don't know what you're talking about," said Old
Mrs. Coventry, finding this best way out.

But Cynthia followed out after her. " I'm trying to

say that either it's right to gamble and take risks, or it isn't. I only want you to be fair to Daddy, who, after all——"

She managed no more, for her grandmother, scenting defeat, brought up all the additional battalions that her age gave her, and various other irrelevant units, and overran the impudent girl: an excellent method this, and one that she often employed. "I don't want to be talked to. It's not right of you to speak to me like that. Anyone would think that it was I who had lost all your money for you. Do you *want* to be turned out of your home like this?"

"Oh, but why don't you speak some sense?" Cynthia almost screamed. "Don't you see that you're not condemning him for gambling, but for being unlucky and losing. If he'd won, you'd be all over him. It's not fair. It's a beastly shame."

"I am not listening," said the old lady, tossing her head and turning towards Hilda, as to an ally. She folded her mittened hands in righteousness, and sat down—not the first old admiral to discontinue a battle and announce to everybody that it was no defeat.

But Cynthia was on fire. Her cheeks flared, and her eyes too; and she spluttered forth her indignation.

"Oh, it makes me so sick," she cried, hating the words because they filled so poorly the ideas that leapt and jostled in her head. "Granny goes to church and pretends to believe in charity and forgiveness and all that, and it means nothing at all really. It doesn't make a ha'porth of difference to anything she does. When one's own people are down, surely it's time to be decent to them, not to—not to——"

"I am not listening," the old lady announced again.

"Of course you're not!" retorted Cynthia. "It's very wise of you not to, because what I'm saying cuts too near the bone, doesn't it? You don't want to listen. I think you're being cruel and caddish. You pretend you don't believe in gambling but you'd give your soul if Daddy'd done it and made a lot of money for you. You pretend you don't believe in dishonesty, but you'd much rather he went bankrupt and let his creditors down than that you had to do without your little bits of comfort. I think he's the only one of you with decency at all."

"I am not listening," repeated the old lady, nodding furiously over her folded hands. "This is what one expects from children to whom one's given up everything."

"Then *don't* listen!" screamed Cynthia. "And I don't believe you've ever given up anything for anybody in your life. If you ever did, you must have got out of the habit very quickly, because I've never noticed you doing it, and I've lived with you for eighteen years."

"Cynthia!" cried her mother, shocked.

"Don't mind her, Hilda," soothed Old Mrs. Coventry, who, we must allow, had the monopoly of dignity in this distressing scene. "The child is beside herself."

"Cynthia, you're not to talk to your grandmother like that," protested Hilda.

"Why not? She isn't listening?" And Cynthia lifted her brows and gave her mother the celebrated look of amazement that anyone should correct her when she was so obviously blameless. "She isn't listening, so I can say what I happen to think. And I happen to think all that—and a whole lot more. And now I'm going to see Daddy." And she flung out of the room, showing no more originality than to bang the door just as loudly as it would bang.

In a sense the abuse of Tom Coventry was the best thing that could have happened to him. It drove his daughter up the stairs to the drawing room, two steps at a time. At the door, however, she hesitated. It was shut, and so were the other doors on this landing, and, since the architect of Glastonbury Road had provided little light for this landing except what the rooms could cast out, it was very dark. The shut door and the darkness unnerved her. What was she to say to her father? " I don't want to be sloppy. Oh, why is one so perfectly incapable of saying all-overish things to one's own people? " She had an ideal picture of herself flinging her arms round her father's neck, but she recoiled from such an exhibition now. Come back, indignation; come back, pity; and give her power to pass through this door. What was it her mother had said that so quickened her pity? " He says he doesn't want to be seen here after he has failed." Oh poor Daddy! She opened the door and went in.

He was standing with a note-book and pencil in his hands, quite obviously engaged on arithmetic; and the sight of him thus brought all the pity in a mist to her eyes. She hurried forward and touched his arm, saying, " Oh my dear, I'm so sorry."

Her father's upper teeth shot over his lower lip and held it. When the lips parted, he only smiled sadly, patted her fingers, and murmured, " That's all right, Cynthia; that's all right."

" And you're not to worry," proclaimed Cynthia. " I don't see anything to worry about. I mean, there's me, isn't there. I'm going to earn a lot." And she rose on her toes and kissed his cheek. It was not the embrace she had imagined, being little more than a " peck " ; but it was a good deal to Tom Coventry.

" It's you I've been thinking about more than anyone else," he said. " I don't much mind how I live, but I want you to have every chance."

" Me ! " exclaimed Cynthia, pretending surprise. " Oh, don't mind about me. I'm filling fast with ideas. In fact, I think it's all rather exciting. And, Daddy "— here she nervously put a finger on his watch-chain and looked up into his face—" I understand so amazingly how you want to go from here. I vote we go."

Tom looked at her with gratitude, but he did not know what these words had cost her. The thought of leaving Norman's End was as the thought of death to Cynthia, but she remembered " beauty of action," and was eager for self-sacrifice. " And I think you're so absolutely right about everything else," she added. " About the debts and all."

" Do you ? " Tom drew her against him and kissed her forehead. " Bless you, my dear."

" Yes, well . . ." said she brightly, when freed from the embrace. " Thank you. And now do let's sit down and talk it all over. I'm really rather thrilled. . . . All right, stand if you want to." But *she* chose the arm of the sofa. " It'll be such fun looking for a house somewhere and thinking how we'll furnish it. And we shall be quite well off in it, I'm sure. We don't want a maid, I mean. If three hulking women can't do the work of the house, and earn some money too, they ought to be suppressed. I shall do quite a lot of work when I come back from the city. And I'll give you my screw every Friday night—at least, *practically* all of it, because I may keep back just enough to buy some sweets sometimes.   Oh, where's it to be, Daddy ? "

" No," said her father suddenly, after thrice measuring the carpet with his stride.   " No."   For, if Cynthia was driving fast towards self-sacrifice, Tom Coventry, as we have seen, could be moved that way too.   " I don't think we'll go from here.   Why should we run ?   Tell me frankly, Cynthia : what would *you* rather do ? "

She put her head to one side to look at this question. " Oh, if I were considering only myself—— "

He completed the sentence for her.   " You would rather stay in Norman's End."

" Yes, I suppose so."

" Then we're staying here."

" But, Daddy, will you really like it ?   I mean, what am I ?   Absolutely nothing, if you come to think of it ;   less than the dust beneath your chariot wheel. But oh !   it would be wonderful if we could."

" Yes, yes," he said with decision.   " I've quite changed my mind.   We shall stay here."

" *Cheers !* "

" Happy ? "

" Ra-*ther !*   Oh, everything'll be perfect.   Oh, I think I'm glad it's all happened.   It's an adventure, isn't it ? It's really rather bracing if you look at it like that.   I feel rather alive.   Something's happened at last. . . . I'm going out to-morrow morning to choose a new place.   Oh Daddy, you *are* a darling."

IV.

So the Coventrys moved into a maisonette in Macartney Road, and went down with the neighbourhood. It was the upper half of one of the old stucco mansions. The worst part of it, thought Cynthia, was the staircase leading to its front door. This was a No-Man's-Land belonging neither to themselves nor to the people in the lower half of the house. Once it had been a carpeted staircase, with the children of the house romping up and down it, or with well-mannered guests coming up to the At Homes, but now it was a steep shaft, boxed in with matchboard and ruled by the will of the landlord, who cared little if its linoleum was worn or its dado chipped and blistered. A dark, hateful shaft! She always ran up it quickly; and that part of her which was born of Norman's End and not of O'Kelvie's studio thought with dislike that this must be the first view her friends would get of her new home, before they passed into the large and cheerful living room with all its massive proofs of yesterday's gentility. This was a spacious chamber, having been the drawing room in the large days of the house; though to see on one and the same carpet the heavy dining room sideboard and table and the light drawing room knick-knacks from Glastonbury Road was a little shame-making (an excellent word of to-day which I here do my best to preserve). On the same floor was a kitchen-scullery; on the floor above two bedrooms of which her parents had one and her grandmother the other; and under the roof were two smaller rooms, of which Cynthia enjoyed the front one.

At first she feared that Granny was going to demand this room because the early sun peeped in at one angle and the evening sun at the other, and all day long there was the view up and down the length of Macartney Road; and the old lady did, in fact, look long and earnestly at the room; but the back room on the floor below was larger; it was higher; it was reached by fewer stairs; it had a better fireplace; it was over the kitchen and therefore warm; it was nearer the living room and the bustle of life; so she sacrificed herself, resting a kind finger on Cynthia's elbow and saying, "No. Give the bright, sunny room to the young thing. I am old and do not need the sunlight as much as she."

And she found her way down the stairs again, leaving Cynthia to rejoice.

And was Cynthia ever very much happier than while she was furnishing, painting, and decorating her room? You will forgive her that she attempted an "old-world effect," and even used that detestable phrase. She painted all the woodwork a dark brown to look like old oak; she hung everything with flowered cretonne; she enamelled her chairs black and found a settle to go by the fire-place (which made that toy grate look exceedingly small); and, in fine, any "old-world" tea room that you will visit on the King's highway to-morrow is of the family of Cynthia Coventry's bedroom in Macartney Road.

Her strictures on her grandmother, which were frequent and virulent just now, were, I submit, unjust. The old lady was really admirable at the time of the move. She bore no malice against the child for her extraordinary rudeness that night and forgave her the next morning. Old Mrs. Coventry always forgave anyone she had to live with, because it was so much more comfortable to do so. Just as she puffed up a cushion behind her shoulders to make her seat more comfortable, so she forgave Hilda and Cynthia after a first-class row, even flattering them a little and being very bright and cheerful. Indeed I am not sure that "forgive" is the word, because she enjoyed an occasional row, and, whether she perceived this or not, was grateful to Hilda and Cynthia when they gratified this need. And as she puffed up the cushions for her comfort, and smoothed out the quarrels with a velvet palm for the same primary end, so now she set about making the new scale of living as comfortable a condition as possible for an old woman who had given up everything for her son. She was immensely optimistic. Three hundred a year to live on? Well, that wasn't so bad! And now they wouldn't have to pay that wicked income tax of a shilling in the pound. Scandalous, that imposition! And surely, after all the years Tom had served the office, the Trustees would raise his salary when they heard he'd lost so much money on the Stock Exchange. And Cynthia could be a governess and meet some rich young man who would marry her, with her good looks and all. And Tom would pretty soon give up that nonsensical idea of paying his debts. Other men found a way out, and he must do the same. Had their income been reduced to fifty pounds a year, Old Mrs. Coventry would have been just as happy and confident. She had need to be. As she adjusted the cushions, so she adjusted the future, with the happy result that the present was comfortable, and she could rest upon it at ease. Wise old lady. Let us all do likewise.

Such optimism is rarely justified in detail, maybe, but what then ? Each failure provides you with an excellent excuse for blaming this person or that to your neighbours, in pleasant gossip along the pavement, or over the tea-cups in the drawing-room. The Trustees showed no sign of raising Tom's salary because he had lost money on the Stock Exchange ; and Old Mrs. Coventry spoke her mind about them to Mrs. Damien and Mrs. Ingram. Cynthia flatly refused to become a governess, and went off to her father's office in Westminster, where she earned only twenty-five shillings a week and never met a man of her own class except a lot of old ecclesiastical trustees who were married already ; and Old Mrs. Coventry explained that she didn't hold at all with this headstrong move. Not at all. In her day it wasn't respectable for a lady's child to be anything but a governess or a nurse, and even now she didn't believe that any but common girls consented to be clerks in the city. And she had said from the first that, if the child was bent upon this move, it was a mistake to go into her father's office, because Tom, with his silly quixotism, would refuse to pay his daughter a penny more than he gave to other typists, whereas, in another office, some employer might have taken a fancy to her—so pretty as she could look sometimes—and have given her a generous salary. Tom was so absurd. Why shouldn't he stand by his own family ? If *she* were employing her own daughter and had *carte blanche* with the money, *she* would ! Don't tell her the Trustees would even notice if he had given her two pounds a week ! She didn't believe it.

Between us all, Old Mrs. Coventry herself was making a little petty cash. In truth, I think that, of the four persons in this household, she was the best money-maker of them all. Not that she got together even as much as Cynthia, but her methods had genius, and all the freedom of genius. The little black mare was the best grazer in the meadow. The others were hobbled : Tom by his decency, Hilda by her dullness, and Cynthia by her pride ; but there was never a rope of any kind about the ankles of the little black mare. Once settled down in her room on the second floor, and once convinced that Tom wasn't going to give her that allowance any more, she sat in her seat by the window, while a great deal of scheming went on beneath the parting in her hair. And as the months went by, though Tom was too pre-occupied to notice it, and Hilda too blind, Cynthia remarked that her grandmother had plenty of money in her purse to buy herself any trifle that she fancied. To be sure, she seemed better off and freer with her money (so it was spent on herself) than in the old Glastonbury Road days.

How was it done ? The girl's eyes saw how it was done, and her lips curled with anger, and her nostrils dilated with contempt. We are older and need not be so intolerant. We can watch with pleasure as Old Mrs. Coventry walks up Macartney Road arm in arm with one of her friends, nodding her little black head and pouring out the tale of her woes and her indigence. She removes her arm from her sympathetic friend's that she may take a handkerchief from her bag and, lifting her veil, blow her nose and dab her eyes, after which she takes the lady's arm again. At Macartney Road they say that she has gone out on some mysterious visit, but

Cynthia knows that she is sitting in some prosperous drawing-room and hinting how sad and humiliating it is to have lost all at her age and to be obliged to ask a daughter-in-law—" no matter how good "—for every little thing she wants. She is playing the pathetic rôle with tact and skill, till all good people are secretly planning how they can send a little money to poor old Mrs. Coventry without hurting her feelings. Her feelings are not hurt ; she accepts these gifts with many tears at the fundamental goodness of men, and much patting of their generous hands. There are her debts at the milliner's and the dressmaker's—" one must wear *something*," she says, and no one denies it—and what assets she makes of these debts ! She confides to Mrs. Ingram and to Mrs. Ellison how the thought of them, and of the impossibility of ever paying them, is wearing her to a skeleton and preventing her from sleeping at night (though Cynthia has reason to know that she sleeps like a child for nine hours) and sooner or later one of these good Christian women begs her to accept the amount of the debt and to sleep again. She takes it, and declares with a snuffle that her faith in humanity has never stood so high. And now she has a little money in hand, because she has stated the amount of her liabilities in approximate or " round " numbers, while she was about it ; and sometimes more than one person has paid the same debt, which little inaccuracy doesn't vex Granny's conscience because she knows that their real desire was to be good to her.

Granny's principle is simple enough : that pride is an excellent possession if you have other possessions as well, but, if you lack them, why, it is to be exchanged at any time for gold and gifts. A sensible principle, surely.

If she doesn't come away with hope of money from these sympathetic drawing-rooms, she comes with the promise of gifts.   She will admire a cushion or a tablecloth, and say how much she wishes she could still afford things like that ; and the next morning the article comes round as a little offering from her friend.

Bravo, Old Mrs. Coventry !   In this way she collected cushions, pictures, an eider-down quilt, a rug, and even a comfortable bedroom sofa for her tired old back. These were the larger things. Omitting such perishable goods as crates of wine (because she was looking out of sorts), fruit, poultry, jellies, and currant cakes, we may mention that she collected such small affairs as writing blocks, ink-stands, old clothes, water-bottles, crucifixes, and devotional manuals for her bedside table. Nothing came amiss to her. Her skill was astonishing and deserved something better than her granddaughter's censure. It was genius, I contend, to take so much from these ladies and yet to make them like her all the more because they had been so good to her. She worked Mr. Guilder for a contribution at the beginning, but after that he was not very fruitful ; he was seeing as much as Cynthia saw, and his eyes were twinkling. From a Legal Society she obtained a pension on the score of her husband the judge—not a great one but an acceptable. Tom knew about this, because, in order to get it, he had been obliged to sign papers ; he did not know—for she was becoming very secretive these days—that she had also succeeded, by suppressing all information about this pension (in a word, by committing perjury) in getting a small annual grant from the Masons, the late judge having been a past-master of several lodges. When two years later

Mr. Lloyd George introduced his Old Age Pension scheme, she suppressed her loyal and ardent Conservatism and had a good look at it, to see what was in it for her, and she was fully prepared to apply for it, without mention made of the kindness of the Legal Society or the Masons. Splendid, splendid! Here was an old lady living in perfect comfort in a household with a minimum of eight pounds a week, and drawing a weekly ten shillings from one society and a five shillings from a second society, and casting about for a third. A guilty conscience? Not a trace of it: she went as regularly as ever to church. What had she done wrong? Was she not a judge's widow—*and* a mason's widow— and had she any money of her own? Wasn't it all Tom's and Cynthia's?

In yet another way she was better off than in her Glastonbury Road days. Having established the legend of her poverty, she need no longer give presents at Christmas that cost her anything. Instead she gave pretty little trifles worked by her own hand, bewailing, as she offered them, that she couldn't afford to give something more commensurate with her feelings. "It's only very small, I'm afraid, but my heart goes with it," she would say, and feel for her handkerchief again. She gave a great many of these pathetic little offerings, her experience being that a hair-tidy for the dressing table was quite likely to produce in response a half-dozen of port, or, better still, a cheque. So she sowed them widely and wisely, working on them throughout the year. And thus she was able to keep her money and satisfy her generous instincts, for which she was famous.

V

MRS. DAMIEN came often to the living room at Macartney Road. It was "so nice and close." Macartney Road running parallel with Conyers Road, she had but to swing round Wentworth Avenue and walk thirty yards down the pavement, and she was at Hilda's door. As a rule her hour of call was between three and four of a week-day; so it was a surprise this Sunday morning when Cynthia, drawn to her lofty window by the bell of St. Alban's and a cloudless sky, saw Rose Damien hurrying along the pavement. It was half-past ten, and normally Mrs. Damien should be preparing for church. But she didn't look in the least ready for church. She had neither veil, nor parasol, nor gloves; and her toque had obviously been pinned on as she ran. Her bosom heaved beneath the broad expanse of ruchings and tuckings. Her two hands lifted her long, fluted and frothing skirt out of the way of her scuttling toes, else they must have become involved in the folds, and she been thrown on her face. One could almost hear her sigh; and one knew that there was no common flurry within the summer draperies of Mrs. Damien. They disappeared from Cynthia's view, under the portico; and in a second the door bell rang.

Since the Coventrys had only a daily maid, who didn't come on Sundays, Cynthia had a good excuse for getting ahead of her mother and opening the door herself. She flew down the stairs, opened it, and exclaimed as if in surprise, " Mrs. Damien ? "

" Yes . . . Let me come in . . ." said Rose breathlessly.   " Let me come in."

" Yes, do come in," invited Cynthia, impotent in the face of an unexplained alarm.   She led the way up a few stairs to the living room, secretly thrilled that the still and sober Sunday should have come alive like this. " Mummy," she called up to the bedrooms, " here's Mrs. Damien."

" What ? " answered a voice up there, but no one heeded it.

" Yes, I'll come in for a minute," panted Mrs. Damien.

They went into the living room, and pretended not to see that the breakfast things were still on the table.   Or perhaps Mrs. Damien was in no condition to consider such things.

" Oh, sit down, won't you ? " begged Cynthia.

" No, I don't want to sit down.   I can't stay."

" Mummy," called Cynthia again.

But at that moment Hilda came in.   And two paces behind Hilda came Granny, her eyes fixed and keen, behind her spectacles.

" Oh my dear . . ." said Rose, hurrying forward to Hilda and accepting both her hands.   " Oh my dear . . ."

This conveying nothing more definite than distress, Hilda looked only alarmed ; but Old Mrs. Coventry, whose emotion was always interest rather than alarm, looked only curious—sharply, staringly curious.   Her eyes were two corkscrews boring into Rose's head. Cynthia, without knowing it, had run up her fingers to her mouth, in a gesture of her childhood.

"What is it? Has something happened?" asked Hilda.

"Yes," panted Rose. "Oh, I don't know why I'm tormented like this."

"But what is it?"

"He's disappeared again."

"Who?"

"Leo. He's run away."

"Where?"

This was just the sort of inept question that Hilda would ask.

"How should I know? But he's gone for good this time. Such a letter as he's written!"

"But I saw him only yesterday!" exclaimed Cynthia. "I saw him on the station, going to town."

"Yes, he was here yesterday," agreed Rose.

Old Mrs. Coventry, impatient with these exchanges which led nowhere, took the matter in hand. Gently she guided Rose to a chair, murmuring, "Come now; sit down and tell us all about it"; and Rose obeyed. How annoyed she would have been if told that this old lady was really a stronger character than herself, and the one most likely to shape events, when she, Hilda, and Mrs. Damien were in the same room! But it was so: Rose obeyed and fell into a chair; Hilda, something dazed, lowered herself slowly on to another; and Old Mrs. Coventry, pulling up the nearest of the small drawing-room chairs, sat deliberately on its edge and leaned towards Rose, that she might see and hear well. "Now?" she ordered.

And Rose told her story. Leo had gone as usual to town yesterday in his bowler hat and black coat. No one would have suspected anything. At the office he had worked quietly and well; and at midday, when Saturday's work was over, he had casually told his father that he was spending the afternoon with a friend and might not be home till late. Abbott had never given a second thought to this—why should he? Abbott and she had gone to bed about half-past ten, knowing the boy had his own latchkey. But this morning about breakfast time a letter had dropped on the mat, pushed through the door by some accomplice of his. Such a letter. He was never coming back, he said—but here Rose's mouth shook and twisted so that she could tell no more. "This is the letter," she concluded.

Hilda took it, and started reading it to herself; which didn't suit Old Mrs. Coventry at all. "Read it aloud," she ordered. "Read it aloud, Hilda, can't you?"

So Hilda read:

"*Dearest Mum and Dad, Don't be too upset when you get this. I want you to understand why I have left you, and why it would be futile to try to get me back. I am fond of you, but you must see that I am quite different from you both, and shall be much happier leading my own life away from you*——"

"Tch, tch!" muttered Old Mrs. Coventry. Hilda, after looking up at this noise, continued:

"*I have a hatred of Conyers Road that I can see is exaggerated and irrational, but there it is, all the same. It is something to do, I dare say, with unhappiness as a child. I just can't breathe its atmosphere. And if you will let me lead my own life, I feel we shall be able to love each other as never before*——"

"Come, come," said Old Mrs. Coventry, more hopefully. "That's nicely put. The boy may not be so bad, after all"; and, leaning forward, she touched the stricken mother on the knee and left her comforting hand there. "Go on, Hilda."

"I am awfully sorry if I have let Father down at the office, but I didn't see what else I could do. You see, by accepting Father's offer and going into his office for a year or so I was able to save the money I wanted, and I may say that I had chosen this course of action from the minute the police brought me back last time——"

Cynthia, listening, perceived that, honest and tender though Leo had tried to make the letter, he was still too young to be above "getting his own back" in these few lines. That setting of the police on him, and that sending of him back to school to "take his medicine," had left a wound never healed till the moment when he wrote these words.

"Please don't try to find me this time. I don't know what the law is, and whether it can force me to come back till I am 21, but it would be silly to make me do that, and quite futile in the end. I am perfectly determined to carve out my own life in my own way. If I find that you are going to leave me in peace, I will let you know where I am and what I am doing; though I must warn you that, with your ideas, my profession may come to you as something of a shock. But if my happiness is your happiness, you will have no need to worry about me. With more love perhaps than ever before, Your affectionate son, Leo."

Hilda had finished, and Mrs. Damien was weeping. Old Mrs. Coventry was also wiping her nose. "What are you going to do?" she asked, dropping the handkerchief to her lap.

"What can we do?" Mrs. Damien dabbed at her nostrils. "The boy is nearly nineteen. Abbott says he gives him up. Apparently he is quite safe; and he may tire of this nonsense."

"Where do you imagine he is?" asked Hilda.

"Not the faintest idea," said Rose, glorying in the completeness of her despair. "He saw to it that the letter was delivered by hand and bore no postmark. I don't like all that cunning."

"Could he have gone to sea?" suggested Old Mrs. Coventry, who had lately been reading, with deep interest, a boy's book where the hero ran away from school and signed on as a cabin boy.

"I can't imagine him at sea," said Mrs. Damien, and began sobbing anew. She had come to enjoy a breakdown, and this was the moment for it. "I don't know, I don't know. The boy has always been a mystery to me. What he has made me suffer in my life! Abbott says I am never to speak of him again, but he is my son. And the only one I've got——"

Cynthia wondered, as children will, whether clearness of vision was a faculty of youth alone, or even a faculty that had first appeared in her own generation, which was now introducing it to the world. Couldn't Mrs. Damien see, as Cynthia saw, and as Leo would have seen, that Abbott, being an unoriginal person, was playing the part that the books had written for him— "You are never to speak of him again!"—and that she herself was doing the same. She was unhappy, doubtless, and one was sorry for her; but she was also luxuriating in some maternal sentiment because she enjoyed it and it sounded well.

"I don't know why he should treat me like this," she sobbed. "I'm sure I've always tried to be a perfect mother to him. What else should I do? Isn't he the only child I've had? 'Unhappiness in childhood'— what does that mean. When was he unhappy? I've done everything to make his childhood happy."

All this weeping was an element in which Old Mrs. Coventry was as happy as a trout in a freshet or a salmon up the tumbling stream. She took Rose's hand and stroked it. "He doesn't mean all that, my dear," she soothed. "He can't mean it. And don't worry: perhaps it's all for the best. While he's away from you he'll learn all you were to him; and then perhaps he'll come back to you. Like the Prodigal Son, you know. Don't you think so, Hilda? Now you mustn't worry. I'm sure there's a lot of good in him —somewhere. And tell us directly you hear from him, won't you? We shall be anxious to know all."

It was a month later that Mrs. Damien came again with a letter from Leo in her hand. Hilda was alone in the room when she arrived; and if there was any difference between Cynthia's race to the living room door and her grandmother's, it was that the younger woman would have laughingly admitted her curiosity, while the older one would have indignantly denied that she possessed such a quality.

"Well?" they all asked.

"I've heard from him."

"What is he doing?"

"He is a market gardener."

" A *what ?* " Both Hilda and Old Mrs. Coventry were inexpressibly shocked ; and Cynthia gasped too.

" Yes, he really is. He's hired himself out as a common labourer to some nurseryman or market-gardener."

" Where ? "

" Somewhere in Kent."

" Goodness gracious ! . . ." What could they say. They were speechless—mazed. Old Mrs. Coventry repeated under her breath, " Somewhere in Kent ! . . ." but that didn't seem to be the point to worry about.

And Mrs. Damien could only nod despairingly—and yet triumphantly : " It is so."

" Then he really meant it when he always said that that was what he wanted to do."

" Apparently so," said his mother.

It was bewildering. Defeating.

" What are you going to do about it ? "

" Nothing. He must go his way. Abbott is disgusted. He is quite broken down by it."

The two elder listeners nodded ; but the other of her hearers suspected that Abbott was bearing up pretty well.

" A common working man ! " Rose emphasised. " Was it for this that we slaved to give him the best education, and the best home ? Was it for this that we took him to church and tried to make a religious man of him, and hoped he might delight our old age by being a clergyman himself. Now—a common workman in the fields ! "

" I know," both ladies sympathised. " What does he say ? "

She showed them the letter, with the apologetic words,

" He writes well, of course." It told how he was earning fourteen shillings a week and living in one room of a tiny cottage, and had never been so happy in his life. He was up with the dawn, and got an extraordinary pleasure from merely handling the earth and the things of the earth. He rejoiced in his old gardening clothes, and in the sweat that dropped from his brow to the soil, and in the ache in his back when he walked home in the evening. A whole new world was opening before him, and what an incredibly exciting world it was ! Sometimes he stood in the woods, appalled to think that up till his nineteenth year he had been unable to distinguish between one bird's song and another's, or to recognise any wild flower except those that grew in the wastegrounds of London. Why, a sparrow had been the only bird he could recognise, a plane tree the only tree, and a privet the only shrub ! But now he was getting good at all these things, and the pleasure they gave him had to be experienced to be believed. Sometimes when he crossed a meadow, ablow with wild flowers and grass, he decided that it was good to have been a townsman for eighteen years, so that these things might break upon one like a revelation. And the nights brooding over the Kentish weald ! Did they realise, Mother and Dad, that the gas lamps of Conyers Road put out the stars and turned the moon into one of themselves ? But he didn't regret it. He was glad to have been held back from the country till he was old enough to love and study its every mood and season and change. It could never be commonplace to him now. " I'm so happy, Mum, and thank you and Dad for letting me choose my own way."

Old Mrs. Coventry had read the letter after Hilda,

and she waited till Cynthia had finished it.   Then she said, " That's very nice about the birds, and the moon —I liked that part—but what does he mean by his last words—show it to me, Cynthia—what does he mean by, ' I finish at five o'clock and I occupy my evenings with work that I really love ' ? "

" I don't know," said his mother.   " What do I know about him ? "

So Old Mrs. Coventry turned to the words again, to see if she could get a little more out of them.   " Work that I really love."   But they gave no more on a second reading.

She handed back the letter, and, removing her spectacles, folded them up.   " Well, we must be glad that he's happy for the present," she said.   " But keep up a brave heart, my dear.   He's bound to weary of all that soon.   It must be so rough and uncouth.   You'll see ! He'll come back one day to his comfortable home."

VI

WHILE Old Mrs. Coventry was looking well to it that Tom's losses didn't narrow *her* life unnecessarily, and with her admirable realism was securing money and goods, Cynthia also was giving many hours to thought. She was often silent in these days. At first she had not seen that the move to Macartney Road would mean a maiming constriction of her life—but she saw it now ; and sometimes the knowledge would come upon her like an unhappy shadow. If her loss could be summed up in a phrase, it would be one that she often used to herself : " No parties now." With only one living room, and Granny sitting in the best chair, it was difficult for Cynthia to give so much as a tea-party to her friends ; and when things are difficult like this, one is inclined to abandon them altogether. Granny sat in possession of the sitting-room ; and it had become the territory of the middle-aged and the old. " No parties now." And parties, she told herself, were really terribly important. Without them, old friends fell away and no new ones came ; and in the end, you were asked nowhere and saw no life. She was nearly nineteen —already two years beyond that seventeenth birthday which had seemed the fullness of time—and no one was having a chance of falling in love with her. In theory she was still in love with Rugg, but, after nearly three years' absence from him, she was ready to accept the adoration of another man, and to give him her second-best love. It might be an affection rather sad and sweet, she thought. And if she married him, the thought of " what might have been " would add only a fragrance to life, softening and not spoiling it.

But opportunity sat not in her mother's living room or in her father's office. Life had narrowed for her, and there were times when she saw this narrowness symbolised in the dreary staircase leading to their front door.

Trying to comfort herself in the silences, she would think, " Oh well . . . my love of Daddy, and my self-sacrifice for him, are all experience of a sort. It's spiritual experience. Perhaps I shall be better for suffering." From any other view-point it had been a mistake to go into her father's office. Who could say what gaiety she might not have met in some other place of business, and what attractive men ? But to go daily with her father to his office in Great Smith Street was simply to convey Macartney Road with her to Westminster, and to bring it back with her at night. " Still, if it makes him happy, poor darling. . . ."

She had hardly any friends now. Nearly all the boys of her day had scattered abroad, and the girls had their own interests. The Pantomime was in possession of a new generation of children ; and she was of the audience. She sat there, a forgotten actress, thinking of former triumphs. On the other side of her, perhaps, sat Miss Preestham, Miss Merthyr, and Miss Massey ; and unwittingly she drew her shoulder away from these faded and empty ladies, for they were portents. They frightened her now that she was nearly nineteen and unloved. They frightened her a little from holiness too. She had a great desire to be

good, but a great determination not to be like Miss
Preestham, Miss Merthyr and Miss Massey. " I'm not
going to be like Miss Preestham," she would tell herself.
" I'm *not*, I'm *not*, I'm *not* ! "

And her nineteenth birthday went by, and she watched
it pass with dismay. I suppose this is a story that
repeats itself wherever a child is born, and fills with
health, and grows up to be nineteen. We say she is
" crying for life." Should we see deeper things if we
said, " Life is crying for room " ? As the meagre
weeks followed one another into the past, she would
tot up the " bits of life " she had enjoyed. If she went
to a theatre with her mother and father, she would
come home in the train, thinking, " Well, that was
something." If she went to a Parish dance at St.
Alban's Hall, even though Miss Preestham was
there, she would think as she undressed after it,
and combed her chestnut hair, " Well, it was one aspect
of life, anyhow ; it was experience." Once a lady
reporter took her to a fashionable garden party, and
she went in a cloudy dress and a large leghorn hat
with streamers ; and as she moved over the green
lawn, she was comforted, thinking, " Well, this at least
is something new." On another occasion the same kind
friend took her to a Literary Dinner, where great and
famous men were shouted by a functionary in a red
coat ; and she sat against the wall, thinking, " Now
this really *is* something ! "

A theatre last week—this Literary Dinner to-night—
really she wasn't doing too badly. And yet—and yet
—in less satisfied moments she saw clearly enough
that all this was to be a beggar grateful for thrown
morsels of life, not a rich man enjoying it to the full.

And only richness of life was worth while—Rugg had taught her that. " There's no doubt about it : Lazarus and I are a pair. We might have paired off very nicely." And you might think and think like this, but nothing happened. Time just flowed on.

And then one evening, as she would put it, " something extraordinary happened inside her." She was sitting in her antique room, at the little oak bureau which she had placed slantwise to the window, and her chin was on her hand. On the top of the desk was a paper bag of sugared almonds, such as she sometimes treated herself to, for companionship in the long dull evenings. And she was staring out at the long street with its row of gas lamps.

There had just been a loud, exalted, and boisterous row between herself and her grandmother, in the living-room downstairs ; because she had ventured to defend Leo Damien and to say that she thought none the worse of him for his Socialism. And Granny, who had not had a good row for some time and felt she could do with one to-night, had blustered up and down the room, refused to listen to anyone but herself, shouted her down, declared that she was asking for revolution, that she shouldn't talk so ignorantly, that she should read about what happened in the French Revolution, that, for *her* part, she'd be guillotined with the aristocrats when the time came, that, look back as far as she might, she could only see Service and Professional men in her family, that, once you had divided all the money equally among the people, the clever and industrious ones would quickly enlarge their share and the wasters lose theirs, that it was an absolute disgrace to become a market gardener when you were offered a gentleman's position in a stockbroker's office, and did Cynthia *want* to be guillotined. Cynthia said she wanted only to talk sometimes to people who could talk sense, and strolled from the room, whistling sadly.

And here she was, sitting at her desk by the window, chin on palm, sweet in mouth, and looking out at the lamps of Macartney Road, and at the stars twinkling over Norman's End. And suddenly she saw Norman's End.

I say she *saw* it; and the word must hold an abundant meaning. The scales dropped from the happy, uncriticising eyes of childhood, and a portion of O'Kelvie's spirit looked out. Her eyes saw the tall houses with their porticoes and areas; with their clean holland blinds and lace curtains; with their window-boxes on every window sill; but her inward vision saw —what? It is difficult to say, for she could not grasp intellectually what she was feeling intuitively. It is too much to say that she saw the solid houses as halting-places no surer nor more permanent than the bivouacs of the Bedouin under the desert stars; that she saw the Square Quarter Mile as an English kraal, with all its tribal fashions and taboos enclosed behind its frail ring-fence, and the eternal sky above; that she saw the lace curtains as prison walls, and the long pavements too—but it was something of all this. And the quiet, the quiet! It was not the quiet of the meadows or the spinney; it was a menacing thing. It was another wall, holding them in. And they didn't see it—they didn't see it. Or they dimly saw it, with a secret discontent.

It was a moment of vision that would escape quickly, and elude recapture afterwards, for she was young, and her mind a muddle. But for the present it was enough to drive her through the prison walls for a spell in the open country. With her chin on her hand, she thought and thought. How get out? She put a sugared almond in her mouth to help her consider. There was only one way out: Rugg. " Come back when you feel you may," he had said. She would go and tell him everything: confession was always so easy with him. She could go to him and say, " I am not living. Please will you take me to some parties." Should she do it? Yes, yes! Oh yes! Her hand flung up to her mouth in her excitement—and her fear. Plans raced in her head, and their pressure was such that she threw back her hair. Her heart raced with them. Where? At the studio, of course. Since Mike had left him for Canada, he had gone from the flat, but he came always to the studio. And when? Driven by joy, and in a passion of decision, she exclaimed, " Next Saturday. Absolutely the first minute I've got ! " To which a voice seemed to answer from the distance, " So soon? . . . Prestissimo, Prestissimo ! "

" Yes, next Saturday—or I might give it up."

And she took her chin off her palm, that she might draw from a pigeon-hole in the bureau her engagement diary (so empty) where, quite unnecessarily, she wrote down this appointment for Saturday.

This is only a tale of the London streets, but does any child in such an hour differ greatly from Monte Cristo, determining to tunnel a way out of his cell in the Chateau d'If, or Columbus, looking at the horizon over the sea, and deciding that the Old World was too small?

VII

TIME ! It was Saturday afternoon ; and she must do it now, or despise herself for ever. Best go to the studio quickly, and perhaps he wouldn't be in—and then she would have saved her self-respect, and absolved herself from going—for now that it was Saturday, fear sat in her breast and was playing a drumbeat there. Her fingers shivered as she dressed. She had given much thought to her dress. She put on her white lace-inserted muslin which fitted tight to her figure and belled out round her feet. Over her puffed-out hair, ornamented with a black bow at the knot, she pinned her large falling hat of pale blue straw, draped round with lace. Three carnations she tucked in at her waist. Then, guiltily taking from her drawer the packet of " Bloom of Ninon " which she had bought yesterday so warily (" Please I want a packet of powder for a friend ") she dusted it on to her face. It smelt beautiful. A pause to gather captaincy ; and she drove herself out of the house and along the roads to the old mansion.

She must approach the studio through the garden of the deserted house, not by the door in Ashgar Terrace, lest old Miss Hackett sat on her balcony with eyes dropping downward from her handiwork. Here were the magnificent coach-gates of wrought-iron, between their high brick piers. Half open, just as they were three years before—or seven years before, when she

threw her ball into the garden—for no one worried
them ever, and their hinges had rusted and their feet
sunk into the cobbles. She slowed her step . . . then
forced herself through, much as a diver, who has
mounted to the highest platform before a staring crowd,
forces himself to spring, even though, at this great
height, he is wishing he had left his boasts alone. She
crossed the cobbled courtyard with the step of a woman
perfectly at ease, but with the quaking heart of a burglar.
And, as quickly as possible, she passed under the low
arch of the coach-house to the friendly seclusion of the
garden at the back. Here she halted on the untended
lawn, with nothing between her and the studio except
the long dividing wall and the orchard trees beyond.
She stood there in the long grass, a slim white figure
under her pale blue straw. And the trees behind made
of her a figure oddly pastoral, since London closed this
garden on every side.

She had stopped, for now, if ever, she wanted to
turn back—but the diver does not turn back : his
fear of contempt is greater than his fear of death, and
the Cynthia in the grass feared the watching Cynthia
within, who would despise and revile her. She would
go on—but she would wait a little longer for courage.
It was very still in the garden. Behind her the old
empty mansion ; on either side the old garden walls ;
about her the elms and cedars which had looked down
upon Johnson and Boswell and Garrick ; in front of
her the unkempt orchard trees. Always when she had
stood here before she had felt as if she stood in the
eighteenth century. There was nothing to disturb the
illusion ; a blue sky, such as any century might have
known, spanned the world ; and O'Kelvie, halting at

her side, used to encourage her in the fancy. "There are market gardens over the wall, Prestissimo, and some of the cabbages may find their royal way down the gullet of King George the Third. Glance over the wall, my child, and you'll see the highway from London, not two hundred yards away. We are expecting the coach of my Lord Harry to pass at any moment. He is on his way to Richmond where he lies with my Lord Twickenham to-night. He pays his court to the Lady Betty, as of course you know." For a second, as she remembered this, a treacherous idea rose in Cynthia's mind: "Lucky Lord Harry and Lady Betty, whose troubles are all over! They sleep for ever, and nobody can ask them to do the high dive any more." But she thrust the thought down, and went through the apple trees to the studio door.

Here she paused again. Was anyone in? Yes, she could hear a tread on the bare boards, and it was the tread she knew. Oh, but supposing someone was with him? A model! Or friends! Then she would turn back, unashamed. She listened for voices. None— except that once or twice Rugg's voice broke into humming, perhaps as he put a canvas against the wall, "It was only a beautiful picture In a beautiful gilded frame. . . ." He was alone there. Her knuckles rattled on the door. But, in her fear, she hadn't done it loud enough. She did it again, and she knew that the man within had paused and was listening. And now his tread was approaching the door. It flung open, and he stood before her, just as he had done when she first came knocking at his studio, a twelve-year-old child. He seemed exactly the same, with his dusty blue overall and his tousled curly hair. They had made no difference to him, the seven years which had lifted her from twelve to nineteen.

For the space of a second or two he stared at her.

"Yes, it's me, Rugg dear," she said, in an effort to jest and be at ease.

O'Kelvie was a witty man; and he quickly saw that the wittiest thing to do now was to express no surprise— nay, not by the lift of an eyebrow to treat as other than commonplace this cataclysmic event.

"Come in," he said. "Come in. And we'll have tea."

And he turned back into the studio, Cynthia following with a stuttered explanation, "Yes, I rather wanted to see you for a minute, if I might. . . ."

"By all means," said he, without turning round.

She was now standing in the large room and looking about her. "Oh, isn't it good, isn't it good to be in it again?" she cried. "And that's a new easel you've got, I'm sure. But Geoffrey's still there." Geoffrey was a plaster head. "And the same old smell! Darling old smell! Turpentine and varnish and dust—oh, it makes me feel fifteen again!"

"I'll deal with you when the kettle's on," said O'Kelvie. "Sit down. Your peculiar couch is still there, if you'll hustle off the junk." He filled the kettle and put it on the trivet, and turned towards Cynthia, who had remained standing.

"Now then, Cynthia Copenhagen, doff your hat and let's look at you."

"Cynthia Coventry, please."

"Tut, tut! As if it mattered! . . . H'm . . . Yes. . . ." He stared her up and down, while her mouth trembled to a grin, as happens to a person under scrutiny. "Well . . . P'raps so . . . Yes. . . . Yes, Prestissimo, you're almost beautiful."

"What stuff!"

"And you've learnt nothing. Same old pretence at modesty when you're as vain as Venus. Same old insincerity. Why can't you admit that you really go further than I and think yourself *quite* beautiful?"

"Because I *don't!*" screamed Cynthia. "Sometimes I look in the glass and get such a disappointment that I say, 'Oh bother!' and turn away to think of other things."

"Liar."

"All right . . ." conceded Cynthia, as one who scorned to argue. "I'm a liar then."

"Yes," agreed O'Kelvie. "Certainly."

"Rude pig!"

"Now then! Now then! None of that hot little temper that used to be such a source of unpleasantness between us! Calm! Calm! And listen: you've looked into your glass sometimes, haven't you, and come away quite satisfied?"

"Well . . . sometimes."

"Exactly. And you are really, all things considered, quite pleased with your face?"

"Sometimes."

"And you think your figure one of the nobler works of God?"

"Certainly."

"Very good then. Now we will tell you the truth. You are very nearly beautiful, but not quite. As an idiot of a woman once wrote to me, 'Yours is my ideal face, not over handsome, but full of character.' That's you too, Prestissimo. Taking you all in all, and by and large, and in the mass, and in the lump, your figure is better than your face."

She looked at him with a simulation of lasting distaste. "You think you know all about it, don't you?"

"Surely!" he averred, staring at her as if wondering what she might be leading to, with such an unnecessary question.

"Well, I wonder if you really do."

"Don't waste your time wondering. Sit down."

"I'd rather walk round, if you don't mind. I want to look at everything. Absolutely everything. I love it all so."

O'Kelvie pretended to scrutinise her again. "A strange creature," he said, summing up his view, "but not unlikeable." And with that he turned to the cupboard for a loaf and some butter.

Cynthia was now standing opposite the windowless north wall which stood between them and Ashgar Terrace.

"I wonder," said she, "if that old woman is on her balcony—old Miss Hackett, who split on us last time."

"Dirty old slut," said O'Kelvie, into his cupboard.

"Yes," agreed Cynthia. "I always say there's no one I really hate, but there are some for whom I feel a less active love than for others. And Miss Hackett is one of them."

"I hope she fries in hell," said O'Kelvie, putting plates and knives on the table.

To do this with any success he had to shove paint pots, turpentine tins, modelling tools, mahl-sticks, palettes and books in a jumbled crowd along the surface of the table. When he had laid two places, he suggested, "Let's see if she's there. This way;" and, still holding a bread-knife, he went towards the long perpendicular slit in the wall through which the large canvases were pushed into the road. He pulled open the panel; and together they peeped through it, one head above the other. Miss Hackett's balcony was deserted.

"I make no doubt she's behind her curtains somewhere," said he, pointing with the bread-knife, and then replacing the panel and locking it with the wooden bolts.

"Wouldn't she have a fit if she saw me here?" asked Cynthia; and she spread her fingers at the end of her nose, addressing the gesture to the wall. She also put out her tongue, and then left Miss Hackett for ever.

When they sat at tea on either side of the table, she said it was quite like old times, and, immediately afterwards, suggested that her conversation wasn't being very bright; an observation with which O'Kelvie associated himself, enabling her to retort that his own was no better, anyway. And with this promising opening she asked if she might tell him what she had come for; and he nodded, with a mouth full of bread.

"Well. . . ." She drew her brows together and then tossed back her hair. "Oh, I don't know! I can't say it now that I have come. I think p'raps I had better go back and write it. You put me off, sitting there eating. I could have written pages and pages of it two nights ago. You see . . . you see, Rugg dear, we're—we're direful poor just now."

"My *dear!*" exclaimed he with sympathy.

And then she poured it all out. She was serious now, and her eyes grew wide and large and sad, as she spoke of all that she was missing and all that she longed to do. O'Kelvie did not interrupt, save now and then to exclaim, "Splendid!" or "Glorious!" or "I knew

you would ; " after which he chewed his bread and
butter with a new vigour, so enthusiastic his endorse-
ment.   This greatly encouraged her, and she filled with
happiness and hope.

" Is that all ? " he asked, when she seemed to have
finished.

" I think so."

" Dear, dear ! "

" I wish you wouldn't say, ' Dear, dear ! ' like that.
It's really rather serious."

" You think you're getting no life ? "

" Yes.   Only thrown scraps of it—like Lazarus.   I'm
a Lazarus at your gate, while you're an old Dives,
gorging away to your heart's content.   It's really
rather disgusting of you, when you come to think of it."

" My dear, it's always the other chap who seems to
have all the fun.   Perhaps he doesn't really.   However
. . . You say that no one takes you anywhere ? "

" No."

" No nice parties."

" No.   Never was a woman so thwarted."

" Ah !   Never was a woman so thwarted.   Well,
have some more tea, my love, till I think it all over.
Never was a woman so thwarted.   Glory be to God,
but it's good to see someone catch fire !   Now then,
what shall we do ?   What's your idea ?   How can I
help you ? "

She said she imagined he went to marvellous parties
where there were lots of interesting people——

" Do I ? " he broke in doubtingly.   " Yes, I suppose
I do at times, though they'd probably seem more
remarkable to you than to me.   They're dull enough
sometimes.   Still, I could take you to shows where

you'd meet, say, Aldorf Hall, and George Ritchie, and Solomon Iles—— "

" Oh ! " She clapped her hands together as he named these famous men.   " Oh, that'd be absolutely marvellous ! "

" Well, that's easily done.   But, Cynthia, that's not my idea.   Parties like that are often silly and affected ; and in that way—strange as it may seem to you—they're not very different from all that you're trying to get quit of.   A shade more intelligent, maybe ;   but wherever there's affectation, there's an end of reality.   No, Cynthia, I'm fast coming to the belief that the real-est life is Low Life "—his eyes lit up with the old fire.   " Give me costers and criminals and Salvation Army bands—— "

" I don't quite understand," interrupted Cynthia, slotting her chin into her two palms.   " Please, I want to."

" I don't know that I do, either.   I just *feel* it.   I think I mean life free from frills.   You may find it among the artists when they're living straight from the earth, so to say, but such men are damned few.   One knows it when one sees it.   If I wander among the costers I catch it occasionally in their wit and their oaths and their rogueries and their decencies ;   and I feel I must rush home and paint.   I catch it in the poor, struggling people who walk from barrow to barrow on a Saturday night, pricing the red meat and the green apples, under the naphtha flares.   I see it in their weary eyes and bent hands and in the children dragging along behind them—especially in the children, who, as a rule, are quite as full of zest and beans and impatience, and therefore quite as happy, as any other children—which is food for thought—food for thought—— "

"Go on," begged Cynthia, staring at him, her chin in her palms.

"I like the hot gospellers at the street corners, if I think the fire in 'em is real, and the lines in the people's faces as they stare up at them and wonder if it's all true. I like the splash of the naphtha flares on the brass instruments of the Salvation Army bands, and the bonny faces of the Salvation Army lasses under their poke bonnets. I empty my pockets into their beastly money boxes. Can't help it, Prestissimo, because they're real and sincere, God's blessing on them, now and at the hour of their death, Amen. I love all real saints. I admire them humbly from my pit of sin. And I love their opposites too—the out and out rogues ; because there's always something extraordinary bright and real about a thoroughgoing rascal. Iago, I mean. Magnificent ! Or a good humbugging, oily, humourous hypocrite—what a joyous phenomenon to study ! I can watch him for ever. Would you like to come round with me sometimes—anywhere, Islington or Whitechapel or the Old Ford Road—— "

"Oh yes, yes ! " she cried. "I know that anything on earth would be interesting if *you* took me round. You'd make anything come alive. Will you really do it ? "

"I will. Isn't it meself that's weary with the telling you I would ? "

"*Joy !* " she breathed.

"And I'll take great care of you, since you've been tenderly nurtured, my child."

"Oh, shut up ! But I say—— "

"What ? "

"Don't let me be a nuisance, will you ? I'm so

afraid I'll be worrying you too often. You see, I've hardly any real friends—at least, not any exciting ones."

Her hand was now resting on the table, and O'Kelvie put his own palm over it. " I don't think there's any danger of that, Prestissimo dear. I've shoo'd you out before now, haven't I, and I shall certainly do it again."

" Really and truly ? "

" Really and truly."

In an excess of delight she snatched her hands from the table and, clasping them together, pressed them down upon her lap. " Oh ! " she cried. " I'm so glad I came ! Oh, Rugg ! "

VIII

LIFE was all joy again. The vistas ahead were spangled. And in such a happy mood it was amusing, as she waited on the platform next morning, to see an enormous young man, very wide in the shoulder and thick in the thigh, and to recognise Rob Ingram. He was exceedingly well-dressed. His blue suit was perfectly cut, his boots had patent-leather toes, his bowler hat was clearly the latest design, and something in the very slight tilt at which he wore it enabled it to carry around for him the atmosphere of Bond Street and the Pall Mall clubs. He was strolling up the platform with an erect carriage ; and, as he turned to stroll back again, she looked up into his face with a grin till he should recognise her ; which he did not do till he was nearly opposite her, and then only after a concentrated stare. At once he raised his hat and drew off a glove to shake hands. " It's Cynthia Coventry, isn't it ? "

" Yes. . . . And where are you off to ? "

" Just going back to the Regiment after a short leave," said he. " And you ? "

" Oh, I work in town now."

" *Do* you ? " This had confused him, she saw ; and he turned his face away : he mustn't show her that he considered it a fall in the world. Best drop the subject, since it must be painful to her.

Perhaps they could travel a little way together, he

suggested, as a proof that he was no snob ; and at that point, with a scream of grating brakes, an electric train came in, shod with sparks.

" Do let's," said Cynthia.

" You travel . . . ? " he began awkwardly.

" Yes, yes : third," she said hurriedly.   " But don't you trouble about me."

" Oh no, no," he laughed.   " I'm coming with you." His freedom from snobbery enabled him to do this for her.

So they got into a third-class coach, and sat side by side, with their backs to the windows. The train grated off with them ; and soon, at her request, Rob was telling her all about his present life.   He mentioned with an air almost too casual his shooting, his fishing, his servant, his friend Lamper—" Lord Lamprey, you know "—and a country house party he had been to " where one of the Connaught girls was present."   As he spoke, Cynthia, three years younger than he, felt a generation older.

" You *do* have a gay time," she said, to please him.

" Yes ; not bad," he allowed ; and they began to talk of what the other children of Norman's End had done—the supposition at the back of Rob's mind being that they hadn't done as well as he.   Lance Guilder was on the stage, and so was Aline Guilder, but —and Rob pursed his lips, so that Cynthia inquired what such an expression might mean.   Well, said Rob, for a chap like Lance who went to Oxford, it was a funny profession, all said and done : there was such a deuce of a lot of riff-raff on the stage, wasn't there ? Jack Trevelyan was touring the provinces too.   Funny ! Mike O'Kelvie ?—Mike went off to Canada, of course, but they were always rather a rough lot, those O'Kelvies. Grant Ellison was going to be a parson, and so was Gus Campion—extraordinary the influence of old Guilder! "Why, I rather thought of being one myself," said Rob, "and I think I should have been, if I hadn't got into the Army; but the church isn't what it was, is it? They're inclined to take anybody now."

"Oh, I think you're better in the Army," laughed Cynthia.

"Yes. The Army at least doesn't take every Tom, Dick and Harry, and never will."

"No," agreed Cynthia, who really thought this was true. Never would the British Army invite the Toms, Dicks and Harrys. . . .

The noise of the train rumbled through their silence, on and on. The walls of the dark tunnel roared by. Perhaps, if we could hear Time racing past us, it would sound like this. Created of our own movement; very near; steady and measured and relentless.

"But where does it lead to?" she asked, after listening to the rhythmic song of the wheels that carried them on and on.

"Lead to?" repeated Rob, amazed at the question. Surely the Army was an end in itself. "*Lead* to?"

"Yes. Where?"

"I don't know. . . . Unless there's a jolly old war soon, which we rather think there will be."

"Oh *no!*"

"Oh *yes!* We aren't building the Dreadnoughts for nothing. And Germany hasn't brought in her new Navy Law for nothing. I say, Cynthia! the *Dreadnought's* a wonderful ship. I went over her a little while ago, and she did my heart good. She carries ten twelve-inch guns, does twenty-one knots, and is capable of inflicting the maximum destruction at the maximum distance. Golly! It warms you, somehow, to look at her guns. And soon we shall have a dozen like her, and they say a battle-line of ten Dreadnoughts is equal to twice that number of the old ships. No wonder she's put the fear of God into the Germans."

"But why? We don't want to fight Germany, do we?"

"No . . ." agreed Rob, hesitantly. "No, of course not. . . . But Germany wants a navy as big as ours, and we can't have two navies cock of the walk. If they *will* be silly, I mean. . . . Did you see what Jacky Fisher did the other day?"

"Who's Jacky Fisher?"

"*Cynthia!*" He gaped at her as if he were her Divinity teacher, and she had asked who were Abraham, Isaac and Jacob. "He's First Sea Lord. Or is it First Lord of the Admiralty? Anyhow he's Boss. And he's just shifted practically the whole strength of the Navy from the Mediterranean to the North Sea; which shows what *he* believes—and I *must* say I think he's right. We calculate that their ships'll be ready by 1912."

"Oh well; that's a long way off."

"Only a few years. By Gad, sometimes I wish I'd gone into the Navy, because they'll have all the scrapping that's going. By the way, what did Leo Damien do? You remember—old Face? Face Damien. Is he still with his guv'nor in the city?"

"He's a market gardener."

Rob whisked round in his seat to stare at her. "Go

on ! " he exclaimed, all decorousness of phrase deserting him.

" Yes."

Rob shook his head, and glanced at the station they were coming to : it was where he must get out. " I was always afraid he'd come to grief, that chap. A market gardener ! God !—excuse me, Cynthia—but, by gad, that's a bit of a fall, isn't it ? Not that the Damiens were ever—well, quite the thing, don't you know ; but I didn't think he'd come to that. Funny isn't it, how some people seem destined to revert to type ? Of course, poor old Leo was always a bit of a waster. Still, I'm sorry for him, somehow. This is my station. Good-bye."

Cynthia, through the window, watched him go along the platform, his hat at a perfect angle and his stick under his arm, while he drew on his gloves.

IX

So Pat O'Kelvie and Cynthia Coventry picked up the threads of their friendship and wove its odd, pleasing pattern anew.

Many a time that autumn and winter a large bearded man in a wide-brimmed hat and an Inverness cape, and a slim, happy girl might have been seen walking the streets of London, or stopping to gaze, with smiling faces, at a sight that enchanted them. Perhaps it was a factory chimney, rose-flushed in a pearly autumn evening, and the man would sound his delight in it with an abrupt oath and a " Look, child, look ! " Perhaps it was six o'clock of a winter dusk, and they were on the pavements of Shoreditch, passing the old clothes shops and the fried fish shops and the Hebrew ironmongers, or standing to watch the barefoot children dancing around a piano-organ, while the face of the man became lost in thought. Or the same two stood on Tower Hill, listening to a mob orator, and at times the man, taking a block from the pocket of his cloak, would sketch an impassioned movement of the orator's arm, or the falling jaw of one of his listeners. And the girl, glancing over his shoulder at the work, would turn her eyes upon its subject and see it with new eyes. Or they went to Chinatown and wandered along narrow, disreputable streets, with the smell of the river coming up the cobbles, and a cold air off the water touching their cheeks. And O'Kelvie would stop and gaze in a fine frenzy at a gull flying above the drunken chimney stacks, against a windy sky. They walked down to the stairs and steps of the river, and looked at the silken sheen on the slack water, or the waves fanning out from a tug and its load of barges. From the doors of gin palaces came the sound of concertinas and the shrill laughs of drunken women ; and round dark corners they heard the shuffle of Eastern shoes. Evil figures of the waterfront loafed past them, their eyes slanting to the girl's face ; and O'Kelvie asked, " You're not afraid, Prestissimo ? Take my arm " ; to which she answered, " Oh, I'm not in the least afraid. You look big enough to knock any of them down " ; but, as the evening darkened, she slipped her hand under his arm.

Sometimes at sunset they would stand upon a bridge to look down upon the Pool of London, watching perhaps a ship for the Baltic put out from Hay's Wharf, or another load its cargo at Wilkin's Stage. And O'Kelvie would point to the rhythmic movements of the stevedores and the visual beauty, unavoidable, of all work that was well done. Then he would go off into a dream, leaning upon the balustrade of the bridge, as the low sun flung their shadows on the deck ; and she would try to see what he was seeing, and when she supposed this sight had come to her, she was pleased and stimulated and a little vain. When the sun was down, leaving a glow along the southern sky, he would point out the beauty of the Surrey side, with its high chimneys, bare warehouses, and soaring cranes, silhouetted against the light. She was astonished at first to hear that he preferred the straight lines of the chimneys, and the bare faces of the warehouses to the " crotchety nonsense " of the Houses of Parliament or the " disgusting jiggery-pokery " of Tower Bridge ; but his judgments were often violently phrased like this, and she would argue violently against them. O'Kelvie could stand for an hour on a public bridge, hot with argument and forgetful of time ; and she, for her part, declined to surrender easily. Gradually, however, when he had calmed down and become conciliatory, she saw what he meant and admitted that " simplicity, honesty, and seemliness must always be more beautiful than affectation," and thought with dismay of her antique bedroom at home.

Nothing for it but to risk all and describe it to him, fearing disaster. She got all the disaster she feared. " Oh no, Cynthia," he said, but without excitement. " No. You must scrap all that " ; and she was appalled to find that what she had liked so much a year ago could now seem so awful. Appalled to find that her taste had been vulgar.

" Oh, I'm afraid I'm vulgar," she would lament ; and he would comfort her, saying, " Oh no. Only untrained. Still, you must destroy that room."

And the darkness fell upon their talk ; and silence ; as they waited to see a ship with red and green riding lights come up the tideway and dip its funnel to make the bridge. Then they would move on.

Sometimes, on a Saturday night, they would " see life " among the costers, in Bermondsey or Islington or Hammersmith, she holding his arm ; and he would point out the receding vista of the pavement with the barrows on this side of the gutter, all gaily coloured with apples and oranges and sweets and many-tinted stuffs, and the streaming, sombre-coated crowd on the other, and the wind-blown flares playing a light upon all. She would see the play of light on faces quickly lost, and the mass of shadows moving against the shuttered shops, and a great ring of darkness surrounding all.

" A splash of light falling on a few passing faces, and darkness all round—what else is our short term of life, my lady ? " asked O'Kelvie.

And the vision he gave her pleased her so much— though God knows why, for it wasn't very encouraging —that she pressed his arm in gratitude.

Perhaps her reaction to the streets was more the literary person's, and his the painter's ; but there was enough of the artist in her now, and enough of the poet in him, for their common ground to be large. The geniality of the raucous costers could move her sharply. She worshipped the friendliness of men, when she heard a beefy butcher calling to an ugly and tired old woman, " ' Ere y'are, *Mother !* " or to a hobbling old grandfather, " 'Ere y'are, *Dad !* " or to any girl, however unlovely, " 'Ere y'are, *my dear !* " and to any little street arab offering his halfpenny, " 'Ere y'are, *sonny !* " Bless them for their good fellowship ! They were adorable, all of them.

Once or twice they went to theatres, delighting especially in the melodramas of the people. They sat in the Lyric Opera House at Hammersmith, with a smell of oranges coming up from the pit, while Mr. Melville's excellent fancies, *The Ugliest Woman in the World* and *The Worst Woman in London*, were played to soft music and thunder before them. At the pathetic parts O'Kelvie would mutter a comment into the darkness, and she enjoyed for the next ten minutes the ecstasy of forcing back her laughter.

He kept his promise and took her to parties where she might meet the famous men and their wives, or their mistresses—a word she met for the first time in these places. But she didn't really enjoy the parties so much as the walks alone with him. The hold of Norman's End on her was strong, and would not release her yet to mix with these people. She felt a watcher by the wall rather than a mingler in the midst of them. She shivered at the freedom of their language and their jokes ; and at the obvious tipsiness of this woman or that man ; but tried to be brave. Listening to their talk, she sat appalled at her ignorance, and dared not speak. While the talk rattled and shrilled about her, she thought with much criticism of her home, where no one had ever dreamed of going to an art gallery, or to a symphony concert (she didn't even know what a symphony was) or of reading any book but Marie Corelli's and Seton Merriman's, who were apparently a joke to these people, or of taking any interest in trees and flowers and birds. How could she hope that O'Kelvie really cared for her company, and she so " abysmally ignorant ? " These people must mean much more to him than she did—of *course* they must, she decided ; and grief sat beside her at the party.

But there was a gentleness in O'Kelvie, and, quickly perceiving her discomfort, he would ask if she would like to come away ; to which she would reply, " Oh no, no. Why ? " as if she were completely happy. And when she got home, she added the party to her swelling total of life seen and lived.

Cynthia, sheltered by the high walls of Norman's End,

was very ignorant, but she wasn't such a fool as never to wonder what these people said of O'Kelvie and her. Nineteen, she did not yet know that love could go farther than an embrace and a kiss, and she imagined that this was the entertainment that a " mistress " provided for a man ; but she was pretty sure that these people thought her O'Kelvie's mistress. The idea didn't worry her at all ; it flattered and delighted her, that they should think O'Kelvie loved her enough to want to kiss her. And she was sure that, if one day he really did kiss her, she would kiss him passionately in return, to show that she was ready to give herself to him, heart and soul. " Heart and soul "—that was all she supposed she could give.

But O'Kelvie did not attempt to kiss her. Only when they were alone in the studio, and talk had died between them, and she was looking at him and wondering what he was thinking of, did he sometimes gaze at her in a curious way. But she feared it was only the way in which he gazed at the men loading their ship in the Pool of London. And one evening when tea was finished, and his pipe alight, and she, who had been sitting on the couch, flung her weight back on both arms and then lifted one to the nape of her neck, he stared at her for quite a while and then said abruptly, " Cynthia, I want to paint you."

" Oh, but how lovely ! "

" Your movements are good. Yes, they are the best thing about you."

" Thank you, Rugg." She bowed. " That might mean anything. . . . But did you really mean that you would paint me ? "

" I think so."

" Oh, how gorgeous ! "

" Yes, but——" and he turned his eyes from her and pressed the tobacco into his pipe—" do you understand what it means ? "

" I ought to by this time, oughtn't I ? It means a canvas, an easel, some brushes, and——"

" No," he interrupted impatiently, and then hesitated. " You're an odd child, and I never like to say anything that'll frighten you. But—I shouldn't want you to wear all those clothes."

She flushed to her hair, but tried her hardest to be brave. " What ? " she laughed. " Not without any clothes at all ? "

" No."

As a matter of fact, he had wanted this, but couldn't bring himself to ask it of her. " No, but——" he began to pace to and fro—" I have a picture of you forming in my mind. We could call it ' Morning,' perhaps. I see you rising from your bed with the weight of the body on one bare arm, while one foot reaches to the ground, and your drapery falls from a shoulder, exposing one breast." He stopped in his walk, and stood looking down upon her. " It has never occurred to you, I suppose, what a lovely thing to a painter is a girl's breast. And so is a factory chimney," he added hastily, " as we've both agreed."

" No, I don't think I have thought of it," she murmured for answer, hardly knowing what she was saying.

" Well, it is . . . And so is the upward swell of her thigh. Your leg would have to be bare, of course."

" I see."

" Well ? "

Her eyes flew anywhere, but she continued in the

brave course. "Oh, I suppose all that could be supplied."

"You wouldn't mind?"

"No." Arching her eyebrows, she pretended surprise at his question. "Why should I?"

"I don't know. You're a funny kid."

"I'm not. I think it's awfully decent of you to want to paint me. Make me as pretty as possible, won't you, Rugg?"

"Pretty? God save us, no!"

"Oh *yes*."

"No, not pretty. Vital, urgent, ugly even—not pretty."

"Oh, I won't be ugly," she protested; and then repented. "At least, I don't want to be. Oh, I *wish* my tastes weren't so vulgar. Never mind, I'll resign myself to being ugly in your picture."

"You'll be quite beautiful in it," he said, rather seriously for him.

That evening she went home dazed into a dream. And in her bedroom at night she stood before her glass and left fall her chemise to expose one of her breasts. A foretaste of the nervousness that must be hers when first she exposed it to him touched her now, damping her forehead so that she flung back her hair. She covered her breast again, hoping he would not be disappointed in it; and went and sat on the bed, putting herself in the position he had suggested, with a bare leg reaching to the ground. She studied the upward swell of the thigh. Yes, she could see what he meant. To anyone who didn't own it, it might seem beautiful. It swelled in a good line from the knee, and was round and firm, and the skin was unspoiled as a child's.

X

WHEN one Saturday afternoon Cynthia came running into the studio for her first sitting, she met the considerable heat that she had sometimes found there before, when O'Kelvie had been working with a " life " model. In the furnace room below, the fire was evidently flaring; and here was a heat that curled up the papers pinned to the wall and, while muttering in the pipes, filled the large room with the smell of overheated wood, as an oven fills with the smell of cooking cake. The larger of the two thrones, she noticed, had been drawn towards the centre of the floor, and her own favoured couch stood at an angle on it, with a white sheet covering its threadbare upholstery and a width of some material in an apricot hue thrown across its foot. One of the light easels stood at the desired distance from the throne, with a drawing board and paper already in position. Some dozen paces behind this easel was a heavy rack-easel, with the large mirror hoisted on to it, to reflect the progress of the picture. The screen zig-zagged round that homely corner of the studio where the armchairs and book-shelves looked at the broken asbestos of the gas-stove. O'Kelvie, in his butcher-blue blouse, billowy trousers, and gay carpet slippers, stood by the trestle table, idly arranging his charcoal and his brushes, and occasionally testing a brush on the palm of his hand.

He turned to face her; and she came to a halt in front of him, flourishing a smile that was meant to show her freedom from all embarrassment and most effectively unveiled the opposite.

" Pleased ? " he asked, to give her confidence. " Happy ? "

" Ra-*ther* ! I think it's absolutely ripping. I've never been so excited about anything in my life."

" Well then, we'll make a fine picture together, Prestissimo . . . Yes . . ." and he looked her up and down. . . . " Yes . . . we shan't be able to have your hair like that. You understand that, don't you ? You'll have to let it down."

" Joy ! " she exclaimed, and immediately pulled off her hat and, by force of habit, patted the hair into the very position he had condemned.

" Why ' Joy,' pray ? "

" Because I'm always so much happier when it's down."

" Set it free then. Take out the wires and the rivets and the staples and all, and I'll have a look at its quality. We shall probably plait it, I think."

She pulled out the pins, let the thick chestnut hair fall behind her shoulders, and shook her head till it hung comfortably.

" Yes . . ." he mused aloud. " Yes . . . it's a good colour. Lucky girl ! But we'll plait it, I think. . . . Yes. . . ."

" Do what you like with it—such as it is," she agreed facetiously, since this was the best way to appear at ease. " It's yours to work your will on."

" Of course," agreed O'Kelvie.

" I don't know that there's any ' of course ' about it,

but have it your own way if it amuses you. What comes next? "

" Next comes this." And he lifted from a bundle of draperies a length of shimmering green silk. " You won't be able to wear your night-shift, as I hinted at first. No, no, we can do nothing with a night-shift. You'll have to drape this around you."

" Crums ! " she exclaimed.

She said it merrily, and hoping that the warmth which had flooded her face was not showing lurid through the skin.

" That's all right, isn't it? " he inquired a shade anxiously, for he had noticed the flush.

" Oh yes. Absolutely. But let me down lightly, Rugg dear. I'm not quite accustomed to this sort of thing yet. I may gasp now and then."

" *You'll* be all right," he encouraged her tenderly. " There's nothing to be afraid of."

" Afraid ? I'm not afraid."

" Of course not. Then nip behind the screen and get ready."

And he pulled out his pouch to occupy himself with his pipe while she should be gone.

Her heart galloping like a restive colt that her will could not rein in and subdue, she ran behind the screen and undressed. She threw off the clothes with agitated fingers and laid them on an armchair. Her knees trembled, but to prove her courage to herself and to him, she sang at her occupations. With the same end she called through the bedraggled walls of the screen, " Can I keep on my shoes ? " and his voice came back, " Yes . . . For the present ; " and his humming over his pipe, " Sweetest little fellow, Everybody knows,

Don't know what to call him, But he's mighty like a rose. . . ." When standing in nothing but the shoes, she swathed the green silk about her hips and flung the rest of it over her shoulder, and called, " I think I must be ready now."

" Come along then."

Feeling rather like a child running out from a bathing machine, she ran from the protection of the screen and jumped on to the throne.

O'Kelvie continued to hum. Plainly he was trying to keep her at ease by an appearance as business-like and mechanical as possible.

" Now then ! " he commanded, half smiling. " *La Pose !* "

Throwing herself on the couch, she tried to put herself in the pose they had discussed, the weight of her body resting on one arm behind her, her leg reaching to the ground, and the drapery falling away to expose a breast.

" Yes. . . ." He had stepped back to consider the pose ; and his head went to one side in thought. " H'm . . . Don't know . . ." and he came forward to rearrange her slightly. His touch on drapery or limb, on hair or head or chin, was considerate of her naïveté, in so far as it was conscious of her as a living person and not as mere paintable substance—and indeed Cynthia, who was always thrilled when his fingers touched her could almost have grieved that there was not the least symptom of any corresponding thrill in him ; that he should be so *completely* mechanical. In one enthusiastic and careless moment he pulled her arm into position, as if it had been the crank of an obstinate engine.

" Help ! " she complained.

"Sorry," he apologised, "but that's all right now. Yes, that'll do. . . . Yes, we shan't improve on that for the moment. . . . No, we won't have the shoe . . . no." And off came the shoe, and he pressed her foot on to the floor. Then, turning to the table for a piece of chalk, he drew an outline round the foot where it touched the floor, and did the same round the ball-feet of the couch.

"Whatever's that for, Rugg dear?" she asked.

"Is it a brain you have? To know our position next time, of course."

"Well, who'd have thought of that?" said she, in a good imitation of a housemaid. "Will you only look at that now?"

"Comfortable?" he inquired, when erect again.

"Yes."

"Can you hold that pose for some time?"

"I think so."

"Good." And he went to the easel, stepped back from it, gave one more look at her—then, stepping forward, began to rough out the preliminary study, his charcoal at arm's length. Between almost every line, it seemed, he stepped back his six or eight paces and studied her, but with a gaze that appeared unconscious of her as a living being.

"May I talk sometimes?" she asked at last.

"Certainly not."

"Crums!" said she.

But he didn't hear. He had turned to the mirror behind him to study the drawing in its reflection, and now was coming forward to amend a line. Once when he stood with his back to her and his face to the mirror, swinging his gaze from the drawing on the easel to the model on the throne, he trapped a sparkle in her eye. The rapt look fled, and he fixed his eye on this new phenomenon. "Is it laughing at me you are?"

"No."

"Holy Mary, Mother of God——"

"I'm not laughing," she declared indignantly to his reflection in the glass.

"Not laughing?" he demanded again of hers. "Do you mean to say that you were not finding something humorous about me when my eye fell upon you, to your surprise and chagrin?"

"I tell you I didn't laugh."

"I'm thinking it's a lie you're after telling."

"All right, think what you like. I may have *smiled*. I suppose I may smile sometimes, can't I?"

"Certainly not."

"Glory!"

"You may not smile at me; you may smile once or twice at the light and frivolous thoughts that flit through the empty chambers of your brain——"

"I see, Rugg."

"——but you mustn't in any way regard me as a figure of fun."

"I see. Thank you, Rugg."

"What do you mean, 'I-see-thank-you-Rugg'?" he demanded, still standing with his back to her and using the glass as a medium of exchange. "Have you come here in a spirit of ribaldry?"

"Not at all; but I should have thought that for a picture called 'Morning' a nice, fresh smile was indicated."

"And who said the picture was going to be called 'Morning'?"

"You did."

"When?"

"When you first suggested it."

"Pah! That was only sugar to please a digestion fundamentally weak. I could not tell you the truth all at once. I shall probably call it No. 1367."

"But I'm not a convict."

"*You?* Don't run away with the idea that I am painting *you?* You're not the specific interest of the composition."

"Well, what *are* you painting then?"

"A picture. You are no more important in the total scheme of things than the couch beneath you or the background behind you. And as for the apricot counterpane, it leaves you nowhere. You are no more than a series of lines and a few colour masses—a few pleasant tints—a sculpturesque mass in one part of the general harmony."

"Help!"

"Besides, 'Morning' wouldn't be appropriate. You have the quick athletic lines and the fresh skin and all the outward appearance of a figure that might symbolise the dawn of a new day, but what's the good of that when your soul is still dark with an almost mediæval twilight—— "

"Oh, but it isn't! I've improved a lot. I've done wonders since you took me in hand."

"Ah, bless you," said he, his accents abruptly changed, the voice affectionate and the eyes looking very kindly on the face in the glass. "'Took you in hand,' poor child! Me? Who am I? I am nothing—a thousand times less than nothing. Don't treat me too seriously, Prestissimo. I am only a poor dauber with a few small ideas and a conceit as large as the world. A trifler, and a gas-bag to boot, when the last word is said, and the last door shut for evermore."

"I think you're wonderful. I've always thought so."

"Ah, now I can't go on with this quarrel. You've unmanned me. 'I'll lie me down and bleed awhile, And then I'll rise and fight again.' Enough, enough; I'll paint." He spun round from the mirror and faced her directly. "But we'll give you a smile, my dear. We'll just part your lips as if you were only now remembering that something delightful was going to happen to-day. We'll concede so much to those who love a story in a picture, and to you who want to be the most important thing in it. We have sometimes observed such an expression about your mouth; and we will allow that we have not been unattracted by it; and now cease your clacking."

The drawing was resumed, and the silence, and he was gone from her again. He drew for another hour, and then gave her a second interval for rest, but did not talk during the interval; for he was lost in consideration of the picture on the easel. Back to the throne again, and he gently touched her position and her drapery into place, and returned to the work. There followed another hour, silent except for the sound of his steps back and forth from the easel, his marks on the paper, and the creaks of her couch if she moved. Then she yawned, and at once patted her hand over her mouth, murmuring, "Oh Cynthia! Cynthia Coventry, behave yourself!" and he looked up at these words, as if they had brought him back to cognizance of her.

"Tired?" he asked.

" Not very."

" Well, we'll stop in a minute. You've done splendidly, and the light's going. Just wait a minute. . . . Yes, that'll do for to-day. Now we'll eat."

" Thank heaven," said she, jumping down. " I've had nothing to eat since breakfast."

" *What ?* " he cried.

" It's so."

" But how's that ? "

" Well, you bet I came here just as quickly as I could get here."

" Child, child ! What can we do for you ? We've only bread and cake in the place. Go at once and see if Benito, the hot chestnut man, is at his corner, or if it is Suleiman (on whom be peace) the baked potato man ; and get sixpennyworth of whichever the Lord has provided. No ; *you* can't go, because there's the lousy old woman opposite, the terrific Miss Huckable—— "

" Hackett," corrected Cynthia.

" Eh ? . . . All right, Hackett, if you like ; but damn her anyway for an evil old slut. *I'll* go. Go you and get dressed, and we'll have a meal for you, directly you're ready. Nothing since breakfast ! My poor, poor darling ! "

Just as he was, in blue blouse and slippers, he left the studio and went up the road, while she ran and took a good look at the drawing, and then hurried behind the screen to dress. Soon she heard him returning, and his voice calling, " It was Suleiman (on whom be peace) so be you quick and get dressed while I balance his potatoes on the hot water pipes ; and then let me get at that gas stove. We've done a good day's work, Prestissimo. I'm pleased with it—pleased with it.

x

Something's going to come out of all this. Something good."

" Oh, cheers ! " said she.

They had many such days. And often she would find a bag of sweets or several bars of chocolate on her couch, because, as he said, " I know you have a childish fondness for such things, and besides, I can't have you feeling hungry. You may gollop a sweet now and then, if I'm not at work on your face." He was painting now ; and his palette was rested on the arms of a chair by the easel's side. Sometimes he was silent for hours on end ; sometimes he was singing at his work ; sometimes he was roaring at it, " *All* that I arst is luv . . . " and on other and talkative days he would break up the work with patches of jubilant quarrelling, standing above palette and chair and demonstrating his points with a brush. But were the days calm or gusty, they were the happiest she had known.

XI

AND O'Kelvie? What was he thinking all this time? Let us free ourselves of the notion that there was villainy in his request that Cynthia should pose as his model. On the contrary, the gentleness in him, as we have seen, was at issue in this matter with the artist's desire, so that he floundered when he spoke of it. The truth is that there were two responses in him to Cynthia and her self-offering : one, the artist's, and the other, the man's. The artist's response was empty of sex—or as empty of sex as any æsthetic reaction can ever be. During that winter and spring, in the hours when he was painting her, she attracted him exactly as a column in the sunlight, or a beech bole, might attract him—no more. An artist, painting a nude figure, if really inspired by it, forgets he is a man— and only paints. Cynthia was never safer with him than when posed on the model's throne with the light and shadow on her breast and thigh. But sometimes, when she wearied and yawned, she would offer one of her childish remarks, such as, " Wouldn't Mother have forty fits if she saw me here ? " and, for a moment, O'Kelvie came to earth to meet his manhood again, and remember how much she charmed him.

For it is plain that, once the artist was laid aside, she charmed the man. Clearly he liked her company, not because he was a painter, but because he was an " average sensual man," and she a young girl with pretty ways, lively spirits, and an eager affection. He would not have given up two or three evenings a week to escorting a young man among the places and people he liked— especially if the young man was as callow as Cynthia. Such a youth would have had nothing to give him ; Cynthia had much. He had other women come to his studio, but none with such a freshness as she. He liked that fragrance of " Bloom of Ninon " which she brought through the garden door into the dusty studio, and left behind her when she went. It was a small, frightened fragrance, modest but peeping ; and the scent of the other women seemed coarser after it.

Often after she had left him he stood at his easel and thought of her. And the hand that held the brush fell to his side, and he left the easel to walk about, for he was an artist no longer but a hungry man. What to do about her ?—but at once he saw how futile it was to argue what he would do, when he knew very well what he would do. It would happen. God, but it was amazing that he, Patrick O'Kelvie, had kept her by him so long, and not even kissed her ! Which of his friends would believe it of him, if he told them ? She had revealed to him as still alive a buried part of himself that he had thought long dead. Her simplicity —the " innocence " of which her father had spoken— had proved a white breastwork around her which this other self was loth to carry. It had weighed heavier in the scale than the self-offering. But with the deepening intimacy the self-offering must win. He was no ascetic, to hold back from all she offered. It was so clear that she loved him, and that he could win her to anything. And why not ? If his philosophies were right, why not ?

But a philosophy of life is a thing of the intellect : it seldom comes, as he saw plainly now, from the whole man. A man is much more than his brain's philosophy, though it be the sincerest. There are ancestors in his blood, and they lift their protests from below. He had had too many ancestors of the puritan breed to be perfectly happy about the taking of Cynthia. And in his childhood he had worn the puritan strait-jacket ; and though, in his vigour, he had cast it off, its impress remained. When he thought of Cynthia and knew what would happen, he found that unwittingly he had shaken his head, as if, alas, it was a heavy business. That shake of the head was ordered from far below his intellect and his will. He could not free himself from guilt and pity.

But were these emotions strong enough to fetter him from going forward ? He knew very well they were not.

They were stronger than he supposed, however. The winter lengthened into spring, and he put off and put off taking even so much as a kiss from Cynthia. And perhaps the painting of her, by changing their relation, had delayed a forward step. But his was a light and rapid brush, and the canvas was nearly complete now, and laid against the wall. And April broadened and brightened into May, and the grass grew lank again, and here and there on the unkempt orchard trees the blossom stood like the last relics of snow, as Cynthia ran through the garden to the studio door. The blossom faded and fell, and the dust of summer settled on the darkening leaves . . . and one could not go on like this for ever. So there came an evening when Cynthia arrived by the garden door, fresh and eager as yesterday, to be taken out into the rioting life of the streets ; and he, not without a catch in his speech, said, " No, let's stay . . . Let's stay and talk . . . I'm tired to-night."

And at once she threw off her hat and light coat, and smoothed her dress into place, for she was happy whatever they did, so long as they were together. She threw herself on the couch, (which was back on the floor again) and curled her feet under her, while he sat himself—almost stiffly—on a hard chair. He tried to run the talk through its accustomed wild and lively country, but his efforts were laboured. Very strange. He, Pat O'Kelvie, felt as uncomfortable as any young simpleton who was trying for the first time to speak a word of love. Silences fell between them, during which they caught each other's glances, and turned away. She had let an arm fall down the side of the couch to the floor, and at last he leaned forward and picked up the hand as if to examine it. But he had not touched it before it trembled. Looking from it to her face, he saw that her eyes were fixed on him. They were frightened but ready, and he drew her to her feet.

" Come," he said with a smile. " I've never kissed you, have I ? "

She was silent; but her eyes lit up. Without a word she put up her face to his.

It was a movement to stir any man's love, and for that second he loved her almost passionately. He took her into his arms and kissed her ; then, lifting his face, looked down upon her and murmured, as her eyes opened, " I love you, little Cynthia."

She only smiled back, and closed her eyes, and raised

herself a little higher on her toes that he might not have to stoop so far. And now he held her very close and kissed her rapturously, passing his hand over her hair and down her shoulder and arm. He pressed his palm upon her breast; and the sweetness of its yielding inflamed him, and he was gathering her against him with strangling arms.

And Cynthia—behind her closed eyelids she burned in an ecstasy. It was as if some power had rushed up in her body, and must consume her in a bliss of the mind and a tingling, sensuous delight. Pulses that she did not know her body possessed beat against the body of the man who held her. Never when dreaming of his kiss had she imagined it would be an uprush of agonising happiness like this. So far as she had thoughts at all, they were, "Hold me! Hold me! Keep me!" and "Is this it? Is this the thing of which people never speak? What more can there be than this?" Which drew another question up into the white dazzle of her mind, "Am I doing my part? Am I doing all he wants?" This last thought diluted the bliss with a flavour of doubt; and when next he lifted his mouth from hers, she opened her eyes and looked up into his face and said, "Forgive me if I don't know what to do."

In a whisper he asked her meaning; but how could she explain? She could only smile and shake her head and say, "I am always rather lost in a new experience."

The innocence of the words was so complete that they pierced him with the old pity. He kissed her in affection rather than in passion, and whispered, "You are all that's wonderful, my dear." And he smoothed her hair and stroked her arm. Then, sated with kisses, and disturbed by her simplicity, he gently put her away.

And she, unaware of his thoughts, held his hand and supposed it was over. If he was happy, so was she.

Speech was impossible for a little while. They could only look at each other, half smiling; till O'Kelvie lifted up her hand and kissed it, and said, " Cynthia."

" Yes."

" Go now, my dear. I want to think."

" All right," she agreed, simply as a child who is told that it is time to leave the bright day and go to bed. She dropped his hand and went to her coat and hat and put them on, while he stood watching her. Her dressing finished, she asked, " When may I come again ? "

O'Kelvie threw out his under jaw, while attempting a debate within himself. But his mind stood still. Conflict of equal forces had stagnated thought. Behold, he was the fettered one now, and she the free. Impotently he asked, " Do you think we had better ? "

" If we love each other, yes."

That " if we love " expressed no real doubt in her mind, for had he not said, " I love you, little Cynthia " ? But the words filled with a different meaning for him, who knew that there were loves and loves.

" Tell me," said he, " has no one ever kissed you before ? "

" No. Not really. Not properly."

" How is that ? " He asked it, as if amused.

" I have never let them. I have never loved anyone but you. I see that so clearly now."

Oh, why did she punish him like this ?

" But I thought you once told me . . . ? "

" Oh yes. But that was when I was only a child. I didn't know what love was, as I do now."

At which he shook his head. " Don't love me too much, little Cynthia."

" Why ? "

" Because you mustn't give the best of your love to me."

" Why not ?   I give it where I choose."

" No." And here was he, Pat O'Kelvie, speaking like any citizen of Norman's End. " I am not worthy of you."

But she didn't take him seriously. " It's too late now, Rugg dear."

" It mustn't be too late."

" But it *is*," she insisted, with laughter in eyes and on lips. " You should have told me that before. I am past praying for now."

" Cynthia."

" Yes."

" I mean it."

" And so do I. I shouldn't mind if you were a hundred times more unworthy than you are. Besides, it's me that's the unworthy one. You're so frightfully clever, and I'm only just beginning to be. But I'm going to try hard to be worthy of you ; oh ! I'm going to try ever so hard. And I *will* be—I *will* be, because I could do anything for you ! I may come again fairly soon, mayn't I ? " And she put up her face for the good-bye kiss. " Please : when may I come again ? "

" As soon as you like, my dear," he answered. " I so love you to come."

He had accepted the oncoming thing. He could not fight against it.

XII

Cынтнia is returning along Macartney Road, and her step is nervously hurried. Her body feels exquisitely empty and tired, but her mind is a room of scintillating light. Never has she known such exultation. And the exultation is also peace; for an old curiosity is laid to rest, and a new confidence fills her. Somewhere below this unresting joy there is stillness and calm. I am reminded of her father returning along the pavement after Evelyn had suffered him to kiss her; but this is a larger triumph.

Up in her room she opens her window and looks out upon the night. She sees the starlight and shadows on the houses opposite, and, down below, the gas lamps zig-zagging and narrowing along Macartney Road till, at the vista's end, they meet the cross-wise lamps of Glastonbury Road. Glastonbury Road where she was a child, and imagined she was happy, in the pitifully empty years before Rugg whispered, "I love you, little Cynthia." She has no dislike now for Norman's End. It has lost all power. Released from it, and free, she can feel an affection for it, and a loyalty. She has left it behind. And the future? But the present is too dazzling for her to see far into the future, or for the future to matter much. She loves, and is loved; and the future can wait. "I love you, little Cynthia."

How soon could she be with him again? Ever humble

and afraid of being a nuisance, she thought, "Not to-morrow, but the day after. I can wait as long as that."

It was good to get into bed, and curl up under the clothes, and think the happy thoughts. To count the hours. Only about forty-four of them. And when she slept, there was a glow over every dream, which the dream did not justify or understand, so that, when she woke to the light, she woke also to the incredible joy. "You are all that's wonderful, Cynthia."

And eight of the hours had been destroyed in sleep. Only thirty-six now.

As she dressed she thought, "Perhaps there'll be a letter from him. Such a letter as I should have longed to write—pages and pages and pages of it." And she hurried down to the living-room and the breakfast table. No; no letter. But she took only a prick of disappointment. It had been a silly fancy. Why should he start writing to her a few minutes after he had seen her? That was the sort of silly thing that *she* would do.

Now she was at work in the office, and lifting her eyes too often from her typewriter to the clock on the mantel-piece. Two more hours had gone. Three. Some-times her fingers paused on the keys while her thoughts ran far away. What was he doing now? If she "willed" a message to him, would he receive it across the miles of London? "Oh, I am thinking of you, dearest." The joy of saying "dearest!" Yesterday she had not the courage to do it, but she would do it to-morrow. She would whisper it between the kisses. Her hands still arrested over the keys, like the hands of one who listens, she imagined his answer coming back, "I love you, little Cynthia."

It was poor work that she did that day; for some-times she wanted to remember how he had stroked her arm and her neck, and laid his palm upon her breast; and since our words may be crude when we talk to our-selves, she thought, " Oh, when he touches me like that, it makes me want to babble ! . . ." Twenty-nine hours. . . .

The day's work over, she escaped from her father that she might travel home with no company but her thoughts. And as she sat with them in a coach of the District Railway, one came suddenly, " There may be a letter when I get back." But no, she wouldn't imagine it : why should there be ? Men were different.

There was no letter. But her need of joy was too great to tolerate more than a second of disappointment. One second's sorrow, and she was happy and expectant again.

All that evening she sat without speaking much, pretending to read. And all the while she was longing for bed, where silence awaited her, and warmth, and thought. As soon as possible, she went there. And she pulled up the clothes and bathed in warm, luxurious thought.

To-morrow was here, slanting through the window down the sunlight of a May morning. Only twelve hours to go. On her dressing table was a little ornamental clock that a school fellow had given her to consolidate a friendship that " time could not sever "— which, alas ! had died long ago—and it ticked on ; and every tick was a landmark passed. There was another clock, we have seen, in the office. It may be that, a good old veteran, it is ticking somewhere still ; but on a May morning of a quarter of a century ago, it took the eyes of Cynthia a hundred times, as its hands went round and round—austere and passionless and dutiful. Ten o'clock. Eleven. A steady, unhurried beat. *It* was advancing towards her ; it was an hour—two hours nearer ; and the ticks went on. Already the expectation of it was almost a torment. So stupid ! She had moments of addressing herself sternly, " Pull yourself together, young woman ! " and rattling long and conscientiously on the typewriter's keys.

But there was no captaining her thought. It tossed from irrelevance to irrelevance. It was one picture transfiguring into another, with no apparent connection. Pictures of streets or rooms or gardens she had known long ago—the big class-room at Lammas—the waste-grounds at evening—the gardens of Earls' Court Exhibition—the dimmed interior of St. Alban's Church —what had suggested them ? Nothing. They had leapt into mind capriciously. And little snatches of scripture—of which some had no relevance at all, but others were astonishingly apt : " Like as the hart panteth after the waterbrooks. . . ." " My body is a thirsty land. . . ." Or was it " My soul . . . ? " What had made her say, " My body . . . ? "

In the luncheon hour she escaped from everyone, for she wanted to walk alone. Food was impossible. And leaving Great Smith Street, she walked up and down Victoria Street, and into Ashley Place where the great Italianate cathedral was a-building, so that these streets, and the high campanile of the cathedral, held for ever after the wistful wraiths of this day's thoughts.

Back in the office, and tea-time came at length ; and she was glad to drink, for her mouth was dry.

And now—was it possible ?—the office hours were

over. It was very near now. She was in the train, and it rolled her and a thousand more from one familiar station to another. Callous and indifferent, the train and the people in it! Those who observed Cynthia sitting with enlarged eyes fixed before her must have thought her lost in trouble. They did not know that each dim and raucous station, as they grated out of it, was another posting-house left behind, on the happiest highway known to man.

In a dream she arrived at Macartney Road, and hurried up to her room to dress. Her impatient hands made many mistakes. And absurdly the scripture sentences kept leaping up, astonishingly apt. " The King's daughter is all glorious within. . . ."

She went out on to the pavements with a quick heart and quivering limbs. Useless to try to control either. They would not be stilled till she was in his arms.

She went across the cobbled courtyard of the old mansion, and over the high grass, on to that moss-green path, between lawn and dividing wall, along which, eight years before, Rugg had walked with her and Aline Guilder, pointing out the mulberry tree. She passed through the door in the dividing wall, and ran through the grass beneath the unkempt orchard trees. And now she stood at the studio door. Yesterday, and many yesterdays, she had knocked loudly or humorously, but not this evening. This evening she knocked timidly.

But he heard, and his step was approaching. The door flung open.

" May I come in ? " she asked, as she always did ; and she hid to-night's timidity behind a smile.

" Come. . . ." He had been sitting there, waiting for

her, wondering if she would come, thirsting for her. "Come, my dear one. . . ."

The door slammed behind them, and she was in his arms. And between their kisses she said her word, "Dearest, *dearest !* "

As before he stroked her neck and arm and shoulders, but said nothing.

"It's so wonderful when you do that," she said. And again for a moment his pity touched him. But it sank from sight in the mounting sea of desire, where no frail thing could live.

"I love you, Cynthia," he whispered. "I love you."

"And I you—madly—dearest."

He drew her to the couch, and laid her there. And she closed her eyes, and said good-bye to the world.

XIII

CYNTHIA left the studio very quietly that night. The hour before she went she had been dazed and silent, but happy. Very happy, and yet . . . was there a vein of sadness in the happiness? Happy in Rugg's loving words, as he lifted her again to his side, but she could not answer him. When he asked her " Happy ? " she looked up with a bright smile, and said, " Yes. . . . Oh yes . . ." but . . . she couldn't admit that she was fighting down a little shame, and telling herself again and again there was no need to be ashamed. " No need. . . . No need. . . ." And at last she said, " I don't want to talk, somehow. Perhaps I'd better go."

Without a word, but with many loving touches, and one last grateful kiss, he let her go.

Bedazed. She walked home as one might who has been stunned, but is now better and glad of the night air on his brow. She was very tired, and longing to lie flat on her bed. She turned into Macartney Road. It was the same as she had left it four hours ago. . . . and yet strange. It was not hostile, but it had shrunk : it seemed smaller and more compact. And very odd the effect of this change upon her : as she put her key into the lock, she felt an overwhelming desire to cry.

In her bed she lay awake for a long time. She was trying to understand an inescapable feeling of loss. " Completion is loss," she told herself. " Fulfilment is loss." Though their parting had been very sweet and tender, she felt that something had gone from their kiss. Why this homesickness for the old dear ways of diffidence and raillery?

And as the night wore on, she was tortured by the thought that she had " made herself cheap." She was obliged to crush the thought down with reiterated phrases, " No, he will not think like that. I loved him. How else could I show my love? He will love me more, not less. He will love me more. . . ." Again and again the phrase passed—like an army of soldiers in single file, for the guarding of her happiness. Unending the army, that the old doubt might not ambush her. " He will love me more." She fell asleep saying it.

In the morning when the sunlight was on the wall, and her body was refreshed by heavy sleep, her mood was very different. Now exultation was livelier than the doubt and guilt, though these were not quite at rest. " Soon I shall see him again," she thought, and could have skipped on her bedroom floor. All her longing for him had returned. And within the heart of her exultation there was a peace. Completion had seemed to be loss last night, but this morning it was peace. The peace of completion. The peace of arrival. Her love had passed into a haven, quiet, safe, and still. Some of this stillness was due, though she did not see this, to the simplicity of her worship. " All, all of me is yours for ever and ever," she said to him across the distance, as she stood still on her floor.

It was so simple that it was peace.

Dressing, she told herself that she desired nothing else but to serve him as long as he lived. He was twenty-two years older than she, and would die before

Y

her—oh no! as she pictured his death, she prayed of
fate to slay her first—but then, with the old love of
self-sacrifice, she changed the prayer, "No; let me be
left, so that I can save him from this awful pain. Let
me bear it for him."

When would she see him? As ever, her shyness
would prevent her going to him that evening, unless he
sent for her. "But if he sends for me, I will run all
the way." She looked for a letter the whole of that
day, but he did not send one; and for a while the silly
doubts and anxieties worried above the surface. She
was sure they were silly, but they hurt—oh, the joy of
loving, but the suffering too! It was joy in its escape
from loneliness, and yet it was pain and loneliness too!
Again sentences repeated themselves in her head: she
seemed at the mercy of these reiterating sentences.
"Oh dearest, ask me to come."

There was a letter next morning. There it lay, when
she ran down to the living room before all the others!
Hope and fear shook the fingers that tore at the envelope;
and then hope had all the field to itself.

"*My very dear Cynthia, why did you not come and see
me last night? Come to-night, dear one. There is much
we must talk over. . . .*"

"My very dear Cynthia," "Dear one"—forgive
her that she whispered "Oh! Oh!" to the ceiling, and
pressed the letter against her breast, and raised it to
her lips.

She was very absent-minded at her desk that day.
"There is much that we must talk over." What would
he say? Marriage might not be possible for them for a
very long time. Perhaps he would suggest that for a

while they continued this secret loving. Perhaps (for
Cynthia had never dared ask him how stood the separa-
tion between himself and his wife) he would ask her
to live with him as his mistress, but she would say,
"I can't do that, because it would hurt father and
mother so ; but I will come to you at every possible
moment." Perhaps—oh perhaps, he would ask her to
marry him as soon as possible, and she had her answer
ready. "All of me is yours for ever and ever."

She had typed a letter all wrong, and with a sigh
drew the spoiled paper from the machine and took
another sheet.

Married. She tried to imagine their children ; and
was surprised that children didn't seem to matter so
much compared with him. But it was sweet to think
of them.

Then liveliness dismissed the dream. Very soon she
would be seeing him again. And her fingers played a
merry jig on the typewriter, and her feet were impatient
for a step-dance.

Half-past six.

Here again were the wrought-iron gates of Ashgar
House. Dear gates ! Uncared for, and ever ajar,
but how she loved them ! She ran through, and over
the cobbled courtyard, from whose kidney stones, so
sunken now, the horses of the periwigged charioteers
had kicked the sparks, as the postilions drew rein. The
dead windows of the mansion watched her as she crossed
them and passed under the coach-house arch. She
skirted along the dividing wall, passed through its door,
and was in among the apple trees.

She had knocked at the studio door ; and his steps
were approaching. He was opening it.

"Come in, dear one."

She took the welcoming hand; and it drew her into the room and into his embrace. There was a peace and a quietness about his kiss, she thought. And she rested her head on his shoulder, as if that were home. And, resting there, she seemed to have shed away five years of her life. All independence and assertiveness had dropped from her, and she could feel no older than when she was fifteen and wore her skirts short and her hair in a plait behind her back. It was a tranquil joy to feel dependent and childish again.

"And now we mustn't delay," said he laughingly, "because we're going to a theatre to-night."

"Oh are we? Joy!"

"Yes. We have half an hour only."

And she jumped for joy; and then there was all the fun of cooking a meal. This little household task gave her a pleasure that she did not speak of. It was almost as if their domestic peace together had begun.

"You don't say much," said he.

"I am so happy."

"Why?"

"You know why?"

He only smiled in return. "I want you to have a lovely time to-night."

So they ate their scrambled meal; and she didn't wonder that he made no reference to the "much to talk over." Too shy to ask what he had meant, she expected that he would break the topic after the theatre.

The fun of hurling themselves into the old red bus that would take them to Hyde Park Corner, and then the grander fun of jumping into a hansom (because time was short and a hansom swift) and jingling along

Piccadilly! He was holding her hand, and staring ahead of him at the hindquarters of the horse, while she was content to stare up at his profile, and smile if he turned his eyes to her.

The driver reined in his horse before the doors of the Alhambra, brightly lit, though daylight was still in the streets. Cynthia skipped out and looked up at that Moorish facade, lifting its domes and crescents into the pearly evening sky.

" Oh ! " she cried, in sheer joy.

O'Kelvie touched her elbow and guided her into the swim of bright opera cloaks and dark swallow-tail jackets that poured through the doorways past the huge commissionaires. He and she were not dressed in satin and silk like the others, but Rugg didn't seem to care. He guided her along the carpeted corridors to the auditorium, where the band was already playing ; and they sank into plush stalls, as the house-lights went out.

The Alhambra, that old gay, winking mosque, is with us still. And I sometimes think : how many have built for themselves within its gilded walls, when the house-lights went down and the proscenium blazed up for the ballet above the sawing bows of the orchestra, an hour's paradise of luxury and love. It is strange to muse upon those individual paradises, thousands upon thousands of them, built there side by side, or night after night, in an unreal land whose substance was woven of nothing more durable than music, cigar smoke, spectral faces along the tiers, loud laughter in the darkness, and, within the square of light, the entrancing movement of dancing girls. We have business with one night only, and one paradise only ; when a far-off summer darkness fell upon the domes and crescents of the Alhambra, and the street lights sprang up about its island block, and a race of hansoms, limousines, four-wheelers and taxis swirled around it, and at its doors, under large feathered hats, the eyes of the wantons plied their allurements; while within, gazing at the ballet but seeing little, Cynthia sat, feeling the hand of O'Kelvie about her own; and sometimes leaning her shoulder that it might touch his, and bringing over her other hand to stroke the hand that held hers.

The house-lights went up, and smartly she sat alert, and pretended to tidy the hair at the nape of her neck.

The performance was over, and they stood in the rattle and lights of the Charing Cross Road. It was a time of transition in the London streets: a few taxi-cabs moved among the hansoms and the growlers; a few motor omnibuses among the old horse omnibuses; and there were private broughams as well as limousines waiting for the opera cloaks and crush hats that poured from the theatre doors. A year later, and the taxi-cabs and the motors had spread their conquest everywhere, leaving the horse to the brewer's dray and the trader's van.

"We'll have a ride in a taxi-cab," said O'Kelvie, as if offering a novel addition to the night's entertainment.

Cynthia skipped.

"Yes, we'll go all the way home in it," declared he, perceiving her delight.

"Oh, but can we afford it?" objected Cynthia. "Hadn't we better go by train?"

"No, I want you to myself as long as possible," said O'Kelvie.

In the dark little room of the cab, she hoped he would gather her close to him, but he contented himself with holding her hand as before, and once or twice lifting it to his lips. No doubt he was waiting till he reached the studio. Then he would ask his questions of her, and take her to himself. . . . Her breath shortened with foretasted bliss, and her throat contracted. Who in the world so happy as she?

And they rolled along, she in her dream, and he abstracted and gazing before him.

The cab purred up to the blistered door in Ashgar Terrace. What of Miss Hackett now? Who minded Miss Hackett? Defiantly Cynthia waited on the pavement, while O'Kelvie paid the driver.

"Good-night, sir."

"Good-night."

Their voices echoed in the empty street; the engine roared, the gears grated, and the cab went away with a diminishing brawl; and Cynthia glanced up at Miss Hackett's windows. Midnight. But who minded? Nay, one was proud of the taxi.

In the studio she threw off her coat and made sprightly talk, pretending that she expected nothing. Rugg did not take her into his arms at once, but stood by the trestle table fumbling with the articles on it. Was he seeking words for what he wished to ask? So far he had not even invited her to stay, so she feigned a readiness to go. "I suppose I had better be going now."

Then he swung round to her.

"No, don't go yet. . . . Come and sit down." And he led her to the couch, and sat her beside him, and took a hand very gently. "It is coming now," thought Cynthia.

" Cynthia." He looked full into her face. " Don't love me too well."

She shook her head, and brightened her eyes. " It is too late now. The damage is done."

" No, no," he answered hastily, as if he didn't want to joke. " Dear, I've been thinking it all over since the other night. I mustn't let you love me."

" But why ? " she demanded, the laughter still in her eyes.

" Because you're too young, and you give too much."

" But what does that matter if I like it ? In all my life I have never been so happy as in the last few days. Since you said you loved me, I haven't known if I've been on my head or my heels."

" I love you, of course ; but——"

" But what, then ? "

" I don't think it's in me to love you as you love me."

" I don't mind," she affirmed happily. " You love me all you can, don't you ? "

To her surprise he met this with silence.

" *Don't* you ? " she begged, turning to him ; and the sudden alarm in her note went through him like a knife.

" I love you—who could help doing so ?—but not—not as you think or mean."

Her answer was a single " Oh ! " like a gasp. Sharply she drew her hand away from his, and held it tight in her other hand. And her face went pale. Not a word could he find for her that seemed worthy of her pain. And it was she who spoke first.

" Don't you love me better than anyone else ? "

Resolved to go forward on the road he had chosen, he gave her no answer, but stared at the ground.

" Please tell me," she pleaded ; and if O'Kelvie

deserved punishment, he was taking it now. No whip-lash could have hurt him like her simple question.

He lifted his eyes from the floor and looked at the blank wall before him. "I love you too well to say ' yes,' " he answered, taking her hand again.

Cynthia's lower lip fell ; and O'Kelvie's hand contracted about hers, as he saw her anguish. "My dear," he begged, " I've never loved anyone as you want or need to be loved. I think my work has drained away all power for that. I have never done more than trifle with women—there are others besides you in my life, Cynthia, and they bear with this—but not you. *You* mustn't. I know I've been a cad to let you come so far. I know it. But I'm only a weak man. And I'm trying to do the right thing now—because I love you enough for it. Help me."

She turned her white face to him. " And you mean . . ." she began.

But he saved her from the question. " I shall miss you so terribly. But—I think we ought to call it off. I—I'm sure of it. For *your* sake."

" Let me think," said Cynthia, staring before her.

But how to think, when all the world was in ruins about her ? She turned to look at him, and looked long. It is the last time you will see him. Look well. His hand was still lying on hers : she would leave it there a little longer, to feel its touch. A few minutes, and it would be no more than a memory. Let her feel it a little longer. The tears—no, drive them back, and order the lips to stay still. Oh, but it was hardly bearable ! If only she could run along Macartney Road, and up the narrow staircase to her room, and there, unseen, press her face into the friendly pillow, and let the agony tear through her. " I must hold myself together," she thought. " I must endure it a little. It will come all right." And her teeth came over her lip.

Better jump up and go. Better run through the torture quickly. . . But that would mean letting go of his hand ; and it was difficult to do.

" Well ? " asked O'Kelvie at last.

His voice gave her strength to move ; and she jumped up, and picked up her coat, which was across the sofa's foot. " Good-bye, then."

" Cynthia ! "

They were standing opposite each other, without words.

" Good-bye," she repeated.

" You do know that I have done this, because I—I love you very much in my way."

" Oh yes, yes," she answered wearily.

" Tell me you don't hate me."

She shook her head and faintly smiled. " No."

" And you're not too sorry it all happened ? "

" Oh no," she answered. " No. I'm sure I'm not that. I don't want you to think that. I know that you have enlarged and deepened me, as no one else could have done. Do always remember that." And for a second she touched his hand, as if in gratitude.

" But you mustn't suffer, Cynthia. You're too dear to suffer."

" That's all right," she said. " Don't worry about me. Please, I must go."

He put out his arms. " Kiss me."

" No, no," said she, hurriedly. " Not that."

" Good-bye then, my dear."

" Good-bye."

"*Cynthia!*" But she had turned and was hurrying to the door. His hand dropped to his side.

And for the last time Cynthia passed through the studio door and between the apple trees. She was longing for the lee of the old dividing wall, where she might release her tears, and let the sobs rack through her. Now she was under it, screened from the studio ; and she stood still, and gave them vent. "Oh, Rugg . . . Rugg. . . Rugg. . ." Then, a long way off, a clock struck one in the morning ; and she threw back her head, and went shivering through the coach-gates into the empty road home.

PART IV

I

VERY often the atmosphere of sad days will distil itself into a single air of music, so that you have but to hear that air sung in the distance, or to hum it to yourself on a lonely walk, for the old sorrow to rise around you. It was the air of a mock-melancholy song that, for years, afterwards, set the ache in Cynthia's heart. " There is a tavern in the town, Where my true love sits him down, And never, never thinks of me. . . ." She heard it only a few days after that parting. A trio of sailors, arm in arm, on leave and in liquor, went singing it along the pavements of Norman's End. And because there is no room for humour in a grief like hers, she sat still and listened to it, wondering that people could make a jovial song of the greatest suffering in the world. And in that craving for heartbreak which seizes people in the sickness of loss, she would hum the air to herself, that she might suffer the more. In her thoughts the " tavern in the town " was one of those noisy rooms where Rugg had taken her to crowded parties. She saw him sitting among the chattering throng, laying down the law in witty and violent phrases, and laughing his gusty laugh. " With a damsel on his knee. . . ." She shut tight her fists and shivered.

There is a pain that in its first weeks is almost beyond bearing. The tormented soul has to find escape from a little of it. And one day—suddenly—Cynthia saw a door of escape. What if Rugg, for her own sake, had lied to her, when he said he didn't love her as she supposed? He hadn't meant it. He couldn't have meant it. He had said it because he loved her with a self-sacrificing love, and knew that it would be best for her to hear this lie and be free of him. Oh, if she could believe this as the truth! Only let her still believe in his love, and she could bear never to see him again. It was not the absence of Rugg, but the absence of his love, that slew the heart.

But was she only deluding herself? Was she only seizing on a hope without which she could not live? Her intelligence was keen enough to ask the question often; and she would walk alone with it, or sit alone with it, while it turned round and round for her inquiry. Indeed, whenever Cynthia was silent in these days, she was keeping company with her question. It sat with her in trains, it broke the work at the office, and it lived at her side from supper-time till bed. And if you saw her abruptly throwing back her head, it probably meant she had decided to think defiantly, " What's the good? I shall never, never know. I will worry it out no more." And a few minutes later the remoteness was in her eyes again, for she was back with the old debate.

In the end she had to believe in his love. She had to hug this hope as the only life-buoy. Meaningless, that ecstacy of love she had felt for Rugg? Over and done with, like a wilted rose? No, it could not be. " I love you, little Cynthia. . . . Come, my dear one. . . ." He had meant it then; he had loved her then—and his love couldn't be a meaningless, purposeless, finished thing. Her very upbringing, with its talk of God, drove her to believe that this story of herself and Pat O'Kelvie was no purposeless accident but a climax to both their lives, God-designed, whose fruition was only withered in this world, and not blasted for ever. In some other life. . . .

Thus for the present she escaped the uttermost pain. She had not the courage to take annihilation.

You would not have seen that she was suffering. Her parents and her friends saw little of it, for it was one of her comforts to take pride in hiding it from the world. The face she gave to the world was hung with cheerfulness, laughter, and interest in other people's poor little topics—but the effort wearied her quickly each day, so that she longed for her bed, where she could lie alone with her thoughts, and in the hope that she would dream of him.

It greatly helped her saving belief that, within a month of their good-bye, Rugg went from these parts, and the studio in Ashgar Terrace stood empty. Surely he had gone for her sake. Perhaps, even, he could no longer bear these parts, and the old untidy studio, with their memories. It was so with herself. Once or twice her journeyings took her along Moyland Avenue, which ran across the top of Ashgar Terrace, and then she walked quickly, keeping her eyes away from the vista of that road, with the long wall of the garden and the high wall of the studio, while the cry of her heart was, "Oh *no!*" No, she must not see it. She could not bear it yet.

And month pushed month behind; and every Sunday morning the church bell of St. Alban's rang across the roofs to her window in Macartney Road.

For a long time she passionately resisted its call. But St. Alban's Church sat deep in her heart, and Mr. Guilder, too, and the old psalm tunes rolling down from the choir, and the voice of a thousand people singing in the dim interior a familiar hymn. The longing grew and grew. Why not, why not? Did she believe any longer in the freedom that Rugg had so merrily proclaimed? She had adventured out joyously towards it, and it had shattered her on the threshold. Dimly she saw that there had been a wrongness in his taking of her; and lo! the vision of that lovely free world was marred. She had seen it, as it were, through his window, and at his side; and now a mist had dulled the glass. If Rugg had sinned and knew it, then was the free man so much better than the prisoners he despised? There was sin in both, and virtue in both. If freedom was good, so too was self-discipline. It was nearly joy to think that she would turn home to the peace she had known when she loved the " beauty of holiness."

" I must try not to be superstitious," she thought, remembering much that he had taught her; " I must think it out properly "—but the emotion was gathering, gathering. . . .

And there came a Sunday when the sun was bright, and her pain at the flood, and the church bell ringing; and she yielded to an overpowering presentiment that, if she went to the service, she would catch from it words that would sound like a direct message from God. Superstition? She was not sure. Perhaps yes, but again, perhaps no; and she hurried to the church in case, in case. . . . She ran there in the spirit of " Lord, I believe, help Thou mine unbelief." And the dim interior, crowded with waiting people, over whose heads the music of the organ waved softly, met her with a welcome, silent, but rich, enfolding, and warm.

She went to a seat about half way up the nave, and sat there, resting without thought in the stillness, the dimness, and the music.

The service began. And as the organ pealed forth the music of canticle or psalm, she knew how deeply she loved these things. She followed in her prayer-book the well-known words, waiting for those, if any, that should have a special meaning for her. At the time of the First Lesson she sat and gazed at the reading priest, wondering if now the message was at hand. Mr. Guilder went to the lectern for the Second Lesson, and " Now, now ! " she thought—but no, not yet. Nothing had called to her yet. With some suspense she listened for the announcement of the first hymn—but it brought nothing. Well, if she had been mistaken in her presentiment, she would know that it had been mere superstition, but she hoped not, for she so loved this hymn they were singing, and she longed, she longed to come home.

Cynthia might have known that it is well-nigh impossible to attend such a service, with its psalms and lessons and sermon, without sooner or later hearing the words you desire. They came in the sun-shot church this morning, and at so remarkable a moment, that she accepted them as a friendly miracle. Mr. Guilder ascended the pulpit, the music died out, and the congregation sat down and looked up at him, while he leaned an elbow on his lectern. Cynthia looked up at him also, and thought that he looked ill. In the selfishness of her love she had given no heed to Mr. Guilder, almost for years ; and it was like seeing someone after long absence : he seemed much older. But now he was speaking, and with a voice sure and pleasing as ever. " In the second chapter of Philippians, and the thirteenth verse, you will find these words : ' It is God which worketh in you both to will and to do.' "

Ah, that was no accident ! That was designed ! Then all this suffering was of God ! Mr. Guilder, as he waited for a dramatic moment after announcing the text, did not know that one of his congregation was gazing up at him, wide-eyed in wonder. He did not know, as he suggested that suffering was often " a mark of God's favour " that this listener was almost frightened by the miracle ; nor, when he quoted, " It is good for me that I have been in trouble, that I might learn thy statutes," that a tired traveller was coming home with joy, with joy. A last hymn, and the congregation sank to its knees for the benediction : " The Lord lift up the light of His Countenance upon you, and give you His peace, this day, and for evermore." Cynthia knelt and buried her head in the crook of her arm. And she stayed thus, after the people had risen again, so full and keen her surrender. Slowly the patient, halting, oft-arrested feet went past her down the aisles, but she did not see the people thronging out, for her head was still upon her arms :

> " *Just as I am, young, strong, and free ;*
> *To be the best that I can be,*
> *For righteousness and truth and Thee,*
> *Lord of my life, I come.*"

II

THIS new rest upon God only strengthened the consoling belief that there had been a purpose in the love of herself and Rugg, and so they must be destined to meet again one day and blend for ever. At times she wondered if she had been sent out into the empty wilderness that she might improve her character so as to be worthy of this bliss hereafter. The idea had fixed itself now that Rugg, in consideration for her, had lied, and that he loved her still. She waited in quietness —or she tried to do so—for sometimes the old anguish flowed over her like a tide. And she went about, trying to be kind and good. She made no new friends in these days, because she didn't seem to want them ; she wanted only the loneliness of thought.

And in her thought she was turning all things to contributory proof. The picture that he had painted of her—nothing was heard of it. Now and again she saw a record of his paintings in some journal, but never word of a picture called " Morning." He had thought it one of his best, and doubtless he had suppressed it for her sake. Oh, she was sure that in some sense he and she were one, forever one. When she read in " Wuthering Heights " Catherine's words about Heathcliff : " My great thought in living is himself. If all else perished, and *he* remained, I should still continue to be . . . Nelly, I *am* Heathcliff ! He's always, always, in my mind ; " she cried, " Oh yes, *yes !* "

The new fashion for Bridge had drained slowly into Norman's End at this time; and if occasionally she went with Hilda and her grandmother for a game at Rose Damien's, she would make mistakes, because, while her eyes gazed at the cards in her hand, or the trick on the table, her mind was seeing a path through the apple trees and the garden door of the studio, and hearing a voice which said, "I love you, little Cynthia."

Another small thing, though scarcely worth recording here, for it was of so little moment in her life, was that Rob Ingram came on leave to his father's house, and began to notice her. He was always seeking her out, and at last asked her if she thought she could ever consider him as a suitor; and she was obliged to put him away quickly but tenderly, assuring him that, if ever she married anyone, she would have to feel very much more than she felt for him. And Rob left her, not greatly hurt, she suspected, because his opinion of himself was good and he would go on hoping, till someone else attracted his eye.

In this manner of life she walked down the empty avenue of a year. Soon she would be twenty-one. That birthday came, and fell further and further behind; and sometimes it appalled her to watch the years wasting behind her. Then she would think, "It will get better if I only wait"; but it didn't. It remained exactly the same. And when the torment of longing visited her, she would ask herself, could it be that more than a year had gone since that midnight parting? More than a year, and she was no better of her sickness. "Oh, Rugg, I am yours always—always. Are you thinking of me?"

One Saturday in autumn, when she had nothing to

fill her mind, the tide of anguish rose so high that it drove her out of the house and along the pavements to Ashgar Terrace, where she could stand and stare at the studio and the fruit trees behind the old wall, and suffer more . . . more . . . all. . . . With a falling lip and a leaden heart, and a head shaking sadly, she looked at the old blistered door that opened on to the pavement and the long perpendicular slit with its wooden shutter, through which the great canvases used to come out to the vans. She remembered the day when Rugg and she had opened the long panel to peep out and see if Miss Hackett was at her post, and, if not, to grimace and make long noses at her balcony.

And as she thought of this, she put her palm on the panel, as one does on something one loves.

How endure ? How go on living ? There swelled within her a passionate desire to tell someone. To tell every word of it to someone, and to ask him to stablish again her faith and her aspiration, which were trembling. She could endure it alone no more. And suddenly— unsought—as she lingered by the grey wall—there stood before her mind the figure of Mr. Guilder. After O'Kelvie's criticism she had not her old illusions about him : she no longer thought him a saint, but suspected that he was a man of passions like any other, and one who loved the limelight well, but she knew also that he was kind and really loved the young. And she had loved him so as a child. And this lovingness, because thwarted now, was ready to run back to any familiar channel that would receive it. This sudden vision of him—was it a message ? Perhaps—for she had picked up all her old superstitions, at least to play with—it was a message from Rugg who was thinking about her at this moment, and unhappy about her. " Go and talk it over with Mr. Guilder. I want you to be helped, little Cynthia." Yes, it was a message from Rugg. Oh, when could she go to Mr. Guilder? Now. *Now.* " So soon, Prestissimo? "—oh, not that—not that thought—she couldn't bear it.

Now. " He will be in; he will be in; he will be in; because this is fate." With a quick step, and a quicker heart, she went from Ashgar Terrace and along the pavements—right across that district we have called the Square Quarter Mile—till she came to St. Alban's Vicarage.

The Vicarage was the only detached house in all this part—the only one with something of a rural charm. Standing on the ecclesiastical land, under the north wall of the church, it was a two-gabled house with bow windows. These windows looked across a narrow stretch of garden to the road; the door was at the side facing the church. Between windows and road were planes and chestnuts; and between the door and the church wall a spatter of privet, laurel, and holly. And a wisteria ran over the door, and draped itself along the yellow bricks. The Vicarage! Within these walls lived and worked Mr. Guilder, with his unknown thoughts and disappointments and ambitions. Its charm in this softening light of evening seemed an earnest of relief. Relief at last!

With a suspense like that before a doctor's home she stood in the gravel path between the front door and the shrubs—and knocked. If he was in, she would know that it had been a message; if he was not in, well, it had been only a silly superstition. But he *would* be in; he *would* be in.

Mrs. Swan, a plump and faithful servant of the Vicar, opened the door.

"Oh . . ." stuttered Cynthia.   "Is the Vicar in ? "

"No, miss."

"What !   Are you *sure* ? "

"Yes, miss."

(Not in ?   But he must be !   It was if a bolt had fallen and knocked a castle to ruins.)

"No, miss.   He's not at 'ome.   He's an appointment in town.   An important one, I fancy."

"I see . . .   Well . . .   Oh, all right. . . ."

"But he should be back any time now, miss.   He said he'd be back in time for Evensong.   I expect he's not far, if you'd care to step in."

(Was the castle rebuilding ?   If he returned within half an hour, she would try to believe that it was built again.)

"Oh, thank you . . .   Yes, I think I will."

"Yes, miss.   Step in, do."

And Cynthia passed into the vicarage, and the door shut on her.

III

Mr. Guilder left Norman's End Station to cross the Square Quarter Mile; setting his feet for the same pavements that Cynthia had trod twenty minutes before. His face was grey. If ever Mr. Guilder's face was "striking"—and seldom a man but used this word of it—it was so this evening. A year or two ago, the hair, waving down from the central parting, had turned to silver, though he was not sixty then; and this evening the grey pallor of the skin matched the silver of the hair brushed back over his ears, under the shining silk hat. And a refinement like the refinement of death lay over the face, as if the blood had withdrawn, leaving the skin pure and the thin features in their first perfection. It might well have been a dead man's face, except for a brilliance in the eyes and a queer, sad smile about the lips.

At the corner of Norman's End Lane and Macartney Road a newspaper shop displayed its row of placards under the window. And the day after a man was dead, thought Mr. Guilder, these placards would blare forth the announcement of things he had not seen; and the next day, and the next. The stream of life would hurry on, indifferent to the passing out of a single man. Old Heraclitus and his Everlasting Flux! Each moment the new thing came to birth, and, with hardly a glance at the old, the newsmen hurried to catch it—the new thing, the "news." And it perished even as it bloomed.

In Macartney Road the children, free of school,

kicked a rubber ball from one to another; and the
expression in Mr. Guilder's eyes, as he went by and
looked at them, was a little like the expression seen in
grandparents' eyes when they play with their sons' sons:
it was the kindly-smiling look that those who are at the
end of their game give to those who are at the beginning.
As he went on, Mr. Guilder noticed every symptom of
social decay in the windows, doors, and basements of
Macartney Road; for that had happened this afternoon
which gives a man new eyes.

Very different Macartney Road from when he
came to it twenty years ago. The northward "tubes"
were open now, and garden cities were building
on the northern heights of London; the westward
tubes pushed further west, and daily a popu-
lation of millions moved under the ground; and the
people who once upon a time came to Norman's End
would come no more. Decay. The law for flowers
and streets and men. Movement and decay. Was
there nothing *still* anywhere? Truth must be still.
Yonder was his old friend, the travelling tinker, pushing
his gaudy barrow, and looking up left and right at the
windows, as he chanted his trade: "Any *knives* to grind.
. . . Any *chairs* to mend. . . . If I'd as much money as I
could spend, I shouldn't be crying, Any chairs to mend.
. . ." Somewhere near-by his old partner would be
sitting on the kerb, mending the cane seat of a chair.
Here she was, at the corner of Macartney Road and
Wentworth Avenue: she always chose a corner for her
seat. Her jaws mumbled as she threaded the cane.
Yesterday he would have pitied her, in her dirty clothes
and man's boots, with her bearded face and horny hands
—but now? Should he not envy her? She still

possessed that which had just been taken from him. He shrugged his massive shoulders ; while, from behind him now, came the melancholy cry, " If I'd as much money as I could spend, I shouldn't be crying, Any chairs to mend. . . ."

In Wentworth Avenue a woman parishioner passed him, to whom he gave his usual smile ; and she went on her way, unknowing. Was he going to tell any of them ? At first his old love of the dramatic showed him the drama of his news, but in the next second he shook his head. What had happened this afternoon was a wonderful purifier of a man's values. It and vulgarity could not house together. For the present he would tell his wife and no one else ; not even Lance and Aline. No, not a soul.

A few steps would bring him into Parson's Road ; and he would see again—after this experience of two hours ago—his home and his church. There they were. It was but twenty strides now to his gate, and, as he took them, he looked up at the north wall of St. Alban's. He did not at once turn into his gate, but paused that he might look at the church a little longer. Many triumphs had been his within that building ; and he had cared so much for them. Fame. He knew, if no one else did, that he had tried to drive two horses together, the fame of Mr. Guilder and the gospel of Jesus ; and to the world it had looked a pretty successful business, but his conscience was not a fool. Where the priest is no saint the people suffer, though they find no fault in him. And how looked the mundane glory now when set against the long white silence of eternity ? Why did one labour for it when the best of one's mind knew that the hour approached relentlessly which would pronounce it of little worth? Like all else it was subject to decay and death; and there was no immortality on earth for any name. The everlasting flux saw to it that sooner or later it perished. It might take many a thousand years to wipe it out; but time moved very quickly; and after you had passed the meridian of your days, you could almost watch it racing by. On and on, diminishing the life-time of every name, so that the greatest men, like the smallest, knew that the hour was there in the distance when they must go out of memory for ever, and shut the door quietly behind them. And when one saw this— and when one had been told what he had been told that afternoon, one believed in nothing any more but kindness and good friends.

Mr. Guilder turned and walked to his front door and let himself in. He hung his silk hat on its accustomed peg, and stood staring, with his new eyes, at the letters waiting on the hall stand. He picked them up, and flapped them unopened on his palm, while he pondered something, not without sorrowful amusement. And then Mrs. Swan came out from her kitchen parts to say that a young lady awaited him in the study.

"A young lady? Oh, no," he began, "I can't see anyone——" and then remembered his last thought at his gate. It turned his eyes, with the resigned smile in them, to the old quaker's motto that hung in the passage for the edification of his waiting visitors: "I shall pass through this world but once. Any good thing therefore that I can do, or any kindness that I can show . . ." and he answered, "All right. I will see her. Who is it?"

"It's Miss Coventry. Miss Cynthia Coventry."

"Very well." And he passed into the study, which

was the second of the two large rooms on the ground
floor. It was a long room receding from the bow
window ; and as he entered, the figure of Cynthia
Coventry rose from an armchair before the fireplace and
moved between him and the daylight where the plane
tree fluttered. He walked towards her ; and, as her
face was flying a smile and had run up a blush too, he
saw only what seemed to him, in his present mood,
perhaps the most beautiful of created things, a girl in
the time of her blossoming, and aglow with life. He
saw—and loved her for what she was.

The next thing his eyes fell upon was his desk littered
with the business of the parish. The business of the parish!

" Well, Cynthia ? "

He, like his visitor, was hiding a sadness, so the look
he gave her was a merry one.

" I say, shall I be an awful nuisance ? " asked Cynthia.
" I so badly want to tell you something."

" No. Sit down. Sit down and tell it."

" But what about Evensong ? " she reminded him,
gradually sitting down on the edge of her chair. " It'll
take rather a long time."

Mr. Guilder drew out his watch. " Well, never mind
about Evensong. I am not bound to go. Now,
Cynthia, what is it ? "

The long room was rather dark, because of the plane
tree without, and because of the heavy furniture and the
dark carpet and the books rising to the ceiling. Cynthia's
back was to the window, and Mr. Guilder's face in its
light ; and she tried to look him straight in the eyes, as
she answered, " You see, I'm really rather unhappy."

" Well, *you* mustn't be unhappy," he laughed. " Tell
me all about it."

Then it all poured from her. It came in a spate that beat impatiently against any question that interrupted her, and hurried round and passed it. The stream carried many emotions on its surface : inconceivable relief, pleasure in mentioning O'Kelvie's name, pride in the statement that he had loved her once, a swell of tears as the pain came nearer, shame at what she must shortly confess. The shame stayed the rush ; and her eyes sought the floor and the fender ; but Mr. Guilder encouraged her, " Go on, my dear. Don't be afraid " ; and she lifted her eyes and gave him the truth. He helped her by showing no shock, but only murmuring " I quite see . . . I quite understand." The worst of her story told, the rest was easy again : oh, the relief, the relief, to pour out the agony of the last long months !

It was over. And after a pause in which he didn't speak, she added, " I don't know why I wanted to tell you. It's not guilt, I'm afraid, so much as—oh, that I couldn't bear it alone any more."

" Of course you couldn't," he answered softly. " I quite understand."

And there was a long silence.

" Do you think I'm very awful ? " she asked.

He shook his head, and if he didn't speak, his expression was kind and understanding.

" Some time ago I seemed to get things right—in church one morning," she continued, " but now I'm losing hold on life again."

Losing hold on life ! Losing hold !

" Tell me how you mean, dear."

" Oh, I don't know : it all seems so meaningless, and I don't seem to want to go on with it."

" Yes, you do, Cynthia. God forbid that I should belittle your pain, but you want to go on."

And just then the bell began to ring in the church tower. It had not a good note, but to Cynthia it was the most familiar bell in the world. This evening it sounded very close—almost over the room.

Absent-mindedly Mr. Guilder glanced at his watch, and then rose and went to the window, where he stood with his fingers interlocked behind him. After a while he lifted the hands to the hips. He seemed to be deliberating something, deeply.

The light coming through the leaves beyond the window threw a dancing lace-work on the wall ; and a late fly buzzed in the warmth of the room.

The bell stopped, and he came back to his chair.

" I am going to tell you something, Cynthia, that, a half an hour ago, I vowed to tell no one. And, Cynthia, I'm quite glad to tell you. It's going to be good to talk to you over a trouble of my own—because I've got something on my mind too. So we'll be companions in distress, shall we ? "

Touched by his confidence, and eager to thank and encourage him, she lit up two bright lamps in her eyes.

And Mr. Guilder, sitting well forward with his elbows on his knees and his hands meeting, told her his story. He told her how for some time past he had been suffering from severe headaches, and that day he had gone to a doctor who had diagnosed a rapidly growing tumour in the brain which was inoperable and must " finish him off " within a year.

She stared. She gasped, " Oh ! " Her lips shook ; and she put out a hand of sympathy and laid it on his.

" Yes," nodded Mr. Guilder, smiling his resigned

smile. "It's a funny experience to be told that. It's rather interesting, really."

"Oh, I'm so terribly sorry," began Cynthia. "But—but words sound so poor. You do know that I—I'd do anything in the world for you?"

"I'm sure you would."

"Oh, why did I come to you with my trouble, when yours is so much worse than mine?"

"Is it so much worse?"

"Oh, it's awful."

"But you said just now that you'd like to die soon? Wouldn't it be a good thing, then, if someone told you that you had only a year to live?"

To this she did not answer. In that darkening room there was place for nothing but truth; and the truth didn't seem to be "yes."

"So you see how much hope there is in you," Mr. Guilder pointed out. "You're full of hope, really."

"Oh, but don't let us talk about *me*," she pleaded. "I can't get over what you've just told me."

"We'll talk about both of us," said he, cheerfully. "Come along: now, my dear, I didn't tell you my story just to say, 'You see how much worse my loss is than yours,' but because I wanted to be able to give the force of—well, let's say a condemned man's sincerity—to all that I may tell you of my beliefs. It isn't likely now, is it, that I shall say a word more than I really and truly believe? You see that, don't you?"

"Of course, of course."

"Very well, then. I'd so like to give you some absolutely certain things to go on with. Let me see what I really believe. I believe—— "

He crumpled his brow, compressed his mouth, and

stared, unseeing, at floor or window, while he ransacked in his brain to find the few pure certainties.

When his eyes were on the window, Cynthia, staring unseen at him, saw its light reflected in them. The moment seemed very solemn : two people wrestling with the world for its truth.

He spoke at last, and it was to say that for the last two hours he had been seeing very clearly what things were first, and what were second. Fame and praise and power were jolly things, but they were very poor seconds when one's days were numbered ! They fell away into such a quaint unimportance then ! You saw then that the great teachers had all been right, and a universal love was an easy, easy first. "You don't suddenly *believe* this, Cynthia ; you suddenly *know* it. You know it, and you loathe all the selfishness that has prevented you from achieving enough of it, till now when it's so late."

Cynthia nodded—nodded vigorously.

"I believe in nobility," he continued. "I don't know it for truth in the same way as I know the other, but I believe in it firmly and truly. Yes, I'm afraid I've preached it too long to be able to lose my belief in it now. But you say, it's sometimes so difficult to know which of two actions is the noble one. But is it ? I always test it like this : if I were telling a story, which of the two actions would I rather make my hero do ? That's the one that seems to be beautiful. That's the one I really believe in. And I believe in Meaning." And as Cynthia frowned her failure to understand, he explained, "I can't believe that life is purposeless— no, I can't even now. I do violence to my thought if I try to believe that. There *must* be meaning in it.

What this meaning is—" and he shrugged his shoulders
—" God knows !   An excellent phrase, Cynthia, and the
last word on the subject—God knows !   Yes, I am
content to shrug my shoulders in humility, and to trust
. . . Nobility, then, and Meaning.   Well, that's much
of religion, isn't it ?   Those are only two other
words for Righteousness and God.   And with all my
heart I believe in them—and I want you to believe in
them always.   Will you remember that I told you
this, Cynthia ? "

She could only press his hand in gratitude.

Then he sought to deepen her sense of the word,
Meaning.   We saw all things change and decay, including
ourselves, he said, but the " I " that watched this change
was still—quite still.   It stood there, watching the
stream go by.   It was the measurer, not the measured.
And therefore it would stand unchanged, as it watched
death go by.   This still " I " drew, he firmly believed,
from the abysm ; and in a few great saints it had
quickened to consciousness of its unity with God.
Those who had achieved this knowledge all reported
the same thing, and it was that they had seen the meaning
of the world, and that it was good.   They knew that
all love and all loss would be resolved in a great harmony
one day.   " Laugh as we may at Pippa's song, ' God's
in His heaven, All's right with the world,' these people
report that, in the end, it will be found to be the hidden
side of the truth.   It is what God sees on *His* side of
the withered rose.   And Cynthia, I believe them ; I'm
sure I do ; I've been thinking so all the way home this
afternoon.   Why, my dear, I feel, even now, the
surging creativeness of life in me—" the old pulpit fire
glowed in his eyes and his voice—" *you* feel it—we all

feel it, and its name is zest, and zest is good. And the meaning behind it is good. . . . So much for *me*. And for *you*—do you know it's my belief that, while these saints penetrate to the knowledge of this meaning by their holiness and their mystic power, you and I and the poorest of us tremble close to it whenever we love."

She stared at the carpet. " But may I ask you one thing. It'll seem silly, but—— "

" Ask it."

" Do you think my love for him was the big thing of my life ? I've such an extraordinary desire to believe that. I don't know why. At present I just can't bear the thought that it wasn't the one great thing."

" I'm sure it was a tremendous thing."

" Yes, but was it the biggest thing ? A bigger one would seem so disloyal, you see."

Mr. Guilder seemed to ponder this long. Then he said, " I'll tell you something about the future. You can be certain of one thing about your future."

" What is that ? "

" That it won't be at all like what you think."

" But why ? "

" Because it never can be. Neither with you, nor with any one else. Things are going to impinge on your life from without, and change its direction a dozen times. One after another they will come, and you can't foresee one of them. So it's futile to worry about the future or to fear it. There is only one way to be sure of spoiling it, and that is to worry about it. Look, dear : the future grows out of the present moment, as the oak grows out of the acorn, and if you wither the acorn with anxiety now, you spoil its hope of good growth. You see that, don't you ? You must keep the acorn right if the future is to be right. That means that you must set the present free from doubt and worry, or your future's bound to go awry. Here's one of the truest paradoxes in the world : the one way to secure the future is to defy it joyously. Then the present is healthy and rich, and great things can grow out of it. You must, so to speak, damn the future, that the future may not be damned."

"What a wonderful idea!" she exclaimed. "I see! I see!"

"Good, my dear. Now tell me, have I helped you at all ? I so want to think I have helped you."

"Oh yes, yes. I agree so terribly with all you say."

"Do you ? "

"Yes."

"So much so that it is really a part of you ? "

"I think so."

"Then the future will probably have much better things in it than you can imagine."

Cynthia rose, feeling that she had intruded too long on his sorrow. "I'll never, never forget your talking to me like this," she said. But gratitude is always difficult to receive, so he only smiled and bent their talk away from it, as he led her through the hall to the door. "Well, we'll keep each other's secrets, won't we ? " said he, as he drew the latch.

"Of course." She stretched out her hand in good-bye. "I am so awfully sorry about what you told me. It—but I can't speak of it."

"That's all right," he demurred. "I have great times behind me, and you have great ones before you. you can be sure of that ; and sure that they won't be in the least like what you think. God bless you in them, Cynthia."

IV

I SHALL have occasion to tell how Cynthia announced to her family one day, more in mischief than in truth, that she had serious thoughts of becoming a nun ; and how Old Mrs. Coventry expressed her anger and dismay. But first we must look again into that strange room (or is it so strange ? Is it a little like one in our own homes ?) the mind of Tom Coventry. He did not oppose Cynthia's announcement with the fury of his mother ; he said that, personally, he hoped she wouldn't do anything of the kind, but that all that mattered was her own happiness, and a nun's life could be a very beautiful thing. There were three reasons for this indulgence : first, that he tended always to think his view saner than that of the women in the house, and therefore opposite ; secondly, that he was believing very strongly in self-sacrifice just now ; and thirdly, that he was somewhat pre-occupied with himself. He was reading his retreat from Evelyn as an example of self-sacrifice. It compensated him to decide that it had been a " triumph of the better parts in him." He was wise enough to see that he had been unable to escape the fettering comforts of home and habit, but he knew also that there was pity in him, and he liked to think that this was the larger cause of his resolve to " stay and look after Hilda."

" I will do my duty," he thought. " Granted that I still long for a woman's love, but if I can't have both

416

this and duty in my life, then I must renounce it and get my happiness out of self-sacrifice. Because I *do* believe in self-sacrifice, really."

So now, if the passing of a beautiful face stirred the old hunger (which happened more than once a day) he would say to himself, not without a pleasant melancholy, " It is not for me. Love and beauty are not for me. I have made my choice." It was a good thing that his self-love compelled him thus to believe in self-sacrifice, because it kept him gentle and kind. All remarked the increasing kindness in him ; and he remarked it too. " There is no doubt that I have improved," he would think.

And if he interpreted his defeat as a triumph of his better parts, so he counterbalanced his financial and social fall by taking an active part in public life. He had become a guardian, and a committeeman of the Conservative and Unionist Association, and, finally, unable to resist the overtures of his friends and their promises of monetary help in his campaign, a Borough Councillor. These in the daylight ; in the half-light behind secret walls he had become a mason and sundry other things that entitled him to dress an apron over his middle, a scarf across his breast, or a chain of office round his neck, and to feel a kind heart and a public spirit behind this decoration. To his daughter he seemed always to be setting off to some meeting, service, or ceremony, with a bag of strange garments in his hand. Once the service was in St. Paul's Cathedral, and it fell to him to carry, in a robe like a white gown, a banner round the aisles. Cynthia saw all this and, understanding something of its roots, watched it with a tender amusement.

The year 1909 was a good year for Conservatives, and for Tom Coventry among them. It was the year when the German Dreadnoughts loomed threatening in the North Sea mist to Conservative eyes. Lord Roberts was carrying up and down the country the fiery cross of Universal Military Service as the only answer to the German threat ; and the people applauded, but gave little heed ; they wanted to meet Dreadnought with Dreadnought, and would crowd to the launching of a battleship as to a Cup Tie. By March of three years hence Germany would have seventeen of these looming ironclads to Britain's twenty, and the Conservative Party declared, with an uproar that brought the spice of battle back to life, that, if the Liberal Government, " the worst government of modern times," didn't speed up their ship-building programme and add four new dreadnoughts, they had sold the country. The Government, misliking the storm, suggested four contingent ships, to be laid down if, after careful watching through the North Sea mist, the danger should seem real ; but the Conservative Party demanded loudly, and Tom Coventry with them, that the four new ships should be immediate and unconditional. And the Government flung the People's Budget on to the arena floor.

It flung it there, and bade the Conservative Party and its House of Lords pick up the challenge, if they dared.

It was a dastardly trick. It was the work of that scheming villain, Mr. Lloyd George. He had used their legitimate agitation for their country's honour as an excuse to attack every decent institution in the land, and, if possible, to trap the House of Lords and overthrow the Constitution itself, under cover of a Finance Bill. It was the beginning of revolution.

So said the Conservatives ; and indeed they had some justification for that anger, invariably righteous, which comes when one feels one had been out-tricked by a cleverer hand. Pleading the cost of the new ships and of Old Age Pensions, the People's Budget introduced a super-tax on all earned incomes over £3,000 and all unearned incomes whatever, a land tax on undeveloped land and unearned increment from land values, and a fifty per cent. tax on all licensed houses, and new " crippling " duties on all liquor. It hit every phalanx of the Conservative Party with dispassion and thoroughness. It hit the great landowners, the country gentlemen, the financiers, the wealthy brewers, and the men of independent means. They raised the cry of " Class Legislation," and prepared to fight ; and Tom Coventry, with his upstairs maisonette and his £350 a year, immediately took his stand by the great landowners, as by the men of his own class. In the living-room at Macartney Road, with a faint smell of dinner coming from the kitchen, he had a vision of the great landowner as a " very perfect, gentle knight " who went among his tenants doing good ; and he determined to stand by him. He saw the Idle Rich (for so Mr. Lloyd George had dubbed them) as generous, unpaid, unadvertising servants of the state, and as much that he would have liked himself to be ; and he, who day in and day out travelled in a smoky third-class carriage to his seven hours' work at an office desk, stood by them. If in his heart he was distressed by the unworthy attitude of some great landowners who were threatening to dismiss their game-keepers, stop their charities, and throw their old pensioned servants on the state, he admitted this only to his safest friends and, declining to believe that such men were typical of England, continued to defend his class in club-room and train. And as for those financiers who were vowing to take their money from England and invest it abroad, he declared them to be the few vulgarians found in every country, and no true gentlemen. The average English financier was not like that.

All the more did he decide on battle when Mr. Lloyd George went to Limehouse and delivered a speech which, in Tom Coventry's view, sounded the knell of all decency in public life. " They shouted for their Dreadnoughts," said Mr. Lloyd George. " They screamed, ' We want eight and we won't wait,' and now that I've sent 'em the bill, they squeal." It was vulgar. It was indecent, and, moreover, it was a lie. Every Conservative would pay with his last available penny for Britain's Navy ; but let the payments be fair ; let them be spread justly over the nation. Everybody knew that the Conservatives were the only people who really cared for the Navy. This Budget was a spiteful attack on the Conservatives because they had forced the Government to promise the " contingent ships." Which showed that there was more at stake in this hour than a few taxes. Behind the dust of this Budgetary tournament he saw the grey ships of the Navy at stake, and with them the whole Empire, and England too. And Tom Coventry, in his decaying street, loved England, and would battle for her supremacy.

The Empire was safe with such as Tom Coventry. He was no " Little Englander," and he scorned those who had " a craven fear of being great." He stood for a great Empire and Tariff Reform as a means to cement it and, incidentally, to pay for ships and pensions instead of these crippling taxes. The Election was coming. If the Lords took up the challenge of the Commons and threw out the Budget, there was bound to be a general election, and he would fight as well as he could for that fine old aristocratic England and that Empire she had built across the seas. It was now or never, he thought ; and he was glad he was still active enough to take his part. " These are great days that you are living in, Cynthia. I doubt if you will see greater."

In the autumn the Lords announced that they would take up the challenge. Declaring that the Budget was no pure Finance Bill, but a mass of social legislation masquerading as finance, they threw it out, and invited the people to decide between them and the Government. The Liberal newspapers came out in deep mourning " for the House of Lords which had thus signed its own death-warrant " ; and the Prime Minister announced that, after this unconstitutional rejection of a finance bill, he would appeal to the country to end or mend the Lords. Tom Coventry came home to Macartney Road, alight with the news. " Now everyone must fight," he said.

V

AND the battle he fought was not without wounds. In these days he was beginning to fancy himself as a public speaker. He had proposed " The Guests " or " The Worshipful Master " once or twice at Masonic dinners, and people had come up afterwards and said how much they had enjoyed his speech. He had also spoken at a Conservative Smoking Concert in the Borough Arms, and the Chairman had thanked him, as chairmen do, in glowing terms. And the praise was very pleasant to Tom Coventry.

And, in point of fact, to an uncritical audience, he did not seem at all a bad speaker. There was enough of poetry in his wistful mind to enable him to see the chances of a broad effect ; and if he preferred the heavy and sonorous phrase to the simple and quick, the majority of his audience supposed that this was the mark of good oratory, and applauded it well. Also his mind ran on the same conventional lines as his audience, and his arguments were therefore acceptable. Only the keen, biting minds, which are rare in a popular audience, perceived after his first ten sentences, that he was not really an orator ; that he lacked that palate for words which knows that the short, energetic phrase, not the long and heavy one, whips up an audience to a foam of cheers. But such strangers, even if present, do not come up to a speaker to tell him this. Only the kindly men who found his speech very tolerable, and the women who loved to say a word of flattery, walked with outstretched hand to Tom to thank him. He heard no criticism. And he left the public room very happy indeed, and well repaid for the agony of nerves that had laid waste the previous eight days.

For, just as a man can both love and hate a woman, being equally miserable when with her or away from her; and just as a painter or writer can both love and hate his art, so Tom Coventry both loved and hated this public speaking. He loved it for the prominence it brought him, and the praise; he loved it because of that merciful arrangement in us by which, since our achievements are up to our optimum, we consider them optimum achievements; and he loathed it because, though the speech lasted but fifteen minutes, it made a desolation of the days that went before.

It usually destroyed some eight of them. Eight days before the horrid ordeal its shadow began to loom on the horizon; and thereafter it gained volume and power to lay waste the days till at last it reigned as emperor of his mind, depriving him of appetite and sleep and joy, and playing strange tricks with his bowels. Pride in his powers as an orator forbade him to confess to a soul that he could suffer like any amateur; and he walked alone with his torment between the pavement and the stars. He would even lie about it. Just as some men will deny that they have ever been sea-sick, though they can remember some very queasy hours that God and His angels may have witnessed, but no one else, and some very private salaams to an oval seat—private, if not quiet—so Tom Coventry, if a friend admitted frankly that the prospect of making a speech at a public dinner made wretched

his meal, would say in surprise, " Is that so ?   Really ?
Now *I* rather like it."

The long emotional experience of which a fifteen-
minute speech was the nucleus ran as follows : happiness
—agony—great happiness ;   that is to say, happiness
when they honoured him with the invitation to speak,
and the bills went out with his name ;   distress that
began on the eighth day previous and mounted to agony
right up to the moment when he rose to his feet ;   and
then a great peace and a glow of happiness as he sat
down and waited for the time when the people would
come up to shake him by the hand.

Cynthia, if present, always came up and said how
much she had enjoyed it ;   and he felt happy that his
daughter should have witnessed his triumph.   It is
another merciful arrangement that, unless we are very
bright indeed, we do not perceive the futility, in the
presence of intelligent people (and there are a few of
these about) of trying to publish ourselves to them as
something more than we are.   Tom supposed that
Cynthia saw only the triumph and nothing of the week
of agony that preceded it.   He supposed that she really
thought his speech extempore and did not know that
he had got it by heart after a score or more rehearsals
and held, moreover, in the palm of his hand, a pack of
post cards on which the whole of it was written down,
against a disaster.   How disappointed he would have
been to learn that it was partly in compassion that she
came up after the speech and strained the truth a little
to say, " Well, Daddy, that was very fine."   She had
decided that the lie, if lie it were, was wiped out by the
deed of mercy ;   or, if it wasn't, and she must be
punished for it hereafter, then she must pay that price

for her father's happiness, "because he had obviously worked so hard."

And now when he said "Everyone must fight," she suspected that he was deliberately bringing down upon himself the pains of public speech. As a councillor and a Conservative committeeman he would probably be invited to address one of the smaller meetings ; or, if they did not invite him, he would probably—so does one leap into the flames—offer to do so. And, coming one evening along Wentworth Avenue which passed the entrance of St. Alban's Hall, she saw the figure of her father in his top hat, short coat and striped trousers, with his rolled umbrella in his hand, standing and staring at a bill that leaned against the wall. He must have come all this way round from the station before going home, on purpose to see something ; and as she called out, "Hallo, Daddy," he started guiltily and flushed, and began absent-mindedly to roll the umbrella.

Her eyes went straight to the bill. Headed "GENERAL ELECTION, 1910," it announced a meeting to be held in this hall—for every hall or parish room that the Liberals had not hired for their defence of the People's liberties, the Conservatives had hired for their defence of the People's rights. It stated that the meeting would be addressed by the Conservative candidate, supported by Lord Leydenthorpe, Admiral Grace, and Councillor Thomas Coventry. Lord Leydenthorpe's name was in the biggest type (he was one of those "roving peers" who were stumping the country in defence of the action of the Lords), the name of the candidate in the next biggest, but the names of Admiral Grace and Thomas Coventry were in quite honourable lettering too.

"I didn't know you were speaking so soon," said Cynthia. "Oh, how splendid! Cheers!"

"Yes, they asked me," he explained, demurringly.

"But why didn't you tell us? Why didn't you tell us?"

He smiled down at her tolerantly. "Pooh . . . it's not very important."

She declared that it was most important. She said she wasn't at all sure that she was on his side, but she was coming along to hear him. And that gave him his first gulp. It was good for your daughter to witness your triumph, but what—what if it were not a triumph, what if it were the long-dreaded disaster? The nervousness that must conquer him very soon had fired from over the sky-line its first shot. Things move quickly in a General Election, and his speech was only ten days away. He had perhaps two more days of peace.

Now the official issue at that election may have been the House of Lords, but the people declined to be much interested in the constitutional question. They were interested in Tariff Reform and the Dreadnoughts. And, perceiving this, the Tariff Reform League, with a fine irrelevance, issued thousands of the pamphlet "Germany and England" in which a Socialist, Mr. Robert Blatchford, advocated a strong navy and universal military service. And Cynthia, determined to help the family, whatever her own views, pushed hundreds of this pamphlet under the doors of Norman's End, during the next two days. She thought the action of the Tariff Reform League very immoral, but supposed that it didn't matter very much, because nothing would come of this Germany and England nonsense.

And then Tom's two days of holiday were over; and he rose from the supper table one night, saying, "I have some work to do;" and went upstairs to his bedroom, where he locked the door, lit the gas fire, and began to compose. Cynthia, in the living room below, heard him walking up and down, as he cudgelled his brain for ideas, and his chair creaking, as he rushed to it, to secure a phrase on paper before it slipped his hold and went into the mist again.

The disease was in its opening stages. It would develop slowly for the first day or two; then mount till it reached its crisis the night before the meeting. This critical stage would last the whole twenty-four hours till the moment when he rose to speak; during which twenty-four hours his face would be pale, his mind abstracted, his breathing disordered, and his legs inclined to shake. It would only end when (and if) the speech was a proven success, whereupon his face would come bright with convalescence, and the palsy leave his limbs as in a miracle.

He spent the next evenings in his bedroom, labouring —labouring. Did ever another man give such preparation to a fifteen-minute speech? Dictionaries, anthologies, histories, and other works of reference piled up on the little writing table. The waste-paper basket filled—but only with paper torn into a thousand fragments that no one might guess the nature of his work. And night after night his feet could be heard tramping up and down while he committed the speech to memory or "heard himself" in it. And as the great evening drew nearer, there was that sudden catch in his breath which caused him to gulp a little when talking of quite other affairs over the supper table; and a tendency to stutter and to use other words than those he had wanted; and a further tendency to leave a large portion of his food on his plate.

Then came the eve of the meeting. Only about twenty-four hours now! Returning from his office in the train, he was quite unable to read his paper. He stared before him, and frequently swallowed. If someone spoke to him, he didn't hear immediately, or grasp what the words meant. Walking from the station to his door, he saw the children shrieking at their play and envied them because they were free of his cares. He passed a horse in the shafts of a grocer's van and envied it its place in nature, where the cares of humanity did not run. He tried to sit down to supper but the food revolted him, and after the first course he said, "It's strange, but I seem to have got a slight headache. I think I'll go and lie down." And he mounted the stairs to his bedroom where he could find peace only by rehearsing the speech for the twentieth time to make sure that he was sound in it.

He got through half of it without a mistake, and with all his gestures and facial expressions in good order; and then—such was his nervousness—his brain seemed to stop and his memory to stand still, so that he knew nothing of what came next, and, for that matter, nothing of what went before. Striving to recall what the address was about, he could raise not a ghost of it: the more he strained his eyes into his mind to find the familiar speech, the more he saw nothing but a white, empty haze. And this though in the last few days he had spoken it aright some twenty times!

So horrid was this paralysis of memory that his heart stopped and the sweat burst from his forehead. In despair he whipped up his pack of post cards from behind his back, and his pince-nez on to his nose, but oh heaven! the sweat steamed the lenses, and he could see nothing through them. He waited for the mist to disperse, but it didn't, because he was perspiring more and more in his anxiety. If his post cards failed him, his last life-buoy had gone. Supposing this happened to-morrow night before nearly a thousand people! His imagination pictured them gaping at him while he failed to utter a word. He saw the stir of sympathy as he sat down, having stopped abruptly for no reason at all and left a truncated speech in the air. He saw them after the meeting talking about his failure in little groups on the pavement, or in twos and threes as they walked home. He saw the story told of him down all the years to be.

Sickening picture! Should he give in? Should he withdraw? Should he send word to the chairman, telling him of a slight indisposition and wishing them a successful meeting. No, he would *not* give in. He would never respect himself again if he gave in. And it was a lovely speech! He must try again. He must take his chance that that ghastly stoppage didn't happen to-morrow. By this time he cared nothing for Lords or Commons, Britain or Navy; or even about the collapse of civilisation, which, on the contrary, seemed to have much to be said for it; he could see nothing solid in the world of phenomena except the necessity of getting successfully through a fifteen-minute speech.

His glasses having cleared now, he began the speech from the beginning again. He got through it quite well, though his heart was hammering all the time, till he came to the peroration, and here again the fear of a stoppage in memory caused the stoppage: he had no idea what came next, and was standing in his bedroom with an open mouth, staring at the wall. And there were only about twenty hours to go now! The sensation was so horrid that it worked a dissolution within him, and drove him downstairs to the privy on the landing. Feeling easier after this, he turned with new hope to his task. This time he got through as far as the poem which brought it to a ringing close. But it is unfortunate that a poem is at once the easiest thing to remember and the likeliest to go wrong; and he went slightly wrong in it. Oh, what was he to do? It would be terrible to have to use his cards (even if he could see them through his glasses) in the midst of his fine peroration. Oh, what was he to do? Only free him from fear of this total stoppage, and he could get through all right. The cards were not insurance enough. If only someone could be there to prompt him!

A bright idea came to him. Yes—anything rather than the disaster. He opened his door and called for Cynthia; who came running up to him.

"Yes, Daddy."

"Look here, dear," he said. "I've been putting together a few ideas for this speech to-morrow. I don't as a rule take all this trouble, but I feel it's important enough to warrant preparation. Usually I rely on my mother wit, but this time I've taken the trouble to write it out. I'm particularly anxious to be lucid, you see. Now I have had very little time to learn it, being very busy at the office just lately—so I'm wondering —I'm wondering if you could, so to speak, make a copy of the manuscript and prompt me in it, should I forget my points. You know the hall well, don't you? You could stand just out of sight behind the proscenium, and I would sit just near there on the stage, and—well, I don't suppose for a moment that I shall need your help, but you'll be there in case I do. I shall have my own notes of course, but I am so accustomed to speaking without them, that I may lose my place in them— that's what I feel. I really haven't had sufficient time to give to this speech, and it's important. Do you see what I mean?"

"Of course I do," said Cynthia. "Certainly I'll do it. And I'm sure I'll do it very nicely so that no one can see."

She took the suggestion so naturally that he was comforted. Evidently it was a reasonable request. Now at least there was no danger of a total disaster. And perhaps—perhaps, free from this fear, he might bring off a great performance.

VI

CYNTHIA, in the days when she played Cinderella, had suffered enough from stage-fright to perceive the symptoms in her father and to understand them. She saw that there was but one difference between her sufferings and his; and it was that she had been very willing to proclaim to all that she was wishing herself dead, whereas her father was trying to brazen it out and pretend that he was ignorant of the meaning of "nerves." At breakfast next morning she noticed that his face was pale and drawn as if he had slept ill; and in the office, when she visited his private room, she always found him walking to and fro or standing between desk and window with a preoccupied mien that the business of the day could not justify. When she said, "If you'll give me that speech, I'll make a typescript of it," and he answered, "Ah . . . yes . . . Yes, here it is"; and tried to say more but could not, she understood that the less he spoke of the hateful thing the better his condition. And she took it from his presence without a word. Coming home in the train—nearly six o'clock now !—she observed from the side of her eyes his pallor and his lost gaze and his recurring yawn, and, knowing that talk would be a task to him, she pretended to be deep in her book. By supper-time her sympathy was almost painful, and some of his nervousness had communicated itself to her. Yesterday she had been more amused by it than

disturbed : it is wonderful how people who are compassionate, and who suffer to see others suffer, yet
consider that two of the most odious forms of torture
known to man, namely, sea-sickness and stage-fright,
are subjects for mirth, in whose presence they can be
offensively cheerful. But to-day, as it dragged by, her
sympathy ousted her amusement—or perhaps it would
be truer to say that her amusement had changed its
character and become a nervousness which vented itself
in a silly inward giggle. When the giggle hadn't hold
of her, she was paying out ejaculatory prayers—" Oh
God, make him do it all right "—by the dozen and the
gross. A light, quick supper had been prepared for
the family ; and her father sat down to it with a pretence
of laughter and ease. Oh, poor darling Daddy ! He
looked at the dish, unrolling his table napkin with a
shaking hand. Surely her mother could have had more
sense than to provide cold tongue—than which there
can be few dishes more revolting to a palate that is
the antechamber, and a stomach that is the very throne-
room, of King Nerves. He pushed a few bits of it
into his mouth, but then it defeated him, and he pushed
his plate away.

"Aren't you going to eat anything ? " asked Hilda
" You're not nervous, are you ? "

" Good gracious no ! "

" But you're not eating anything ? "

" It's too early. I can never eat much as early as this.
Nervous ? Pooh ! What's there to be nervous about ? "

" *I* should be nervous," said Old Mrs. Coventry,
champing at the tongue, " if I were going to speak to
so many people."

" I've done too much of this sort of thing now to

be nervous," said Tom. "I used to be nervous when I was a beginner at the game, I confess. Not seriously so, but . . ." and he shrugged, and left his early weakness to their imagination.

"You know your speech, I suppose?" inquired Old Mrs. Coventry, chewing at her mouthful.

"Yes, yes," answered Tom, something irritably. "Of course I know my speech." It was impossible for him to say airily and carelessly, "Oh, I've made a few notes somewhere," when his daughter had the complete typescript in her bag.

"Well, I think you ought to eat something. You're looking a little tired and pale."

Idiots! thought Cynthia. "Oh, why do you notice anything? Leave him alone!" she could have cried out. "Leave him alone!"

If he could not eat, he could drink, it seemed. Again and again he lifted his glass with a vibrating hand and sipped or drank from it. And all the time he tried to talk and laugh on general subjects, as if he were hardly remembering that in an hour he must rise and address a thousand people, or, if he did recall it, he couldn't understand why people made a fuss of such a simple business. But however he might force these laughs from his lips, he couldn't control the gulp which came along with them and tripped them up every now and then. He covered it with his hand, and rebuilt the laugh or the sentence. Amazing, the unimaginativeness of his wife and mother! They actually carried on with the general subjects he opened up, never perceiving that he wasn't in the least interested in them, and desired nothing less, really, than to talk about them. Oh God, why were people such fools?

Directly he could do so without comment, he rose from the table and went up to the bedroom, where, no doubt, he had a last look at his notes. Five minutes later she heard him coming down the stairs to the little intimate room on the landing and retiring behind a bolted door with his loneliness and his distress. She heard him yawn.

Upstairs again, and, unseen of Cynthia or anyone, he was putting neat touches to his hair, moustache and tie, because he would have to rise before a thousand people, and, if he did his performance well, he would like to charm their eyes as well as their ears, and, if he perished, *bien*, he would at least perish looking like a gentleman. He dusted his coat, arranged a handkerchief in its breast-pocket, and polished his watch-chain. Next, though it was twenty-five minutes too soon, he was putting on his hat and coat and calling most cheerfully, " Come along, Cynthia ! Come along, you people ! Time ! Time ! " Well done, Tom Coventry. Go bravely, and let the people see no hint of fear. " Give me thick garments," said Charles Stewart before going to the block, " lest if I shake with the cold, they say I tremble with fear."

They set off, all four of them, along the roads to St. Alban's Hall. Old Mrs. Coventry and Hilda talked fluently ; Tom said little—only enough not to appear afraid ; and Cynthia said nothing at all, but wished with occasional curses that the other women would keep quiet. For instance, when they came in sight of the hall, her grandmother exclaimed, " Oh, *look* at the people pouring in ! You're going to have a huge audience, Tom."

" Yes," he said.

"And nearly all men, it looks like."

"Yes," he said.

"Will there be reporters there?"

"Yes. No doubt."

"Oh, fancy having to speak before all those men! I *should* be nervous! He must do us credit, mustn't he, Hilda? Here, where everybody knows us so well. You'll do your best, won't you, Tom?"

"Yes."

There was indeed a strong river of people flowing through the central doors, and tributary streams coming down the neighbouring roads. Stealing a glance at father, Cynthia saw his lower jaw come forward.

They went in at the stage door which she knew so well, having run through it so often with a cloak thrown over her pantomime dress. Not a soul was on the cold stone stairs within. They struck silent and chill. Only through distant doors came the sound of feet and voices as the audience crowded into the big hall. Sure that her father would rather be left alone, even in this cold emptiness, she said, "Well, we'll secure our front seats, I guess"; and as Old Mrs. Coventry was as eager as she to make sure of a good position in the reserved seats, they passed through the side door into the hall, and left him there.

Cynthia, sitting in the front row between mother and grandmother, asked herself why people who suffered from nerves always came twenty minutes too soon, thus giving themselves twenty minutes of misery while they listened to the audience arriving or tried to talk at ease to the caretaker who came into the waiting-room entirely free from anxiety and abundantly talkative.

Old Mrs. Coventry had promptly put on her glasses

that she might study the stage and its furnishings. Cynthia studied them too.

The caretaker had done his best. Deciding that politics were a domestic business and not suited to a woodland scene, and thinking, perhaps, that they were a matter for Lords and gentlemen, he had built up the old box set which had done duty in many a pantomime as the Hall of the Wicked Baron. Had they known the history of this dear old scene the radical wags in the audience might have made very merry about it. In the centre, down stage, was the chairman's table, draped with a large Union Jack and a bill, " The Lords say, Trust the People." On either side of this table a dozen chairs were so set as to form the arc of a circle. Behind were two rows of chairs for privileged persons with platform tickets. A vase of blue and yellow flowers—the Conservative colours—stood near the caraffe of water on the table. And this picture was framed by the looped-up curtains of the proscenium arch, on either side of which hung a bill, one proclaiming " Tariff Reform means Work for All," and the other asking, " Who gave South Africa back to the Boers ? "

Now she turned round to consider the hall behind her. It was filling fast, mainly with strange men, though here and there she descried a familiar face from the congregation of St. Alban's. It was evident that the place was going to be crowded to the window-sills : stewards in blue and yellow rosettes were bringing up chairs from the smaller halls below. The Doré pictures round the dado looked strangely inappropriate encircling this throng of men politically minded ; so did the travelling rings, trapeze and climbing rope looped up above their heads. As always they were a lively crowd, attracted to the meeting, less by a desire to save the country than by hope of fun or a fight. Every now and again a fellow with a muffler stood up to shout at a pal whose dial he had espied floating in with the crowd.

"What cheer, mate? Lord, if it ain't Charley! What are you doing here? Thought you belonged to the other shop."

"Nah! Always like to 'ear the enemy."

"Well, mind you be'ave yerself."

"Gaw, I like that!"

"Well, this is a gentlemen's meeting, this is."

"Looks like it with *you* here. Are you going to make a speech?"

"Nah! We've got Lords and Edmirals speakin'. We'll show you what speakin' is."

"Well, thank Gawd we shan't 'ear from you."

"Oh, I may arst a question or two."

"Gawd!"

"'*Ullo*, Gen'ral!" This to a new face floating in. "Strike me blue if there ain't the Gen'ral! I'm awf! It's no place for me. Gettin' too low class altogether. He's another bloomin' radical, he is."

"Sit dahn, before they put you aht!"

"Well nah, I like that! Didjer ever? 'Sit dahn from '*im*! It makes yer think, don't it?"

And often there was the smothered laugh of a woman who rebuked the antics of her male. Or the comments of other women on the thickening crowd. Cynthia could hear two of them talking in the row behind her.

"Oh my! How will they get them all in?"

"It's to be hoped there ain't a fire. Reg'lar death-trap it'd be."

"You're right."

" I never like these places where there's footlights and things.   You never know what'll happen."

" No.   You're right."

" Do you know anything about any of these speakers ? Any of 'em any good ? "

" Oh, Admiral Grace, he's a fine speaker, he speaks lovely.   I like him ; you know—breezy ; gives you a charnst to laugh now and then.   But I don't know nothing about the Lord."

" His lordship . . . yes . . ." said the other voice richly, and for the mere pleasure of savouring the succulent title.   " And Councillor Coventry—what's he like ? "

" Don't know anything about him.   But he ought to be all right ; he's a councillor."

" Well, I hope so, because I can't say that politics interest me really—not as you'd say, ' *inter*-est.' "

" Oh, I don't know ; I like a good speech."

" I wonder if there'll be any suffragettes about.   I can't say I hold with their goings-on, do you ? "

" No, not as you'd really say, ' *hold* with them.' "

And now the privileged people were beginning to sidle to their seats behind the chairman's table, followed by the muttered jests of the humourists.   " She ain't a beauty, is she ? "   " Nah.   Seen better."   " Who's this ole cock-sparrer ? "   " He's the feller what spiked the guns in the Crimea."   " Well, I don't reckon much to his dial, anyhow."   " Nah.   One of the guns went awf too soon and stove it in a bit.   It was all right before."   " 'Ere !   This cove ain't a Scotchman, is he ? MacSolomon's his name, I *don't* think.   Oi, oi, vot you say, Abe my dear ? "   " Yes, he's a Scotchman all right. One of the Jordan Highlanders, he is."   " Come awf it ! You'll make a joke in a minute." "Crikey, Bill ! Here's a nice little bit ! What's *she* doin' at a political meetin' ? " " P'raps the Admiral's her fancy boy. Naughty 'ole man ! " " Nah ! She's a suffragette, I shouldn't wonder. It's gettin' even the pretty ones now, though Gawd knows why. That's what she is : a suffragette." " I don't believe yer. I believe she's his lordship's barst'ud."

And all the while Tom Coventry waited behind the scenes. Cynthia wished for his sake that the business would hurry up and begin.

At last a rattle of applause lifted her eyes from the floor and showed her that the chairman was leading his little procession of speakers and officials on to the stage. They diverged to this side and that of his table, and sat down, studying to appear as little self-conscious as possible. Councillor Coventry who had come in last of all took the outside seat nearest the wings. It was not their fault, but the caretaker's, that, when they were all seated in the arc of a circle and waiting for the chairman to rise, they looked a little like the Moore and Burgess Minstrels with the illustrious Mr. Johnson in the centre. Some waggish radicals at the back observed this, and called out, " Now for the opening chorus, sir ! " and since the chairman only smiled and continued to glance among his papers without rising, they obliged with a chorus of their own. They burst into the Land Song :

" *The land, the land !* '*Twas God who gave the land.*
The land, the land ! The ground on which we stand !
And why should we be beggars with the ballot in our hand ?
God gave the land to the people."

Good-humouredly the chairman allowed them to finish, and then rose and thanked them, saying that he was glad to see so many of their opponents at the back of the hall, because doubtless they would leave the meeting converted.

" I *don't* think ! " scoffed the loudest of them.

" No, that's why you're a radical," retorted the chairman pleasantly—a palpable score, which the audience clapped and cheered.

An excellent beginning. The chairman was in very good form, as he could well afford to be (thought Cynthia, suffering with her father) because he had very little to do. He announced that Lord Leydenthorpe would speak first, followed by their Candidate ; after which Admiral Grace would propose the vote of confidence, and Councillor Coventry would second it.

" 'Ear, 'ear ! " shouted the vocalist at the back ; and the chairman said that evidently he had converted one of them already, and now he would call upon Lord Leydenthorpe to convert the rest.

To this first speech Cynthia gave little attention. Her eyes and thoughts were drawn to her father in his corner by the curtain. She watched him crossing and recrossing his legs restlessly. She saw his sad eyes examining the audience, as a man might examine the pool into which he must plunge and die. She saw him recognise a familiar face here and there, and slightly raise his hand to them in greeting, while he arranged for them a smile —a rather sickly smile. Now he was yawning, and she remembered exactly similar tricks of the breath when she was waiting on this very stage for the curtain to go up. Lord Leydenthorpe had finished, and her father was giving formal and belated applause, which revealed to her that he had heard nothing of the speech.   Now the Candidate rose, and all the audience rose with him, to give him musical honours ; and her father, suddenly coming to the surface and perceiving what they were doing, stood up with the rest on the platform, and tried to sing too.

" What a mixture of heroism and cowardice is ours ! " she thought.

And she alone noticed that his song inadvertently perished in a sigh, as he sat down, with the whole vast audience.   Only one more speech after this, and it would be *his* turn.   She noticed that he was putting a hand into one side-pocket and drawing out a handkerchief on which to wipe his palms, and then into the other, to draw out his notes and have a last look at them.   Oh, she wouldn't allow him to fail !   If he showed signs of stopping, she would jerk him on somehow.   She had read the speech, and it wasn't at all a bad speech.   There was a part in it that was really good : it pleaded for the ships-of-war ; and, though this had reminded her, with a pang, of Rugg standing before her in the studio and declaiming that the people of Norman's End were saving their greatness by loading the future with their children's death, she treated this jocose judgment no more seriously now than then, and thought her father's plea the best part of his speech. The poem at the end disturbed her rather, but perhaps it would sound less flamboyant when delivered from a platform than when read in an office.

The Candidate finished, and must leave the building to go on to another meeting, so there was a considerable break, while all cheered his passage down the centre of the hall.   Her father waved his agenda papers with the rest, and smiled; and very well did his daughter know that every delay was irking him, who wanted to get the ordeal over as quickly as possible.

The chairman called upon Admiral Grace; a wag called "Ship ahoy! All 'ands on deck"; and the gallant admiral, rising to his stocky legs, set about being the bluff and hearty old sea dog. Clearly he was off for a long voyage; and this was making her father more and more restless. He moved this way and that in his chair, crossed and uncrossed his legs, and suddenly— to her alarm—rose quietly and slipped from the stage. At first she dreaded lest he had run away altogether; but then she understood. He would be back in two or three minutes. As a child she had been driven that road herself, in the last few minutes, when the overture was playing.

She was right. He returned to his place just as the admiral seemed to have sighted port. As the admiral said, "And in conclusion . . ." she fixed her eyes on her father. He was swallowing with difficulty, and snatching a last look at his notes. Her heart thumped as fast as his. She slipped from her place, passed through the door that led to the stage, and took up unseen a prompter's position in the wings. She was not three feet from her father.

"I have now much pleasure," said the voice of the chairman, "in calling upon Councillor Coventry."

Her father rose and put his hands behind his back. In the palm of one she could see his pile of post cards. Some applause greeted him, but it was formal and unrecognising: her father was not one of the resounding successes of the world.

He was off. He was going rather well. Whatever

wild alarm his thoughts might be indulging, unconscious cerebration was guiding his voice along the lines of his speech. Word by word, in absolute perfection, the sentences on her typescript reeled out from the speaker. The gestures and expressions came at the right moment and behaved themselves properly. The audience was listening because the sentences, having been polished in the study and learned by rote, were at least coherent and lucid, and arrived without accident or side-slip at their full stops ; which was more than could be said of most of the Admiral's. Half the speech was through— splendid ! Enthusiasm rose in Cynthia, as if she were a spectator watching the successful running of her horse. It looked as if he would stay the course and reach the winning post. He had spoken in defence of the Idle Rich ; he had given them his picture of the faithful landowner, he had held forth on Tariff Reform and the Empire, and now he was at his last pages which dealt with the Navy and its share in the greatness of England.

Now Tom Coventry had written with real feeling here. He did not know the true source of his feeling : he did not know that he saw the ships of the Navy as the grey walls of Norman's End, protecting his security ; he did not know that he saw them as the grey hulls in which his unachieved greatness put to sea ; he did not know that they carried much of his imprisoned poetry and thwarted enterprise in their bottoms ; he knew only that he loved them. And you write vividly of that which you love, and Tom Coventry's words were potent at last, nor could he have had a better audience than this to hear them. They began to clap him at the end of his carefully-turned sentences—and Cynthia was delighted. Already she had turned the last page. No doubt now that he would get through. His peroration was a pæan in praise of England as a seafaring nation ; and it ran for its final coda on to Henley's lines :

> " *Mother of Ships, whose might,*
> *England my England,*
> *Is the fierce old sea's delight,*
> *England, my own——*"

and he arrived at this point with great vim. Then—well, in the last six days he had not had the least difficulty in continuing, " Chosen Daughter of the Lord, Spouse in Chief of the Ancient Sword " (though he had had very little idea what these titles meant) but now, such is the treachery inherent in verse, his memory halted like an idiot mule ; it refused to go one inch further ; he could remember nothing. Those who think that Henley went a good mile too far in this resounding fanfaronade may feel glad that they are not to be asked to suffer shame for Tom Coventry, that he uttered it from a platform to an audience of English humourists ; but if they feel this, they can have little idea of the agonised moment he suffered when it would not come at his bidding. The hand that held the cards moved spasmodically ; there was a silence that seemed to him and to Cynthia to last an eternity—though, thank God, the audience had not perceived it yet—he turned his face towards his one hope of safety in the wings ; his eyes met Cynthia's and most plainly—most pitiably—asked, " How does it go on ? " Cynthia, nervous as he, had no sooner caught those eyes and perceived the ludicrousness of his question than that silent, inner giggle seized her like a paroxysm ; it stopped speech ; she would have given worlds to be able to whisper, " Chosen Daughter of the Lord," but the wretched, racking, silent giggle would allow nothing to pass ; her father turned his face sadly from the support that had failed him ; she could have wept bitterly for him, if she hadn't been giggling ; it seemed to her and to him that the dreaded disaster had happened—and then the poem (as is the way of poems) threw up the last lines of quite another verse ; they were not very appropriate but they were in the same metre ; and Tom Coventry seized upon them as a man seizes a life-line before he sinks for the last time :

> " *Life is good, and joy runs high*
> *Between English earth and sky* ;
> *Death is death* ; *but we shall die*
>   *To the song on your bugles blown, England,*
>   *Round the world on your bugles blown !* "

He sat down. What was this ? The people were applauding. Thunderously applauding. After giving him a nightmare moment Fate had treated him kindly, for these were the simplest and most effective words in the poem, much better than the shameless boast about the " Chosen Daughter of the Lord " and they went to the heart of the audience. The audience, having had no time to catch their inconsequence, were moved by them and applauded him noisily, continuously. He sat down. The applause, going on and on, surprised him. He had imagined that every person in the world had noticed that failure of his memory, and pitied him, while, in pure fact, one only of his hearers had so much as suspected it. In the kindly mood of Fate, the pause had actually added emphasis to his last quiet words. The applause endured long enough to amount to a triumph; and a peace—almost an exultation—alighted upon his face.

But that awful moment had left a wound that must fret him for the remainder of the evening. And when, as they were walking home, Cynthia looked up at him and said, " That was good, Daddy; you surpassed yourself. I liked that part about the ships "; he only sighed, shook his head, and answered, " No, no. Nothing is ever perfect in this world."

VII

If Cynthia giggled at her father's meeting, it was not that her grief had ended; it was partly in hysteria, and partly because no one is for ever occupied with his sorrow; a prisoner will smile wistfully in the first year of his sentence, and more easily as the months go by, only remembering his sorrow afterwards. Mr. Guilder had helped her much; and a greater help still was the saving belief that Rugg had lied about his love when he sent her away. The Election had been a distraction; and when it was over and the dust had settled, she sank again, almost with relief, into the familiar sadness.

The Election was over. The Liberals had been returned with a reduced majority, and were deciding to mend, not end, the Lords. And Tom Coventry, if disappointed that the Conservatives had been able to do no more than snatch a hundred seats from the swollen majority of the Radicals, could yet take comfort in the thought that Norman's End had returned to its true allegiance, and his efforts had helped the victory, and in the secret knowledge that a Liberal Government was not really so disastrous a thing as he had represented to the people. They had conceded the contingent ships.

And so we come to that morning at breakfast when Cynthia announced that she had serious thoughts of becoming a nun. She said it, as I have told you, more in mischief than in truth. It was true that she did gaze

fondly sometimes at the idea, as at a gentle messenger
who came with benediction in her face and quiet in her
hand. She had accepted easily and with joy those three
words that Mr. Guilder had given her, love, nobility
and meaning ; and what a way to achieve them would
be the way of the wimple and the black robe and the
rosary dangling from her belt ! She was for ever
steadying her faith, when it rocked, by a repetition of
those three words that was as rapid and rhythmic as the
ticking of a clock. What fools we should feel if our
secret mental tricks were revealed to our friends ! She
would have loathed anyone to know that, as sure as
doubts and dismays attacked, she gabbled three words to
herself for some fifty or a hundred times, till she had
forgotten what they meant or why she was doing it.
When she recovered their meaning, she would think,
Yes, it might be a sweet solution to incarnate them in
the figure of Sister Mary Cynthia—an attractive figure,
as she saw it, with an expression so serene that all who
looked upon it were brought to a lively sense of their
sin. But then the hard rocks of reason and humour
would rise above the tide of feeling : it ebbed, and she
saw clearly that her impulse towards life was stronger
than her impulse towards asceticism, and if she took her
vows, it must drive her either into morbid regrets or
over the nunnery wall.

So there was more mischief than truth in her announcement at breakfast that morning. Or more wrath. It
was designed to shock. She was feeling very impatient
with all her family. She was offended by the furniture
in the room, which was the measure of her mother's
dullness ; she was annoyed by some observations of her
father on the socialistic legislation of the Radicals ;

and she took one look at the hard, little beady eyes of her grandmother and told herself that the old woman had never, for all her piety and sentimentalism, been in sight of love, nobility, and meaning; she felt artistically, intellectually, and spiritually superior to them all, and announced that she had thoughts of becoming a nun.

A nun! It brought a storm to the breakfast table. Nowadays there were often rows over the breakfast table; and the chief protagonists were Cynthia and Old Mrs. Coventry, because these were the two who really enjoyed them. Cynthia enjoyed them because they gave relief to her pent-up irritation with the old lady, and Old Mrs. Coventry enjoyed them because she had long learned (what is the simple truth) that to lose one's temper and to rampage about the room are worth doing for their own sakes. They constitute an enlivening experience. They please like wine. And Old Mrs. Coventry always took, if possible, what pleased her. The methods of the two combatants were dissimilar, but equally infuriating to each other: the older lady was unconsciously infuriating, the younger one most deliberately so. (Nobility and her sisters were put from the room for a while, when Cynthia was in battle with her grandmother.) Old Mrs. Coventry's weapons (or some of them) were a torrent of words, a rising voice, a refusal to listen, an independence of all logic and relevance that would have fired a stone to flame, a storming about the room, and, finally, a majestic climb to the very summit of Mount Pathos. The girl's weapons were fewer and slighter, but they stung. They were, in the main, a selection of barbed sentences, which she sharpened, pointed, and poisoned, during the body of her opponent's tirade, and shot neatly in, when the old lady's invention flagged and hesitated, or her breathlessness compelled a pause.

I cannot deny that Cynthia sometimes fired the first shot.   When you are frustrated and unhappy and restless, there are two ways of relief, and both are often employed by the same person contemporaneously : one is to seek your happiness in the happiness of others, and the other is to let fly at your parents or other available targets at home.   The furniture in this living-room was the source of one memorable row.   The room had always been overcrowded, and now, thanks to Granny's acquisitiveness, and her excellent trading in the streets and drawing-rooms of the district, it was beginning to look, Cynthia thought, like the store of a dealer who had been obliged to crowd his China and Glass, Silk, Rugs, Second Hand Furniture, and Old Curiosity departments all into one.   Granny's acquisitiveness was growing on her ; her methods were improving with practice and the presents came with perfect regularity.   She was beginning to expect them as a right, and to grumble behind the donor's back if they were below standard. And as she much preferred the living-room to her bedroom, and liked to " have her things about her " she insisted on finding a place for each new offering as it came in.   " Oh my God ! " thought the girl, watching it into its place.   And Cynthia had learned from O'Kelvie what a room might be.   So one morning when, on coming downstairs, she had been more than usually chafed by the room, she shot into the silence over the breakfast table the words, " Can't we do something about this room, mum ? It's getting more and more littered every day."

So often the technique of shooting a provocative sentence differs from other archery in this, that you direct your eyes and your voice at the person before you, while desiring the words to hit someone at your side. Cynthia's words, blandly addressed to her mother, registered a direct hit on Old Mrs. Coventry.

" What do you mean ? " she demanded. " What's wrong with the room ? "

" It looks like a Second Hand Furniture Store," explained Cynthia. " If we could scrap half the furniture and nearly all the bric-a-brac——"

" Don't listen to her," counselled Old Mrs. Coventry.

But Cynthia, determined that her mother should listen, in the few moments left while her grandmother got up steam, hurried on, " and if we could put that awful Dresden china in the bedroom, and those awful old books which nobody ever reads, we might be able to make a start. I'm sure I could paint the walls, and with some new, unpatterned rep——"

But Old Mrs. Coventry's engine was now primed and ready.

" I hope you won't listen to her, Hilda. You're surely not going to listen to her. In so far as these things are mine I won't have any of them touched. Not one! I know what she's hinting at ; I may be old but my wits are still sharp. My few little presents were given to me by good friends who have some consideration for my comfort in my old age, if *you* haven't, and I wouldn't hurt them by putting them out of sight. I can't help it if people like me and give me presents, can I ? Do you *want* me to have no friends ? Do you *want* me to go friendless to my grave ? Is that what you're hinting at ? As long as I live, I hope I'll keep about me the souvenirs of my friends. Please allow me to do this. *Please ;* I *beg* of you. It is not much to ask. I suppose you'll be wanting to take the very cushion from my back next. When I'm dead, you can scrap them all, as you put it, and that won't be so very long, if you can only exercise a little patience. I'm seventy-seven now, and I can't live so very many more years. Leave me in peace for that brief time, *please*. Please ! "

" Oh dear," sighed Hilda, and rose to go from the room, since there was a row developing.

" And those old books," continued Old Mrs. Coventry, " I won't have one of them moved. I'd have you know that many of them belonged to my dear father, and some to my husband, who, after all, was your grandfather, you seem to forget. Are you *ashamed* of having had a distinguished man for your grandfather, and one who was fond of books, and who knew more about them than *you'll* know if you live to be a hundred. You may call them dirty old books, but——"

" I said ' awful old books,' " corrected Cynthia.

" What ? " demanded Old Mrs. Coventry, who didn't want to be interrupted.

" I said ' awful.' Still, I'll give you ' dirty,' and then you'll be able to go on."

" They're awful, are they ? Well, let me tell you that if ever you know as much about books as *he* did, you'll be able to talk. Are *you* an LL.D. ? And I don't see why you need get up and go, Hilda. I think you might stay and take my part against your daughter. You might tell her that I am seventy-seven and merit a little consideration from a chit of a girl who's——"

" I suppose there are other people who inhabit this

room and are entitled to a little consideration?" suggested Cynthia.

"Consideration! Isn't that just what I'm complaining of? Isn't it time you learned to treat *me* with a little consideration?" cried the old lady, magnificently catching Cynthia's arrow and using it as a spear for herself. How free are the actions of a fighter unfettered by logic or sense! What advantages are his who can change the rules at will, and play boxing one second, wrestling the next, and single-stick the next, and the hundred yards race at the end! "Consideration! I should have thought that you were the last person in the world to talk about consideration. Are you going then, Hilda? Surely you're not going to leave her to say just what she likes——"

"I can't stand it," sighed Hilda, and disappeared.

"Stand what?" cried her mother-in-law to the lost figure. "Stand what? Do you mean—— " but, since it was hopeless to reach Hilda's ears, she turned her question to Cynthia again. "If she means that I started anything, let me tell you that I did nothing of the sort. I'm sure I was sitting peaceably enough when you opened this attack on my few little things. Why can't you leave me alone? Why can't you leave me with my few little possessions around me? Is it that you want to drive me out of the house? Why can't you wait till I die?"

"You'll outlive me at this rate," said Cynthia.

"And what do you mean by that? How can I outlive you? I am seventy-seven, and you are twenty-one. I have ten more years at most, if I am lucky. No doubt you wish that I'd go to-morrow, but I can't help it if I am healthy and vigorous. All I ask is to be left alone to spend my last years in peace. Surely I have earned my rest."

" I have no objection to your being utterly selfish, but I could wish "—Cynthia felt that if her opponent was employing irrelevance, she was going to wield such a convenient weapon too—" that you didn't go to church quite so much."

" Selfish ! Church ! What ? Oh, you wicked, wicked girl ! Selfish ! Selfish because I want my few little things about me ! Am I to go on sacrificing myself to the end ? And now are you going to throw my religion in my face—one of the few comforts I've got ? It's only because I'm poor that you taunt me like this. If I had a big house of my own and many servants, you'd speak to me with respect. Young people are all the same. But because I'm poor and a nuisance you want to drive me out into the street. And I'd go if I had anywhere to go to. But you know I've nowhere to go. You know that it's safe to say what you like to me, because I'm poor and old and alone. I'm too old to go out and earn my living now. Don't you see that I must have a roof over my head ?—— " she almost screamed—" Don't you see that I must have somewhere to die ? There now ! I've said it ! "

And, completely overcome by the pathos and drama of this last remark, she went weeping to her chair, where she blew her nose vigorously and pummelled her cushion, while Cynthia left the room, tossing her head and exclaiming, " Lord, how I hope I don't get peevish when I'm old ! "

" I am not listening," proclaimed Old Mrs. Coventry from her chair.

But this skirmish was as nothing compared with the

battle which ensued when Cynthia announced she was thinking of becoming a nun. I fear we shall not see Cynthia at her best in this scene, as we seldom do when she is playing opposite her grandmother, but I must give you the truth. Old Mrs. Coventry gaped. In the bottom of her heart she could see no real reason why her granddaughter should not become a nun, but she didn't deal with the things in the bottom of her heart. Things were too steady and simple and dull on that sea-bed; she preferred the wind-blown surface and the liveliness of the high waves. A nun! Here manifestly was a chance for getting excited, being dramatic, picturesque, and very suggestive in one's talk, working up to a good heat, and steaming up and down the room—in short, of enlivening the empty days with the gaiety of a row. Her mind raced to all that she had read of nuns; and she had read some very tasty things when relieving the monotony of days with pungent and interesting matter. She turned on the child.

" How can you talk so, Cynthia ? Tom, tell her not to say such things. What does she know about nuns and nunneries ? You think it's nothing but saying prayers and doing good, but it's very different. It's not so simple as that—not by any means—but there ! you're not old enough to understand. I'm sure I've heard of terrible things happening in convents. The temptations are shocking, everyone knows that—shut away as the poor creatures are from all natural enjoyments and—er—all natural activities, but, as I say, you're much too young to understand. Don't let her do this, Tom. Don't let her sacrifice her young life like that. It's unnatural, and, what's more, it's a wicked return after all we've done for her. Very wicked, I think."

"No, Granny," said Cynthia with an angry light in her eyes. "I should like to make you a return for all *you've* done for me. Would sixpence cover it?" and then the row was in full swing. Hilda said that that was very rude; Cynthia asked innocently, "Was it?"; Tom corroborated that it was; so Cynthia made the sporting offer that if Granny would write down on a bit of paper what she'd done for her, she would willingly add it up and make a proper return. Hilda muttered, "Tch, tch!" and suggested that her grandmother had always been kind to her; Cynthia, with her celebrated look of innocence, submitted that she had always been kind to her grandmother; Granny, addressing Hilda, begged that no one should worry about *her*, as she expected only rudeness and ingratitude from children, and, anyhow, she wasn't listening; Cynthia said, Of course Granny wasn't listening, because it was impossible to talk all the while and listen too; Tom went from the room, saying he'd leave them to it; and Hilda thereupon expressed her neutrality by sighing and beginning to clear away the breakfast crockery. Meantime Old Mrs. Coventry strode back and forth, straightened cushions, picked up objects and tossed them down again, while her angry words gushed forth like water from a hose-pipe with a hole in it; and Cynthia, who had a few minutes to spare before going to her train, kept the pipe gushing strongly by giving it a sharp and handsome prick every time it showed signs of dwindling to a trickle. Between the fireplace and the far wall, and between the table and the window curtains (which she adjusted *en route*) Old Mrs. Coventry spoke of nuns craving for love in their cold cells, of their longing for little babies of their own, of the

cowardice of withdrawing from temptations into the
security of convent walls, of the well-known fact that
temptation was quite as much with you in the solitude
of your cell as it was in the crowded world (which
seemed to cancel out the previous argument, but that didn't
trouble this high-hearted old fighter), of the wicked-
ness of the Anglo-Catholics in trying to drag the Church
of England back to Rome, of unsavoury goings-on in
the confessional if all she'd heard was right, of the disgraceful political interference of the priests in Ireland who
wanted to take that country from its natural possessor,
England, of the Spanish Inquisition, and of Irishmen
who had fought against us in the Boer War.   Did Cynthia
want the Inquisition back, she asked.   But Cynthia said,
No, she only wanted to catch the train, so good-bye,
and she went; and, this forcing a silence on the old
lady, she puffed up the cushion of her chair (which she
had already done twice), sat vigorously in it, sniffed and
snorted, dropped the ball of wool that went with her
knitting, and picked it up smartly as if she would vent
on it a little of her anger, and then, her lips indignantly
moving, waited for Hilda to return that she might
continue the topic with her.

And in the next days she took the topic among all
her friends, whether she were walking arm-in-arm with
Rose Damien along the pavements or leaning forward
from her chair to chat with a visitor in Mrs. Ingram's
drawing-room, or sitting with three other ladies at a
table of the Working Party in St. Alban's Hall.   To
these people, of course, she wasn't rude.   She played
the part of the gentle old lady who was unhappy about
a beloved child.   She said what a pity it was that such
a bright young girl should turn away from the fullness

of life, and how they would certainly send her to work among unhealthy people who would give her all manner of diseases ; she spoke of the morbid condition that arose when the hunger for maternity was unsatisfied, and asked how she could explain this to a bright and innocent young girl who knew nothing of life ; she suggested that a bonny child like her was obviously made for marriage and a home, and (moistening at the eyes) that she had always hoped, before she died, to see Cynthia with a little baby at her breast. They offered their sympathetic words ; and she apologised for feeling it so much, but justified herself on the score that she was like an old hen with one chicken ; and, being quite worked up by this time, concluded, " It's too awful ! It worries me night and day lest she goes into a nunnery. I'd rather see her dead first. There now ! I've said it ! "

As she was now weeping, they plied their consolations, suggesting that perhaps there wasn't much in it, dear Mrs. Coventry ; perhaps it was only a passing fancy. But she shook her head, vastly preferring to believe the worst. " No, I'm afraid there's a great deal in it—a great deal in it. Tom and Hilda decline to take it seriously, but I think they're very wrong, I *must* say ; very wrong. I'm sure the child wanders about alone sometimes and looks so unhappy that it quite distresses me ; and she seems to have given up all her nice little friends. I'm afraid she means it. What an end for that dear child for whom we've laboured so much and had such hopes ! What an end ! "

VIII

THERE was another watching Cynthia as she walked in her loneliness; and thinking too that she looked unusually beautiful when the sadness lifted her eyebrows and enlarged her eyes. From his pulpit or his lectern he would see her sitting in her pew with her eyes turned up to him and taking a brilliance from the lamps above her. In the roads of his parish he would meet her walking by herself, and she would watch his approach with a grave smile very different from the ardent and impudent welcome of a few years ago. Sometimes in her own high room, when he was calling on the Coventrys, he would find her seated at her desk, with the supply of chocolate or the bag of sweets at hand, wherewith she comforted her loneliness.

And this was Cynthia Coventry! Walking through life alone! "She walketh alone"—that was a true and beautiful lot, he knew, for some of the mystical children of God, called to solitude, but the more he thought of Cynthia Coventry, the more he was sure that it was not the truth of her. She was built for eager, personal things; her citizenship was among people of the warm, present earth; and in her breast she carried the heart of a lively companion, friend or lover. And now she was stilled and futile, like some delicate mechanism whose spring had broken.

And he so longed to help her, before the end. She

had come to him with her story, and quickened in
him a love that, always there, was now running full
and strong like a tidal stream. But he could see clearly,
and more and more clearly with every passing month,
that there was only one way. And it must hurt her so.
Did God ask of him that he must be the one to hurt
her, before he went? It was asking much. But He
did ask these deeds of His servants. Once they were
dedicated to Him, He never complimented them so ill
as to ask of them less than much. Mr. Guilder's thoughts
ran to the legends of those who, with hearts twisted in pain
but hands strong in duty, had broken again the broken
arms of those they loved, or pressed the burning iron
on to flesh dearer than their own. And often as he
passed through his hall, the old Quaker's motto arrested
him. When he had hung it there with easy—nay,
almost hypocritical—sentiment twenty years ago, he had
little thought that the days would come when it would
take to itself a power sharp as Michael's sword. "Any
good thing therefore that I can do . . . let me do it
now; let me not defer it nor neglect it, for I shall not
pass this way again."

A love pure and perfected wins an insight nearly
perfect; and Mr. Guilder, as he walked in his road,
knew the thoughts of Cynthia, as she walked in hers.

She was thinking all the thoughts he gave to her.
She was not seeing nunnery walls, because her every
solitude was engaged with other pictures: the old
wrought-iron gates standing ajar on the cobbles, and
the moss-green path between the grass and the long,
dividing wall; Rugg meeting her at the studio door
and saying, "Come, my dear one"; the door shutting
behind them, the blank studio walls screening them

from the world, and Rugg taking her into his arms and whispering, "I love you, little Cynthia"—oh, he had meant it!—surely he had meant it when he looked like that and said those words. Sometimes, in the quiet of her room, she recalled the words with which he broke the farewell, "You give too much. I love you —who could help doing so?—but not as you think or mean"; and her heart burst out in protest, "No, no! Rugg, no!" The second anniversary of that parting came, and died down in darkness; and as it passed at midnight, Cynthia, lying awake in bed, thought, "Now it is the third year. I shall get better soon. It can't go on for ever." And she tried to remember all that Mr. Guilder had said, that she might wrap it round her for warmth and comfort, and so find sleep.

But the third year piled week upon week, and she was still listless and uninterested in anything but her thoughts. A young clerk at the office began to follow her as Rob Ingram had done; and she put him away quickly that he might never reach to suffering like hers —poor boy. But this showed her that she would never be able to love anyone so long as she believed that Rugg still loved her, and yet knew that they would never meet again. And then she would think, "I can't go on like this. Perhaps it would be better to get rid of the idea that he lied to me. Perhaps it would be better to believe that our story meant nothing, and it *wasn't* destined to be the great central love of my life." The assurance would mean a few weeks of agony too terrible to contemplate—the agony she had shirked so far—but after it, she would be free. She would be able to lift her head and say, "*That's* all over! Now I'll begin to live." But as sure as her thoughts reached this point, she cried out, " Oh Rugg, no, no. I don't *want* to love anyone else."

Her mind was swaying like this when, walking one evening, she saw Mr. Guilder coming towards her. She saw the thin, kind smile with which he recognised her, and, remembering that many months had gone of the year that he supposed to be his last, she wondered what it was like to be he. What was it like, knowing what he knew, to dress every morning in that clerical frock-coat and to swing that watch-chain from vest-pocket to vest-pocket—to look sometimes at the watch !—and, when duty took you into the street, to put on that silk hat and take an umbrella against the rain ? And to meet a girl parishioner, and give her a thin, kind smile ?

Now he stopped in front of her and asked, " Well, how are you, Cynthia ? "

" Oh, all right," said she, laughing.

" No, but really tell me the truth. I don't see you looking happy again yet. Not as I want to see you."

Sympathy pierced to the spring of tears ; and Cynthia, though forcing them back, yielded to the weakness of saying, " I don't think that I shall ever be happy again " ; but immediately was ashamed that she had indulged self-pity before this man, and added laughingly, " Oh yes, I shall, though ! Of course I shall ! One gets used to anything, doesn't one ? "

" Yes . . . anything," he answered thoughtfully, and stared down the vista of the road.

She would have liked to ask him about his own illness, but somehow she felt that it was a ground too sacred to visit, and she knew that he would understand her silence. So neither spoke for a while. Then Mr. Guilder asked, " Do you still love him ? "

She nodded, attempting a shamefaced smile. " Yes. I'm afraid so."

" I see. . . . Where are you off to now ? "

" I don't know. I'm just walking."

" Well, walk along with me. I want to hear more."

" Oh, I'd love to." And she fell in beside him, and they started off together.

" Now tell me all sorts of things," he invited. " Anything."

" Oh, but I'm so afraid of being a bore. People with an unrequited passion can be such a ghastly trial for everyone else, can't they ? "

" Perhaps it depends on the ' everyone else.' Go on."

" Oh, but I know I shall never stop once I get started. You don't realise what you're drawing on yourself."

He half turned his face to her. " You and I are each other's confidants, aren't we ? "

Unable to answer this with words, she felt for his arm and pressed it. And she told him how, though the years must, of course, have made *some* difference, she still felt imprisoned in a sadness, and that she sometimes thought that she would be better if she knew definitely that he had spoken the truth, when he sent her away. Not to appear too sorry for herself, she spoke in her slang. " I shall take an absolutely imperial jar, of course, but perhaps I should be better after it."

Mr. Guilder pondered this for a long time, and they crossed from one road to another, and went half-way down it, before he turned his face to her and spoke again.

" Would you like me to find him and ask him for you ? "

For a second her heart stopped as if Rugg had

suddenly come into sight.   So near these words brought him!   And fear, fear came with them.   Did she really want to know the truth?   Could she bear to hear it? . . .   No. . . .

But yes she must.

"I should like to know, but you mustn't trouble. It's not as important as all that."

"I think it's very important," he said.   "Shall I do it?   Shall I get you the real truth?"

"I don't like worrying you."

"My dear, I am here to serve you.   I will do it; and I will send for you when I have seen him."

In the next days the eyes of her mind flew always to one thing: the expected message from Mr. Guilder. As in the old days, when she looked for a letter from O'Kelvie, so now: she hurried home from the office wondering if a message had been delivered by hand, or she came down in the morning with a shaking heart, wondering if the post had brought it.   But in those old days her expectancy had been alight with hope and happiness; now she hardly knew if hope filled it, or dread.   Hope that the message would be an acute joy, or dread that it would strike her down?   On the whole, hope.   An aura of happiness hung around her watching.   The little automatic voice in her head kept repeating, "I am going to hear about him again! I am going to hear about him again!"

But a week of days went by, and Mr. Guilder sent not a word.   A thought came, "Perhaps he has forgotten."   Perhaps she had built up this great house of hope for no tenant to occupy.   Should she remind him? No; she had a fixed fear of being a bore, and couldn't bring herself to do it.   Besides he might be suffering.

He had cares enough of his own to fill his day. Then another thought came, " Perhaps he has failed to trace Rugg. Perhaps he has learned that Rugg has left this country long ago, and he doesn't want to tell me."

A second week lagged by, and gradually the fullness of her disappointment showed her how much greater had been her longing to hear than her dread of hearing. The week brought a second Sunday, and, living always with the one thought, she went to church, where she gazed up at Mr. Guilder, in stall or pulpit, half hoping to convey to him by a thought-wave an impression of Cynthia Coventry that would put her again into his memory. And when the service was over, she dawdled out among the last of the congregation, hoping that he would see her from the distance and remember her.

She calculated that, if she had achieved either aim, he might see Rugg on the Monday, and send for her on the Tuesday. But Tuesday brought nothing ; nor Wednesday. Then the old resigned despair set in, and she went about her business, thinking, " It can't be helped. Nothing ever happens right, now."

It was Saturday morning when she saw the summons on her plate. " Come and see me any time this evening," it said.

Saturday was her half holiday, and she could hardly wait till the evening. " Evening " meant after tea ; so it was not five o'clock when Cynthia set out for the vicarage. A white, trembling glow was in her head as she walked along. Why this happy excited glow ? Perhaps because she was going to speak to someone who had just seen him, and that was the next best thing to being near him herself. Perhaps because a halo of happiness surrounds ever the memory of the beloved, however great the pain. Perhaps because she was going to hear the truth at last, and she did not doubt—she did not dare to doubt—that the truth would be good. If not—but thought recoiled from the " if not." No, he had truly loved her, and she was going to hear this said. A bell struck five as she came in sight of the Vicarage gate ; and, ashamed at her earliness, she passed the Vicarage and walked on, hoping that no one had seen her from the windows. Best kill another quarter of an hour ; so she wandered round the church, and into Wentworth Avenue, and past the entrance to St. Alban's Hall, and so back by Parson's Road toward the Vicarage, slowing her step as she came nearer. " Ah well . . . *Now*, then " ; and, with a bracing of her will and a toss of her head, she turned on to the Vicarage gravel, between the front door and the north wall of the church. It was an evening of early summer, and the smell of lilac drifted from the shrubs under the wall. Sparrows flew and chirped between the eaves of the house and the steep roof of the church ; and she could hear some children singing a hymn in one of the lower rooms of St. Alban's Hall. " There is a green hill far away. . . ."

Mrs. Swan opened the door and showed her into an empty study ; but very soon Mr. Guilder came in. She greeted him with a smile as if she had come on some small parish matter.

" Sit down, dear," said he ; and they fell into the chairs they had occupied in the previous interview, one on either side of an empty summer hearth. The window was open to the bright day ; and the smell of the lilac drifted in, with the chatter of the birds. Every limb of Cynthia was trembling ; and her heart was as water inflated with air and palpitating. But her eyes were steady—fixed on him, and waiting.

" Well, he began at length. " I've seen him."

" Yes ? "

" I didn't of course tell him that you had sent me. I said only that, more than a year after it had happened, you came to me as to a very old friend and priest for my help and advice. . . . When I told him that, he said, ' Poor, poor darling. . . .' "

Cynthia nodded, her eyes still fixed on Mr. Guilder.

" I told him that I wasn't altogether happy about you. I said that I believed you still thought he loved you, and that, for your own ultimate happiness, you ought to know the absolute truth. Either of the two answers that he might give, I said, would make for your peace in the end. Then he told me."

Mr. Guilder paused, lifted the hands that rested on the arms of his chair, and dropped them again. He rose and went to his desk where he trifled with a paper-knife, beating a little drum-tap with it. Then he returned to the fireplace and stood with a hand on the mantelshelf.

Cynthia crumpled up her forehead, as if asking a merry question. " Well ? "

" His first words," said Mr. Guilder, " were ' Give her my love.' "

Again he paused ; and Cynthia hardly knew whether the message had inflated her with hope or pricked her with dread. " Love "—he had used the word " love " ; but, on the other hand, the words had a ring of farewell. So again she crumpled her brow merrily and asked, " Well ? "

Mr. Guilder answered her by shaking his head.

This was the greatest fall of Cynthia's life. Her heart seemed to sink like a dead thing. Her breath came short and difficult, as in the minutes before death. Her eyes stared. Where her heart had been, there seemed nothing but a sick emptiness. And her first thought was, " I can't bear what is coming. I can't bear it."

" I am so sorry to have to tell you this," continued Mr. Guilder, " but I know it is best. He said that of course he loved you in a way, and your memory was dear to him still, but you were a child of your upbringing and couldn't understand a selfish man who loved more than one woman, and none so well as his art. He said that he had admired you greatly. His actual words were, ' Her every movement is lovely, and cries to be caught in marble ; I have never known anything like the lift of her eyebrows when she asks a question. All the wonder and all the questioning in the world is in it. Or her raised eyebrows and wide eyes when she tries to look at once blameless and impudent—I'd have given much to catch that fleeting look on canvas and hold it in trust for the world for ever—but it is so quickly gone, and one could not get it to order. . . .' I think that was how he put it ; and he went on, ' Tell her how much I loved those things about her—but—but——' he added this very emphatically—' she mustn't think that I am still in love with her. No, she mustn't think *that*.' "

Still staring, Cynthia tried to grasp what she was hearing ; and Mr. Guilder waited a while to help her.

" Please go on," she said.

" I think," he explained very gently, " you frightened him a little by your intensity."

" I see."

She rose. " I will never make a fool of myself to anyone again."

To comfort her, Mr. Guilder shook his head and smiled unbelievingly. " I hope you will, my dear. All excessive love is foolish and irrational, if you like, but it chances to be such a much better thing than sanity. I see that so clearly."

She shook her head : " Never again."

" Oh yes," he encouraged. " Perhaps all this will help you to do it again, because it will have moved an obstacle from the path."

" Never again," smiled Cynthia ; but she was hardly listening. A last gasp of hope had come to her. " Did you—did you believe him ? "

" Yes," said he, perceiving the nature of her thought. " Yes, I'm certain of it. Don't hold on to an impossible hope."

" I see. Do you mind if I go now ? Thank you so much for what you've done. I think it's been wonderful of you."

Her courage broke him. Taking her hand, he said, " My child, I know what you've got to go through. But not quite alone. I want you to think that I'm with you all the time. And I believe with all my heart that this will turn to good in the end, because you *had* to be free of him ; but that's no comfort to you now, is it ? "

She shook her head, but with her lips tight closed, for if he spoke like this, she must break down. Only at the door she turned and asked, almost beseechingly, " You were not unkind to him, were you ? "

" No, no," he assured her. " *I* don't judge him."

" No," she agreed, but rather hazily. " No, of course

not. He's awfully good in many ways. . . ." And then, " Good-bye ; and thank you a thousand times."

" Good-bye, Cynthia. God be with you all the road, my dear."

Then she was walking home. How was it that one's limbs served one so faithfully when one's mind was a disorder, and one's body a shivering, captainless state. Her mind could find one phrase only, " It didn't mean anything." It had been only an episode. They were not destined to blend together hereafter. Rugg didn't want to. The love had had no light of eternity on it, as she had imagined. " It didn't mean anything." How could she believe it ? How could she have deceived herself so ? " I am not in love with her. She mustn't think *that*. . . ."

Well, it didn't mean anything, after all.

Here was her door, and she rushed upstairs to the safety of her room. There perhaps she could cry. In inadequate words, as she hurried up the stairs, fearful of being met, she told herself that she had never taken such a blow. There was no other such blow. There was no other such pain. The death of the beloved left at least a memory of the past and a whisper of reunion in eternity. This left nothing. It was annihilation. She had shirked this final blow, but the Gods were resolute that she should take it.

In the bedroom she put her forehead against the cold mirror of the wardrobe, and threw up one hand to grasp the cornice, letting the other fall limp at her side. She rested her body against the glass. " It didn't mean anything." A belief built up in the last two years must be knocked down. She must hammer it down slowly. He *hadn't* been loving her all the time. He hadn't even been thinking of her. He hadn't been sending messages, nor receiving those she sent through the air, because he had almost forgotten her. And—and she still loved him.

Pressing her brow against the cold glass, she murmured to herself—none but the slang words coming to her aid—"I am *for* it now. I've got a long bit of suffering in front of me, and I had best begin on it straightaway. How long it will last I haven't the foggiest, but I must get ready to bear it. Every day will be a day nearer the end." And she lifted her face from the glass, and sighed, and went to her desk to see if there was any work she could pick up and do. "Because I'm *going* to be happy again," she vowed, as she sat down. "I'm *going* to be . . . one day. . . ."

IX

"Granny's late," grumbled Hilda. "Supper's all spoiling."

Tom Coventry, in his armchair, pulled out his watch and glanced at it. "It's only a little after half-past seven. Give her till eight o'clock." And he turned to his book again.

"But where can she be?" worried Hilda. "She's not usually as late as this. Can anything have happened?"

"Oh don't *fuss*, mummy," begged Cynthia, forcing her needle into a hat she was trimming. "It's only that the scandal's being extra rich to-night, and she doesn't want to miss a word of it."

"You shouldn't talk of your grandmother like that, Cynthia. Why are you always so bitter about her?"

"Bitter? Not at all. She delights me rather. I think she's a very bright spot in Norman's End."

"If anything happened to her, you'd be sorry."

"Of course I should! But nothing ever happens to people like Granny. They look after themselves too well."

"I'm not at all sure. She's getting very shortsighted, and she *will* wander off alone."

"She's out looking for a little fun, that's all. Some-one's illness to discuss, or a reputation to destroy, or something jolly like that. Or, better still, the prospect of a new baby somewhere——"

" Oh, that'll do ! " snapped Tom. " Can't you see I'm trying to read ? She's come to no harm. It's broad daylight still."

" And it'd have to be very dark for Granny to fail to see where her advantage lay. Even then she'd smell it."

" Cynthia, *will* you not be so bitter ? " rebuked Hilda. " She's your grandmother, after all ; remember that."

" But that, strange to tell, hasn't made her a saint."

" Be quiet, Cynthia ! Tom, tell her she isn't to speak about your mother like that."

" What ? " began her father, who had heard very little of this, but was ready to oblige. " Cynthia, don't——"

" All right, Daddy," Cynthia interrupted him. " She's an old darling. I love every button in her dress, and she hasn't a fault in the world."

It was a Thursday evening, about a month after Cynthia's visit to the vicarage. June was still over England, and its light was still in the streets, and the birds were gossiping in the back gardens, so it didn't seem very odd that Old Mrs. Coventry should be twittering somewhere too. Tom relapsed into his book, and Cynthia into her trimming, while Hilda wandered between the living room and kitchen, or stood by the table with her hand at her mouth and indecision in her eyes. The clock ticked on towards eight.

Suddenly Tom looked up. The unmistakable step of Old Mrs. Coventry was on the staircase leading up to their front door. Old Mrs. Coventry, nearly eighty, was getting rather breathless ; and they could hear her panting as she came quicker than was wise up the first stairs, paused for a moment of recovery, then addressed herself anew to the climb, and later hesitated again.

Something in the shortness of her breath to-night, and a sound that might be the snuffle of a person in tears, turned Hilda's eyes in the direction of the door, and lifted Cynthia's face from her needle. The old lady came puffing up a few more steps, halted again, and called between heavy sighs, " Hilda . . . Tom. . . ."

This drew Tom quickly to his feet ; but Hilda, running before him, met her mother-in-law, who had begun the ascent again and now reached level ground, just inside the front door.

" What is the matter ? Is anything wrong ? "

" Let me get in . . . let me sit down . . ." panted the old lady, " and then I'll tell you. . . . It's not me ; *I'm* all right . . . But it's terrible, terrible. . . ."

" But what is it ? " asked Tom and Cynthia together, who were now at the room door.

" Oh, haven't I said, Let me get in ! " cried the old lady angrily, and pushed past them. " Let me sit down. The shock has quite taken my breath away."

They had followed after her ; and now waited while she sat heavily in an upright chair near the door, threw open her short black coat, and pushed her bonnet back on her forehead. Finding her handkerchief, she blew her nose, wiped her eyes, and fell to fanning herself. The others stood around.

" He went off to the place this afternoon," she said. " Abbott, being churchwarden . . . and Mr. Bennett . . . saw him before he went off."

" Who ? "

" Mr. Guilder."

" Mr. Guilder ? " exclaimed Tom.

" Yes. Rose has only just heard. . . . Abbott, being churchwarden, was the first to hear. . . . Rose told it all to me only an hour ago, and I . . . went round and told a few people . . . because of the service. I felt they ought to know. It was all I could do. . . . I went round to several, and I'm quite worn out. It's at noon to-morrow. Or at eleven forty-five, rather."

" *What* is ? " asked Tom, impatiently.

" The Service of Silent Prayer."

" But why ?   What service ? "

" The service for poor Mr. Guilder. He's gone off to hospital, and they say there's very little hope. They're going to operate on him at noon to-morrow. It seems he's believed for about a year that he was going to die, but now that he's lived so long, they've decided that there's a thousand-to-one chance in an operation. And not a soul's known anything about it all this time ; not a soul. And oh ! I've laughed with him about looking worried and tired with us all, and I didn't know, I didn't know ! And he used only to smile back at me." At this memory she broke down and could not speak.

" Tell us about the service," said Tom, when her handkerchief was put down.

" He went away so suddenly that it's been difficult to arrange anything. He's known about the operation for a fortnight, but he only told Mr. Kenneth about it this morning—even Mr. Kenneth who would have to carry on in his absence. Why didn't he tell us all last Sunday so that we could have spoken to him before he went ? And now Mr. Kenneth and Abbott want all those who knew him to come to the church to-morrow at noon, so as to spend the hour of the operation in silent prayer for him ; but how are they to let people know ? I said it was a lovely idea, and I myself would go off and tell everybody I could, and I've been going round doing it. I am quite worn out with it. Give me a sip of water, will you, Hilda? I shall of course go myself. It's all we can do now. But there's very little hope— Mr. Kenneth says Mr. Guilder made that quite clear to him—he said, 'Well, Kenneth, it's a thousand-to-one chance that this is good-bye, old man.'" At this she was sobbing again. "Poor, poor Mr. Guilder!" she said over her handkerchief. "Oh, what can we do for him? And on a Friday too! Why must he go and have it on a Friday? But if we all pray our hardest, surely God will do something. He mustn't die. They say that if he dies, he'll die quickly, and we shall never see him again; and it's all so absurd: he's only sixty or so, and I'm nearly eighty, and never so well. I've got his address. After supper I'll write to him. He'll get it in the morning and know that we're all praying for him. It may be the last thing he'll hear from us." And her mouth twisted again, and she broke into tears.

Cynthia, watching, felt sorry for her recent bitterness. That her grandmother enjoyed any alarm because it brought interest into life she saw well enough, but also that the relish was unconscious, and not the whole of her emotion to-night. Affectionateness and pity and kindness were there too. The tears that she was dropping to her lap were good tears, and the prayers that she would pray in the silence to-morrow would rise from what was best in her. Cynthia was glad to see and feel all this. She was happier in this moment, feeling kindlier towards her grandmother.

They sat down to a very quiet supper. Old Mrs. Coventry was silent all the time, withdrawn into herself that she might compose her letter to Mr. Guilder. And whenever she thought of a phrase particularly affectionate and sympathetic, her eyes filled, and her old mouth twisted. Her lips moved with the sentences, and her head shook. Sometimes she was even whispering one aloud. And if Hilda spoke to her, she was irritable at this interruption in her work, and answered her curtly, remotely. Towards the end of the meal she was restless on her chair, because impatient to be up and gone to her room, where she could get her rich composition on to paper. And as Hilda rose to clear away, she pushed back her chair and rose too ; and now that the moment of writing had come, and she was walking to her task, the tears reassembled in force, her head shook from side to side, and her mouth trembled under the effort to control herself. Cynthia, still in her chair at the table, put out an understanding hand and touched her grandmother's as she passed ; and Old Mrs. Coventry, nearly overthrown by this touch of sympathy, pressed the child's fingers, murmured, " There, there ! And he was always so fond of you," and hurried on, and out of the room. Cynthia heard her creaking up the stairs, wretched and enthusiastic, to her task of love.

Tom had retired to his chair ; and Cynthia went to another and picked up the hat that she had been trimming. But soon she let it fall to her knees, and sat with useless hands folded over it, and eyes gazing into vacancy. She was thinking of Mr. Guilder, and how quietly and quickly he had gone. No dramatic last sermon to his people, such as in the past years he would have loved. Last Sunday he had preached a simple and wholly impersonal sermon on forgiveness. Forgiveness—what had he been thinking of, as he put it together in his study ? He had chosen no striking text such as they might recall when they heard the news.   Death was a great master in the art of living.   Let Death come and habit with us for a little before the end, and he schooled us to dignity. Mr. Guilder had gone in the dignity of silence.

Rising, she went and sat on a low stool in front of her father, her elbow on his knee.

" Daddy."

" Yes, dear ? "

" Daddy, do you mind if I don't go to the office to-morrow.   I want to be there at the service.   I'll make the day up some other time."

Tom Coventry, seeing that her eyes were wet, pushed back the hair off her forehead and then pressed her hand. " Of course you must go to the service.   I want you to go.   You have lost a good friend.   He was very fond of you, from a child."

So the next day, just before noon, the three women walked along the road to St. Alban's.   From everywhere people were streaming towards the church.   Granny needn't have been afraid that the parish wouldn't hear in time : the word had gone from lip to lip like news in an Eastern bazaar, and not a soul of the seventeen thousand parishioners but knew that Mr. Guilder had gone last night to the very door of death.   And now the bell was ringing in the steeple—the familiar, unlovely, single bell ; calling across the huddled roofs to all, of their charity, to come and pray.   And every one of them who could spare a half-hour was hurrying towards the church.   The nature of the service, and its very suddenness, had appealed to a sentimental, good-hearted, dramatic people, both in residential street and slum. They were coming in crowds ; and Cynthia, seeing them, thought how Mr. Guilder, in trying to avoid drama, had achieved the most dramatic thing in his life. Old Mrs. Coventry, seeing them also, unwittingly quickened her pace, though her mouth was working with unshed tears. The old habit had taken command, and she wanted a good place.

They passed up the steps of the church—slowly because of the congestion at the doors—and as soon as they were in its comparative darkness, after the summer brilliancy of the streets, they saw that it was likely to-day to hold such a congregation as it had never held before —no, not at the time of the old queen's death, nor at the coronation of the king. And nearly all were kneeling. It still wanted ten minutes before the time of starting, and yet there was hardly a vacant place. With a quick anxious step Old Mrs. Coventry led them to the top of the nave, but nowhere could they see three seats together. They separated, the two older women found seats near the front, and Cynthia went far back.

She was glad to be far back. She knelt, and remained kneeling. For some minutes she prayed ; and then lifted her face from her palms, and allowed herself the luxury of thought. What an assembling of the people ! It swelled one's throat. Chapel and choir stalls were packed ; and people were standing near the doors and against the church's back wall, mostly with bowed heads. And still more were coming in, and men were giving up their seats to tired old women. Working women came in, dandling their babies lest they should break the silence with a cry. Women who had snatched a half-hour from their shopping came in with string bags of parcels, which they lowered to the floor beside them. Shy young labourers, who had an odd hour, and seemed rather ashamed to be coming to church on a week-day, loafed in, and finding no seats, went back and stood by the door. The children from the church schools filed up the south aisle and occupied all the pews against the wall, shuffling on to their knees, beneath the stained-glass windows, through which the sun, lifting to a summer meridian, played dazzle patterns on their heads. Sprinkled among the congregation were " ladies' children " with whom Mr. Guilder had laughed and joked so often. These children recalled to Cynthia the old pantomime days, and, looking round, she saw Lance Guilder, with Aline at his side. And there—yes, it was he—was Rob Ingram who must have heard from his people of the service and hurried from his club—just the soldierly thing he would like to do : he would feel it his duty to be on parade. Rose Damien and Abbott were in the churchwarden's pew, of course—was not Abbott the Vicar's Warden ? And the servants from the homes she knew. It touched her to see them. The Damiens' two maids were there together ; and the Ingrams' old cook ; doubtless Mr. Guilder had often exchanged a pleasantry with them, and they were praying for him now.

One minute before the service started, her father came in. This was a surprise, for he had gone to the office that morning. But there he was, returned from London, and dressed in his best, and walking up and down in search of a seat. The verger, who had been tip-toeing about, tapped him on the arm and led him up into the chancel, where he could stand between choir stalls and altar rails. In this high place he seemed a little self-conscious, and fingered his tie : then he rested both hands on the handle of his rolled umbrella and bowed his head. Not far below him sat Old Mrs. Coventry, sobbing into her handkerchief. This will be our last glimpse of Old Mrs. Coventry, and her son, Tom ; and I am glad that we take leave of them like this.

Astonishing the silence where such a multitude was packed together ! A silence only emphasised by the sound of a newcomer's feet, an occasional cough, the sob of an overwrought woman, or the quickly suppressed cry of a baby. A cart passed in the road outside, and one heard the steps of its horse for a long time, dying away. The only startling thing was the flutter in the rafters of a bird, which seemed frightened by this unusual assemblage below. The midday sunlight poured through the clerestory windows ; and the motes of dust, disturbed by a thousand feet, danced in its beams. These were the high-lights in the sombre picture, but the eyes of the people did not fall on them. They turned always to the vicar's stall just above the chancel steps. It was empty ; the only unoccupied seat in the church. Cynthia looked at it, and up at the pulpit too, and thought of the days when she was a child.

Now Mr. Kenneth, the senior curate, alone and with no ceremonial robe save his cassock—the other three curates were kneeling in the body of the church—came to the steps behind the Litany desk, and faced the congregation, a plump, bespectacled, commonplace little man after Mr. Guilder ; but a good heart, and he told the congregation how he had seen the surgeons that morning, and they had promised to begin their work at noon, so that Mr. Guilder's people might be praying for him.

"It is now nearly noon," said Mr. Kenneth. "If I may, I will say a few prayers with you, and read you a passage of scripture ; and then, as our church clock strikes, we will join together in silent prayer. That will be all. After the quarter strikes, we will say the

Lord's Prayer together; and after that, perhaps you will disperse as quietly as possible."

He did not mount to one of the priests' stalls, but turned with his back to them and knelt at the Litany desk, as if he would kneel in front of this great company, to lead it. He read a few collects, to which the people said Amen; and all remarked the number of men's voices in those low Amens. He stood up and read them St. Paul's description to Timothy of a good priest —" If thou put the brethren in remembrance of these things, thou shalt be a good minister. . . . Take heed unto thyself, and unto the doctrine; continue in them, for, in doing this, thou shalt both save thyself and them that hear thee . . ." and then, as he looked at the watch in his cincture and said, " Let us pray," all knelt again. They waited in silence for the church clock to strike midday. Soon its machinery moved in the tower, offending the silence, and, after a premonitory pause, it began to strike. A great many of the people standing near the doors fell to their knees. The twelve strokes seemed to bruise the listeners after the quiet; but when their last reverberation died away, they left a silence all the deeper for their passing.

Far away, in another silence, the white-coated surgeons bent to their task.

All that afternoon they waited for news. Rose Damien had promised that, directly Abbott heard anything, she would " send round and let them know." But the afternoon softened into evening, and not a word passed from Conyers to Macartney Road. At suppertime Rose sent the news that he had rallied a little and the doctors were not without hope. A spring of joy rushed up in Cynthia. "He's going to be all right! He's going to be all right!" cried the little repetitive voice within her. "He's going to be all right! Oh joy!" And because it was her nature to recoil from too much pain, she believed all through the evening that he would have a miraculous recovery and live and move among them once more. After supper she went up to her room and tried to read. Nine o'clock struck—she shut her book sharply—she went to her desk by the window. Better to occupy herself with letters than to stare at the pages of this book and read a few lines and then wonder what they were about.

Her bedroom window was thrown open to the July night, and for a few minutes she rested her hands on the sill and looked out. It was not yet fully dark, and the light in the windows on the opposite side of the road had the look of lamps lit too soon, which always made for melancholy. So also in the sky overhead: the stars, in a sky not empty of day, looked like the visitors to a ball who had come too soon. Down below a boy, without a care in the world, went whistling along the pavement. She closed the lower half of the window, and sat at the desk. She busied herself there for half an hour broken by mindless pauses during which she knocked the end of her pen against her teeth. It may have been about ten o'clock, it was already fully dark, and she had forgotten Mr. Guilder in the task of finding words for a letter, when a sound struck on her brain like the sound in the last second of a dream, whose reality one wakes to doubt. Had she really heard it or not? Fear that it was real turned her heart to lead. She lifted her face and sat motionless, and listened. Nothing. The emptiness was just giving her hope again when, cruelly, indifferently, the sound rang in the night a second time.

" Oh ! "

Rising up and staring through the window, she tried to deny her senses and waited throughout another long pause. Useless—hopeless : it came again. The bell of St. Alban's. It was telling to all the parish that John Wilfred Guilder was dead.

For one hesitating moment she stood there while the mass of tears welled up. Then, since uncontrolled grief turns everyone into a child again, she ran down the stairs to the little kitchen where she heard her mother moving at her last tasks. Running to her and crying, " Oh mummy ! " she flung her arms round Hilda's neck and her head on her breast, where she let her tears have their way. " He's dead. He's dead," she sobbed. And Hilda held her there, against the warmth of her breast, stroking her head or gently patting her shoulder.

X

At the morning service on Sunday Mr. Kenneth, ascending the pulpit, told another great congregation that their vicar had passed away at about ten o'clock on the Friday night, and his body was now resting at the vicarage. Before he went to the hospital, said Mr. Kenneth, he had left a last message to be given to his people in the event of his seeing them no more. "But first I will say all that I have to say, and then read it to you, so that his words shall be the last you will hear and unspoiled by comment of mine." The funeral was to be on Monday at midday; and after Evensong to-night they would bring the body of their vicar into his church where it would rest throughout the night. A chain of parishioners would watch beside it from the close of Evensong till noon to-morrow. He invited all who would like to give up an hour of the night to come and share in this watch. After this invitation he said his words of praise, and, then, putting up his spectacles and unfolding a paper, began to read.

"My dear people, If this letter is read to you it will mean that I have gone from you somewhat discourteously. But I did not know what the outcome would be—I do not know as I write this—and I decided that, if all was good, why then, a leave-taking would be unnecessary, and if not, why then, dear people, I could say my good-bye to you in a letter. For with all my

heart I want to give you a last message if I am to see
you no more. I want to ask your forgiveness for all
my failings of which I am deeply conscious in this hour ;
and I want you to know that, in spite of these, I really
loved you. Why God was so good as to give me such
a loyal people, I do not understand. I could wish now
that I were about to face Him with a sense of work
among them discharged more fully and offered with a
more single mind. But at least it seems to me that any
word I write to you will carry much weight ; and
therefore I do not let this opportunity pass of saying a
word that may have a greater chance of growth in your
hearts than many I have spoken to you before. Some
of you may be visited at times by doubts about the
dogmas of your faith—I have known them myself—
but of the substance of the Christian teaching I ask you
to believe that there can be no doubt whatever. Oh, I
wish I could convey to you how certain I am in this
moment that its cardinal trust in the goodness of God
and its two mutually dependent counsels to men, that
they should love one another and judge no one, will
remain the truth about the world so long as the world
shall last. I have never in my life been so certain as
now that, though it may be our duty to correct the
offenders, we can judge not one of them—no, not the
worst of them all. I will not weary you by justifying
this certainty ; it must come to you as vision. But
each of you who is a parent has the beginning of that
vision in you, when you look with clemency on the
waywardness or the ill-temper of a little child. If you
have no more of the vision than this, watch out for it,
and it will come. And the other : it is told of the
Apostle John that when he was a very old man and

almost beyond speech, they would carry him into the church at Ephesus and ask of him one word for the congregation, and he would answer, in his failing voice, " Little children, love one another." Humbly I copy him to-day and give you those words as the only wisdom. I know that where I have obeyed them I have been happy, and where I have resisted them, I have missed happiness ; and I so want you to be happy. Good-bye and God bless you, my good and loyal people."

Mr. Kenneth folded up the paper and, removing his spectacles, came down from the pulpit.

Cynthia knelt in the church. It was after Evensong, and the greater part of the congregation had gone. Only here and there among the pews knelt a few watchers like herself. The body of the church was rather dark, because no lights had been lit as yet, and nothing but the half-light of a July dusk came through the stained-glass windows. Before the Litany desk, at the meeting point of nave and chancel and transepts, the coffin of the vicar rested on its trestles, its foot toward the altar. She knelt at the end of a row, some eight pews back but not very far from it ; and often she looked up the nave at the coffin under its black and purple pall, with no flowers anywhere about it, but only the white stole of a celebrant priest folded up as for the end of a day, and resting on its top. Mr. Guilder lay there quiet, in the scene of his triumphs.

She had cried bitterly as the bearers brought him up the nave and laid him there. But they had gone now, and for half an hour she had tried to pray. She was coming back at midnight, to watch again till one. And now her thoughts had deserted prayer an begun to stray. Thoughts are a wayward and selfish flock, be their shepherd never so eager for self-forgetfulness ; and if he weary and rest for a moment, they will wander into the fields that they favour most. She forgot where she was ; she saw nothing of the chancel arch, choir stalls and east window, and barely noticed when the verger tip-toed across to a switch-board and lit one light in the centre of the church and one before the altar ; she was seeing a path through some orchard trees and an old grey studio wall. She was seeing the interior of the studio, and Rugg in his smocked overall as he stood with his hands on his hips and stared at a canvas. Then her thoughts went back to the years before this central episode, and she saw herself as a child full of hope and confidence that life was going to bring her great days. And slowly—to her surprise— as she saw these old lost and lively scenes, a very terrible darkness of despair began to gather around her. Perhaps she had endured too much in the last months. The death of Mr. Guilder, her one friend who knew all and supported her, had been as if she had dwelt on a desert island and found at last a companion and then lifted her head to see that he was gone. The world to the horizon was empty again. And now faith was falling from her, falling from her—leaving her heart dead. Like love for a person, faith in the future, or in anything, can fade from us in some dark moods, and we are our lonely selves again. And the loss is a sick despair. In her desk at home was a letter that he had written to her, perhaps just after the letter to his people ; " Keep courage, Cynthia. All will be well. Who knows, perhaps I may be able to help you still, and better than before ? And I am so sure that good things are coming to you, because you are made for them." Good things are coming to you. But why should they? Why should they when that had happened which had slain the desire to love and the power to hope? If only she could hope for something! But she couldn't : nothing seemed to be worth looking forward to but death, and death, to-night, seemed release and rest. But there was such a long time to live. Forty or fifty years at least— what a dreary avenue to wander down, neither loving nor hoping! Nor believing anything. For in this sudden, beaten mood she could feel only sick recoil from the lofty ideals that Mr. Guilder had once put before her. And she knew that she was recoiling from them with aversion just because they were high and good. She was ready to call good evil, and evil good—no, not evil itself seemed good. Evil was evil too. All things were alike worthless. There was nothing worth doing, or hoping for, or striving for. The despair was now pitch black ; and out of it she cried " Oh God, help me ! Oh God, save me from this ! . . ." Then she remembered where she was, and how selfish it was to use this time in prayer for herself. Glancing at the quiet bed of her friend, she thought how different he had been. On the very day that he had heard he must die, he had said, " The future will have better things in it than you can imagine. I hope I may be there to see some of them." Oh for the dignity of unselfishness again! She left her prayer for rescue unfinished, and prayed for him instead.

And at that moment she heard footsteps in the silence behind her. Someone was coming up the nave. The steps must pass close to her, who knelt at a pew's end ; and she halted her thinking till they should be by. A

tall shadow passed her; and when it was a few paces
further on, she saw a tall man who stood by the coffin
with his head bent thoughtfully. She could see only
his back, and the instantaneous impression was of a
figure singularly strong and graceful. It looked a
youthful figure, but who could yet say? Her wearied
thoughts, no matter how she might try to drill them,
were ready to travel to any distraction; and soon her
eyes, trained by O'Kelvie, were noticing the fine column
of the neck, the wide shoulders, the neat lines from
arm pits to waist, and the narrow, shapely loins. This
was a figure that Rugg would have liked to model.
The hair, as far as she could see, was fair, and the skin
at the nape ruddy with weather. Though the figure
was dressed in a good grey suit, well cut, the hands,
when soon they met behind the back, were rough. But
they were powerful hands; as were the square wrists
that showed below the sleeve. One of the hands now
grasped a wrist, and the other closed into a loose fist.
Who was it? Who was it that cared to come at this
late hour and look thoughtfully on Mr. Guilder? She
was quite unable to lower her face into her palms again
till he had turned round and revealed himself.

He turned, and at once she knew. But what a
miracle! Five years had worked a miracle, no less.
His face had taken on that charm, invisible to its owner,
but very visible to women, when fair hair meets a skin
tanned and chiselled and engraved by the wind. And
as might have been expected, the eyes, alight with
thought and humour, were of that pale blue which is
said to come to sailors and to all who watch the weather.
She saw all this, because, as he came down the nave
again, he caught her eyes and paused a second as if to

greet her, and then, remembering where he was, passed on.

Leo Damien. But what a Leo! The surprise was enough to jerk her out of her self-centred thought. She felt kindly disposed towards him at once. She liked him for the sake of their quaint old memories, and because he had cared to come this evening and take his farewell of a man who had been a big figure of their childhood. Sunday, she supposed, was the only day that he was free to leave his market fields. Oh, she would like to hear all about his work, for never had she seen anyone who looked less like a labourer of the fields. Oh, was there no chance that he was staying with his parents that night, and she might yet be able to hear his news? Almost she would have liked to run after him and stop him, and she felt that Mr. Guilder would have forgiven her for this moment of desertion and smiled tolerantly. But she remained on her knees, and soon she heard the door swing behind Leo Damien.

XI

SHE remained on her knees even longer than she had intended, because she wanted to prove to herself that the temptation to desert had no power over her. And then, since she was coming back later, she left the church—but only to find Leo waiting for her in the road.

" Oh good ! " he exclaimed. " Hallo, Cynthia."

" Hallo, Leo," she answered ; and, remembering whence she had come, added, " Isn't it awful about Mr. Guilder ? "

" Yes," he agreed. " I only heard about it all from Mum this morning, and all day I've felt I'd like to come up and see the last of him. Shall we walk along ? A great man in his way. But tell me : how are *you* ? "

" Oh, I'm all right. But this has upset me a little. He . . ." and she left speaking of herself to talk only of Mr. Guilder. He alone, she felt, had a right to her words to-night.

Leo, perceiving the thought and respecting it, listened to her praise ; often supporting it with a " Yes . . . yes, he was," or a " Yes, rather amazing in his way . . ." but she felt, none the less, a kind of suppressed eagerness in him that was impatient of too much preoccupation with the dead. Mr. Guilder, of course, had meant nothing like so much to him as to her, and she saw that he was hard put to it to prevent the impatience from bursting through his politeness and his timely reverence. And when they were in sight of her door, which was soon, he did burst into her talk with, " I say ! Let's walk round the streets a bit. Do you mind ? " to which she answered, " But shan't I see you to-morrow ? " and he replied, " No, I must get back to-night " ; and she, halting on her doorstep which they had reached, and putting her head a little to one side, waited for the battle to end between her feeling that she ought to deal only in the things of Mr. Guilder to-night and her desire to yield to the urgency of Leo Damien. And when, glancing up, she saw a look on his face, a look of mingled anxiety and disappointment, which was almost comical, she shrugged her shoulders, said, " Well . . ." and they were in the road again, talking.

She asked for information about himself, and he told her that he had never been a market gardener, but a gardener to a firm of Nurserymen and Garden Craftsmen —" Mother makes these small mistakes sometimes "— and now he had risen to be Second Manager and spent his time designing gardens to be made with other's people money. He imagined the Boss had given him this job because he generally got enthusiastic about his own designs and ended by inducing the clients to spend twice as much as they had intended—which pleased the Boss no end. It didn't exactly distress him, either, because he got a commission as well as wages, and so was making all the money he wanted. He had his own cottage now and a patch of garden, which by golly ! she must come and see one day. It overlooked two-thirds of England.

There was a recurrent flash in his eyes as he spoke rapidly, eagerly, urgently of the things that interested him ; and Cynthia, perceiving it with a smile, said, " Yes, I should think you'd make quite a good manager."

Instantly his lower jaw went slightly to one side, as if praise, in some strange way, hurt him, while it pleased. Perhaps it pleased so much that it hurt. He swung his eyes from her face, and the talk from her remark, and began to pour out his ideas about gardens, his plans for his cottage, and his schemes for the future ; for he had forgotten all about Mr. Guilder. The excited flash returned to the weathered eyes as he got safely away from praise ; and Cynthia, listening and sometimes throwing a glance at his profile, wondered what her old feeling of pity for him should have changed to this present feeling of—well, comparative smallness. She felt as if she were walking by the side of someone bigger and stronger and alas ! cleverer than herself— and certainly much quicker in his pace : she had to keep begging him to slow down, reminding him that she had a skirt, with such things as " gathers " which were liable to rip out at the first provocation. He apologised, fitted his step to hers, and was back in the rapids of flashing talk, his step in danger of being carried away by them once more. Funny ! When she walked with Rob Ingram she felt much older than that callow young man ; walking with Leo, who was only about two months older than she, she felt—what ? of an age but less assured ; a little dependent. With Rob, who had despised Leo, she was the counsellor and the giver ; with Leo, the listener and the receiver. Strange turning of the tables.

" You can certainly talk," she said. " But there ! I never knew a man who couldn't."

" H'm. Can I ? Yes, I suppose I do hold forth a bit, if I'm interested. And I *am* interested in gardens. I'm sorry."

" Oh, don't be sorry. I'm quite enjoying it. It interests me too, as you put it. I'll tell you when you get on a subject that's boring me to distraction."

" Well, it occurs to me that I might now talk about someone besides myself, for a change. How are *you ?* "

" All right, thank you."

" Are you happy ? "

" Oh yes . . . so, so. . . ."

" What does that mean ? "

" Well . . . oh, but I don't want to talk about myself, Leo. *You* sound terribly happy, at any rate. Are you ? I hope so."

" Yes. I think so."

" Oh joy. I'm so glad. Go on telling me all about it."

She had turned the talk back to him because she had suddenly felt disloyal to the dead. And Leo, perceiving this and anxious lest he had been offensively egotistical, gave all the talk to Mr. Guilder and old times : evidently he was still very sensitive. They walked on through the streets of the Square Quarter Mile, speaking of the Children's Service, and the Pantomime, and the boys who had gone off to become priests, till the church clock broke on their gossip, striking ten. Leo waited till its last note had died away, knowing that it must be recreating for her the scene in the church ; then, after a loaded silence, his eagerness burst up again, and he exclaimed, " Oh, don't let's talk about death ; let's talk about you. *Do* tell me something about yourself. Tell me all your past life, and your future plans. *Please !* I've got to go soon. I've got to get back to-night."

" *Mine* won't be very lively," she lamented, laughing.

But, though she pretended to this gloom, she suddenly knew that she was pleased with the request. Liking him, trusting the intelligence in his eyes, and feeling that a sympathy had sprung up between them, she was quite ready to use him as a receptacle for all her problems. She heard herself in fluent description of her discontents ; and she noticed that, when he endorsed them with a most convincing and enthusiastic " Yes, *yes !* *Don't* I understand ! My God, yes ! " she became enthusiastic about them, too, and then impetuous and torrential, and at length completely indiscreet. She had opened the floodgates dangerously far, and the pent-up emotions were doing the rest. She spoke of loneliness and longing and the fond illusions from which it was such a searing grief to wake. She deplored the ultimate isolation of every living creature and the impossibility of ever really *knowing* people so that you could possess them as you longed to, and they could possess you as you longed to be possessed, and how this final fact of the world meant that nothing—*nothing* was really worth while, because what was the good of doing anything by yourself and for yourself, alone—absolutely alone, when you came to work it out ? She said she didn't know the real heart of anybody living, neither father nor mother nor friend ; and no one knew hers ; and she wanted to know and to *be* known, as she was sure every decent person did. She even spoke in guarded terms about her love. " Of course I went and fell terribly in love with someone, and it all went to pieces. It ended rather more than two years ago, and all the rest has been this—this wilderness. It ended hopelessly and for ever, and the idiocy of it is that I love him still."

She had come to an end ; and Leo, who had

accompanied her rhapsody on loneliness with a series of endorsements that were almost joyous in their enthusiasm, walked with his thoughts for a while—lips compressed and pace quickening—till he surprised her with the words, " I'm rather glad you're lonely and miserable, Cynthia."

" Why ? "

" Because so am I."

" You ? " She knit her brows in laughing protest, feeling that humour was due, after her outburst.   " But you said you were terribly happy ? "

" Yes. So I did. And it's quite true in a way, but——" and he explained that he had no one to talk to ; no one to whom he could talk as he wanted to talk. In a small country town his spade and his gaiters shut him off from all women of education like her—" Lordy ! Me ? *Educated ?* " interrupted Cynthia—and from most men friends as well, except his pals in the pubs whose tap-room chattiness he quite enjoyed, but if he wanted to discuss Schopenhauer, they'd stare and say, " 'Oo's 'e ? "

" Well, who *is* he ? " asked Cynthia.

Leo ignored this. And the long and the short of it, said he, was that his trouble was exactly the same as hers : he so badly wanted a real friend. And now they would meet once a week at least, and talk over their miseries, which was the one way to turn the disgusting things into delightful ones.

" I should love to," said she, simply.

" Oh good ! Well, what's wrong with next Saturday ? Let's see : you leave your office at twelve. I'll be in Victoria Street at twelve-ten, and we'll go to Victoria Station and take the first train that looks good, and get out at the first station where the fields are pleasant and the cows look kind."

"Oh *yes!* Oh *let's!*" cried Cynthia, lifted out of her woes.

"And we'll have tea at the first pub that delights us, and in the evening——"

"Evening!—but that reminds me! That reminds me of something. Something I've been burning to ask you for five years. Please, Leo: what is the mysterious work you do in the evening? You remember: you wrote to your mother after you ran away, saying that you were happy because, in the evenings, you could do the work you really cared for. What is it? I've scarcely had a wink of sleep all these years wondering what it was. What is it, Leo?"

"I shan't tell you."

"Yes, you will. *Please.*"

"No."

"But why?"

"Because it might shock you. When you know me much better, and can stand the shock, I may tell you."

"That won't happen, because, if you don't tell me now, I shan't come next Saturday."

"No?"

"No."

"All right. Shall we be parting now? That, I think, is your door over there."

"Please tell me."

"No."

"You really won't."

"Certainly not."

"Then that seems to be the end of our friendship, Mr. Damien?"

"Certainly."

"The shortest friendship in history?"

"Absolutely."

"Oh, confound you!"

And this brought them to her door.

"Well, good-bye for the present," said he. "Next Saturday, in Victoria Street, at twelve-ten. And don't be late."

"Here!" protested Cynthia, one foot on her doorstep and the other swinging, "I'm not one of your hired labourers." And then, with the kindest look, her head thrown to one side and her hand stretched forward, she said, "Good-bye, Leo. It's been wonderful to meet you again. And I shall live for Saturday." He pressed her hand, and went; and she laughed and waved him out of view.

Laughed and waved, because excited by hope of a friend. In the silence of the church, a quarter of a mile away, Mr. Guilder lay as she had left him, with the few watchers kneeling among the pews. I think that she was right, and he would have smiled tolerantly.

She returned to the church much sooner than she had intended, because, when Leo was gone and his figure fading, she wondered if she had been guilty of desertion.

XII

ALL that summer they gave their Saturdays or their
Sundays to each other. And later, when the companionship deepened, they sometimes gave both. They went
to any part that could be reached in an hour's journey
by train, and here they wandered across meadows and
over hills. Cynthia would bring a picnic lunch, and
they had tea in a farmhouse or village inn. Sometimes
when the day was very fine, and a wide, cloudless sky
arched over them, and there was never a house in sight
anywhere but only the meadow-flowers at her feet and
the hedgerows and woods far away, Cynthia, from sheer
joy, would break into a run, the wind taking her hair,
and would cry back to Leo, " Oh, isn't it gorgeous ?
How can you just *walk* like that ? It's *too* foolish " ;
and she was singing, " Cynthia was a housemaid, Modest
and content . . ." or (with exquisite appropriateness,
as she quickly maintained) " When the Pipes of Pan are
calling, . . . Oh, follow, follow, follow the merry,
merry pipes of Pan." Early in their friendship he took
her to his own place, and they peeped over hedges
and walls at gardens he had made, and went on to
his cottage. As a building it was not beautiful, being
no more than four brick walls and an old roof, but its
garden was such an exhibition as a gardener's plot
should be, and the view from its windows justified
some of his boasting, if not all. It stood near the

brow, on the southern face of a hill; and if it didn't overlook two-thirds of England, it did command a great prospect of rolling valley that was not shut in till the far hills were blue. From his study window on the upper floor she looked out over a chequered carpet of fields and farms and parklands; and she said, " Well, it certainly has a nice view, but it doesn't overlook two-thirds of England."

" Yes, it does."

" No, it doesn't."

" Yes, it does."

" How ? "

" Because two-thirds of England are just like that."

" Clever, aren't you, Leo ? " said she, with marked distaste; and, after a quick glance round his study with its books, pianola, and untidy desk, that she might guess at his interests, she turned to the window again, and allowed, " Yes, it is certainly a better view than mine, I'm afraid. But come, let's get out into it. Let's be part of the view." And then they were part of it, walking across a ten-acre meadow, and talking, talking.

In these talks they exchanged their frivolity and their earnestness; their laughter, their life-stories and their hopes. It was a friendship in the grass and on the hills, as the friendship of Cynthia and O'Kelvie had been a friendship in a studio and along the London streets. Perhaps Leo did most of the talking. His step quickening with the rush of thought, and his fist hammering one mighty idea after another into her obstinacy, he stuttered his philosophies as only young people can. And she, after a little resistance mainly designed to annoy him, responded with interest and delighted enthusiasm, for

Cynthia, though she may not have had a strong original genius, had a gift for friendship. She was able to listen, and to be interested and curious and encouraging, when he talked at hearty length about himself; and this, as far as I have been able to discover, is something that only women can do. She had to take much of it, for imagine what it was to Leo, after five years, to have someone at last who would listen to his self-revelation! As O'Kelvie had done, he would often, towards the close of a long harangue, catch the smile trembling on her lips and demand what the devil she was laughing at.

" Well, you men are all the same," she explained. " You do lay down the law so."

" Not at all," protested Leo.

" Yes. Every bit at all," insisted Cynthia. " But don't worry. It's only what one has learned to expect."

" That's absurd," said Leo.

" It isn't. If you listened to yourself instead of leaving that part of the entertainment to me, you'd just *hear* yourself. It's ripping. It goes on and on. . . ."

" My dear child," began Leo in explanation—

" Don't my-dear-child me. You seem to forget that you're exactly the same age as I am, even if you *are* twice the size."

" I'm not the same age as you. I'm two months older."

" Well, what's that ? "

" It's a lot. You can learn a great deal in two months."

" Still, I've no great opinion of men," said she, irrelevantly.

" Haven't you ? "

" No. But go on. Go on with your tale. You

are more entertaining than some. Only, for mercy's
sake, don't walk quite so fast."

"Sorry. But when I get excited with the talk, I
always walk *prestissimo*."

"Oh !"

"What ? "

"Nothing . . . nothing . . ."

"But I thought you spoke ? "

"No, that was nothing, Leo. Go on with the tale."

She had soon discovered that the miracle of Leo was
less complete than she had supposed. Of the change
in his face and frame there was no question. Sometimes
when he toiled in front of her up a hill, in his workday
clothes of breeches, leggings and open shirt, she would
get as keen a pleasure as O'Kelvie would have done
from his athletic shape and his long powerful limbs.
Sometimes, as he sat beside her with his rolled-up shirt
sleeves, she noticed the modelling of his forearm, large
and round at the top and tapering to an iron wrist,
with the pale hairs glistening on the tanned skin all the
way ; and she would be moved by an odd, impersonal
wish to grip it once with her fingers. But his mind was
not so perfectly changed. There remained a sensitive-
ness, an easily hurt pride, and a craving for praise,
though he shied from the first breath of it, like a horse
from a shadow in its path. He seemed to fear it almost
as much as he wanted it. And the wounds of his youth
had developed an assertive egotism which beat at the
kindlier walls he had built around it ; but he disarmed
criticism by seeing this even more clearly than she, and
deploring it with self-ridicule. And when you can see
it yourself, it is partly controlled.

"I think I always rather admired you for running

away like that," said she one evening, as they sat together under a hedge, " and living your own life. Getting free ! " And her eyes gazed over the fields at the far-stretching freedoms that lived in the evening light, just beyond the horizon.

" Free ? " Leo picked a blade and trifled with it. " But I'm not free. And I don't know that I ever shall be. The tyranny of those who held your childhood endures too long. You may dethrone it from your brain, but it still works in you. Down below somewhere."

" I wish you'd talk intelligibly. Please : what does all that mean ? "

" It means that Father and Mother and Rob Ingram and the whole of Norman's End still exercise a tremendous power over me. What they think and say—I tell myself that I ought to be majestically indifferent to it, but I'm not : it matters to me. It matters hugely. In fact, I sometimes think it's been the biggest driving force of all. You see, they despised me. Oh yes, they did ! They laughed at me. If I were as free as I should like to be, I should laugh at their laughter. Instead I dream night and day of doing some colossal thing in the world that'll overthrow them with amazement, and then I'll march in triumph over their prostrate bodies. I want Rob Ingram to gasp in surprise and secret jealousy. It's contemptible of me, but it's there, Cynthia. Can't help it. And Mother and Father too. I've got quite fond of them since I left them, but I want to walk over their prostrate forms—over Mother's more than Father's, because, all said and done, Abbott's a harmless little fellow. And when I've sufficiently impressed them all, I'll begin to be good. I'll be above such pettiness then, but not before!" His eyes flashed. "Perhaps it's good to have been despised, Cynthia. It fills your boiler with steam enough to get you anywhere. It gives you strength to move mountains. Lord, when I do it, he *will* look cheap!"

"Who?"

"Rob Ingram."

"What are you going to do?"

"I've done it. As a matter of fact, I've done it already. I'm sure I have, but the world hasn't recognised it yet. It will one day. Of that I'm just as sure as I'm sure of anything between the heaven and the earth." Now his eyes were staring at the distance. "We must keep Rob alive till that happens. And Rose and Abbott too. How long will Abbott live, do you think, Cynthia?"

"I don't know. He looks pretty healthy."

"Good. Take care of them all, won't you? Fatten them up for the sacrifice."

"Yes; but what is it you've done?"

He pretended not to hear. Rolling up the blade of grass, he continued, "Tyranny, when you're a child, compels you later on to think that you're a great lad. Napoleon and Shakespeare aren't in it with you. It induces the most disgusting vanity. That's why I can't bear criticism really, Cynthia; at least, not at the first shock. I pretend to welcome it, but it pricks like hell. I want only praise. However, I think I'm getting a little of all this out of my system, but it's a battle . . . it's a battle. . . ."

Cynthia looked at the ground. "I understand."

When he talked like this, and she could see that he was speaking out of his real self, some of the old pity would come back to her and mingle with her new admiration for his fine body and dancing intellect ; and she would put out a hand and just touch his bare arm sympathetically. It was an excuse for doing what she had longed to do.

They fell to talking about the past. "You are not to say anything against Mr. Guilder," she declared, "because I believe there was something true in all he said. I saw it, and got hold of it, and you're not to unsettle me ; else am I the poorest soul alive."

"I am *perfectly* sure that much about Mr. Guilder and St. Alban's was right, and will always be right," agreed Leo. "I felt it with a curious certainty when I heard of his death. I felt driven to come up and take a last look at him, and to see if, by sitting quietly in the old church, I could catch hold of what it was."

"And I think that was nice of you. And what did you get hold of ? "

"Oh, I don't know. It is difficult to put into words. I saw that, in so far as he and his people were really righteous they were beautiful, and in so far as they were hypocritical they were ugly."

"Well now ! Isn't that simple ? Oh, why doesn't my brain work clearly like that ? Here have I been puzzling for at least five years over Norman's End, and you've summed it up in a sentence. It's so humiliating. I hate to think you're cleverer than I am. I don't think you are, really. It's just that you've a better brain."

Instantly he drew aside from the praise. "I think we're both the same. St. Alban's is in our blood for good and all, and we've got to come to terms with it."

"Oh, I'm so glad you think that ! " she exclaimed. "And I'm so glad you think we're alike. But doesn't that mean that you ought to tell me at once what is the marvellous thing you've done ? "

" It may do ; but I'm not going to tell you."

" Well, you're a pig ; and I think I'll be going now."

" Shall you ? "

" Yes, I think so."

" Right." He jumped up. " I'll walk back with you to the station. It's getting cold, I admit."

Cynthia stood up, scorning to answer this. The shadows lay long on the grass, and they walked across them in silence, till Leo inquired, " And where shall we go next Saturday ? "

" I'm not coming next Saturday."

" Oh yes, you are."

" Oh no, I'm not. I'm not coming any more."

" You most certainly are."

" No."

" Yes."

" *No.*"

" Why ? "

" Because you won't tell me what it is you've done."

A smile broke on his lips as he looked down on her, " Cynthia, are you sulky ? "

" Certainly."

" Oh my crikey ! "

" I don't want to see you any more. At least, I don't think I do. You encourage me to talk all about myself, and then you won't tell me a simple thing like that."

" Well, should we say good-bye here ? "

" If you like. I don't mind."

" Good-bye, Cynthia."

" Good-bye, Leo."

" Well, why don't you go ? "

" Why don't *you*, you great booby ?   Just standing there, trying to look clever ! "

" The idea was yours, I think."

" All right.   Then we shan't see each other any more ? "

" No.   And you'll be sorry when I'm a great man."

" I shall bear up."

" Shall you ?   I shall see that you don't.   Hell, I've got another spur to drive me further than ever.   I've got *you* to impress now."

" I suppose you think all that's clever ? "

Leo shrugged, as if he neither admitted nor denied it.

" *Tell* me," pleaded Cynthia, turning and looking up at him.   " *Tell* me what it is you've done."

" But I've never told a soul !   I've always felt I couldn't till the work was proved to be good by the applause of half the world.   They wouldn't believe in it till that had happened.   They'd pity me again, for my foolish ambitions, God damn them !   Why should I tell *you* ?

" Oh, because I *want* it."

" I see."   And he smiled at her, as one smiles at a child.

" Yes, that's why.   Now what *is* it ? "

" If I tell you, you will come to supper at a pub, and resume operations next Saturday ? "

" Of course, of course ! " cried she, impatient at such a stupid question, and rising up and down on her toes.

" Well, here it is."   And he drew a long fat envelope from his pocket.   " I've had it in my pocket all the time. I should probably have given it to you in any case to-day —only you made such a little beast of yourself—asking for it, and all that . . .   No, not now ! . . .   You're not to open it till late to-night.   Listen, Cynthia : you've got a room, haven't you?—with a door?—and a bolt to the door? Shut it and bolt it. And wait till you're certain they're all asleep. Especially Granny, because Granny's got eyes that'll see through a wall, I'm sure. And she might come knocking, and I should suffer agonies if you were disturbed in the midst of it. No, don't peep at it. Remember you're sworn not to open it till all the world's asleep."

" Oh, but I'm——"

" That's enough. Not another word. I'm inclined to shiver if it's even spoken of. Come along to supper."

XIII

Cynthia opened it that night in her room, with the door shut and loyally bolted. Poems. As she had suspected, the manuscript of a book of poems. And immediately a slight nervousness assailed her lest they should fail to please ; for what should she say to Leo then ? This nervousness put her heart out of its true beat : she was anxious for him, because he had been so confident about his work. That he was clever she had no doubt, but that didn't mean that he could write poems ; and that he was confident the world would one day acclaim them proved nothing : hardly a person yet who, having written poetry, supposed it less than remarkable. What if she should, in spite of her desires, find them weak ? What then ?

"I shall lie," she decided. "I should have to."

And comforted by this resolution, she threw herself on to her bed to look at the manuscript. It began with a title page. Leo was young enough to have enjoyed printing out this page. "A WINDOW OVER ENGLAND, And Other Poems. By Leo Damien. All Rights Reserved." Next, two pages of "CONTENTS." Glancing further among the pages, she saw that the earlier were shorter poems; the later long ones ; till at last she came to the longest of all, which gave its name to the book, "A Window over England."

She began with the first and short ones ; and soon she was giving quick little murmurs of pleasure. They were good ; oh, they were good ! If most of them were not good, she knew nothing about poetry at all.

In the simplest words they caught and imprisoned the stirs of delight that a child of the pavements feels, who comes late to the pastures and the woods. Men had written before of leaves and grass and flying and creeping things ; of labouring men and shepherds, and the light from tap-house doors, and the laughter and wisdom within, spilt with the ale on the sanded floor ; but had anyone caught so well the sharp wonder, the quick delight, of the escaping townsmen who comes to these things at eighteen and finds that he is coming home ? Of his weakness Leo had made his strength. Men had written before of flowers and sapling trees ; but seldom, surely, had a journeyman gardener sung with such knowledge of their roots and seeds at work in the slow earth, of their enemies tunnelling forward to their overthrow, and of a good labourer's war for their life and beauty, and their inheritance by other men. Again and again she enjoyed that thrill which is the gift of a new thought exquisitely phrased. To almost all his pictures of country things her response, sharp on the last word, was, " Oh, why haven't I perceived that ? Why haven't I known that ? Oh, why have I wasted my days ? " After reading those verses that enshrined his vision, tender and amused, of the homely characters of bar-parlour and lane, she loathed her preoccupation with herself, and its consequence, the lack of a wide humanity like his. " Oh, I see nothing ! I'm looking into myself all the time. It's awful." After smiling at those lines that were humorous, salted, or witty, she felt annoyed with the ordinariness of her thought. " Oh, why didn't *I* say that ? Why should I never have thought of that without being helped ? Oh Leo, I'm afraid you're wittier than I am."

Only a few poems left her frowning in a failure to understand.

Then she came to the long poem at the end. She began it ; and she had not read far before her pleased approval lifted to something more. Whatever critics might say, here was a poem charged in every line with power to move and thrill mere ordinary people like herself. It would reach the plough-boy and the ruddy, illiterate squire, the poet-shy Pall Mall clubman, and the " tired business man," as well as the earnest bookworm in the train. It would stir her father to his depths, if he read it in print instead of in manuscript and didn't know that it was by Leo Damien who had lived in the next street and was still unrecognised. It was made for all, except the arid few who distrusted emotion of any kind. Leo had thrown all hypercritical rationalism, all disabling diffidence, to the winds, and written straight out of an emotion that was for ever surging in himself, and that lay incipient in every man ; and the result was a poem to which all, if they trusted their first response, must cry, " Yes ! "

And in all this judgment Cynthia was right. Though she did not know it, she was reading the poem to which, four years later, the chances of war gave so unusual a fame. Little wonder that the press seized on it, that Authority circulated it, that pulpit and platform quoted it, that parents and wives, left at home and longing for faith and justification and the strength to go on, sent it to their men in all parts of the world—by an odd accident it was ready for the moment.

" *My window looks on England, pasture, wheat, and hill. . . .*"

Sentimental, as the song of a lover must always be, it yet sang one aspect of the truth, as love always does. It spread before the reader a wide prospect of England, touching in with fond precision the copses and the quilted fields, the grazing cattle, the spires lifting from the huddled roofs, the quiet parklands, and the rolling hills with their woods on flank or crown. Over this manifold and chequered scene it played the changes of the year : spring with the orchard blossom and the pale skies and the flutter and song of mating birds ; summer, brown on the pasture and dark on the leaves, but turning the acres of arable into golden pictures of God's mercy ; autumn with its low sunlight and opalescent cloud, and the grass never so green against the rusty trees ; and winter, brown and purple in the woods, while rain-pools stared at the low, grey sky.

" *My window looks on England, pasture, wheat, and wood ;*
I watch the seasons drift across.   See, winter goes
Over the hill with driven cloud, and leaves the spring behind,
A scattering of white and rose
And tender green where yesterday the empty orchard stood ;
And pale, transparent light, unending, still ;
And plovers sailing up the laden wind. . . ."

Then the poet mused. England had many faults, but she had also a truth. " I saw it from my window yesterday." No art culture hers to equal those of Athens, Florence, and France, but a culture of humanity which, " if far this side perfection yet," was better than the best of other lands. And in the main it was a culture bred from her earth and her sky. What other earth had such differentiation in valley, garden, wood or flower-bank, or in the pattern of her counties ? And differentiation bred individualism; and individualism at its best, and as England on the whole had understood it, meant toleration, liberty, humour, and fair opportunity for all. Her grass, far-famed, had bred her games of ball which had meant so much to her culture, and the quiet of her pastures which had meant far greater and rarer things. He painted her wet winds, her driving clouds, her white mists, and all her moody weather; and, seeking a true audit, scored to the credit of these, not only her blazing hearths and her full gardens with such domestic virtues as were their fruits, but also her " grin-and-bear-it " laughter which had steadied her in a hundred trials. To her hills and her thousand bays she owed her exploration and enterprise; and lastly, but most significantly, to her ring of sea she owed that deep, innate, unconscious sense of security and self-confidence, which had been such a marvellous psychological wall behind which to attempt the structure of liberty.

And on the words " structure of liberty," Leo burst into his avowal:

" *And so, if any come to waste her, I shall bare my arm,*
And not the blood will bid me rise and stand my ground
Within the rank of those whose bodies fence her round,
And not the haughty scorn, the sullen grudge, the old alarm
Of those who guard their own,
But because I can no other;
Because I saw her from my window yesterday
And knew her for the matrix and the mother
Of the best liberty the world has known.
Grant that the tocsin call; what can I do but say
' I yield my freedom up, if thus alone
Can England, fashioner of freedom, stay.' "

So wrote the Leo Damiens in 1910, and Cynthia
Coventry, more and more deeply moved as she read on,
longed at last to be done with the poem, that she might
rush to her desk and write to him about it all.   Ideas for
phrases she would use jostled with the ideas of the poem.
Creativeness is infectious, and Cynthia in this condition
was a poet too, surging with delight and praise which
must be got on to paper before they slipped her.   She
scamped the last words and rushed to the desk.

It was midnight then, and she was writing her letter
and adding to it and destroying some of it, and rewriting
that part, till the clock struck two.   As she wrote, her
thoughts ran so far ahead of her pen that the writing
could only race and stagger shakily after them, dropping
important letters here and whole words there, and
sometimes falling into one prone line, so that it was
impossible to recognise its features at all.   There is joy
in writing pages of praise and affection, and she was
exalted as she wrote her last words.   " I am absolutely
certain that your poem must —simply *must* be recognised
some day.   Oh Leo, there's not a hope for poor Rob
Ingram.   Poor old Rob !   Why, even he will be moved
and stirred by it, probably wishing all the time that he
wasn't getting the funny sensations from Leo Damien.
It's a shame to take such a vengeance on him !   And
Rose and Abbott, won't they stare, poor darlings !
Only *I* shall be able to say, ' I told you so ! I told you so !
So sucks all ! '   You see, I always thought you were
clever, but I'm afraid I didn't know you were as clever
as this.   Oh, Leo, I'm very proud to think that you
are my friend."

XIV

THE lane leading from the main road and the station up to the mossy gate was straight and over-arched with trees. It lay east and west, so that in the middle hours of the day the sunlight flung across its floor the shadows of the southern trees. By one pillar of the gate a lanky ash soared up and spread its branches high in the air, like a rocket. By the other pillar a beech suffered the opposite fate : it stayed low and stunted, spreading its branches over the gate like an awning. The lane ended at the gate, running through it, under beech and ash, on to a country road.

If one stood within the gate, as Leo was standing now, and looked across this road, one saw over the hedge the slope of Tetterten Hill. The hedge was low, so that the most of Tetterten Hill could be seen above this fringe of blackberry, hazel, and old-man's-beard. Bare of all foliage itself, as a chalk hill should be, and in shape like a shallow dome, it gave its check to the October sun, and caught its yellow light.

But the top of Tetterten was not the sky-line. There was a dip beyond it, and then the far higher summit of Olafden ; after which the chalk hills went sweeping on and on, but not to be seen from the gate, for Olafden was top-dog of them all.

Leo waited within the gate, a tall, youthful figure whose rust-brown jacket seemed to focus in itself all

that was autumn in the leaves.   Sometimes he leaned
back against the top-bar, and idly smacked his leggings
with a stick.   Sometimes he walked a pace or two, with
both hands thrust deep into his breeches pockets.   And
ever and again he looked down the avenue of the lane
to see if Cynthia were coming.   It was the Saturday after
her reading of the poems, and he was eager for more
praise—if a little shy of it.   But the lane was empty.   He
saw only the shadows and the sunlight splashed on its
earthy floor.   His drifting eyes remarked how few were
the flowers in the green verges and up the banks ; except
for a thistle or two the verges were unspotted green—all
nettles and bramble and high drooping grasses.   If he
turned sideways, resting an elbow on the bar, he saw
how the dappling shadows were brown on the lane's
floor of earth and blue on the macadam of the road.
A cock chaffinch hopped across the lane, and flew
up into the trees, flashing the white of its tail.   How
silent !   An acorn dropping among the trees seemed to
shatter it—but then he wondered if it had really been
silence at all, because now, when awakened to them,
he heard birdsong and the rustle of air in the leaves.

And soon another sound : the chunking of the second
train that might bring Cynthia, for the first had come
and gone without sending her this way.   The train
puffed out of the village station and away ;   and he
kept his eyes down the vista of the lane.

He had not long to wait.   There she was at the other
end of the lane, coming towards him ;   and, though
she was still a long way off, he knew that she was made
self-conscious by his eyes, for once or twice she switched
with her cane at the grass or knocked an acorn from
before her feet.   He guessed the embarrassed smile

about her lips, and maliciously heightened her discomfort by keeping his stare as merciless as a searchlight. And when she was close to him, she said, " Oh, isn't it awful to walk all that way towards someone who's standing still ? Especially if he has never the decency to turn his eyes away."

He didn't answer, but only grinned.

Standing opposite him, she inquired with the celebrated lift of the eyebrows and the incomplete smile: "Well?. . ."

He pulled himself straight, shook his clothes into position, and drew back the gate. " Come along," said he. " We've a long way to walk to-day " ; and, putting out his hand, took her fingers, so that they went through the gate thus lightly linked. Such a thing had never happened before, and Cynthia at once said so. " This is very unusual," she said.

" Never mind," said Leo. " It's friendly."

The hedge through which they must break if they were to climb Tetterten Hill forced them to unlink the fingers ; and when they were through, they did not rejoin them. Instead they walked up the slope a few paces apart, without saying much at first. Let us stand at the gate to see them go. In a minute their figures appear above the hedge and bend themselves to the hill. They move rapidly at first and then more slowly, for it is further than it looks, and the girl at least is tiring. Sometimes, to secure an innocent halt, she stands and points with her arm : it may be to the ever-enlarging view, or it may be to a white asterisk of thistle-down floating along the wind. The same careless wind drives her dress against her figure, and tries to send her hair on the same journey as the thistle-down. Higher up, and she has found another excuse for a halt : it is probably the transparent and diminishing light of a clear autumn day, which goes back and back, further than thought can reach.   Swallows are swarming and soaring high above their heads, as if at last they are looking over the autumnal mists for the sea.   A cow lows in the distance ; and far below, behind the tiny trees, there is a column of blue smoke where they are burning off the harrow.   On again ; and now the two figures are at the top, and dipping down into the first hollow.   It would seem that the girl, in a burst of good spirits, must have run, for she drops from view so quickly, and one catches her voice as she calls back.

But the hollow is not deep ; and soon they can be seen again toiling up the slope of Olafden, the girl a little behind the youth, as if, really, she will shortly give in.   She does so : she seats herself on the grass, leaning her weight back upon her arms ; and the boy comes down a few steps and throws himself on his side, two yards from her.   A hot argument begins up there —possibly about the poem—for the youth is often sitting up abruptly and gesticulating, that he may hammer a point into her contumacy.   Once or twice his loud laugh, even at this distance, can be heard.

The girl puts an end to argument.   She jumps up and dusts her skirt.   The youth rises too ; and when she is ready, they resume their walk up the hill.   We may suspect that they are laughing and abusing each other, since at times their paths diverge and at others come together again.   There is a halt, that they may compare the busy individual things on the crust of the earth with the brilliant nothingness of the sky.   Down there the sun makes a passing beauty of the smoke-wraiths and the mists ; above, there is only light, going back and back to nothing—or to all. They move upward again, getting smaller now, their voices lost, and their form and character difficult to define. They drag on to the top of the hill, dip down on the farther side, and sink from our view.

We shall see them no more. Some years of measured happiness are theirs, and then the grey ships put to sea.

ERNEST RAYMOND'S
TRILOGY

ONCE IN ENGLAND

In one volume comprising:

A FAMILY THAT WAS
THE JESTING ARMY
MARY LEITH
Entirely revised and reset.

Daily Telegraph: "It is a superb achievement, this
trilogy of Mr. Raymond's—a 'Cavalcade'
among novels which touches the heart and
memory. The fortunes of a middle-class
family from 1890 to 1930 are intermingled with
a magnificent panorama of England's story
during these four decades."

Sunday Times: "If Mr. Raymond had written
nothing else, 'Once in England' would give
him a sure reputation . . . a great trilogy."

Times Literary Supplement: "He has a remarkable
vis comica."

Nottingham Guardian: "Mr. Raymond is in the
front rank of living novelists, and this is his
chief book. It should earn him lasting fame."

Newsagents and Booksellers Review: "A great book
in every sense of the word."

ONCE IN ENGLAND 1,190 pages 500,000 words

CASSELL, 8s. 6d.

'The story of the most comp
told with greater clarity, insight and wit. Charting the route to ruture
discoveries, this is a masterpiece.' Adam Rutherford, author of *The Book of Humans*

'Not only is this a work of phenomenal erudition, but it has the rare
distinct   nong books on the brain of promoting no premature
"exp!   ɩ" of how this astonishingly complicated organ does its
jo⊦   , Cobb offers an honest appraisal both of what we know
and   ... s still a mystery. There is no better primer to one of the most
profound questions facing science today: how matter creates thought and
consciousness.' Philip Ball, author of *How to Grow a Human*

'Thoughtful and thought-provoking, this is a book I wish I could have
written, and one that I will be thinking about for a long time. It is a down
payment for future brain research.' Marina Picciotto, editor-in-chief,
Journal of Neuroscience

'Humanity's quest to understand the brain has led us to some of our most
important ideas, but as Matthew Cobb shows in his riveting, eye-opening
book, that isn't all it gave us. In fact, the road to our hi-tech present was
strewn with brutes, eccentrics – and victims. Highly entertaining and
deeply authoritative. Read it.' Paul Mason, author of *Clear Bright Future*

'*The Idea of the Brain* is a superb book describing the surprising history of
research on how the Universe's most complex object produces memories,
consciousness and volition.' Jerry Coyne, author of *Why Evolution is True*

'This exquisitely researched and thrilling book charts an epic quest to
understand our deepest selves. Its scale and scope is phenomenal, and it
leaves us with a profound sense of wonder about science and humanity, as
well as the brain itself. Altogether a feast.' Daniel M. Davis, author of *The Beautiful Cure*

'A scholarly and wonderfully entertaining guide to the advances that have
driven our knowledge of the brain, and the extraordinary people who
have made them.' Chris Frith, author of *Making Up the Mind*

'A masterful examination of the vast history of humans trying to figure out
how the brain does its tricks. The scope, sweep and insight are stunning.'
Michael Gazzaniga, author of *The Consciousness Instinct*

'Cobb is a reliably sceptical but sympathetic guide to the murky world of
mind exploration, offering plenty of diverting stories along the way. You
may be no closer to understanding your brain after reading this, but your
brain will be richer for it.' Gaia Vince, author of *Transcendence*

ALSO BY MATTHEW COBB

Life's Greatest Secret: The Race to Crack the Genetic Code

*The Egg and Sperm Race: The 17th-Century Scientists
Who Unravelled the Secrets of Sex, Life and Growth*

Smell: A Very Short Introduction

The Resistance: The French Fight Against the Nazis

Eleven Days in August: The Liberation of Paris in 1944

MATTHEW COBB is Professor of Zoology at the University of
Manchester. His previous books include *Life's Greatest Secret: The Race
to Discover the Genetic Code*, which was shortlisted for the the Royal
Society Winton Book Prize, and the acclaimed histories *The Resistance*
and *Eleven Days in August*. He is also the award-winning translator
of books on the history of molecular biology, on Darwin's ideas and
on the nature of life.